Wizards
at War

Diane Duane's
Young Wizards Series

DIANE DUANE

Wizards
at War

Harcourt, Inc.

Orlando   Austin   New York   San Diego
Toronto   London

For James White

Requests for permission to make copies of any part
of the work should be mailed to the following address:
Permissions Department, Harcourt, Inc.,
6277 Sea Harbor Drive, Orlando, Florida 32887-6777.

www.HarcourtBooks.com

Library of Congress Cataloging-in-Publication Data
Duane, Diane.
Wizards at war/Diane Duane.
p. cm.
Summary: Nita and Kit rejoin forces when a strange
darkness of the mind overcomes the older wizards,
stealing away their power, and forcing the younger
wizards to go to war to save the world.
[1. Wizards—Fiction. 2. Fantasy.] I. Title.
PZ7.D85415Wiz 2005
[Fic]—dc22 2005002439
ISBN-13: 978-0152-04772-6 ISBN-10: 0-15-204772-7

Text set in Stempel Garamond
Design by Trina Stahl

First edition
A C E G H F D B

Printed in the United States of America

Contents

"Never, never, never believe any war will be smooth and easy, or that anyone who embarks on the strange voyage can measure the tides and hurricanes he will encounter.... Once the signal is given, he is no longer the master of policy but the slave of unforeseeable and uncontrollable events."
—Sir Winston Churchill

...Moon reflected on the water:
The moon doesn't get wet, nor is the water broken.
Although its light is broad and great,
The moon's reflected even in an inch-wide puddle.
The whole moon and the entire wide sky
Lie mirrored in one dewdrop on the grass.
—Dogen, *Genjokoan*

To be the miracle,
Get out of its way.
—Distych 243, *The Book of Night with Moon*

Situational Awareness

IN THE BRIGHT LIGHT of an early spring morning, a teenage girl in faded blue jeans and a cropped white T-shirt stood in her downstairs bathroom, brushing her teeth and examining herself with a critical eye. *Have I lost weight?* she thought, pulling the T-shirt a little away from her as she looked down. *This doesn't fit like it did two weeks ago...*

The view in the mirror was more or less the usual one: light brunette hair cut just above her shoulders, a face neither unusually plain nor unusually beautiful, a nothing-special figure for a fourteen-year-old. But there were changes besides the fit of her T-shirt. Nita Callahan racked the toothbrush and then leaned close to the mirror over the sink, pulling down the skin above her right cheekbone with one finger. *My tan looks pretty good, but are those* circles *under my eyes?* she thought. *I look wrecked. You'd think I hadn't just had ten days off on a planet that was almost all beach.*

"I think I need a vacation from my vacation," Nita muttered.

She started to turn away from the sink...then stopped, noticing something in the mirror. Nita leaned close to it again, pushing her bangs up with one hand and eyeing her forehead. *Oh no, is that a pimple coming up?* She poked it, felt that telltale sting. *Great. I really need this right now!*

She sighed. "Okay," she said. Normally she wouldn't have been enthusiastic about spending any significant part of her morning talking to a zit, but if she talked the pimple out of happening right now, it'd take her less effort than if she waited until later.

"Uh, excuse me," she said in the wizardly Speech—and then stopped. *Wait a minute. I don't know the word for "pimple."*

Nita frowned. For a moment she considered the tube of facial scrub on the shelf by the sink, then shook her head and reached out toward what otherwise looked like empty air beside her. Into that "empty air," the pocket of otherspace where she normally kept her wizard's manual, Nita's arm disappeared up to the shoulder. She felt around for a moment—*I really have to clean this thing out; there's too much stuff in here*—and then pulled out what to most people would have looked like a small hardbound library book an inch or so thick.

Nita started paging through it. *Let's see. Pimple, pimple...see "aposteme."* She shook her head, turning more pages. *What's an aposteme? Sometimes I really wonder about the indexing in this thing.*

"Nita?" came a shout, faintly, from the other end of the house.

"What, Daddy?" she shouted back.

"Phone!"

Nita raised her eyebrows. *At this hour of the morning? It's not Kit; he wouldn't bother with the phone.* "Thanks!"

The word for "phone," at least, she knew perfectly well. Nita held out her hand. "If you would?" she said in the Speech to the handset in question.

The portable phone from the kitchen appeared in her hand, its hold button blinking. She hit the button, meanwhile balancing her manual on the edge of the sink while she kept paging through it. "Hello?"

"Nita," Tom Swale's voice said. "Good morning."

"Hey, how are you?" Nita said.

"A little pressed for time at the moment," said her local Senior Wizard. "How was your holiday?"

"Not bad," she said. "Listen, what's the Speech word for 'pimple'?"

There was a pause at the other end. "I used to know that," Tom said.

"But you don't anymore?"

"I'll look it up. You should do that, too. How are your houseguests doing?"

"They're fine as far as I know," Nita said. "Probably having breakfast. I was just going to get some myself."

"You should definitely do that," Tom said. "But can you and Kit and the visiting contingent spare me and Carl a little time afterward?"

"Uh, sure," Nita said. "I was going to call you anyway, because I heard some really strange things from Dairine about what went on here while we were away... and the manual wouldn't say anything about the details. Where did you guys vanish to? Assuming I'm allowed to ask."

"Oh, you're allowed. That's what I'm calling about. I have a lot of people to get in touch with today, but since you two and your guests are just around the corner, we thought we might drop by and brief you in person."

"Sure," Nita said. "I'll let everybody know you're coming."

"Fine. An hour or so be all right?"

"Sure."

"Great. See you then."

Tom hung up, leaving Nita staring at the phone in her hand. She pushed the hang-up button and just stood there.

"Wow," she said. She looked down at the manual, which now lay open to one of its many glossaries, and was showing her fourteen different variations on the "aposteme" word. "Kit?" Nita said.

A slightly muffled reply came seemingly from the back of the manual, along with the sound of barking somewhere in the Rodriguez household. "I can't believe we're out of dog food," Kit said. "I leave for a week and a half, and this place goes to pieces."

"We were doing just fine without you," said another voice from two blocks away: Kit's sister Carmela. "It's not *our* fault you forgot to put dog food on the shopping list before you left. Neets, is it true he destroyed a whole alien culture in just ten days?"

Nita snorted. "It wouldn't have been just him, 'Mela," she said. "And we didn't destroy it. We just happened to be there when they were going on to the next thing."

"'Just happened'?" Carmela said. Her tone was one of kindly disbelief. "You're so nice to try to share the blame! See you later on..."

After a moment Kit said, "Am I allowed to *think* about teleporting her to Titan and dumping her in a lake of liquid methane?"

"No," Nita said, feeling around under her bed for her sneakers. "It'd upset those microbes there... the ones Dairine's been coaching in situational ethics."

"The thought of *Dairine* coaching anybody in ethics...," Kit said. "No offense, but sometimes I wonder if someday our solar system is going to be famous for having entire species made up of criminal masterminds."

"Well, if the Powers That Be have slipped up, it's too late to do anything now. And speaking of the Powers, you should get over here in about an hour. Tom and Carl want to talk to everybody."

"We're not in trouble, are we?"

"I don't think so," Nita said. "In fact, I think maybe they are."

"And here I thought we were going to have a few quiet days before spring break was over," Kit said.

Nita shook her head. "Guess not. But now we get to find out why nobody could find them anywhere."

From down the hall, toward the front of the house, she could hear voices in the dining room. "Sounds like they're having breakfast out there," Nita said.

"Should I wait to come over?"

Nita shrugged and turned away from the mirror. "What for?" she said. "You might as well come have some breakfast, too, if you haven't had anything."

"I have," Kit said, "but another breakfast wouldn't kill me. Give me ten minutes, though. I have to talk to Ponch."

"Why? Are all the neighbors' dogs sitting around outside the house again?" This had been a problem recently, apparently due to some kind of wizardly leakage. Diagnosing its source had been difficult with so much wizardry happening around their two households lately... and with the present houseguests in residence, the diagnosis promised to get no easier.

"Nope," Kit said. "Everything's perfectly quiet. He just has some more questions about life."

Nita smiled. "Yeah, who doesn't, lately," she said. "Take your time."

Nita paged briefly through the manual, looking at the pimple words. *There are too many ways to have this conversation,* she thought. *And I'm still pooped. If Tom hadn't called, I'd just go back to bed.* She yawned—

In the moment when her eyes closed during the yawn, the darkness reminded Nita of something. *Another darkness,* she thought. *I had a dream* . . . She had been standing on the Moon, and it had been dark.

Bright lights were scattered all around her, throwing strange multidirectional shadows across the rocks and craters, but the sky was as blank of stars as if the whole thing was a stage set. And something was growling.... Nita suddenly got goose bumps.

She opened her eyes. The bathroom, the morning light, the mirror, all the things around her were perfectly normal. But the memory left her feeling chilly.

It means something, of course, Nita thought. *Lately, what doesn't?* Every wizard has a specialty, but the specialty can change. Nita's initially straightforward affinity to living things was now turning into something more abstract—an ability to glimpse other beings' realities and futures, or her own, while dreaming. She was struggling to master it, but in the meantime all she could do was pay attention, and try to learn as she went along.

Great, she thought. *News flash: It was dark on the back side of the Moon. I'll make a note. Meanwhile, as for the zit...*

She looked one more time at the pimple words in the manual, shrugged, and shut it. *Later,* Nita thought, and headed out of the bathroom.

"All right," her dad was saying from the kitchen as she passed through the living room, and Nita started walking a little faster as she caught the smell of frying bacon. "*How* many are we for dinner tonight?"

"The usual," came the reply. "Three humans, one humanoid, one tree, one giant bug—"

"Humanoid *king*," said another voice.

"Yeah, fine, whatever."

"And who were you calling a bug?"

"Or a humanoid? *I* am the human. *You're* the humanoids."

Nita came around the corner from the living room and paused in the dining room doorway. The room's slightly faded yellow floral wallpaper was bright in morning sun, and the polished wood of the table was covered with cereal boxes, empty plates and bowls, various cutlery, the morning paper, and several girl-teen magazines of a kind that Nita had sworn off as too pink and clueless a couple of years ago. At the head of the table, poring over the international-news section of the newspaper, was a slender young man with the most unnervingly handsome face and the most perfect waist-length blond hair Nita had ever seen. He was dressed in floppy golden-colored pants and high boots of something like glittering bronze-colored leather, unusually ornate—but over it all he was wearing an oversized gray T-shirt that said FERMILAB MUON COLLIDER SLO-PITCH SOFTBALL, and he was sucking on a lollipop. Sitting at the right side of the table, turning the pages of one of the too-pink magazines and eyeing it with many, many red eyes like little berries, was what appeared to be a small Christmas tree, though one without any ornaments except a New York Mets baseball cap. Across the table from the tree was Nita's sister, Dairine, in T-shirt and jeans, her red hair hanging down and half concealing her freckled face as she paged through the paper's entertainment and comics section from last weekend. And at the end of the table opposite the blond guy was a giant metallic-purple centipede, reading several different columns' worth of classified ads with several stalked eyes.

"You're too late," Dairine said. "All the French toast is history."

"Knew I could count on you," Nita said.

At the table, the centipede pointed a couple of spare eyes at the Christmas tree. "You done with that?" the centipede said.

"Yes," the tree said, and pushed the pink magazine over to the centipede.

"Thanks," said the centipede. It tore the cover off the magazine, examined it with a connoisseur's eye, and started to eat it.

"Morning, everybody," Nita said as she headed through the dining room and around the corner into the kitchen, where her father was. "You all sleep well?"

"Yes, thank you," said the Christmas tree and the centipede.

"Adequately," said the slim blond guy, nodding graciously to Nita as she passed.

In the kitchen, Nita's tall, blocky, silver-haired dad was standing in front of the open fridge in sweatpants and a T-shirt, considering the contents. Nita went to him and hugged him. "Morning, Daddy."

"Morning, sweetie." He hugged her back, one-armed. "Didn't think I'd see you so early."

"I'm surprised, too," Nita said. "Didn't think I'd get over the lag so fast. Tom and Carl are coming over in a while. Oh, and Kit."

"That's fine."

Nita rummaged in the cupboard over the counter by

the stove to find herself a mug, then put the kettle on the burner for tea. She put one hand on the kettle and said to the water inside it, in the Speech, "You wouldn't mind boiling for me, would you?"

There was a soft rush of response as the water inside the kettle heated up very abruptly. Nita took her hand off in a hurry. It took only about five seconds for the kettle to start whistling with steam.

Nita stood there and breathed hard for a moment, feeling as if she'd just run a couple of flights of stairs. No wizardry was without its price, even one so small as making water boil: One way or another, you paid for the energy.

"You're getting impatient in your old age," her father said, reaching into one of the canisters on the other side of the refrigerator and handing Nita a tea bag.

"Yup," Nita said as she dropped the tea bag into the mug and poured boiling water on it.

She smiled. Her father seemed to have become surprisingly blasé in a very short time about wizardry in general—but Nita and Dairine had between them put their parents through a fair amount of wizardly business in the past couple of years, and the adults' coping skills had improved in a hurry once they'd come to grips with the idea that the magic in the house wasn't going to go away. *We were lucky, I guess,* Nita thought. *So many wizards don't dare "come out" to their families at all. Or they try it, and it doesn't work, and then they have to make them forget...* She got down some sugar from the cupboard. *But look at him now. You'd think everybody had alien wizards living in their basement...*

"It's almost nine," her dad said. "I should get ready to go, honey."

"Okay," Nita said as her dad headed through the dining room and toward the back of the house.

She wandered back into the dining room with her tea and pulled one of the spare chairs over from the wall, pushing it down to the far end of the table between Sker'ret and where Dairine had been sitting. The centipede—Nita smiled at herself. *I should lay off that,* she thought, *it's so Earth-centric...* The Rirhait was carefully tearing out another page from the teen magazine. He then examined both sides of the page with great care before shredding it up with several pairs of small knife-sharp mandibles and stuffing it into his facial orifice.

"Where'd these come from?" Nita said to Dairine as she came back in.

"Carmela brought them," Dairine said. "They're sure not *mine.* I mean, look at the covers! You could find them in the dark. The publishers must think human females are nearly blind until they're eighteen."

The Christmas tree—*The Demisiv, I mean,* Nita thought—reached out a frond-branch to pull another magazine off the pile. "I think the colors are delightful," he said.

"That's just because you're a sucker for Day-Glo, Filif," Dairine said. "It's a newbie thing. You'll get over it."

Nita somehow wasn't so sure about that. "And as for you, Sker'ret," she said to the Rirhait, "you're a one-being recycling center."

"There's a pile of Dad's old *Time* magazines by the chair in the living room," Dairine said. "For when you want something a little more substantial."

"Oh, substance isn't everything," Sker'ret said. "Sometimes a little junk food is just what you need."

He munched away. Nita drank her tea, watching Roshaun read while he maneuvered the lollipop stick from one side of his mouth to the other. It was like catching some coolly elegant anime character relaxing between shots, because the bulge it produced in the Wellakhit's face looked very out of place against that otherwise flawless facial structure, the emerald green eyes and the too-perfect blond hair.

Roshaun felt Nita's gaze resting on him, and looked up. "What?"

It was exactly what Dairine would have said. Nita controlled her smile. "The lollipop..."

"What about it?"

"I hate to say this, but you're kind of spoiling your grandeur."

"What grandeur he has," Dairine remarked.

"Kings are made no less noble by eating," Roshaun said. "Rather, they ennoble what they eat."

"Wow, who sold you *that* one?" Nita said. She grinned. At the same moment, her stomach growled, and she made up her mind about breakfast. "I think I'll go ennoble a couple of waffles."

Roshaun ignored her and continued to work on the

lollipop, while Nita went back into the kitchen and headed for the freezer. "And you're going to get cavities," Dairine said.

As Nita turned around with the frozen-waffle box, she saw Roshaun deliberately arch one eyebrow. "How can a biped come down with a geological feature?"

"It's *hwatha-t*," Dairine said, turning a page in the weekend section. "Not *emiwai*."

"Oh," Roshaun said. "Well, it's all right: People from my planet don't get those."

"I don't care if you come from Dental Hygiene World," Nita said as she put the waffles in the toaster and started it up, "you'll get them all right if you start stuffing that much sugar in your face every day."

Roshaun merely chewed briefly, and then reached out to the canister in the middle of the table for another lollipop. Nita winced. "Oh, Roshaun, don't chew them up like that. It hurts just listening to you!"

"You sound like Sker'ret," Dairine said, turning another page.

"Sker'ret is if nothing else enthusiastic and robust in his approach to the things he enjoys," Roshaun said, "so I'll take that as a compliment." He got up and wandered out the back door.

As the screen door slammed behind him, Nita glanced over at Dairine. "You've got a live one there," she said.

Dairine glanced up and shrugged. "Listen," she said, "at least he's not complaining about our food anymore. You should have heard him last week."

"I didn't understand it, either. All your food's

lovely," Sker'ret said, and munched another page of the teen magazine.

Nita's waffles popped up. She went to the cupboard for a plate and pulled the waffles one by one out of the toaster, hissing a little as their heat stung her fingers. Dropping the waffles on the plate, she turned to root around on the shelf next to the stove for a bottle of maple syrup. "Got my hands full here," she said in the Speech to the silverware drawer by the sink. "Would you mind?"

The drawer, well used to the request by now, slid open. Nita tucked the maple syrup bottle into the crook of her elbow while holding the plate in that hand, and went fishing in it for a knife and fork. "Thanks," she said to the drawer.

It courteously closed itself as Nita headed into the dining room. Filif drifted past her in the opposite direction, brushing Nita with the fronds on one side as he passed. "You need anything?" Nita said.

"No, I'm just going out to root for a little," Filif said, levitating gracefully past her and toward the back door. "I'll be back shortly."

Nita headed into the dining room; the screen door creaked open and banged shut behind her. She sat down and poured syrup on her waffles, then started to eat. "So what're your plans for the day?" Dairine said.

"To stay right here until Tom and Carl turn up," Nita said between bites.

"They're coming *here*?" Dairine said, looking alarmed.

Sker'ret looked surprised, too. "They're your Seniors, aren't they? Wouldn't you normally go to *them*?"

"Yeah, but what's been normal lately?" Nita said.

The screen door creaked open again. A moment later, a black four-legged shape burst into the room and began jumping up on the people at the table, one after another, putting his front paws on them and licking them until they protested they'd had enough. When the large Labrador-ish creature got to Nita, he started the same procedure with her, and then paused, looking with sudden interest at her waffle.

"Oh, no, you don't!" Nita said.

But it smells so nice, Ponch said silently.

"And it's going to keep smelling nice until it's all gone," Nita said. "Oh, come on, don't give me those big sad puppy-dog eyes. Kit gave you breakfast."

He might not have. You haven't asked.

There was no lessening of the puppy-dog–eyes effect. Nita went back to eating. "I don't have to ask," she said. "I know he did. You're really pitiful, you know that?"

Not pitiful enough, it seems, Ponch said, in a tone of mild regret. He dropped to the floor again and went to sit by Sker'ret instead.

Sker'ret looked at Ponch with several eyes, then offered him a strip of torn-off magazine page. Ponch sniffed it, mouthed it briefly, and then let Sker'ret have it back, somewhat damp. *Tastes like my dry dog food,* Ponch said.

Kit came in from the kitchen in Ponch's wake. "Did I hear you bad-mouthing breakfast?"

Not hers, Ponch said. As Kit flopped down in Roshaun's vacant seat, Ponch got up and went to rest his head on Kit's knee. *I don't mind the dry food so much when there's some wet food. But when you have to eat it by itself—*

"It tastes like cardboard, is that what you're trying to tell me? Okay, we'll try another brand." Kit ruffled Ponch's ears. "Boy, when you got smart, you sure got picky…"

I was always picky, Ponch said, with an air of wounded dignity. *But now that I'm smart, I can tell you why.*

Kit looked over at Nita, amused. As he did, it struck her that he looked a little different somehow. "Is it just me," she said, "or are you having another growth spurt? You look taller today."

"I am taller," Kit said, looking toward the kitchen as the screen door creaked open again. "Probably so are you. Looks like ten days in eight-tenths Earth gravity makes your spine stretch. My mom picked up on it last night. She measured me and I'd gained half an inch."

"Huh," Nita said, turning her attention back to what was left of her waffle.

"I, too, am taller," Roshaun said, coming back into the dining room. "Your gravity is somewhat lighter than ours at home."

"You're the last one around here who needs to be any taller," Dairine said as Roshaun reached for the lollipop canister again. "I have to stand on a step stool to get your attention as it is."

"You finished that last one *already*?" Nita said, taking a bite of waffle as Roshaun sorted through the canister, pulling out a couple of the root-beer–flavored pops. "Roshaun, you're not going to have any teeth left by the time you get home."

"We shall see. And what is this delicacy?" He reached down into Nita's plate and snitched a chunk of waffle off it just as Nita was about to spear it with her fork. As it was, she nearly speared him instead, and wasn't terribly sorry about it. "Hey!" Nita said. "Cut it out!"

Roshaun ignored her, chewing. "A naive but pleasing contrast," he said. "And I wouldn't be so concerned about *my* sugar intake, if I were you." He smiled at Nita.

"I don't eat this every five minutes, Roshaun!" Nita said, but it was too late: He was already sauntering out again.

Kit smiled as the screen door slammed once more, but the smile was sardonic. "Is he for real?" Kit said under his breath.

"He's real enough to fix a busted star," Dairine said, giving Kit an annoyed look.

Kit raised his eyebrows. "Finish explaining this to me," he said to Dairine as she got up, "because you didn't get into detail yesterday. He's a prince?"

"A *king*," Dairine and Sker'ret said in chorus, sounding like they'd heard the correction much too often lately.

"The 'upgrade' happened the other day," Dairine said.

"And he won't let us forget it," Sker'ret said. "I think maybe I liked him better as a prince. He was so much less self-assured..."

Dairine rolled her eyes. She made her way around the table and out, heading through the kitchen after Roshaun. *Squeak, bang!* went the screen door.

"Sker'ret, my boy," said Nita's dad as he came in from the living room, now dressed in jeans and a polo shirt for work, "your mastery of the art of irony becomes more comprehensive every day."

It was hard to be sure how she could tell that an alien with no face was smiling, but Nita could tell. "You going now, Daddy?" she said.

"I want to get some bookkeeping done before I open the shop. See you, sweetie." Once again, the screen door banged shut.

"Something going on with Dairine and Roshaun?" Kit said after a moment.

Nita shook her head. "At first I thought it might just be a crush," she said. "But now I'm starting to wonder..." Nita speared the last pieces of waffle, and a thought hit her. "Hey, did Filif hear that he needs to be here?"

The wizards around the table looked at one another. "He went out as you were coming in, didn't he?"

Nita nodded. "He's probably out back," she said. "I'll check."

She got up and put her plate in the kitchen sink; and with Kit in tow, and Ponch following him, she went out through the side door, down the brick steps to the driveway. The morning was a little hazy, but the sun was warm on their faces. The view up and down the driveway would have seemed clear enough to any non-wizardly person who happened to pass by, but Nita's vision, well trained in perceiving active spelling by now, could see a tremor of power all around the edges of their property, a selective-visibility field that would hide the presence or actions of anything nonhuman. Inside it, across the driveway, the leaves on the big lilac bushes were out at last, and the flower-spikes were growing fast. Nita was glad to see them, though they also made her sad. The winter and the earliest part of the spring seemed to have lasted forever, some ways: Any sign of things being made new was welcome. But her mom had loved those lilacs, and wouldn't be seeing them again. Nita sighed.

"Yeah, I'm tired, too," Kit said, glancing up and down the driveway as Ponch wandered off down it. "You wouldn't think a vacation would leave you so wiped out."

"And there won't be much time to get rested up now," Nita said. She looked down their street, where the branches of the maples beside the sidewalk, bare for so long, were now well clothed in that particular new spring yellow-green. The leaves that had been small when they first went off on their spring break were now almost full-sized. "At least there's stuff to do…"

"And five whole days left before we have to go back to school." Kit looked at her meaningfully.

Nita rolled her eyes. "Yeah, I know, the Mars thing. I've been meaning to talk to you about that. *When* did you get the idea it would be cute to carve my dad's cell-phone number on a rock in the middle of Syrtis Major? He *hates* it when people call me on his phone."

Kit gave Nita a resigned look. "Sorry," he said, "I couldn't resist."

"Well, *resist* next time!" Nita said. "Anyway, we can't just run off and start digging up half of Syrtis on our own. We have to talk to the rest of the intervention team and see if they've got any kind of idea where to *start*."

"Yeah, but they said individual research was still okay," Kit said as they walked up the driveway toward the gate leading to the backyard.

"You don't fool me," Nita said. "You just want to run all over Mars like some kind of areo-geek, and you want *me* to split the labor on the transport spell with you!"

"Oh, wait a minute now, it's not that simple!"

Nita grinned, for he hadn't denied it outright. Kit had developed a serious case of Mars fever—serious enough that he'd added a map of the planet's two hemispheres to his bedroom wall and started sticking pins in it, the way he'd been doing with his map of the Moon for some months. "It *is* cool, isn't it," Nita said, "standing there at sunset and seeing Earth? Just hanging there in the sky like a little blue star."

"Yeah," Kit said. "It's not the same as when you do it from closer."

"So let's message Mamvish," Nita said, "and see if she feels like getting the team together in the next few days. It'll give you an excuse to go do some 'new research.' And we can take the guests along: They like to do tourist things, from what Dairine says."

The screen door slammed again. Nita looked back to see Dairine wandering down toward them.

"Filif says he knows about Tom and Carl coming," she said. "He'll be up in a minute."

"Okay," Nita said. "Hey, you did a good job on the shield-spell around the yard. The energy for that has to have been costing you a fair amount. You need some help with it? Kit and I can take some of the strain."

Dairine looked briefly pained. "No, it's okay," she said. "If it starts to be a problem before the guests have to go, you can make a donation. Spot's holding the spell diagram for me at the moment."

Nita blinked. "Hey, yeah, where *is* he this morning? I haven't seen him."

"He's up in my bedroom," Dairine said, "under the bed, saying, 'Uh-oh.'"

"I don't like the sound of that," Kit said. Dairine's laptop computer was more than half wizard's manual, if not more than half wizard, and the *uh-oh*ing had proven at least once to be an indicator of some unspecified difficulty coming.

Nita shrugged. "Neither do I," she said. "But maybe Tom and Carl will know what the trouble is—"

The sound of a car turning into Nita's driveway brought all their heads around. It was Tom's big Nissan. "Since when do they drive over here?" Kit said as Filif came drifting toward them from the backyard gate. "They only live three blocks away."

"Yeah," Nita said over her shoulder. "Come on—"

A few moments later, Tom and Carl were getting out of Tom's car: Tom looking as he usually did, tall and broad-shouldered, his hair graying, casually dressed in jeans and shirt with the sleeves rolled up; Carl, a little shorter, dark, dark-eyed, and—today at least—looking unusually intense, with the shirtsleeves down at full length. Nita's attention fastened instantly on that intensity, and on Tom's hair. *He started going gray so fast,* she thought. *What's been going on? What have I been missing?*

Nita and Kit greeted the two Seniors as casually as would have been normal.

"Hey, you three," Tom said.

"Filif?" Carl said, turning to him. "Berries all in place?"

Filif laughed, a rustling sound. *For the moment, anyway.*

"Can we go in?" Carl said. "We've got a lot of ground to cover."

"Yeah," Nita said. "Come on." She gestured toward the door.

Kit pulled the screen door open, holding it for everybody. Nita dawdled a little, watching with fascination as Filif went up the back steps after Tom and Carl. It was hard to see how Filif did it: His people had some personal-privacy thing about their roots, and when they moved, there was always a visually opaque field around the root area, like a little cloud that concealed the actual locomotion.

When they were all inside, Nita slipped past them

and into the dining room to rearrange the chairs a little. As Tom and Carl came in, Sker'ret and Roshaun rose to greet them, the respectful gesture of a less senior wizard to a more senior one—though Nita noticed with some annoyance that Roshaun looked slightly skeptical.

"Sker'ret," Tom said, while Nita sorted out the seating, "I talked to your honorable ancestor this morning: He sends his best."

"Does he?" Sker'ret said, politely enough, but Nita thought she caught some edge behind the words. Roshaun was standing there off to one side, with Dairine, looking superior and skeptical as usual. Carl turned to him. "Roshaun ke Nelaid am Seriv am Teliuyve am Meseph am Veliz am Teriaunst am det Nuiiliat," Carl said, *"eniwe' sa pheir"*—and then he continued, not in the Speech, but in a beautiful flow of language that sounded more like running water than like words. Nonetheless, the meaning was plain, for those who speak the Speech can listen in it as well, comprehending any language. "A sorrow for your new burden, Sunborn. Bear it as befits you, and lay it down in good time, mere cast-off shadow as it is of the greater radiance beyond."

Roshaun looked utterly stunned. He bowed to Tom and Carl as if they were as royal as he thought he was, or more so. "May it be so," he said, "here and henceforward."

They nodded to him, and moved around the table to get settled.

"Now those are *Seniors*," Roshaun said under his

breath as he sat down beside Nita. "I was wondering if your people had any worthy of the name."

"You have no idea," Nita said softly. She wondered yet again exactly what was involved in becoming a Senior. *It's not like they're so old. It's not like they're just grown up, either. Lots of grown-ups are wizards, and they never make Senior level, or even Advisory. What is it? What do you have to do? How do they know so much stuff, and make it look so easy?*

At last everyone was seated. "Normally we'd spend a lot more time being social," Tom said, "but today's not the day for it, so please forgive us if we get right down to business."

He let out a long breath, looking them all over. "Some of you," he said, "will have noticed that the world has been getting...well, a lot more complicated lately. And, seemingly, a lot worse."

"Yeah," Nita said, thinking ruefully of the Manhattan skyline.

"By 'lately,' " Tom said, just a little sharply, "I mean, over the past couple of thousand years."

"Oh," Nita said, and shut her mouth.

"It isn't local," Tom said. "Matters have been worsening gradually all over the worlds; and wizards who study macrotrends have been concerned about it for some time. The Powers That Be haven't had much to say except that this worsening is a sign of a huge change coming...something that's not been seen before in the worlds. And now we know the change is upon us...because the expansion of the universe is speeding up."

Kit looked a little confused. "But hasn't it always been expanding? What's the problem?"

"Bear with me," Tom said. He looked at Nita. "Do you know anything about 'dark matter'?"

"Mostly that it was missing," Nita said. "Astronomers have been looking for it for a long time, maybe a hundred years or so. But now they've started to find it."

"And so have scientists on a lot of other worlds," Carl said. "Know what's strange about that?"

"That it took us so long?" Kit said.

Carl shook his head. "That all the sentient species who were looking for dark matter started finding it at around the same time."

Nita sat there and wondered what to make of that.

"The discovery of dark matter and the increase in the speed of the universe's expansion are somehow connected," Tom said. "Dark matter is being detected in ever-increasing masses and volumes...as if it was appearing out of nowhere. And in all the places where 'new' dark matter is being found, local space is starting to expand much faster than it should. *Thousands* of times faster."

"So everything's getting farther and farther away from everything else," Kit said.

"Right. Now, that's bad enough by itself. But there are also side effects to this kind of abnormal expansion. Mental ones...and effects that go deeper than the merely mental."

Roshaun stirred uncomfortably, and a sort of rustle went through Filif's branches.

"The expansion isn't just affecting space itself," Carl

said. "It also stretches thin the structure space is hung on—the subdimensions, the realms of hyperstrings and so on. If the expansion isn't slowed to its normal rate, physical laws are going to start misbehaving. And since those laws are the basis on which life and thought work, people here and everywhere else are going to start being affected personally by the greatly increased expansion."

"How?" Filif said.

"That's going to vary from species to species," Tom said. "In our case, the case of Senior Wizards—and I don't mean Seniors, but everyone much past latency, what our own species calls adolescence—it's going to look like a slowly increasing physical and then mental weariness. We're going to start finding it hard to care, even hard to believe in what we're all doing. And then our wizardry will vanish."

Nita looked at Tom and thought, with a sudden twisting in her gut, how very tired he looked.

"Yes," Tom said. "It's already begun." He let out a long breath. "Now, of course, this is something we'd try to derail. Most Seniors and Advisory-level wizards from this part of the galaxy were involved this past week with an intervention that was meant to deal with the problem, at least in the short term, for our galaxy."

Nita thought of Tom and her dad sitting in her dining room and talking, some days back, when they'd thought no one was listening. *We have a chance...a better than even chance...* Tom had been saying to her dad, about something the Senior Wizards had been contemplating.

"So that's where you were when nobody could get through to you, even with the manuals," Nita said.

Carl nodded. "None of us was sure when the necessary forces could be completely assembled. When the call finally came, we had to drop everything and go. There was no time for explanations."

"Or for interruptions," Tom said. "To say we were busy would have been putting it mildly... not that it made any difference, in the end. Because we failed. After that we were all sent home to our homeworlds, to start organizing their defense."

Nita went cold in a rush, as cold as if someone had dumped a bucket of snow over her head.

"Why now?" Kit said. "Why is all this happening now?"

"Not even the Powers are sure," Carl said. "Someone's going to have to find out, though... because the 'why' may be the key to solving the problem. If it can be solved."

Kit had a very uneasy look on his face. "So, if you guys are going to lose your wizardry for a while... who's going to take over for you as Seniors?" he said. "Who's going to be running the planet?"

Tom and Carl looked at each other, then at Nita and Kit.

"You are," they said.

Force Support

KIT SAT THERE AND came to terms with what it felt like when all the blood drained from your face. It was a feeling he really didn't like.

"You're kidding, right?" he said after a moment.

Tom shook his head. "I know this is a terrible thing to dump on you," he said. "But in a very short time—certainly within a couple of weeks, possibly within days—we adult wizards are not going to be able to do our jobs anymore."

"We hoped we could head it off," Carl said. "But even a mass intervention involving more than two thousand Seniors from this part of the galaxy couldn't stop what was happening in our neighborhood... or deal with the cause."

"But you said it was the dark matter," Sker'ret said.

"That's the 'what,'" Carl said. "But we're still missing the 'why'... and there's no point in treating the symptoms. We need to find the cause... and we haven't." Carl raised his hands, let them fall again. "We have some hints and possibilities—"

"It's the Lone Power again, isn't it?" Dairine said.

"That'd be an easy first assumption," said Tom. "But the early indications are that something different from the Lone One's usual pattern of attack is going on. We're continuing to investigate..."

"Not with a lot of success," Carl muttered.

Kit squirmed in discomfort, for some of the good-natured humor that was always there when Tom and Carl talked to each other was missing. *They're scared,* he thought. *And they're trying not to show it, because they don't want to frighten the kids...*

"We should start at the beginning," Tom said. He looked over at Carl. "Do you want to do the run-through this time? I wouldn't want to deprive you..."

Now the humor was back, but Kit was still un-nerved. Carl, though, just raised his eyebrows, re-signed. "You go ahead," he said. "I'll have lots of chances to do it by myself over the next few days."

Tom took a deep breath, then reached into the air and brought out his wizard's manual. It was, as usual, larger and thicker than Nita's—more like a phone book than a library book. He put it down on the table and opened it to about the halfway point. "Go ahead," he said, and the manual's pages began riffling by them-selves to the place he was looking for.

When the page-riffling stopped, Tom ran his finger down one column of the print on the right-hand page. "Okay," he said, "here we go." He began to speak, very quietly and conversationally, in the Speech. As Kit watched, the manual and its pages seemed to spread out more and more widely across the table—or maybe it was the table underneath it shrinking. But, no, that couldn't be true; Kit was leaning with his forearms on the table, and it wasn't moving, and neither was he.

Nonetheless, the room darkened, the yellow-flowered wallpaper fading down and out as if someone had turned off the day. The pages of the book darkened; the table darkened, too, and kept on spreading out into the darkness, somehow seeming to avoid everyone who was sitting around it. Farther and farther that flat darkness spread; and Kit and Nita and Dairine and Roshaun and Filif and Sker'ret were all still illuminated, as if by an overhead light that nobody could see. Across the table from them, illuminated in the same way, Tom leaned back in his chair, his arms folded, his gaze cast down as he watched the ever-spreading pages of the book. There on the surface of the page, as it grew, Kit could see the previously prepared spell diagram that Tom had been working from—a blue-glowing, densely interwritten circle of characters in the Speech, the outer circle containing the basic parameters of the spell, knotted with the wizard's knot, and the inside of the circle containing the variables.

As they sat there, the outer circle of the spell rotated up around them out of the horizontal, leaving a hemisphere of incandescent blue filigree overhead, in which various characters of the Speech sparked and glittered as the wizardry worked. For a few moments, as everything got more and more silent except Tom's voice speaking in the Speech, they seemed to be sitting inside an elaborate blue-burning globe, a glowing wire frame. Then, without warning, the globe expanded outward in all directions, as if heading for infinity.

Where it passed, first stars flared into being, and then galaxies. Within a few breaths' time, the kitchen table was at the heart of a viewpoint on the Local Group, the thirty-odd galaxies closest to Earth's Milky Way spiral, which Tom had placed at the center of the view for reference purposes. Close by hovered the ragged irregular patches of starfire that were the Greater and Lesser Magellanic clouds; a little farther off, the great golden-tinged spiral of the Andromeda galaxy hung in its majesty, with the other associated galaxies scattered in various directions around it and the Milky Way. The imaging wizardry's blue sphere shot out past the Local Group, sowing more and more galaxies and groups of galaxies in its wake, until it was as if the eight wizards—and the dining room table— were floating free in a near-infinite volume of space.

"So here's the neighborhood," Tom said. As he spoke, the utter blackness between the galaxies paled to a sky blue, and the light of the stars paled as well. "I'm lightening up the black of space a little, so you can see where our part of the trouble first started—"

He pointed off to one side. Faintly, in the depths of the space between the Andromeda galaxy and its neighbor, the smaller loosely coiled spiral in Triangulum, a dim patch of darkness started to grow in the blue. At first Kit wasn't sure what he was seeing, but it became more and more distinct.

"We first spotted that dark patch about three years

ago," Tom said. "Back then it seemed as if it was just an anomaly, a dark-matter aggregate that was in the process of popping out and would stabilize after a while. Space is always springing little 'surprises' or accidents in interstellar structure that heal themselves up over time. Intervening too soon, or too energetically, can make them worse."

"Like when you keep picking at something," Kit said, "and it doesn't get better..."

Carl chuckled.

"Something like that," Tom said. "At any rate, the wizards over in Andromeda kept an eye on it. The dark-matter area grew, but not much, and not quickly. There came a point where it seemed to have stopped. But then another one appeared..."

They saw it fade in, very gradually, on the opposite side of the Local Group, over by the small irregular galaxy known on Earth as GR8. "And after that, the dark-matter aggregates started appearing more quickly," Tom said. "In rapid succession, over the past couple of years, concentrations of dark matter appeared near 30 Doradus and M32."

The dark splotches were spreading fast, popping up seemingly randomly in every direction. "It's getting closer," Nita said. "There's one right by the Lesser Magellanic Cloud. That's really close, just next door, almost."

Kit didn't know the names or locations of the galaxies as well as Nita did: Astronomy was her specialty. But right now what troubled him most was the rate at which the darkness seemed to be spreading. "Did you just speed up the simulation?" he said to Tom.

Tom shook his head. "No, the spread began accelerating last year," he said. "That was when the Powers That Be first asked wizards to start doing local interventions." He let out a breath. "The early wizardries, which were large-group workings like the one we just came back from, seemed at first to work. The aggregates of dark matter froze, even began to retreat in a few cases. As you see here—"

The assembled wizards watched the twilight-colored virtual space between galaxies and groups of galaxies continue to undergo a bizarre and splotchy nightfall. After a few moments, the darkness grew no darker, but there was still too much of it. And to Kit, the galaxies burning in the simulation-wizardry began to look small and threatened.

"That's how the situation stood until a few days ago," Tom said. "That spot over there"—he pointed at one side of the simulation, and the view of that area leaped closer—"that's where Carl and I were last week. Two thousand Seniors and Planetary-Supervisory Wizards from all over our own galaxy, along with groups from Andromeda, the Sagittarius and Canis Major Dwarfs—we went there to reverse the effect in that one spot. We defined a local control structure, a temporary 'kernel' for that part of space, and operated on it to force the dark matter back out of our space."

"And the intervention did not work," Roshaun said softly.

"No," Tom said. "Instead, this happened."

The darkness began to spread again—and this time, much faster.

"It was as if someone was waiting to see whether we'd be able to pull it off," Carl said. "When it was plain that we couldn't, the expansion took off again at twice the speed. And this is what the projected result looks like."

Kit looked up into what was left of the blue of intergalactic space as the simulation ran. In a frighteningly short time, the blue was all gone. Then, the blackness began to intrude among the stars of the galaxies themselves. Their stars pushed apart; the galaxies started to lose shape.

"But how can it be happening so fast?" Kit said. "That has to be a lot faster than the speed of light. Matter can't go that fast in space."

Nita was shaking her head. "But *space* can," she said. "Sit an ant on a balloon and blow up the balloon really fast, and the ant winds up moving a lot faster than it could ever move by itself. If something's stretching space out of its usual shape, then everything inside space—matter and light and gravity and time—gets distorted, too."

"And that's where the real trouble starts," Carl said. "Physical law is fairly robust, but wizardry is more delicate and subtle. The way this expansion undermines what we do is very simple...very nasty."

"When you do a spell," Tom said, "you have to accurately describe what you're working on in the Speech, or you risk destroying it. And to accurately describe anything, you have to know, and describe, not only what it is, but *where* it is. Now, your manual normally helps you factor in the adjustments you need for the way things in your location are moving: your planet's rotation, its orbit around the Sun, and so on. But if all of a sudden, because of this expansion, things are moving unpredictably in directions or speeds they *shouldn't* be—"

"Then your wizardry doesn't work at all," Kit said. "Or starts to, and then breaks down."

The thought gave him the shivers. There were so many ways that a failed wizardry could be deadly that he hated to give it much more thought. *And what's worse,* Kit thought, *is that up until now, the one thing you could always count on was that a spell always worked. If all of a sudden it doesn't...*

"That would be bad enough," Tom said, "but matters get even worse. The changes in the structure of space then start affecting the thought processes and reactions of all living beings in the area. Their behavior will start to become less and less rational...less committed to Life. This is the point where a wizard whose power levels are below a certain level starts losing the ability to speak or understand the Speech...because you stop believing that you can. Soon you stop believing *in* it."

Kit gulped at the awful thought.

"'Wizardry will not live in the unwilling heart,'" Sker'ret said, quoting one of the most basic tenets of the Art.

"Yes," Tom said. "And nonwizards will suffer, too.

Matters of the heart and spirit will be valued less and less. Shortly only physical things will seem real to people. And when that happens—because most humans will still remember that, once, the heart and the spirit *did* matter—they'll get scared and angry. Eventually anger and violence will be the only things that seem to work the way they used to, the only things left that make people feel alive."

Kit shivered, looking over at Nita. She glanced at him, a sidewise, nervous look.

"Why do I get this feeling," Nita said, "that on a planet with nuclear weapons, we'll probably blow ourselves up a long time before light and gravity start to malfunction?"

"Not that the rest of the known universe won't be just a little way behind us," Kit said.

Carl cleared his throat. "Exactly."

They all sat there in silence for a few moments. Then, after a moment—"If that's all," Filif said, sounding a little forlorn, "please, may we have the daylight back again?"

"Sure," Tom said, and put out his hand. The wizardry surrounding them collapsed itself to a little blue-white sphere no bigger than a ball bearing, and dropped into his palm. As the wizardry shrank away, ordinary afternoon sunshine and the reality of Nita's dining room reasserted themselves: the flowered wallpaper, the dining room table with some of the leftovers of breakfast still on it—a marmalade jar with a knife stuck in it, a couple of crumpled paper napkins.

Tom dropped the imaging wizardry back onto the

open page of his wizard's manual. It flattened itself to the page; he reached out and closed the book again. Kit watched him do it, feeling peculiarly remote from it all. *We're sitting here in Nita's dining room talking about the end of civilization,* he thought, *and not in ten thousand years, either. From the sound of it, it's gonna be more like ten thousand hours... or minutes.*

Roshaun glanced up from the table, where his troubled gaze had been resting for a few moments. "Senior," he said, "why is all this happening *now*? Surely if this is so simple a strategy, the Isolate Power should have enacted it and made an end of us all ages ago."

"We don't know why," Tom said. "There's always the possibility that the Lone One might not have known *how* to do this before. Though they're immortal, the Powers That Be aren't omniscient: They learn, though the exact shape of their learning curves is never likely to be clear to us because of the way they exist outside of time, dipping in and out as it suits them. Or the Lone Power could have known for aeons how to produce this result, but for some reason was waiting for the best moment to spring it on an unsuspecting universe."

"Then, perhaps," Filif said, "something has happened either to embolden It... or to frighten It."

Carl shook his head. "We have no idea," he said. "Another possibility is that something's going on in our universe that the Lone One doesn't want us interfering with—and this inrush of dark matter may simply be a distraction to keep us from discovering what's *really* happening, and dealing with it."

"But you don't have any idea which of these theories might be the right one," Sker'ret said.

"No," Tom said.

"What about the Powers That Be?" Dairine said. "What do they say?"

"Right now," Tom said, "they're waiting for the experts in this universe to give them some more data."

"The experts?" Nita said.

Tom smiled just slightly, but once again that smile had a grim edge to it. "Us," he said. "While They live here, too, They do it on a different level. We're a lot more expert in the business of actually *dealing* with physicality, day to day, than They are."

"It's like the difference between manufacturing something, say a dishwasher," Carl said, "and using it every day. You could say that the Powers know what the universe acted like when it left the factory, but we're the ones who know the little noises it makes every day when it's running. And where to kick it to make them stop."

Kit spent a moment trying to see the universe as a malfunctioning dishwasher, then put the idea aside; it made his brain hurt. Meanwhile, Tom picked up his manual and put it into the air beside him: It vanished. "Anyway," Tom said, "right now we need to stop the dark matter from tearing the universe apart—or at least slow down its growth and buy ourselves some time to solve the problem."

"Or rather, buy *you* the time to solve it," Carl said. "Wizards near latency age—near their peak power levels—are the only ones who'll keep their power long enough to make a difference now."

Kit saw Dairine swallow hard, and Nita raised her eyebrows at him, while Sker'ret clenched its front four or six legs together, and Filif held very still, and Roshaun looked down at the table again, as if afraid what might show in his eyes if anyone saw them.

And then suddenly, Tom smiled. It wasn't an angry smile, though it was fierce, and it had a surprising edge of amusement to it. "Now, after all that," he said, "believe it or not, we have some good news for you. For the duration—for as long as there *is* a duration—as far as wizardry goes, the lid is off. Any wizardry you can build to fight what's happening, any wizardry you can figure out how to fuel, is fair game. Normally we all limit our workings carefully to keep them from damaging the universe, or the beings who share it with us. But now the system itself is on the chopping block, along with everything else. If we don't save that..." He shook his head. "Then not just wizardry, but the Life we're sworn to protect, is at an end."

Kit was immersed in a strange combination of shock and excitement, but at the same time practical questions nagged at him. "When you said we were going to be running things on the Earth," he said, "you didn't mean *just* us... did you?"

Tom's grin became less fierce. "No," he said, "we didn't. Forgive us for making absolutely sure we had your attention when we started."

"Obviously there are a lot of other wizards on the

planet who'll be of use in this crisis," Carl said. "Not to mention a whole lot of wizards elsewhere in our galaxy. Seniors here and just about everywhere else have been selecting out younger wizards in their catchment areas who've shown promise, or have produced good results in the past. You fall into those categories. We've been organizing two main intervention groups—those who'll be staying here, managing the usual problems that come up at home, and those who'll be going off-planet to look for ways to stop the dark-matter incursion. Shortly we'll be putting you in touch with the groups you'll be assigned to. In the meantime, start researching on what we've been up to—it'll all be in your manuals. Anybody you feel will help you handle what's going on, get in touch with them pronto. But you've also got some logistical problems to deal with."

Kit noticed Dairine beginning to squirm a little in her seat. *Uh-huh,* he thought. *Bet I know what that's about.*

"First of all," Tom said to Dairine, "you've made the best of being 'grounded' inside the solar system for the last little while, so—assuming you've learned your lesson—the Powers That Be have cleared us to unground you." Dairine stopped squirming, and started to grin. "But don't *you* assume that this automatically means you're going to be sent off-planet. The team assignments haven't been thrashed out yet, and you may be of more use here."

Dairine sat still and assumed an expression that Kit had long since come to recognize as an attempt to look "serious" and "good." As usual, he had a lot of trouble taking it seriously.

"Anyway," Tom said, "whichever way your team assignments go, you're all either going to have to be on call at a moment's notice to deal with things here, or you're going to have to be away for some time." He glanced from Dairine to Kit to Nita. "Normally, in an emergency, we'd help you deal with your absence from school and 'real life' by issuing you with timeslide wizardries, so that you could spend as much time away as you needed to and come back at the same time you left. But this situation's not normal. Local implementations of wizardry may suffer early on... and if a timeslide fails, you could wind up marooned in the wrong time period, with no way home. So you're going to have to find other ways to handle your absence. Any way that we can help, let us know as soon as you have a plan."

Nita just nodded.

"Uh," Kit said, "right." *I can see it all now,* he thought. *I go to my mama and pop and say, Hey, I need to take some more time off school. Yeah? How much? Oh, just enough to save the universe. Might be a few weeks. But no more than a few months, because everything that exists may be destroyed by then...*

Tom, meanwhile, had turned to Filif, Roshaun, and Sker'ret. "The story's different for you three," he said. "Sker'ret, Filif, we don't have direct jurisdiction over you—your Seniors or Advisories at home have that. But we can advise you while you're here. Both your species fortunately have long latency periods, so that your worlds have plenty of wizards on hand to deal with the local-level threat. Your people in particular,

Filif, have such a high latency age that nearly all the wizards on the planet are still of an age range to be immune to what's going to happen. Officially, you're still both enjoying excursus status. The emergency, naturally, supersedes the 'holiday'; if you feel uncomfortable staying here, you can go home to your people at any time. But there's no need for you to rush home unless you feel you must."

"I am free to come and go as I please," Filif said, "and have no binding ties to draw me immediately back. I am, after all, just one tree in a forest…and I think I might be of more use here."

Tom glanced over at Sker'ret, who gave him a casual look in return. "I'm in no hurry, either," Sker'ret said. "People of my species are legally independent a long time before we're finished being latent. My esteemed ancestor won't mind if I stay."

Kit glanced briefly at Nita, and saw her eyes flick toward him, then away again. *She hears it, too,* he thought. There was something uncomfortable going on with Sker'ret and his family. *Not something that's going to get us all in trouble while we're trying to handle this mess, I hope…*

Tom nodded. "All right, then. But, Roshaun, unfortunately matters aren't as simple in your case."

Roshaun glanced up at Tom with an expression that Kit found totally unrevealing. "Though your species has a longer latency period than ours," Tom said, "your own situation's complicated by your family's unique relationship with your planet, and the way wizardry's practiced there. Since your father, the Sun Lord That Was, is your Advisory, you're going to have to go home and sort out your intentions with him."

Roshaun's expression didn't change. "It should not take long," he said.

"All right. If he's got any questions about what's been going on here, have him get in touch with us; we'll be glad to fill him in on the details. In fact, I kind of look forward to it, because I read the précis in the manual about what you did while we were gone."

Roshaun nodded graciously, his face adding only the slightest smile of pleasure at the praise . . . and Kit suddenly found himself really wishing he could somehow eavesdrop on that conversation. *His father's his Advisory?* The thought made him boggle. Sure, there were families in which wizardry ran; Nita's was an example. But to have such a close relative be a wizard, too, and your superior—*It'd be like having a father who was also principal of your school. It could be super . . . if your dad was some kind of saint. But, boy, if he wasn't . . .*

"So," Carl said, "now you're all up to date. Just make sure you understand one thing: You're not going to be immune from the loss-of-wizardry effect forever. For a while it'll even seem to be going the other way, because as we lose our power, the Powers That Be are going to make sure it's not wasted. It's going to pass to *you.* But unless you work very fast to find out exactly what it is you need to *do* with it to save the world, then all that extra power isn't going to help you for long. You'll lose it, as we'll lose it. You'll lose the Speech, and wizardry, and even the belief that there was ever any such thing. And then the darkness will fall."

Kit felt himself going pale all over again.

"So work fast," Tom said. "We'll do the same, for as long as we can. We'll set you up with all the automatic manual assistance we can before we become nonfunctional." His face hardened as he said it, as if he was trying hard not to let his real feelings out. "But after that, it's up to you."

Kit, glancing briefly sideways, saw Nita swallow. He'd seen that sealed-over expression on her often enough lately; he hadn't ever thought he'd see it on Tom. *You get used to thinking the Seniors will always have a way out,* Kit thought. *That they'll figure out what to do. But when you see that it's not going to be that way...*

Tom glanced around at all of them. "So," he said, "if you have any questions..."

He paused as a faint clicking noise came from off to his left, and then watched with interest as Dairine's laptop walked into the room. A small, rectangular silvery case on many jointed legs, it now hunched itself down on the polished wood floor, put up two stalky eyes, rather like Sker'ret's, and glanced from Tom to Carl and then to Dairine.

"I was wondering when you were going to come out from under the bed," Dairine said, sounding to Kit both annoyed and a little relieved. "Spot, are you okay?"

From Spot issued a small whirring noise, like a cuckoo clock getting ready to strike. Dairine leaned over to peer down at him.

"Three true things await discovery," Spot said. "Darkness overspreading,
A commorancy underground:
And the Moon is no dream—"

He sat there for a moment more, silent, and then got up on all his little legs again and spidered off into the kitchen.

They all looked after him. "Uh, excuse me," Dairine called after him, "but *what was that?*"

There was a pause, then the sound of little feet on the kitchen floor again, and Spot put several stalked eyes around the doorframe, gazing at Dairine. *What was what?* he said silently.

"What you just said."

What did I say?

Kit gave Nita a *Huh?* look. She gave him one right back, and shrugged.

Dairine looked perplexed. "You're the computer wizard here," she said. "You're supposed to be the one with all the memory! What do you *mean*, 'What did I say'?"

Kit said, "You said, 'Three true things await discovery'—"

"'Darkness overspreading,'" Nita said.

"And then something about a commorancy underground," Dairine said. "Whatever a commorancy is—"

"'And the Moon is no dream,'" Roshaun said. "Well, I should say not. It's real enough. Indeed, when we went there—"

Dairine elbowed him. "Ow!" Roshaun said.

Did I say that? I don't recall. And Spot headed off

into the kitchen again. A second later there came a little subdued *pop!* of displaced air as he teleported outside.

"Oh, great," Dairine muttered. "Since when does he have memory errors? This is just *not* the time."

Tom, however, looked thoughtful. "Has he done this before?" he said.

Dairine shook her head. "Absolutely not!"

Tom looked over at Carl. "That certainly sounded oracular to me. How about you?"

"Sounds a lot like our koi," Carl said. "Not haiku, though, more like some kind of poetic shopping list. Better start taking notes," he said to Dairine. "Some of this might turn out to be useful at some point."

"Well, that's just great, because *he's* what I usually take the notes in!" Dairine said, aggrieved. "If all of a sudden he's forgetting stuff—"

Nita put her eyebrows up, reached across the table, and pushed a pad of yellow sticky notes over to Dairine.

"Oh, sure! So we're going to be running all over the place, saving the universe, and I'm going to have to write things down on *stickies* while I'm doing it?" Nonetheless, Dairine pulled one of the notes off and started scribbling on it furiously. "How do you spell 'commorancy'?"

"You're asking me?" Nita said.

"You're the spelling champ."

"It'd help if I'd ever *heard* the word before!"

"Better look it up," Tom said. "Meanwhile, we have to get moving. We've got a lot more people in the area to see today, and some who're a lot farther away than the Island. Any questions before we go?"

For Kit, there were at least ten or twenty, many of them variants on the theme of *How are we supposed to save the world when* you *don't know how?* One question, though, had pushed its way to the forefront and was going to drive Kit crazy until he got an answer.

"Why didn't you tell us about this before?" he said.

Tom and Carl each let out a long breath. "Because there might not have been any need for you to worry about it, if we'd solved it?" Carl said after a moment. "Because you had enough to deal with in your own lives? Because we were fairly sure we could handle the problem—and so were the Powers That Be?"

Everyone was quiet again. "And then things didn't turn out the way any of us thought they would," Carl said, "so it became time to start worrying *you.* Believe me, we wish we didn't have to. But right now, wishing's a waste of time. We've got our work cut out for us. So..."

He and Tom got up. "Thanks for making the time for us," Tom said. "We'll be in touch."

They headed for the back door. Nita got up and went out after them, and Kit got up and followed her, while Dairine finished scribbling on her sticky note, and Roshaun, Sker'ret, and Filif watched her.

Nita peered in Tom's open car window as he settled himself in the driver's seat and Carl got in on the far side. "If you've got all these people to see," she said, "why don't you just worldgate it?"

"We're saving our strength," Tom said as he started the car. "And, anyway, when all this is done, we still need some groceries." His smile, though kind of tired looking, had the usual humor about it. "See you later..."

Tom backed the Nissan out of the driveway, turned, and headed up the street. Neither Nita nor Kit said anything until the car was almost down to the traffic lights at Park Avenue.

"They are both completely freaked," Nita said at last. "I've never seen them like that before."

Kit shook his head. "*They're* freaked? What about *us*?"

"Yeah," Nita said. "I know."

Nita still looked a lot calmer than Kit felt. He envied her composure. "All we have to do now," he said, "is start figuring out what to do until they get us assigned to these teams."

Behind them, the screen door banged. They both turned to look. Dairine came out. A moment later she was followed by Roshaun, who stood there, somehow managing to look regal in a floppy T-shirt, and glanced down the driveway as if nothing particularly upsetting had happened. *And what about* him? Kit said silently. *Completely cool. Or so he wants us to think...*

I don't know him well enough to know what's going on inside his head, Nita said. *Dairine's another story, though. The very thought that she might have to stay home again while we're out in the Great Wherever is driving her nuts. I think she's got her plans made already...*

"You're gonna love them," Dairine was saying to

Roshaun as the two of them came down the driveway. "They're unbelievably terrific."

"Who?" Kit said. "Your little one-celled buddies on Titan?"

Dairine turned a don't-get-cute expression on Kit. "Them, too," she said. "But they weren't who I was talking about."

"Uh-oh," Nita said, glancing at Kit. Then she looked back at Dairine. "Something tells me you're thinking about doing some traveling."

Dairine looked over her shoulder, back up the driveway. Twenty feet or so behind her, Spot was sitting in the middle of the driveway, staring with all his eyes at the sky. They all looked upward to see what he was looking at, but nothing was immediately obvious.

"It's a long way there, and a long way back," Dairine said, looking back at Kit and Nita. "It's not somewhere I've been for a while, except virtually. Not enough energy available for the transit. But now"—she laced her fingers together and cracked her knuckles—"now it's a whole new ball game."

"Don't *do* that," Nita said. "You know it's bad for your hands."

"Like the state of my finger joints is going to matter if the world comes to an end?!" Dairine said.

Nita made a face. Kit had to admit that Dairine had a point. "Doing your own spell to get there's going to cost you a lot of power," Nita said.

"It would if I was going to do one," Dairine said. "But why should I, when the visitors' worldgates in the cellar are fully subsidized?" She grinned at Roshaun.

"And on checking mine," Roshaun said, "I find that as of your Seniors' talk with us, the subsidy has been extended indefinitely. We've retro-engineered those gates before."

"Yeah, but this is going to be a much longer jump," Dairine said. "If you're not careful how you restate the spell's power statements, you're gonna make a mess. Better let me handle it."

Roshaun frowned. "I should remind you that when *I* restated them last time—"

Kit took Nita by the elbow and steered her casually away; they headed down to the end of the driveway. *They're at it again,* he said silently. *How many times is this now since we got back?*

Don't ask me. I stopped counting yesterday.

They looked up and down the street, while behind them the argument started to escalate. "What's your dad going to make of all this?" Kit said.

Nita shook her head. "He's already dealt with the houseguests saving the solar system. After that, maybe saving the universe won't seem like such a stretch."

But she didn't sound certain, and the uncertainty was catching. Kit looked around at the maple trees, the street with its potholes, the across-the-street neighbor washing his car in the driveway, the front-fender rattle of a kid riding by on a mountain bike—and found that everything suddenly felt peculiarly fragile and undependable, as if something far more solid and deadly might break through at any moment. Kit stuffed his hands into his pockets, hunching his shoulders a little.

The day that had seemed mild earlier seemed chilly now, as the spring breeze whistled down the street and rustled the maple leaves.

"Well," Kit said, "even if our parents don't completely get what's happening, it's not like they can stop us."

"I know," Nita said. "But I'm so used to them coping, now. I'm getting spoiled for being open about it... it saves so much time." She rubbed her forehead for a moment. "Time... *What are we going to do about school?*"

"I'm still thinking about that one," Kit said.

Nita looked around, shook her head. "I can't think straight right now," she said. "I'm in shock. And now I'm wondering if I'm going to lose it totally when it starts to sink in. Dairine's right for once: They've just told us the *world* might end in—what, a few weeks? A couple of months?"

"Something like that." Kit's mouth was dry again.

She looked up and down the street. "Makes everything look different," she said. "Look, here comes Carmela..."

Kit glanced to the left, down toward the corner, where his street crossed Nita's. Carmela had just come around the corner lugging a big pile of what Kit could eventually see were more teen magazines, and Ponch was trotting after her. As they came down the block, Nita said, "When she finds out, is she going to be able to cope with this?"

Kit had to laugh. "Carmela? Neets, how would I know? I don't know if *I* can cope with it yet."

She looked at him and shook her head. "You will," Nita said.

Kit shrugged. Her certainty was reassuring. He just hoped it was justified.

"You guys done with your big meeting?" Carmela said as she came up to them.

"Yeah, we're done," Kit said.

"Roshaun still here?"

Ponch jumped up on Kit and started trying to lick his face, as usual. "Having a discussion with Dairine," Nita said.

Carmela snickered. "I'll just bet." She went on up the driveway.

I went home and got some food, Ponch said. *Your pop forgot that you fed me.*

"Yet another criminal mastermind," Kit said. "What are we going to do with you?"

Give me enough food that I don't need to manipulate you. Did you miss me?

"Didn't even notice you were gone," Kit said, which was true, if not terribly tactful.

Ponch snapped at Kit's face playfully. *I didn't think you'd mind if I went. Tom and Carl are nice, but they weren't bringing their dogs.*

"No problem," Kit said. He looked over at Nita. "Look, I'm gonna go home and give my mom and pop the news. The sooner they find out, the sooner they'll get over it. I hope."

"Yeah." Nita let out a long breath. "Telling my dad's gonna be fun, too…at least I have a few hours to figure out how to explain it. There should be a stripped-down version of the story in the manuals."

She reached out to the seemingly empty air and slipped her hand into the otherspace pocket where she kept her own manual. Then her eyes went wide.

"What?" Kit said.

Nita pulled her manual out, and Kit suddenly understood her reaction. Nita's wizard's manual normally looked like a hardcover library book—buckram-bound, a little beat up, and the size of a largish paperback. But now it was twice its normal size, and three times its normal thickness. It looked more like a phone book now.

"It looks like Tom's," Kit said.

"Yeah," Nita said, looking both intrigued and troubled. "Great...See you afterward?"

"Yeah. The usual place?"

"Sure."

He lifted a hand, a half wave.

Kit turned and headed down the sidewalk toward the corner. Ponch followed him, trotting along and looking up at him. *So what was it about?*

"Look out for the tree!"

I know where all the trees are, Ponch said, just barely avoiding the maple he'd been about to run straight into. *What happened? Are you all right?*

"Huh? I'm fine," Kit said. "But we have to save the universe."

Ponch looked up at him, swinging his tail widely from side to side as they walked along. *Oh,* Ponch said. *Okay.*

Kit smiled. He felt weak in the knees at the moment, but there was something about Ponch's matter-of-fact acceptance of the seemingly impossible that made him feel better—for the moment, anyway. "Come on," he said. "We need to talk to Mama and Pop. And then I've got a couple of calls to make."

Initial Reconnaissance

NITA LET OUT A long breath as she went back up the driveway. Kit's uncertainty disturbed her... because she was feeling more than her own share. *I'm so used to having Kit to backstop me,* she thought. *Whenever I get nervous, he's always there to help me get a grip. But for a while I may have to do the gripping.*

Across from the back door, Roshaun was leaning against the fence that ran just this side of the lilac bushes, with yet another lollipop sticking out of his face. Carmela was leaning against the fence, too, on one side of him. Spot seemed to have wandered off.

On the other side of Roshaun, her arms folded, eyes narrowed in annoyance, Dairine was saying, "He's never done this before. How am I supposed to depend on Spot if he can't even remember things from one moment to the next? He's my version of the manual! What if this memory loss thing starts extending to his reference functions? The little spells I can keep in my head...but how am I supposed to do wizardry if he can't feed me the complicated ones?" She let out a long breath. "I'm going to ask Spot's people to check him out. If they can figure out what's going on with him..."

Roshaun took the lollipop out and examined it: It was a red-and-white-striped one. "Everything is changing," he said. "We are all going to have to learn new ways to be wizards, I think, if we are to bring our worlds safely through this." He glanced at Nita's manual. "Some of us have already started work, it seems."

"It's going to take me a while just to get used to how much it weighs now," Nita said, hefting the manual. She glanced around. "Sker'ret went out. He seem okay to you?"

"He was fine."

"Where's Filif?"

"He might have gone through his gate downstairs," Dairine said. "Where are *you* headed?"

"Gotta make a call," Nita said, and went up the steps.

Inside the back door she paused and looked down the basement steps. "Filif?" she called.

No answer. Nita raised her eyebrows and went down the wooden stairs, reaching up for the string that hung down from the bulb at the stairs' bottom. The basement was unfinished—some painted metal posts supporting the joists of the upstairs floor, a concrete floor underfoot, many cardboard and wooden boxes containing old books, kitchenware and magazines, and much other junk: off to the left, the oil burner and various yard tools; off to the right, an ancient busted chest freezer; more boxes, and the washing machine and dryer. Cellar windows high in the cinderblock walls let in a little daylight, except for three yard-wide circular spots on the wall at the back of the house. In those, complete darkness reigned, the visual effect of worldgates in standby mode: two of them Filif's and Sker'ret's original ones, and the third a replacement for Roshaun's, which had become nonfunctional after being stuck into the core of the Sun.

From behind her came a faint clattering noise. Nita glanced that way and saw that Sker'ret was pouring himself down the stairs. "Hey," she said, "have you seen Filif?"

"He said he was going to the Crossings to have a look around, while he still had free time," Sker'ret said. "I'll be meeting him. Do you need him, Senior?"

"Oh, please, don't *you* start," Nita said. "Look at this thing!" She showed him her manual.

He pointed several eyes at it. "It looks like the inside of my head feels at the moment," Sker'ret said. "I wish my people got our wizardry like that: It looks so much more manageable."

"Yeah, well, I wish my people didn't have to keep it a secret," Nita said. "Like yours don't."

Sker'ret chuckled at her. "We all have our little problems."

"The question is how much longer we're gonna have them," Nita said. "Years and years, I hope. How long will you be?"

"Not long."

"Good. And listen—I meant to ask you earlier."

Then she stopped herself. *Maybe this is too nosy... No, we have to start keeping an eye on each other; we may be getting into some dangerous places soon.* "Sker'ret," she said, "if you don't want to go back to your own people for some reason... no matter what happens in the next few weeks... stick with us. We're glad to have you here."

Sker'ret held all his eyes still, the only time since she'd come home from the holidays that Nita could remember seeing him do that. "Thank you," Sker'ret said. "Seriously, I thank you. I'll be back in a while."

And he poured himself through his own worldgate at some speed, vanishing into the darkness of the interface segment after segment, until nothing was left.

Oh, God, did I insult him somehow? I hope not. But now for my own problems...

Nita went up the cellar stairs and into the kitchen. Outside in the driveway she could still hear Dairine's and Roshaun's voices raised, and then Carmela's laughter. Nita shook her head, amused. *Dairine and Roshaun,* she thought. *I don't get it. They're too much alike: He ought to drive her nuts. In fact, it sounds like he is driving her nuts... But maybe that's it,* Nita thought, picking up the wireless phone from its cradle. *Maybe she likes the challenge. I'd say she's picked herself a big one.*

Nita stared at the phone, once more envying wizards who practiced in cultures where they didn't have to work undercover. Though the visual effects of wizardry often went without being noticed by ordinary humans, you couldn't absolutely count on it... and a "passive" effect, like one's absence for three weeks when they were supposed to be in school, would definitely get noticed. *I've got no choice,* Nita thought. *But I wish I didn't have to make the call.*

Nita fiddled with the phone until it consented to display the number that had been given her for use in emergencies. She looked at the name: *Millman, Robert.* And right under it, the entry that her dad refused to erase: *Mom (cell phone).*

Nita sighed and punched the dial button. After a few moments' silence, the phone at the other end started ringing. It rang seven or eight times, and Nita stood there thinking, *What do I say to him, exactly?* She had been surprised enough to find out that the school psychologist even knew there were wizards, let alone that he knew some personally. But she had no idea how much *they* might have told him about what the practice of wizardry was like.

"Hello?"

"Mr. Millman?"

"Speaking; what can— Nita?" There was a second's hesitation while she imagined him putting on his professional hat in case it was needed. "How's your break going?"

"Uh, it's gotten kind of complicated."

"Are you all right?"

"Yeah. But everything else isn't."

"I see. What can you tell me about that?"

Professional hat maybe, but not professional voice. He sounded the way he always did, absolutely unruffled, ready to let you set matters out at your own speed. Nita had found Millman surprisingly easy to talk to, even before he let her know that he knew wizards and wizardry existed. "I'm still trying to figure that out," Nita said.

"You know that what you say is safe with me," Mr. Millman said.

"Yeah. But it's *your* safety I'm concerned about. It wouldn't be very nice to get *you* all unstable."

"I'll take my chances that I can cope with whatever weirdness you're about to drop on me. Tell me what you need."

"Right now ... some time off."

"Meaning time after your spring break ends?"

"Yes."

"On mental-health grounds, I take it?"

"Yeah."

There was a brief silence. "Not that such things are impossible to arrange," Millman said, "but—"

"I wouldn't be asking you about this unless it was serious."

"Okay. If I'm right in thinking that this has something to do with your break so far, you should tell me about how that went."

"Uh..." The question, as always, was just how much to tell him. "We went off-world on sort of a student-exchange program," Nita said. "It was really nice ... pretty much."

"But there were problems."

"Yeah." She had to restrain the temptation to yell down the phone, *Problems? You bet, because they sent us to Paradise, and we found out the snake was still living in it. And if that wasn't weird enough, for once the snake was on* our *side, mostly!* But even had Nita felt comfortable telling Millman about it, she hadn't yet found the words to explain, even to herself, why the experience still unnerved her so.

"From the sound of what you're not saying," Millman said, "I gather you're still processing the results. What's going on that makes you need this extra time off?"

"There's about to be trouble with the older wizards," Nita said.

"The Seniors?"

"All the adult wizards. And there's an incoming threat that we've got to find out how to cope with, in a hurry."

"You couldn't possibly tell me anything about what's causing this threat?"

"I wish I could," Nita said. "Even the older wizards don't understand it completely yet... and they don't know what to do about it. That's what *we're* going to have to figure out. And I really don't know if I feel up to this!"

"But you don't feel you have any choice, it sounds like."

"No," Nita said, "we don't."

"Dairine's having to deal with this situation, too?"

"Yeah."

"Anyone else I should know about?"

"Kit, too," she said. Millman knew he was a wizard as well, but no more than that.

There was more silence. "This is problematic," Millman said. "Especially since I haven't been seeing Kit professionally. The school system would buy into the concept for you and Dairine, since we've been working together for a while. But as for Kit…And I'm reluctant to lie about this, not just because lying is wrong, but because it undermines my relationship and my contract with the school."

"I know," Nita said.

There was another silence. Finally, in a changed tone of voice, Millman said, "This kind of lost school time is *not* good, especially with your aptitude tests coming up."

"If we don't do something pretty drastic right away," Nita said, "there may not be a planet to *have* aptitude tests on for very long. Or there might be a planet… but no one left on it."

She could just hear Millman thinking. "You need to understand," he said after a moment, "that just because we share the same privileged information about your special talents, I'm not to be routinely considered as a get-out-of-jail card. This gambit isn't going to work more than once…just so you know."

Nita rolled her eyes. "Being in this situation again is the very, *very* last thing on my mind."

"Good." He was silent for a little longer. "How long do you think you'll need?"

"I have absolutely no idea."

"Well," Millman said at last, "I can cover for you for ten days, tops. I can pull Kit under the umbrella as well by telling the school that something came up for him over the spring break…something crucial that needs to be sorted out. Would that be true?"

"Yeah," Nita said.

"All right. If his parents will back me up, we'll be okay for that long. But that's all I can give you. After ten days, if you don't show up at school again, you're likely to find the district superintendent banging on your dad's door. Or, if someone at school gets too nervous, the cops."

Nita swallowed. "Yeah. Okay. I'll tell Kit."

"Good. Can you give me some more detail about *what* exactly is going to be happening to the planet... so that I can help people around here deal with the fallout, if things get sufficiently strange?"

Fallout, Nita thought. *I wish he hadn't used that word.* The thought of mushroom clouds sprouting all over the planet was haunting her. "I haven't had a lot of time yet to go over the premission précis in my manual. But people are going to start losing their sense of what's underneath reality. Only physical things are going to seem real, after a while. And even those won't feel right for long. Finally, only violent emotions are going to feel good—"

She wondered how much sense this was going to make to Millman, if any. But the faint scratching noise she heard in the background suggested that he was taking notes. "Okay," Dr. Millman murmured. "Any sense yet of what you'll have to do to reverse this situation?"

"The universe has started expanding too fast," Nita said, "and we have to stop it before it tears itself apart."

There was another of those long, thoughtful pauses. "Um," Millman said. "Okay, I see why you might need a few extra days off for that."

The complete dryness of his voice was bizarrely reassuring to Nita, so much so that she laughed out loud.

"Better," Millman said. "Hold that mood. For my own part, I'll do what I can for people who start having trouble at school. But, meanwhile, keep me posted, all right? If things are going to get a lot worse all of a sudden, I'd appreciate knowing about it. We're all on the same side here."

That was the thought that Nita was still having trouble wrapping her brains around. She was much more used to hiding the things going on with her from everyone at school. "I'll do what I can," she said.

"So will I," said Millman, "and together we'll have to hope it's enough. But, Nita...for you, this has to seem like an impossible burden."

She swallowed hard. "Yes," Nita said.

"Call me if you start to feel the strain. I'll help for as long as I can."

"Thanks."

"Okay. Go well," he said.

"Yeah. Thanks again."

Millman hung up.

She sat there staring at the phone for a moment before sticking it back in its cradle. *Well,* she thought, *at least that's handled.*

So. A total of two weeks to save the universe, huh?

It did seem absolutely impossible. But there would be powerful forces working to help them. And when someone believed in you—

Maybe this won't exactly be a piece of cake, she

thought. *But at least you know people are rooting for you when you start cutting it up!*

Nita picked up her manual, tucked it under her arm, and headed upstairs to her room.

One side of the dining room at the Rodriguez house had a sofa against the wall, and on that sofa Kit sprawled, lying flat on his back and reading his own manual. For maybe the tenth time, his arms had become tired enough that he had to rest the book on his stomach. He was having trouble believing how much new data was in that book all of a sudden. The effect wasn't new—any manual would grow and shrink depending on what information you needed. But this time it *felt* like there was more stuff in there. It felt more important, and somehow more dangerous.

He turned a page and looked once more at the image he'd kept revisiting: a slowly rotating image of the galaxy, seen as if from several hundred thousand light-years away. It was displaying in negative, the stars black against white space, and the space was full of slowly growing fuzzy dark patches.

From the living room came the sound of laughter: Carmela, long since back from dumping her load of teen magazines at Nita's place, was now sitting in front of the entertainment system's big TV and talking to someone in the Speech. "No," she said. "You've got to be kidding. It's too early here to even *think* about grenfelzing…"

Kit let his manual fall closed. "'Mela?" he said over the sound of alien laughter from the TV.

"Kit, I'm talking to somebody. Can't it wait?"

"If I wait, I'll forget. What *is* grenfelzing, exactly?"

"It's kind of like emmfozing," his sister said after a moment, "but with chocolate."

Kit covered his eyes. "Sorry I asked," he said. Since he'd made the mistake of using wizardry to configure the entertainment system, Carmela had been spending what seemed like hours every day talking to the various alien species whose hundreds and thousands of interactive channels had suddenly become available along with the more commonplace Earth TV. 'Mela's grasp of the wizardly Speech had been getting more acute. But at the same time it seemed to Kit that Carmela's sense of humor was getting weird, even for her.

Well, at least she's not turning into a wizard, Kit thought. *It's much too late for that.*

He turned his attention back to his manual. "Did that last message go through?"

Received, the manual page said.

"Okay," he said to the manual, "show me again where all this started."

The image of the galaxy reset itself. "Zoom in on that," Kit said.

The spiral grew and swelled past the ability of the page to show it all. Shortly after that, the page was full of the empty space between the Milky Way and the next galaxy over. "There's nothing there at all," he said softly.

Ponch was lying upside down on the floor with his feet in the air. Now he glanced up. *Where?* Ponch said.

"Here." Kit put the manual down on the floor, stood up. "Walk-in, please?" he said to the manual.

The imagery spread out of the book format and surrounded Kit, obscuring the dining room. He walked into the space between the Milky Way's spiral and the spot that Tom had shown them earlier. Ponch got up off the now-invisible dining room rug, shook himself, and wandered into the negative-image intergalactic brightness, standing beside Kit with his tail idly waving.

"This is where it began," Kit said. "You sense anything?"

Ponch stretched out his head and sniffed. *I don't smell anything,* he said. *But it's hard for me to scent through this. Your manual has its own way of telling what's happening. It's not like the way I scent things.*

Kit shook his head. "The manual doesn't detect anything, either," he said after a moment. He reached out a hand and poked it into the brightness. The manual obediently rolled down a menu showing Kit a list, in the specialized characters of the Speech, for the various forces and energies that had been operating in that part of space when the stretching had happened. "Light, gravity, string structure, everything was behaving itself." He shook his head and closed the Walk-in. "Then this came out of nowhere..."

In the living room, the laughter started again. Kit rolled his eyes, picked up his manual, and slapped it shut. "How am I supposed to save the universe with all this noise?" he hollered.

"Go save it somewhere else?" Carmela said. "I mean,

even if you go read in *your own room,* and shut the door so that the sound of other people having *lives* doesn't bother you, you'll still be in this universe. Right? And you should be able to save it just fine from there."

Kit gave Ponch a helpless look. "She has a point..."

I don't think it would be smart for you to admit that, Ponch said, glancing in Carmela's direction.

"Come on," Kit said, getting up.

He went through the living room as quietly as he could. Carmela, sitting cross-legged in front of the TV, didn't look up as he passed. As Kit went up the stairs, behind him she said, "You're tense. I forgive you."

I hate it when she forgives me and she's right, Kit thought. But aloud he just said, "Thanks," and went up the stairs.

Ponch trotted up behind him, his nails clicking on the wood of the steps. *So you were serious before, when you said about us having to save the universe?*

They came out on the landing, and Kit paused there for a moment with his hand on the banister. Ponch went under his arm and paused, too, looking up at him. "Yeah," Kit said.

I wasn't sure if you were joking, Ponch said.

Kit laughed a single laugh. "Not this time."

All right. Let's do it, then.

Kit laughed again as they went into his room. "You're on," he said. "You point me in the right direction when you see what we need to do." He tossed his manual onto the bed and looked around at the place: desk and work chair, chest of drawers, braided rug, maps of the Moon and Mars, neatly made bed. Every-thing was unnaturally clean, but then he'd been away for the better part of ten days and hadn't had time enough to get things into their normal comfortable mess.

He sprawled on the bed, picked up the pillows at the head of it and started whacking them into a shape he could lean against, while trying to think some more about where to start attacking this problem. *The weird-est thing is that space started stretching in some place where there was so little stuff to* do *a wizardry on. Any-one who could work directly on the structure of space-time is going to be really powerful...*

That was the thought that kept making Kit think that once again the Lone Power was involved. *But Tom and Carl seemed real eager to keep us from coming to that conclusion. And if the Powers That Be themselves think that this is something new...*

He picked up the manual and flipped it open again, pausing briefly to look at the Wizard's Oath, all by it-self in a block of text in the middle of its page. Just after that came a section containing your own personal data—especially about the way the "long version" of your name looked in the Speech at the moment, in-formation that was vital for doing spells. After that normally came the sections on spell writing, special-ized vocabulary in the Speech, and so on. But now, before those sections, Kit's manual contained a "noti-fications" area nearly a quarter inch thick. Every page of it was full of bold headings and blocks of text that rewrote themselves as you read them, constantly updating with real-time information from the physical universe. He glanced down at one heading: METEORO-LOGICAL INTERVENTION:

> Diversion of tropical disturbance/incipient cyclone "Igme" (NOAA) approved JD 2452758.7756. Cyclone centerpoint latitude: 21:11:15N, longitude 141:55:30E, SSE of Iwo Jima. Storm heat energy release presently holding at only 1.6×10^{12} watts/day, making it ideal for "bounce-away" intervention within thirty hours (cutoff time/latest implementation 2452760.8900). Intervention team is scouting for available backup wizards with past experience in tropical-latitude hydro and meteo work (usual SE Asia specs on assignment to master [interim] crisis evaluation group Earth). Seniors are urgently requested to check their local talent for availability.

Kit shook his head, for this was just one small problem on a planet full of them. On all the pages that followed were status reports on more interventions of every kind. Wizards all over the world were doing spells for everything, from melting back an overaggressive glacier to stopping a small southeast Asian "bush war" from breaking out by giving all the potential combatants a brief, profound case of amnesia. They'd instantly forgotten why they were there; by the time the spell wore off, almost all of them had wandered hours and miles away from the battlefield.

Sweet, Kit thought, reading that précis with admiration. *And smart. But that spell must have really cost the wizards ... the psychotropic wizardries are tough to work.*

The trouble was that the smart people who thought up that solution were the very ones whose expertise the Earth would shortly be losing—the typical adult wizards who worked the spells that kept Life going, or stopped bad things from happening, unnoticed by anyone but other wizards, their Seniors, and the Powers That Be. *It's going to be us carrying the weight now. And doing what the real Seniors have been doing... or screwing it up.*

Kit made himself breathe. *Don't get too hung up on how big it looks,* he thought. *Take it a piece at a time. That has to be what Tom and Carl did. They weren't born Seniors.*

Ponch jumped up on the bed and walked up to just behind Kit, flopping down. The springs creaked under them both as he settled himself with his head over Kit's shoulder. Kit turned over a few more pages, looking at team wizardries going on all over the planet. *There are so many things happening,* Ponch said, looking down at the pages.

Kit turned his head to look at Ponch in some surprise. "Can you read this?"

I see things happening on the page there, Ponch said. *Those marks—when I look at them, I see the ice melting. Is that reading?*

"Maybe not exactly the way I understand it," Kit said, "but, yeah, I think so." He turned another page.

Look at all the spells. Everybody's so busy.

"This is what the wizardly world's like every day," Kit said. "And for us, it's about to get a lot busier than this if we're going to solve this problem."

What if you can't?

It was a thought that had been coming up for Kit about every ten minutes. "We have to," he said. "We don't have a get-out clause. We have to do everything to make the 'end of the world' not happen. *Everything.*" He was surprised to find himself shaking a little.

From outside in the hall came a loud popping sound and a puff of displaced air that stirred some of the papers on Kit's desk. A second later, Nita looked in Kit's door. "Hey," she said.

"Thought you were going to meet me 'upstairs,'" Kit said, jerking a thumb toward the ceiling, or, rather, toward something beyond it.

"I thought I'd check here first." She came over to the bed and looked down over his shoulder at the manual. "Yeah," she said, seeing what Kit was looking at. "I've been spending a while with that. Any ideas?"

"I've got a few," Kit said. "But we need to talk to the others—" Kit tipped the cover of the manual shut and got up. "You tell your dad yet?"

"Not yet. You talk to your mom and pop?"

"Yeah, but I think it's not the kind of conversation you can have just once. My pop just said, 'I trust you to do the right thing. You'll figure it out. You always have before.'"

"Oh, God," Nita said. "Well, at least Millman has us covered."

"Millman?" Kit gave her a surprised look. "You and Dairine, yeah, but—"

"No, you, too, if your folks'll go along with it. But only ten days."

I should eat first! Ponch said. He scrambled off the bed, turned several times in an excited circle, and shot out the bedroom door and down the stairs, making small enthusiastic woofing noises to himself.

"I was going to ask you how he was taking all this," Nita said as they went after him, "but I guess that's my answer."

"As long as the end of the world doesn't mess up his mealtimes," Kit said, "he'll be fine."

"Hah," Nita said. "Anyway, you've been looking the problem over again—"

"Yeah. I hate to say it, but I think Tom and Carl and the other Senior Wizards were running down a blind alley." They went down the stairs into the living room. "I think whatever started that part of space expanding was done from somewhere a long way off. There's no point in wasting time sniffing around out there."

"*Ohaiyo gozaimasu!*" yelled the TV and the DVD player together as they came into the living room.

Kit stopped just long enough to bow to them. "Hey, guys," he said. "Anything good on today?"

"...On insponder 2186043, the Gratuitous Transaction Channel presents the sixth-rerun thirteenth episode of *How Much for Just the Planet?* In this episode, Mexev finally hears from Anielle, who reads her an electronic communication from Turun, alleging that Nisb had a clandestine meeting with Keniphna at which they discussed the possible bribery of Twell—"

Kit gave Nita a look. "This is what happens when *certain people* leave the Galactic TV guide turned up to 'verbose.'" He looked back toward the TV and DVD player. "Guys," he said in the Speech, "back it down to 'vaguely tantalizing,' will you?"

"Ahem," the TV said. "The Planetary Acquisitions team is menaced by a strange alien force."

Nita snickered.

Kit rolled his eyes and led the way into the dining room. "Remind me never to use wizardry on anything electronic again," he said. "Anyway, even if the Seniors managed to stop the expansion in that one part of space, what were they going to do then? Patch all the other spots one at a time? Even if there were enough wizards to do it, it'd be like sticking Band-Aids on a sponge. The leakage just starts happening somewhere else."

"I think you're right," said Nita. "Small-scale solutions won't work on this problem. We need to stop wasting time on finicky analysis of the affected space, and find the source of what made it misbehave."

"Wherever that might be," Kit said. He collapsed onto the sofa. "So what now?"

"I think first we should start getting in touch with the younger wizards who've been picked for these intervention teams Tom was talking about," Nita said. "I know he said he'd be in touch, but somehow I don't feel comfortable just sitting around and waiting."

"Neither do I," Kit said. "I had an idea about that, too—"

The back door creaked open. "Another charming bijoux residence," said a cool voice from just outside. "The overall understatement is most effective."

A few moments later Dairine came in, followed by Roshaun, who gazed around him with the vague, polite interest of someone visiting a theme park, or some kind of historical re-creation. Behind them came Filif and Sker'ret, who also looked around at everything, but with more interest. As the screen door slammed shut behind them, Ponch ran over to the new arrivals and started jumping up and down among them in excitement, slurping Sker'ret and sticking his nose in among Filif's fronds.

"You did have your disguises on when you came over here, didn't you?" Kit said.

"Please," Dairine said, putting Spot down. He went spidering away past them all and into the living room. "What's tough now is getting the seemings *off* them." She glanced over at Roshaun in his baggy T-shirt. "Some of us are becoming real fashion victims."

The back door creaked open again, and Carmela came in. "'Mela," Kit said, "have you seen Mama and Pop?"

"They went out for a while," Carmela said. "Pop said something about 'bracing himself for the rest of the explanation.'"

"Okay," Kit said. Then he blinked, for an odd humming sound was coming from the living room. Kit headed in there, with Nita in tow. Spot was crouched down in front of the TV, staring at it with his own stalky eyes, and images and words in the Speech were flickering across the wide screen much too quickly for Kit to follow. "What're you guys up to?" Kit said.

"*Dataaaaa...,*" said the TV and the DVD together, and fell silent again.

"Maybe we don't really want to know," Nita said. "It might be some kind of relationship thing. The secret life of machines."

The two of them wandered back into the dining room, where Carmela had just finished getting some glasses down from one of the cupboards. "Boy," she said with satisfaction as she went back into the kitchen, "this is a whole lot more interesting than just spending the day grenfelzing."

Roshaun looked baffled. "Grenfelzing? What is that?"

"It's like emmfozing, except that—"

"Okay, hold it right there. I've been meaning to ask you about that," Kit said. "Since when do aliens know about *chocolate*?!"

Carmela gave him a pitying look as she came in with a carton of fruit juice and a bottle of cola. "Poor little brother," she said. "You mean you actually don't *know* why Earth has so many UFO sightings?"

"I assumed it was something to do with human beings being convinced they were the center of the universe." Kit snorted. "Like other species have so much time to waste kidnapping us. Not to mention making weird patterns in wheat fields."

"Oh, no, those are just people with boards and ropes," Carmela said, ducking back into the kitchen. She came out a moment later with a bottle of spring water, which she put down in front of Filif. "And, very occasionally, sentient ball lightning. But most of the aliens are here for cocoa plants. The only reason people get abducted is when they have chocolate on them."

Nita looked at Kit. "*Please* tell me she's making this up!" she said.

Kit could only shrug. "She spends half her time watching the alien versions of the Discovery Channel," he said. "It could be true."

"It *is* true," Carmela said. "For silicon-based life-forms, one of the chemicals in chocolate is an aphrodisiac."

"Oh, now, *wait* a minute!" Kit said, and covered his eyes with one hand.

"But most warm-blooded carbon-based species just really like the taste," Carmela said. "Every time a new species finds out about chocolate, they send someone here to get cocoa plants so they can take them home and genetically tailor them to their physiologies." Carmela smiled a bright and infuriating smile. "See, I *don't* 'waste' all my time in alien chat areas. I've been doing educational things. Like telling my chat buddies which brands of chocolate are best."

Kit was left with the image of some intergalactic SWAT team turning up on his doorstep and arresting his sister for being a cocoa pusher. "Why do I get the feeling that you are totally out of control?" he said.

"*Your* control," said Carmela, and wandered off, smiling angelically. "You're just now noticing?"

Kit clutched his head as Nita stifled a laugh. "It's not funny," Kit muttered. "And here I was just hoping we might survive the next month or so! Now I have to worry about my sister getting our whole planet put on probation for corrupting underage species or something."

The doorbell rang.

Aha, Kit thought, and braced himself.

Nita's amusement at the way Carmela was putting Kit through the wringer was diverted by a weird feeling she couldn't quite analyze. It was like feeling the sun on sunburned skin; and it felt directional, so that she could get a sense, in her mind anyway, of where it was coming from. She turned to look toward the front door. *Now what the—*

"Probably just another of the thundering herd," Carmela said, frowning, and heading that way herself.

"Don't let any of your would-be boyfriends in here!" Kit said.

"Are you kidding?" Carmela said. "There's a lot cooler stuff happening in here than mere *guys.*" She vanished around the corner into the living room.

"Someone's being unusually cooperative today," Kit said under his breath. "I bet I know why."

Nita looked at him. *Oh no*, she said silently. *She doesn't think that just because she knows about what's going on, that she might get to go along with—*

If she gets that idea, Kit said, *believe me, I'll help her get past it. Way past it. We have more than enough problems.*

Nita heard Carmela open the front door. The silence that followed was entirely uncharacteristic, so much so that Nita looked in that direction, still wondering at that uneasy "sunburn" sensation.

A voice at the front door said, "Uh, is Kit here?"

Nita's eyes went wide.

Oh … my … God, she thought.

"Or Nita?" the voice said.

"Uh, yeah," Carmela said, after another of those unusually long pauses. "Yeah. Can I tell her who's asking for her?"

Nita stood there for several seconds more getting used to what was happening, and then got up and headed for the Rodriguezes' front door.

Carmela stood there looking up at a tall dark figure dressed in black jeans, black shirt, a black leather jacket over it all, and with that shaggy longish dark hair hanging down over one eye, in just the way Nita remembered.

"Ronan," Nita said.

Ronan Nolan Junior glanced over Carmela's head at Nita, and actually smiled, though as usual for him it was a rather grim and edgy smile. "Hey," he said, *"dai stihó."*

"Dai, cousin." Nita thought for a moment, and then said, "Or is it 'cousins'?"

He rolled his eyes. "Some days," he said, "your guess'd be as good as mine." He looked from her to Carmela. "Can I come in?"

"Sure," Carmela said, sounding rather stunned.

Ronan stepped in and glanced around the living room. "Listen," he said, "normally I wouldn't just show up without warning—"

"Is anything normal at the moment?" Nita said.

"Now you'd be asking."

"It doesn't matter," Nita said. "Believe it or not, it's kind of good to see you."

"Kind of?"

She smiled slightly. Ronan smiled a little, too, then looked down at his feet. Nita followed his glance. To her surprise, Spot was standing in front of Ronan, staring up at him with multiple stalked eyes.

"Three matters unknown but soon to be:
The way of the Gods with the created,
The way of the created with the Gods,
The way between them across the bridge of Being."

Ronan blinked as Spot walked away again, toward the TV and DVD player, where he sat down on the rug and both legs and eyes vanished.

"You remember Spot," Nita said.

Ronan raised his eyebrows. "Had an upgrade, from the looks of him," he said.

"Yeah. Well, he's started doing poetry. Haiku, sort of."

Ronan shook his head. "Triads," he said. "In Ireland we used to get a lot of prophecies that way: everything in threes."

Nita shrugged. "His basic logic's trinary, Dairine says. But at least it beats him sitting in the corner going 'uh-oh' all day."

Ronan snorted. "Been hearing a fair amount of that myself," he said. "That's why I'm here. You've been in touch with your Advisories about the trouble that's coming—"

"Uh, yeah."

"Did they seem a little less helpful than usual?"

"A little," Nita said, hating to admit it.

Ronan nodded. "It's the same all over. Well, things

are moving already, and we have to be part of it. But I need your help. *We* need it."

He looked uncomfortable as he said "we." That, at least, was in character. "Come on," Nita said, and led him toward the dining room. Then she paused and turned, responding again to that sun-on-sunburn feeling. "It's here, isn't it?" Nita said.

"What's here?"

"The Spear. You've got it with you."

Ronan nodded. "Thought you might notice."

Now it was Nita's turn to laugh a little. "How do you not notice *that*?" she said, for she'd been present at the forging of the Spear of Light, and had been more frightened by it than by almost anything else she'd seen or experienced during her practice of wizardry. It wasn't that the Spear was a bad thing: absolutely the opposite. But it was hard to be in the neighborhood of a power of pure goodness for very long. That Ronan could handle the full force of the Spear—had apparently been *destined* to handle it—made Nita as nervous as the thought of the Power that lived inside his head with him and made dealing with the Spear possible.

"Is it a problem?" Ronan said.

Nita shook her head. "Right now we can use all the help we can get—and that means weapons, too. Where have you got it? In an otherspace pocket?"

"No, in this one." Ronan reached inside his jacket and came out with a plastic ballpoint pen.

Nita blinked. *"That?"*

"Mightier than the sword," Ronan said, clicking the

point in and out a couple of times. Nita got just the briefest glimpse of a spark of blindingly white fire at the tip of the ballpoint, as if its ink were lightning. "Don't think I carry it around in its normal shape all day, do you? It's murder on people's woodwork." He slipped the pen back into the inside pocket and went into the dining room past her. "*Dai stihó,* everybody—"

"*Dai stihó,*" said five audible voices and one silent one.

Nita stood there watching them all get acquainted with the newcomer. Ronan looked taller somehow. *Seems a little late for a growth spurt,* Nita thought: Ronan had to be around sixteen now, maybe seventeen. But there was always the possibility that what Nita was picking up was something to do with the Other that lived inside him—a being much older, and far more powerful, than any of them.

She glanced over at Kit as Ronan made his way around to him, and banged a friendly fist against Kit's. "You don't look surprised," Nita said.

Kit and Ronan looked at her, and then at each other, and Ronan raised his eyebrows. "Why would he be?" Ronan said.

"I asked him to come," Kit said.

Nita's mouth dropped open. She shut it.

"I was thinking of coming anyway," Ronan said, "but this makes everything easier." He glanced around at the other wizards. "And I'm glad to meet you folks, because it seems like you weren't sent here by accident."

"No," Dairine said. "We kind of got that feeling…"

Without warning, Carmela came around the corner

and pulled Nita away from behind Ronan, backward and out of sight of the dining room, where Kit had started to ask Ronan something.

"Who. Is. Your. *Friend??*" Carmela whispered, as Nita regained her balance. "Where did he *come* from?"

"Ireland. There's this town on the east coast, it's called Bray—"

"No, no, no," Carmela said. "I meant it in a much more existential way. I was referring to his basic, you know, hotness." Carmela put her head down by Nita's. "Is he attached?" she whispered.

"In ways it would take me days to describe," Nita said, "yes."

Carmela's face fell.

"But none of them are *those* kinds of ways," Nita said.

A smile appeared slowly on Carmela's face. "Oh, *good.*" Carmela then strolled back into the dining room in the most casual manner imaginable.

Nita shook her head. *Did I think things were getting weird around her? We're about to set a weirdness baseline the likes of which the planet's never seen.* She went after Carmela.

Ronan had just sat down at the table. The others got comfortable on the sofa or on chairs or on the floor, each according to his kind.

"As I just said to Nita, things are starting to happen already," Ronan said. "The new 'young Seniors' are starting to meet on the Moon, right now. You'd have found out about the gathering shortly from your manuals, or whatever form of the Knowledge you use. But

I needed to reach you before you left…because I've got access to information that's too sensitive to be entrusted to the manuals."

Nita's eyes went wide.

"*Whoa,*" Kit said softly.

"Here's the short version," Ronan said. "The Powers have learned that hidden somewhere in this universe, there's an Instrumentality, a weapon, that will stop the stretching of space-time—if we can find it and 'arm' it soon enough. They say if we start looking now, there's a good chance we'll find the Instrumentality before things get really bad."

"What are the adult Seniors saying about this?" Sker'ret said.

"Nothing," Ronan said. "They haven't been told."

Nita shot Kit an uncomfortable glance.

"I know how it sounds," Ronan said. "But we can't tell them. They're already losing their power; that's why the intervention last week failed. And that power loss also means they won't be able to guard the secret from the one Power that would benefit most from learning it, and sabotaging what we have to do."

"Which is what?" Carmela said.

Ronan glanced sharply at her. "I'm not sure you should be here," he said.

"I live here," Carmela said in the Speech. "Get used to it."

Ronan looked at her for a moment more, then shrugged. "Well. The One's Champion has passed me a hint of what the solution to the problem might be. But the Powers can't tell anybody straight out, not even me." Ronan looked royally annoyed. "If the Powers speak plainly about this to *anyone,* or put it in the manuals, the Lone One will shortly know whatever it is They know. So we have to go looking for the weapon with nothing but hints to guide us."

Nita was shaking her head. "I don't get it. Why are you the one to get this news? Why didn't the Powers say anything about this to Tom and Carl and the other Seniors who went out on the intervention last week?"

"Because they're the ones the Lone Power would *expect* to be given that news," Ronan said. "I'm sure It was listening to their every thought. But me? I'm a failure."

He smiled one of those particularly grim smiles of his as he said it, and Nita winced a little. With Ronan it was often hard to tell whether he was being bitter because he meant it, or whether he was doing it for effect.

"I've had the One's Champion in my head for a good while now," Ronan said. "And I haven't done much of anything." He shrugged. "The usual wizardry: local interventions, small-time stuff. But nothing to suggest that I've come to any kind of long-term agreement with the Champion, or that I'm anything to be concerned about."

And whose idea was that, I wonder? Nita thought. Ronan had at first fought the idea of the ancient warrior Power, which humans had occasionally called Thor, or Athene, or even Michael, winding up inside him. He'd hoped the presence of that Power would eventually just fade away and leave him in peace to be human.

"And if the Lone One eavesdrops on me and isn't

able to hear what's going on in my head terribly well," Ronan said, "It's likely to jump to the conclusion that it's my fault. Ambivalence...the thing that makes a wizard least effective." His smile wasn't quite so bitter this time. "So I guess the Powers fancy me as an under-cover agent. It was 'suggested' to me that someone I knew would be able to get the search for the Instru-mentality started. Right after the suggestion came, you got in touch with me"—he glanced over at Kit—"which kind of clinched it."

"Great minds think alike," Kit said.

Ronan's grin acquired a sly and amused edge to its darkness. "There'll be other suggestions as we go along," he said. "And the Champion will keep us from being eavesdropped on. But for the moment, to get started, the Champion says we need a Finder. We need the best one there is."

Ponch, lying on the floor, lifted his head. *That would be me,* he said, and yawned, and sat up. *What are you looking for?*

"All I have to go on is imagery," Ronan said. "I don't know where it comes from, and neither does the Champion. But if you really have the tracking gift, my lad, it won't matter. You'll be able to find it."

Kit said, "Ponch is very good. He's 'made' whole universes before, to find what he wanted."

Ponch's tail started to wag. *Squirrels!* he said, and started to jump up and down.

Kit groaned. "Ponch," he said, "this isn't the mo-ment! First you have to find what Ronan and his 'friend' need you to find."

Then the squirrels? Hurray! At least that was how the thought translated from a deafening spate of mental barking.

Kit exchanged a wry glance with Ronan. "The Lone One has to know something about what Ponch can do."

"Probably more than we'd like It to. All we can do is try to cover our tracks."

"Then we should head for the Moon first," Kit said. "If a lot of wizards are there, it'll seem normal that we should be there, too. If after that we go out into space as just one more of however many teams, It may get thrown off our track long enough for us to find what we're looking for."

"Right you are," Ronan said. "So we should get going now."

"What, *right* now?" Nita said.

Ronan threw her one of those *of-course-you-dummy* looks that Nita had hated so much until she came to understand that they were caused by impatience, not cruelty. "There are other kinds of 'now,'" Ronan said, "but, yeah, that was the one I meant." He looked around at the others. "How about it?"

Filif and Sker'ret and Roshaun exchanged glances. "If the Powers That Be want to send us on the hunt," Sker'ret said, "it seems foolish to refuse."

"I have some issues at home that will have to be handled," Roshaun said. "But after that"—he looked over at Dairine—"I have never yet worked directly with one of the Powers That Be." He smiled. "It should be interesting...for the Power, of course."

Dairine shot Roshaun a look that he entirely missed, but Nita didn't. She had to cover her mouth to keep from snickering.

Filif rustled. "I am with you," he said at last.

Kit turned to Nita. "What do you say?"

She let out a breath. "I say we go," she said.

Half an hour later, they were on the Moon.

Engagement

AT THE FAR LEFT edge of the face of the Moon, as it's seen from the northern hemisphere, about halfway between the Moon's equator and its south pole lies a vast triple-ringed crater—the remnant of a huge impact in ancient times when the Moon's surface was still just a thin crust of stone over seas of seething lava. What hit the Moon did so with such terrible force that three consecutive ripples of lava, each as tall as Everest, roared hundreds of kilometers outward across the surface before they froze in place. They became the Inner Rook, Outer Rook, and Cordillera mountain ranges, all surrounding Mare Orientale—the Eastern Sea.

The mountain rings have themselves over time been pocked with countless big and little craters. One of these, at the one o'clock position on the Cordillera ring, is too small and unremarkable to have a name on any astronomer's map. But others familiar with the Moon know it for its unusually dark crater floor, its spectacular view across the vast expanse of the Sea, and the short, sharp impact spike sticking up sheer out of the middle of it; and today it was remarkable for other reasons, too.

"Wow," Nita said under her breath. "It's full of wizards."

The normal darkness of the crater floor's basalt was obscured by what, in the pale blue-white light of the setting near-full Earth, could have been mistaken for gigantic soap bubbles. But they were really force fields full of air—hundreds of them, big and small, scattered right across the near-perfect kilometer-wide circle of the little crater that wizards call Lake View, after the nearby basin of Lacus Veris, Spring Lake. The force-field wizardries gleamed blue on one side with Earth-light, where the crater's Earthward shadow fell over them, and on the other with the light of the Sun, now nearly halfway up the jet-black sky over the Eastern Sea; and about them all was a little shimmer or tremor of a most delicate silvery fog, as the force fields shed out frozen "waste" carbon dioxide into the lunar dusk.

Inside their own bubble of air, which Kit was handling for the moment, Nita looked down at that gathering with a strange feeling that was half excitement, half reluctance. "Anybody down there we know, you think?" she said to Kit.

He glanced at her and laughed. "Like it matters," he said. "We'd better get to know at least some of them, and fast, if we're going to pull this off."

Nita glanced over her shoulder. Behind her, Ronan and Roshaun and Sker'ret were already separating off their own smaller force fields to make the passage through vacuum less of a chore. Filif stood looking down at the gathering, his fronds rustling all over, so that even his baseball cap jiggled.

Nita gave him a look. "You okay, Fil?"

Filif kept on rustling, gazing down with all those red eye-berries at the wizards massed there down in the crater, human and otherwise. "So many," he said at last.

Nita let out a long breath. "I just hope it's enough," she said. Following Filif's gaze, she spotted a force field down below that seemed a lot larger than many of the others, and it didn't seem to be a group field, either. *I'll bet I know who that is!*

Nita reached out to the force field, rotated her own part of the field-spell around to her in a whirl of glowing symbols, and bounced forward as she spun off her own part of the spell. The sphere of air budded out in front of Nita, closed up behind. She paused for a moment to make sure that this smaller segment of the main wizardry had her personal information correctly laid into it.

As she did, Ronan came up behind her and paused with his own "bubble" touching Nita's. Knowing she could be heard while their two fields were in contact, she said, "What do we tell the other wizards about what we're really going to be doing?"

"Nothing," Ronan said. "The odds are better than usual that at least a few of them are overshadowed."

He might be right, Nita thought, uneasy. *But what's going on inside* his *head?* "But we can at least find out what some of *them* are doing."

"Sure."

Ronan headed down the slope. Nita looked over her shoulder at the others, who were now clustering their own force fields up against hers and the one that contained Kit and Ponch. "Come on down," she said to them. "Houseguests, watch the gravity, it's about a sixth of what it is back home—" She turned and started to astronaut-bounce down the slope, kicking up silvery moondust behind her. The others followed after.

Kit caught up with Nita quickly, which was no surprise: He was expert in light gravity. As he bumped his bubble back up against hers, Nita got a look at the expression on his face. It was strange. "What's up with you?"

"Oh, you know. Carmela..." Kit was looking downslope at the bottom of the crater with an expression that suggested his ears were still ringing; their departure from his house had not been a calm one. Carmela had taken it very badly that she was being left behind.

"Yeah," Nita said. "Kit, relax. She'll get over it."

"Well, I still feel like pond scum. I didn't have all day to stand around being oh so tactful." He sighed. "Now I wish I had."

Nita let out a breath. "Look, before we go away, see if you can find time to sit her down and explain it all in detail."

"You've never had to explain something to Carmela," Kit said. "The universe's life span might not contain enough time..."

The others caught up with them. They continued down the slope into the flatter area of the crater floor. The biggest of the bubbles was not far ahead of them, and inside it a huge long figure floated, slightly curved, graceful; the long double-lobed tail of a humpback whale swung upward in greeting as she spotted them, and the tiny eye came alive with a smile to match the artificial one of the great long mouth. Nita bumped her own bubble up against the bigger force field, felt the wizardry that ran it analyze her own and adjust itself to include her personal parameters for oxygen requirements and respiration rates. A moment later she was inside. Nita trotted over, bouncing a little, to throw her arms as far as they'd go—not very far—around S'reee. "*Dai*, big sister!"

"And *dai stihó* to you, hNiii't!" S'reee said, folding a long forefin partially around her in a friendly gesture, one that made her bob up and down a little where she hovered. "I didn't think you'd have too much trouble finding me."

"With the kind of air supply you need for a run like this," Nita said, "it wasn't going to be that hard."

The humpback glanced toward the others following in Nita's wake. "Busy up here today," she said. "And everyone's well loaded with spells, I can feel."

Nita lifted her right wrist and shook it. Her charm bracelet, every charm standing for a spell nine-tenths ready to be used and needing only a few words' worth of activation, jingled gently. "Seemed smart to be ready for anything on this run," she said. "But you are, too."

She glanced up above them at the surface of S'reee's force field; to a wizard's eye, it swirled with faint characters in the Speech, the way a bubble's surface swirls with colors. "That's some spell," Nita said. "It almost seemed to do that inclusion by itself."

"I'm not sure it didn't," S'reee said. "I've been doing things I used to think were impossible these past few days, since it all started to change."

"S'reee!" Kit said, as he came up beside Nita, free of his own force field, and Ponch danced briefly on his hind legs near S'reee's nose, getting her scent. Kit thumped S'reee's broad side in a friendly way. "I didn't know you did space!"

The whale chuckled, a long, slow, bubbly noise that finished in an upscaling whistle like a boiling kettle. "Why not? It's just another Sea." S'reee angled her head very slightly to one side, as Ponch lost interest and ran off underneath her. "And here come your excursus guests! *Dai stihó*, cousins. Welcome to the Moon," she said to Filif and Sker'ret and Roshaun as they came in behind Dairine. Then she glanced past them again, and bent her head as if looking down at the moondust...and kept on bending until her nose almost touched it.

Belatedly Nita realized that what she was seeing was a bow. She looked over her shoulder and saw Ronan coming toward them, bouncing a little. "You know each other?" Nita said.

Ronan stopped his bounce just short of S'reee, waited until he got settled a little, and then put up a hand to rest it on her hide. He smiled, then, an unusually open look for him.

"Both of them," S'reee said. "Rhoannann 'took in the Sea,' once. It was a notable Ordeal. And as for the Other—I'm wizard enough these days to know the Finned Defender when I see him, whatever or whoever he's wearing at the time. Elder brother, well met in the current that bears us!"

Ronan nodded back. *"Dai,"* he said. "And he greets you, too."

"It's good you all got here before I had to leave," S'reee said. "There's a lot to do back home, for I, too, have been 'upgraded.' I am now Wetside Supervisory Wizard for Earth."

Nita's mouth dropped open. "S'reee, you're *kidding*. The whole planet!"

"The oceans, at least. When we first met, and I'd been promoted to Senior so young, I hated it...but now the experience seems like it's going to come in handy." She swung her tail in a thoughtful way. "It almost makes me think—"

"That Someone or other might have planned it this way in advance?" said a rather young voice from the far side of S'reee.

Kit glanced up. He started to grin. "Is that who I think it is?" he said.

A small human shape came ducking underneath S'reee's floating broad, barnacled belly: a little dark-skinned kid, slender and slight in jeans and T-shirt, maybe about eleven years old, with a short afro and quick, bright eyes. "Hey," he said, "*dai stihó,* everybody!" And then he saw Kit, and laughed that peculiarly joyous laugh of his, and went to throw his arms around Kit in a big hug.

Nita looked hurriedly at Ronan. *Listen,* she said, *about Darryl—*

He's a lot more than he seems, Ronan said.

A whole lot. And we don't mention it.

Of course not.

"Darryl, my man, *look* at you!" Kit said as they broke the hug, and Nita headed over. "Are you taller? Are you actually bulking up?"

"Just eating more," Darryl said. "Yeah, I'm growing all of a sudden. I guess I've got the energy to spare now. Don't get into it with my mom—she says that these days I cost too much to keep. *Almost* too much." He grinned, turning away from them and S'reee toward the others as the visitors merged their bubbles with S'reee's big one. "Hi, guys, who are you all?"

Introductions got under way. As they did, Nita saw Dairine giving Roshaun an unusually intense look. Roshaun put his eyebrows up, and then took them right down again. Any wizard in Darryl's vicinity would notice an atypical intensity of power. But once you realized what it meant, it wasn't something you discussed with Darryl, ever. He didn't know about it, and wasn't meant to. The situation was like knowing a superhero with a secret identity. But the difference here was that everybody else knew about the secret identity, and the superhero didn't...which was a good thing, because if Darryl ever found out he was a direct channel of the One's power into the world, the discovery would kill him.

Darryl turned back to Kit after a few moments. "I looked you up in the book, saw you were off joyriding halfway across the galaxy." Darryl looked Kit over approvingly. "Got yourself some tan."

"Nearly got myself a scorched hide," Kit said. "Our old 'friend' again."

Darryl nodded, his grin fading a little. "Well, we're just going to have to screw up Its plans one more time."

"Yeah, and then we can get back to business," Kit said, and looked up at the sky. "Like the Mar—"

"*The Martian thing!*" Nita and Dairine and Darryl more or less shouted in chorus, leaving Sker'ret and Filif and Roshaun and Ronan all looking confused.

"You crack me up," Darryl said, and whacked Kit in the shoulder in a friendly way. "Here we've got the whole universe going to pieces around our ears, and all *you* can think about is going hunting for ancient Martian princesses in skimpy clothes." He guffawed.

"Will you cut it out? It's not about princesses! That's just in a book!" Kit said, but no one was listening. There was too much laughing going on. "Come on, Darryl, give it a rest!"

"Okay, never mind," Darryl said, "you're off the hook till we get present business sorted out. I can't believe how full my manual's gotten in the past few days. Just look at it—"

To Nita's surprise, Darryl reached not into a nearby space pocket for his manual but into the front pocket of his jeans. Dairine stared at what Darryl brought out.

To all appearances it was a sleek rectangular white-and-silver MP3 player, but as he turned it toward them, Nita could see that the apple on its little blue-glowing screen had no bite out of it.

"That is too *slick*!" Dairine said. Spot came up from behind and put some eyes up to goggle in a friendly way at the WizPod.

"Yeah," Darryl said. He pulled it open—which shouldn't have been possible—until it looked like a little book, and then opened it out again, and again, and yet again, until it was more like a flat-screen monitor than anything else, but one you could hold in your hands. Manual data started scrolling down its surface, imagery and spells together. "It's got all the usual spell-storage and display options," Darryl said. "*And* it carries my tunes. Like I've got time for music when this thing's got twenty times the content, all of a sudden…" He grinned as he folded it up again.

Nita looked over at S'reee as a thought occurred to her. "Are there any other Seniors on Earth who were Seniors before but'll still be functioning when things go bad?"

"No," S'reee said.

"Oh, wow," Nita said. "How that must be making you feel…"

"Yes. And just when I was starting to relax about being a Senior," S'reee said, sounding briefly mournful. "But all we can do now is dive deep and do the best we can on short notice, even if we're not sure we have enough data. That said"—S'reee looked less troubled—"we've been given access to a lot more power than we've ever had. It's hard to feel so uncertain when you do a wizardry and it just jumps out of you like a waterspout."

"Yeah," Nita said, "I noticed." Thirty minutes or so ago, when they'd built the wizardry to transit the group to the Moon, it had gone together in record time, and had left no one even slightly tired—unusual for a fairly complex spell. Nita's first reaction had been exhilaration. But then she'd started feeling uneasy, as if something she'd always been used to paying full price for was now suddenly on sale. *What if it's actually a sign that the thing you're getting is about to go permanently out of stock?*

"Well, we're going to need that extra power, because things are already happening out there," S'reee said. "The effects of the unnatural expansion are spreading fast." She looked across the crater at the jumble of bubbles of air; they were splitting and moving around, bumping into each other and merging, as wizards got together to lay their plans. "There are already pockets of space where wizardry isn't working . . . and it's only a matter of time before those pockets start occurring here. About half these people are heading off-planet, following various leads toward ways to stop the expansion. The rest will head back home to try to keep things running steadily for as long as we can. We're going to be spread pretty thin." She sounded wistful. "I don't suppose you're going to be staying?"

"No," Nita said, "we're outward-bound, in two different directions. Right now we just wanted to check in and see what people up here were doing."

"It's all in your manuals," S'reee said. "Check those to see if anything comes up that has any bearing on what you're about to do."

Kit turned to Darryl. "What about you?" Kit said. "You gonna sit tight?"

Darryl nodded. "I'm too new at this," he said. "I've got lots of power, but I'm not sure what to do with it yet. S'reee's taken me under her fin; she's full of good advice."

Nita smiled slightly, privately pleased. She had the idea that Earth might be safer if this one of its precious few abdals stayed home. When she looked back at Darryl, though, he was eyeing her a little strangely. "But, listen, I saw something the other day," Darryl said, "just when I was waking up."

"Lucid dreaming?" Nita said. It was one of a number of techniques that visionary wizards used to more clearly hear what the universe was trying to tell them.

"Not like that," Darryl said. "I just get these hints, you know? Like something whispering in my ear. So far it's turned out to be smart for me to pay attention. But I don't think this hint was for me."

"Why? Do you get 'wrong numbers'?" Nita said. "I get them sometimes."

Darryl shook his head. "First time," he said.

Nita found that interesting, in an uncomfortable way. "What did you see?"

"Bugs," Darryl said. "Giant bugs."

Kit and Nita looked at each other. "Like him?" Nita said, nodding past S'reee. Over that way, Sker'ret and Filif were discussing something.

Darrell gazed over at Sker'ret for a moment. "No, not really. He's a nice guy; you can feel it from here. *These* bugs"—he shivered—"I don't know where they are, but running into them wouldn't be fun. Our 'old friend' owns them, body and soul." Darryl actually shivered. "They're deadly. And I think if you hang around where they are, somebody's going to get killed."

"No problem," Kit said. "If we see any giant bugs, we'll give them a miss."

Nita swallowed. "Now," she said to Darryl, "you're going to tell us a way to beat this, right?"

Darryl's expression was stricken. "I don't know for sure that there is one," he said. "Like I said, it was just a hint. It felt like someone could have said more...and wasn't saying."

"Okay," Nita said. "Thanks. We'll keep our eyes open."

She looked around again, out toward the center of the crater, where hundreds more wizards were milling around. "Ronan?" she said.

"Yeah," Ronan said, and glanced over at Kit. "We should get started. Where's your adjunct talent?"

Kit looked around, then ducked to look under S'reee. "Playing with rocks, as usual," he said. "Hey, Ponch!"

Moondust flew up in a cloud as Ponch ran underneath S'reee to Kit. *I'm here!*

"Let's go hunting."

Oh boy!

"You going to be here later?" Kit said to Darryl.

"I'll be one of the last ones out," Darryl said. "Somebody has to clean up all the footprints when we're done."

Nita squeezed his shoulder. "Later," she said, and went off to where Dairine and Roshaun were deep in conversation and, to judge by their expressions, having one more disagreement. As Nita bounced over, they looked up at her almost in relief.

"You heading out now?" she said.

"Yeah," Dairine said. "Roshaun's carrying his subsidized portal; we'll use that. We're going back to his place on Wellakh first."

"All right," Nita said. "Message me when you're done there. But meantime, listen—"

"Yeah, I'll be careful," Dairine said. She turned away.

Nita took her sister gently by the arm, turned her back toward her. "Dair," she said. "Giant bugs."

"Huh?" Dairine turned to glance over at Sker'ret.

"Not cute bugs. Nasty ones," Nita said. "Darryl says they're bad news, and some of us are probably going to run into them. If you do, avoid them. Understand?"

Dairine gave her a dry look. "With all this extra power we've suddenly got, I think can handle it."

Nita let out an annoyed breath and turned to Roshaun. "I'm not kidding," she said. "Watch your backs, okay?"

"We will do nothing obviously foolhardy," Roshaun said. "But under the circumstances, no situation any of us goes into is likely to lack its dangers." He looked down at Nita from that regal height of his, an effect still somewhat altered by the big floppy T-shirt he hadn't changed out of yet.

"Yeah," Nita said. "I know." She glanced at Dairine. "Take care of yourself."

"You, too," Dairine said. She hesitated, and then she came over and gave Nita a hug.

Nita hugged her back, then pushed her away, trying to make it look casual. S'reee was now talking to Filif and Sker'ret; Nita turned back to them. "What about you guys?"

"We'll go with you and Kit and Ronan," Sker'ret said.

"Great. Let's move out..."

Kit stood just past the boundary of S'reee's force field, having detached his own; inside it, beside him, Ponch was gazing upslope. At first Kit thought Ponch had seen someone coming, but then realized that it was the setting Earth that held his dog's attention. Ponch was staring at the world the way he might watch a tree after he'd seen a squirrel go up it.

"What?" Kit said. "What's the matter?"

It's small, Ponch said. *I never thought it was small before.*

Kit nodded. "That's the way the astronauts saw it," he said. "Like a little thing...fragile. I never thought the world was small until I saw it that way myself. It surprises everybody when they see their own world that way for the first time, all by itself in the dark." Kit looked curiously at Ponch. "But you've been here before."

I didn't notice it then, Ponch said. *Now I do.*

He sounded concerned. "It's okay," Kit said. "It's a point-of-view thing. You get used to it."

I wonder if that's wise...

Kit wasn't quite sure what to make of that. He looked up and saw Ronan heading over to bump his own now-detached force field against Kit's.

"You two ready?" Ronan said.

Kit nodded. Ronan stepped through the interface between their two force fields and went over to Ponch. "So, big fella," Ronan said. "You ready for it?" He got down on one knee by Ponch. Kit hunkered down across from him.

Ponch sat down, his tail thumping. *Show me what you want me to find.*

Ronan and Ponch locked eyes.

Since the time that Ponch began to reveal his ability to find things—stepping between realities, even sometimes out of his own home universe to track them down—Kit had started trying to use the wizardly link between them to "overhear" what Ponch was seeing and hearing. It wasn't always easy. Even a dog who had become much less doggy than usual—because of the frequent use of wizardry in his neighborhood—still sometimes had trouble explaining to Kit just what was going on with him. Now, as Ronan looked into Ponch's eyes, Kit listened hard.

What flowed into Ponch's mind—tentatively at first, and then with more assurance as the Winged Defender became clearer about how to communicate—affected Kit in two different ways at once. Half the message came through as a blinding, confusing series of images overlaying one another: light forms and dark ones, strange shapes that seemed to have too many sides, colors Kit couldn't name. But the rest Kit experienced as Ponch was experiencing it—as scent. And this perception left Kit half dazzled, for Ponch's sense of smell was endlessly more powerful and complex than any human's, making Kit feel like a blind person who's suddenly been given new eyes. The complex of scents was a strange mixture, and Kit could make nothing of it. He thought he smelled metal, flowers, strange green scents like those of growing things, a smell like dry cocoa and another one like old motor oil, those two aromas strongly overlaying many more.

Kit was aware that to Ponch, these scents weren't evidence of concrete things but of conditions, thoughts, emotions. The acrid taste of fear, a distant smoky frustration and anger mingling with that fear, concealing itself within it. *It's not so much that he can smell emotions,* Kit thought. *From his point of view, emotions are scents.* There was information of all kinds buried in the miasma of odors—particularly in one that got stronger by the moment. Kit was unnerved to realize that Ponch had classified this scent as being very like dried blood. *But blood on the surface of an old wound. Something that's not over with yet. Something that's waiting*...Whatever was waiting sizzled behind it all like electricity: powerful, dangerous, yet also suppressed, muzzled—

Kit blinked himself back to the here and now: the powdery gray soil underfoot, the Earth setting over the rim of Spring Lake crater. He looked down at Ponch. Ponch had his head cocked to one side; he was whuffling at the air. Ronan sat back on his heels. "Can you track that?"

Ponch glanced up once more at the Earth hanging low by the crater's rim. *I can find what you're looking for,* he said, craning his neck back to look at Kit and Ronan. *But we have to go closer to where it comes from, and get away from where there are so many people.*

"How come you can't just 'walk' us there?" Kit said.

Ponch stood up and shook himself. *Because it's a real place with life in it,* he said, looking across at Kit. *Finding a place that's already there is different from just making one up. And it's inside the same universe with us. There are a lot of other places that smell sort of the same way: I have to make sure I find the right one. Once we're away from here*—Ponch looked around and down at the wizards—*I can do a lot better.*

"Okay," Kit said. He thought for a moment; then said to Ronan, "I have an idea."

"Yeah?"

Let's hear it, said the other version of Ronan's voice, the one both older and edgier.

Ronan, Kit said silently, *you said your...partner was going to be able to protect us from being overheard. Are you both sure?*

"Yes," and *Yes,* they said.

Okay. A custom worldgating from here would be pretty easy for You-Know-Who to trace. Let's lay a false trail, and go out through the Crossings. Some of the wizards here'll be going that way. And if Ponch's prob-

lem is that all the life here and on Earth is drowning out
the scent, then Rirhath B will be a good place for him to
try again. Their population's a lot smaller.*

"Makes sense," Ronan said. He looked down at
Ponch. "That suit you?"

Ponch was already wagging his tail. *Blue food!!*

Ronan looked at Kit, confused. "Am I missing
something?"

Kit had to laugh. "Uh, he thinks that when we hit
the Crossings, he's going to get a treat."

Ronan nodded and stood up. "All right. Well, let me
know when you're ready." He disengaged his force-
field bubble from theirs, and headed off toward the
center of the crater.

Nita came up behind Kit and bumped her bubble
into his. As she slipped into his bubble, she glanced the
way Kit was looking. "Got a problem?"

"I don't know. Does Ronan seem kind of abrupt to
you sometimes?"

Nita laughed silently. "More like always. But more
now than before. Probably it's something to do with
his passenger."

"I guess so."

"Look, we should think about where we're going,
and how. Dairine and Roshaun are heading off by
themselves, so it looks like our group is you, me,
Ponch, Ronan, Sker'ret, and Filif."

"Okay. Did S'reee mention if anybody around here
has a gate to the Crossings running already?"

"No," Nita said. She reached into her otherspace
pocket for her manual. "Let's do a scan..."

"In a minute. Did you ask anyone else to meet us here?"

Nita looked surprised. "No."

"Then who's that?" Kit looked toward the center of the crater. One force-field bubble was moving toward them. As the bubble got closer, Kit could see that the occupants were two kids of maybe twelve or thirteen, a boy and a girl. The girl was wearing a short cropped T-shirt and baggy cargo pants, more or less in Dairine's style, and had very long, straight, dark hair worn loose; the boy's hair was cropped very short, and he was wearing something that at first glance looked like a suit—though as they got closer, Kit saw that it was actually one of those dark Far Eastern collarless jackets, worn somewhat incongruously over denim flares. Both of the kids looked slender, lean, and perhaps a little small for their ages. They were Asian, delicately featured, handsome, though there was something a little fierce about both their faces.

They bumped their common bubble up against Kit's. "Can we come in?" the girl said.

"Uh, sure."

Their bubble merged with Kit's. "You're the ones who did the Song of the Twelve, right?" the girl said. "*Dai stihó!*"

"*Dai,*" Nita and Kit both said. And Kit laughed, and said, "Well, maybe you both know who *we* are—"

"I'm Tran Liem Tuyet," said the boy.

"I'm Tran Hung Nguyet," said the girl.

"We're a twychild," they said together.

Then they both burst out laughing. "Sorry, it's a bad habit."

"Twin wizards!" Kit said. "Yeah, I guess you would hear each other think most of the time."

"Constantly," they both said.

"But twychilding is more than just being twins, isn't it?" Nita said. "I read about it in the manual a while back. You guys bounce spells back and forth between you, right? And they get stronger." And then Kit was surprised to see Nita blush. "Sorry, I don't know which of your names it's okay to use."

"The last one's like the Western first name," said the girl. "Nguyet's fine for me. But as for the spells, yeah, that's how it goes. The output multiplies, sometimes even squares."

Kit grinned. "You sure you aren't breaking the laws of thermodynamics or something?"

Tuyet snickered. "Probably," he said. "Nguyet breaks most things."

Nguyet glared at him. "I do not!"

"Oh yeah? What about that lamp last week?"

"That was an accident!"

The ground under all their feet suddenly began to vibrate. Kit and Nita looked at each other in alarm. "Guys!" Kit said.

The ground's shuddering stopped. The twins looked at each other. "Uh, sorry…"

"It's him doing it," Nguyet said. "He's younger."

"Oh, yeah, right, two minutes younger!" Tuyet laughed. "That makes me more powerful."

"Are you two going out, or staying in?" Kit said.

"Staying in," Tuyet said. "That's what we wanted to check with you. We're putting together a notification list in the manuals so that wizards who're staying home can cover for the ones who're going on the road when the trouble starts. S'reee told us you guys were probably going off-world, so we added you to the list. You going through the Crossings?"

"Yeah."

"We've got a custom gate wizardry set out in the middle of the crater," Nguyet said. "Been a lot of traffic through there in the past few hours, in both directions. You can never tell . . . it might confuse Somebody." She grinned. When she did, that fierce look in Nguyet's face got fiercer. Kit liked it: It made her otherwise extremely delicate, "porcelain" prettiness look more like the kind of porcelain that's made into high-tech knives.

"I hope so," Kit said.

Tuyet's grin was even more feral than his sister's. "We'll keep an eye on things here," he said. "Get out there and make It crazy."

"That's the plan," Nita said. "Good luck, you two."

The twychild waved and headed on out of the force field, making their way down toward S'reee. "That was interesting," Kit said.

"Yeah," Nita said. "Imagine how it must have been for them. Joint Ordeals . . . never having to find someone to help you with a spell . . ." She shook her head.

"Having another wizard in your head with you all

day, instead of by invitation?" Kit said. "A little too weird for me."

"But if you've been used to it all your life," Nita said, "even before you knew you were wizards, then maybe we're the ones that would seem weird to them." She tucked her manual away. "Never mind. Here come the others."

The center of Spring Lake Crater was empty except for one thing: a large hemispherical force-field bubble. Inside it, laid out on the pockmarked, dusty gray surface, was a huge circle of blue light; and that outer circle was subdivided into about twenty smaller ones of various sizes. The diagram was a duplicate in pure wizardry of the more concrete and "mechanical" gating circles and pads of the worldgating facility at the Crossings. Everyone knew the drill, at this point, and one after another, Filif and Sker'ret and Nita and Ronan went out into the diagram and stood in the middle of one of the subsidiary circles. With Ponch bouncing along behind him, Kit made his way out to an unoccupied circle and stood in it.

"Everybody ready?" Sker'ret said. "I'll do the master transport routine—"

He began to recite a long phrase in the Speech, rattling it off with the assurance of someone who'd done it many times before. As Sker'ret spoke, and that familiar silence of a listening universe began to build around them all, Kit gazed back the way they'd come for a last look at the near-full Earth, the edge of its globe just touching the edge of Spring Lake Crater. A thought came unbidden: *What if this is the last time you see that?*

He shook his head. *Silly idea. We've been in bad places before and made it home, even when we thought we wouldn't.*

But there's something about this time that's different, the back of his mind said to him. *Everything's changing. The things you thought you could always depend on aren't dependable anymore. Maybe it's smarter not to take anything for granted now.*

Kit swallowed as the glow of the working world-gating wizardry rose all around them like a burning mist, beginning to obscure the view.

See you later, he said silently to the fading Earth ... and hoped very much, as they all vanished, that he would.

Target of Opportunity

DAIRINE STEPPED THROUGH THE brief darkness of Roshaun's portable worldgate into the huge, high-ceilinged, overdone space he called home, and waited for Roshaun to come out behind her. Sunlight poured through those tall crystalline "patio" doors off to the left, but it was a fainter color than it had been when she was here before. This light was a weary, dulling, late-afternoon orange that burned, but burned cool. In it, every bright surface in the room gleamed coppery, and the silver gilt of Roshaun's long flowing hair briefly matched the red of Dairine's as he came out of the worldgate.

Dairine put Spot down. The laptop put out legs and quickly crab-walked out into the middle of everything, producing as many eyes as Dairine had ever seen him come up with at one time. He settled himself down flat, pointing every eye in a different direction. Apparently the architecture had him fascinated. This Dairine understood, since Roshaun's living space in the palace on Wellakh closely resembled a three-way collision between an antique furniture warehouse, a jewelry store, and a Gothic cathedral carved and decorated by the artistically insane. Rich overlapping carpets covered the floor everywhere; sofas and wardrobes and tables and chairs ornate enough to be thrones were placed here and there under rich canopies. Delicately wrought lamps hung down from a ceiling almost lost to sight in an opulent gloom, through which the occasional gemstone gleamed down like a lazily observant eye.

Roshaun stood there looking around for a moment, then glanced over at Dairine. "I wish we did not have to make this stop," he said.

"Family stuff," Dairine said. "It's always a mess. You're just lucky to have parents who're wizards."

"Am I indeed," Roshaun said. "You shall judge. For the moment, I have to change."

"Really?" Dairine said in amusement. "You mean there's somewhere in the galaxy that won't immediately buy into Carmela's fashion statement? She'll be horrified."

Roshaun gave her what was meant to be a cutting look, and with apparent regret pulled off the floppy T-shirt that had been covering him to his knees. *Has Carmela got a thing going for him?* Dairine wondered. *But no, now it's Ronan.* She had to smile a little. *Wait till she figures out the ramifications of* that *one.* Dairine spared a second for an entirely clinical appreciation of the lean look of Roshaun's upper body above the soft golden-fabric "sweatpants" he was wearing. *How old is he in "real" years, I wonder? If there's even an approx-imation that makes any sense. Officially, as his people see age, he can't be much older than Nita or Kit.*

Roshaun carefully draped the T-shirt over an or-nately carved chaise longue. "I shall return momentar-ily," he said. "Do you require refreshment?"

Somehow Dairine didn't think Roshaun was likely to have a supply of her favorite soft drink on hand. "I'm okay," she said. "You go do what needs doing."

He vanished behind an intricately carved and gilded screen. Dairine glanced over into the middle of the floor, where Spot was still watching everything with all his eyes.

"How are you feeling?" she said.

"Peculiar."

That made her twitch a little. "Is that something new?"

"Not since this morning, if that's what you're ask-ing," Spot said. "I don't feel like I'm losing my mind. But then again, I haven't 'felt' any of these strange fugues you tell me I'm experiencing, either."

That was one of the things bothering Dairine the most. A computer that was losing memory or files was enough cause for concern by itself. But when the com-puter was sentient, and at least partly wizardly, and was forgetting things it was saying or thinking from one moment to the next—

"I haven't lost any spell data," Spot said, sounding to Dairine's trained ear faintly annoyed. "I've been running diagnostics constantly since this started to happen."

"And they haven't been showing anything?"

"No." Spot sounded even more annoyed.

Dairine sighed. "In the old days, we wouldn't have had these problems."

"These are not the old days," Spot said. "You are no longer half human, half manual. I am no longer just a machine with manual access. Both of us have become more, and less. And the new increased power levels do not make us who we were again. They only make us more powerful versions of who we are now."

Dairine looked out the doors at the setting Wellakhit sun. It looked like a huge shield of beaten copper, sliding down toward the sea-flat horizon. It seemed like an age ago, now, that time when she'd come home from her Ordeal with the constant soft whisper of a whole new species' ideation running under all her conscious thought, like water under the frozen surface of a winter stream. They had always instantly had the answers to any question—or had seemed to, the mobiles' time sense being so much swifter than that of the human kind of computer which was built of meat instead of space-chilled silicon. And the answers they'd come up with, she had always been able to implement with staggering force, since she'd come into her power so young. But slowly that power had faded to more normal levels, and the connection to the computer wizards of what Dairine thought of as the "Motherboard World" had stretched thin, carrying less power, less data. It never entirely failed; that whisper of machine thought still ran at the bottom of her dreams, and if she listened hard while waking, she could find it without too much trouble. But nothing now was as easy as it had been in the beginning. Knowing that this was the fate of wizards everywhere didn't make it any easier. *But I thought I wasn't wizards everywhere. I thought I was something different.*

Roshaun came out from behind the screen. Dairine's jaw actually dropped. *And I thought he looked a little too formal before.*

Those long golden trousers had been exchanged for others completely covered with thousands of what looked like star sapphires but were orange-golden and as tiny as beads. The upper garment was, by contrast, a simple gauzy thing, like a knee-length vest of pale golden mist. Under it Roshaun was wearing a massive collar of red gold with a huge amber-colored stone set in it, a smooth and massive thing the width of Dairine's clenched fist.

The stone shifted as Roshaun swallowed. "How do I look?" he said.

Between the realization that he was actually nervous and the total effect, Dairine was for once sufficiently impressed to tell him the truth. "Great," she said. "Tiffany's would want you for their front window. Why is it always gold with you people?"

"It's Life's color," Roshaun said. "In this way we do Life honor. What about you?"

Her eyebrows went up. "What *about* me?"

"Are you going to meet my father dressed like that?"

"Like what?" Dairine looked down at her own cropped T-shirt and baggies. "I look fine."

"Surely something more formal..."

Dairine made a face. Of various things she hated, dressing up (except at Halloween) was close to the top of the list. "Why not just tell him this is formal wear on my planet?"

"I could tell him that," Roshaun said, "but it would not be true." He frowned at her.

Dairine sighed. "Oh, all right," she said. She pulled out her manual.

"It cannot be a seeming," Roshaun said. "He will see through that."

Dairine frowned. "You're such a stick-in-the-mud sometimes," she muttered.

"And you are so intransigent and disrespectful," Roshaun said, "nearly all of the time."

"What? Just because I don't let you walk all over me, Mister Royalty?"

Roshaun let out a long breath. "He is waiting," he said. "This is going to be difficult enough as it is. Please do something about the way you look. Something genuine."

Dairine grimaced. Still...she couldn't think when he'd last said "please" to her; for a while she'd thought his vocabulary didn't even contain the word. "Oh, all right," she said. "Spot, what're the coordinates of my closet?"

"Here are the entath numbers," he said, and rattled off a series of numbers and variables in the Speech. "Do you want me to set it up?"

"Go ahead, knock yourself out."

A straightforward square dark doorway appeared in front of her. The darkness cleared to reveal the inside of the closet in Dairine's bedroom. As usual, its floor was a tumble of mixed-up shoes and things fallen off hangers; her mother had always said that when the Holy Grail and world peace were finally found, they would be at the bottom of Dairine's closet, under the old sneakers.

Dairine sighed and started pushing hangers aside. Last year's Easter dress and the dress from the year before looked unutterably lame. Lots of jeans, lots of school clothes . . . but none of them suitable for meeting a former king. "This doesn't look promising," Dairine said under her breath.

"Hurry," said Roshaun.

The tension in his voice cut short all the acid retorts Dairine could have deployed. "Oh, the heck with this," she said, irritable. She turned her back on the closet. "Spot, close that. Do we have a routine for *making* clothes?"

"Searching," Spot said, as the darkness went away. "Found."

In her mind, Dairine looked down the link between them and saw the wizardry he'd located. It was a matter-restructuring protocol which would use what she was wearing and turn it into something else. She glanced at Roshaun. "How unisex is what you've got on?" she said.

He looked surprised. " 'Unisex'?"

"Do girls wear that kind of thing where you live?"

"Well, yes, but—" Surprise became confusion. "What is the problem with your own clothes? What do your people usually wear when meeting your leaders?"

"If we've got any guts at all, a real annoyed expression," Dairine said. "Never mind, I can come up with something. Spot, hit it."

"Working."

A second too late it occurred to Dairine that this process might show Roshaun more about her than was anybody's business but her own. A sudden chill ran over her body as every stitch of clothing on her pulled an inch or so away and resolved into its component atoms, then started to reassemble in new shapes. Her first urge was to duck behind the nearest sofa, but it was too late; any movement could possibly result in a dress that came out her ears. She closed her eyes, gritted her teeth, and held still.

The chill faded. Cautiously Dairine opened one eye. Roshaun's expression was confused but not scandalized. *Not that that means anything in particular. Does his culture even have a nudity taboo? Never mind, mine does!* She looked down at herself.

"Whoa," Dairine said.

She was wearing a simple, scoop-necked, short-sleeved, floor-length dress, in a velvet as green as grass. Around her left wrist, where her watch usually went, was a bracelet of emeralds the size of quail's eggs, held together with nothing but a series of characters in the Speech—a delicate chain of symbols in softly burning green smoke, which scrolled through the gems as she watched. Another chain just like it held a single similar stone at her throat.

"Nice," Dairine said. Then she realized there was something on her head. She put her hands up to feel it. Her eyes widened, and then she grinned. Tiaras were back in fashion; no reason she shouldn't wear one. She turned toward Roshaun. "That okay?" she said.

Roshaun looked impressed. "There are likenesses to our own idiom," he said. "To what land of your world is such raiment native?"

"Possibly Oz," Dairine said, "but I doubt the Good Witch of the North is going to come after me for stealing her look."

"Good," Roshaun said. "This way—"

They headed toward those crystalline doors, Spot spidering along behind them. Out beyond the doors lay a goldstone terrace with a broad stone railing, and beyond that, a huge formal garden full of red and golden flowers and plants. Past the garden, the surface of the "sunside" of Wellakh spread: miles and miles of unrelieved flatness reaching straight to the horizon on every side—the everlasting reminder of the catastrophic sunstorm that had blasted half the surface of Wellakh to slag all those centuries ago.

Just in the doorway, before stepping out onto the terrace, Roshaun suddenly paused. He stood there for some seconds simply looking at the setting sun— straight at it, blinding as it was. Finally he dropped his gaze. "This is not good," Roshaun said softly. "Still, let us go."

They walked through the doors and out across the terrace, and as they did, Dairine thought she saw something stirring out there, a waving movement. Her first thought was that she was seeing the motion of wind in the garden plants. *But there isn't any wind,* she thought as they came closer to the rail. *Is there a—*

She froze. There were people out there…about a million of them. *Maybe two,* Dairine thought. *I don't know anything about counting crowds—*

Two million, six hundred and eight thousand, four hundred twenty-four, said Spot silently.

The multitude of Wellakhit men and women started just past the formal garden and went on and on, seemingly all the way to the horizon. The slight motion Dairine had seen was the million-times–multiplied tremor of people shifting a little in place as they stood waiting for someone to appear.

Roshaun walked up to the railing and just stood there, resting his hands on the broad rail. As he came to where everyone could see him, a sound started to go up from the crowd nearest the balustrade, and rolled back across it like a wave: a murmur of comment, curiosity…and straightforward hostility. These people wanted to see Roshaun, but not because they liked him. The murmur sounded to Dairine like the thoughtful sound an animal makes deep in its throat when it sees something it considers a threat, an utterance just short of a growl.

Roshaun simply stood there with his head up and let it wash over him. The sound got not necessarily more angry, but more pronounced. Roshaun moved not a muscle, said nothing. Very slowly the murmur began to die away again. Only when the crowd was quiet did Roshaun move at all, to look over his shoulder.

"Don't stay hiding back there," he said. "They know you are here. Come out and let them see you."

At the moment, it was the last thing Dairine wanted. No one could ever have called her shy—but not being shy in front of a classroom full of kids, or a crowd of wizards, was one thing. Not being shy in front of a couple of million pairs of staring, hostile eyes was something else entirely.

Dairine swallowed and stepped forward to stand beside Roshaun at the railing. She couldn't think of anything to do with her hands. She put them down on the balustrade as Roshaun had, and held very still.

She had thought it was quiet before, but she was mistaken. A silence fell over all the people at the edge of the garden, rolling back from them right across that vast multitude. The stillness became incredible.

Dairine didn't move a muscle, though she desperately wanted to bolt. The pressure of all those eyes was nearly unbearable. The faces closest to the two of them wore a look very like Roshaun's normal one: proud, aloof, very reserved. They were all as tall as he was, or taller, which made Dairine feel, if possible, even smaller than usual. And the expression in the eyes of the closest people held a hostility of a different kind than what they'd turned on Roshaun. *Alien,* it said. *Stranger. Not like us. What is* that *doing here?*

Dairine manufactured the small the-hell-with-you smile that she usually applied just before getting into a fight with somebody. "You might have mentioned this beforehand," she said under her breath.

"Why?" Roshaun said. "Would you have worn something different?"

Maybe a force field, she thought. "Who are they all?"

"My people," Roshaun said. "They have come to look at their new king."

"How long have they been here?"

"I have no idea," Roshaun said. "Perhaps since the time they heard that my father had abdicated."

Dairine tried to figure out when that might have been. A couple of days ago? She wasn't sure. "What do they want?"

"What I do not think I can give them," Roshaun said.

He turned his back on the great throng of people. Reluctantly—for to her it felt somehow rude—Dairine did the same. "Our transport will be here in a moment," Roshaun said. "We have very little time. However casually you may enjoy speaking to me, believe me when I tell you that such a mode would not be wise with my father. He may have resigned his position, but he keeps his power as a wizard—"

"However much of that anyone his age is going to have for much longer," Dairine said.

Roshaun looked at her, and for the first time Dairine understood what it was like to see someone's eyes burn. That sunset light got into them and glowed, impossibly seeming to heat up still further in Roshaun's anger. "I would not put too much emphasis on that if I were you," he said. "Not with him, *or* with me. He and I may have our differences, but anybody who would find humor in a wizard losing his power should probably consider how it would feel to them. Or *does* feel."

Spot came spidering along to her. Dairine bent down to pick him up, glad of the chance to get control of her face, for she was blushing with embarrassment at how right Roshaun was. "Sorry," she said.

"Yes," Roshaun said. And more quietly, over the upscaling scream of an aircar that Dairine heard approaching, he said, "I, too. Now stand straight and properly represent your planet."

Dairine stood straight. Between them and the crystalline doors of Roshaun's residence-wing, the egg-shaped aircar, ornately gilded like everything else here, settled onto the terrace and balanced effortlessly on its underside's curve without rocking an inch to one side or the other. Dairine looked up past it to what she had partly forgotten—the mountainous bulk of the rest of the Palace of Wellakh, bastion upon bastion and height above height, all carved from and built into the one peak that had survived the solar flare that slagged down everything else on this side of the world. The palace was not only a residence but a reminder to the kings who lived in it. *Your family saved us all once,* it said in the voice of the people of Wellakh, *and you showed such power then that now we fear you. We keep you in wealth and splendor now; just make sure you protect us. Because if the Terror by Sunfire should ever come again, and you* don't— And the message was far stronger than usual with them all standing there, silent, watching.

What will you *do now, new young king? We are waiting...*

Manservants dressed in quieter versions of Roshaun's "normal" clothes, the Wellakhit long tunic and soft trousers, appeared from the front of the aircar and came around to bow before the two of them and touch the car's surface. It opened before them, and Roshaun turned to Dairine and nodded; she picked up Spot and stepped in. Inside were luxurious cushioned seats that followed the curved contour of the aircar, and as Dairine sat down and Roshaun sat across from her, she saw that the aircar's surface was selectively transparent—they could see out, but no one could see in. As the car rose, Dairine looked out past the palace and toward the horizon, clutching Spot to her, gazing out a little desperately across the widening landscape to see where the people ended and the landscape began. It took a long time before she got a glimpse of the plain stone of the "sunside," golden colored or striated in blood and bronze, barren and desolate.

Turning back to Roshaun, she was surprised to see him looking at her with concern. "Are you all right?"

"They scare me," Dairine said after a moment.

"You would not be alone," Roshaun said.

The aircar kept rising past the face of the palace; terrace after terrace, building after building fell away beneath them as the peak into which the palace was built narrowed almost to a needle. Beneath the final height was one last terrace, and the aircar made for this, lifting just slightly above it and settling down onto the polished paving.

The door opened for them. Roshaun got out first,

and then turned to help Dairine down. She was surprised to feel, as he took her hand, that his was sweating.

Without warning, she found herself starting to get angry. *Here's one of the most arrogant, self-assured people I know,* she thought, *and just the thought of going to see his father has him freaked. That's not the way things should be!* As she stepped onto the paving, she squeezed his hand a little.

He gave her a look she couldn't read. Dairine dropped the hand, unsure whether she'd misstepped, and followed him toward the pair of huge bronze doors that faced the sunset and were emblazoned with the sun.

That sun split before them as the doors ponderously swung open. Dairine put Spot down, and they all walked in.

Their footsteps rang in the huge and echoing space they entered, and their shadows ran far before them down the length of the polished floor, to merge with the dimness at the far end of the severely plain great hall. *Use the time to compose yourself,* Roshaun said silently.

Like you're *doing?* said Dairine. She could feel all too clearly what was going on inside his head. But then that had started to be a problem lately.

Roshaun didn't reply. But by the time they were actually getting close to the throne, the racket inside his head had started to die down somewhat.

Throne was not the best word for the chair in which that very tall man sat waiting for them. It was backless and had arms that rose from its seat on curving up-rights; it sat not on any dais, but on the floor. However, the man sitting in it made it look like a throne by the way he sat, both erect and somehow completely casual about it. He watched them come without moving a muscle, and as they got close enough to get a decent impression, Dairine tried to size him up. His clothes were like Roshaun's, though in a darker shade of red-orange; his red hair was shorter than Roshaun's by a couple of feet, and he wore it tied back, so that the angles and planes of a face very much like Roshaun's, sharp and high-cheekboned, were made more obvious. His eyes, as emerald as Roshaun's, were more deeply sunken, a little more shadowed by the brows; his face looked both more thoughtful and more dangerous.

Roshaun stopped about six feet from the throne. Dairine half expected him to bow, but he simply stood there, silent, waiting.

Slowly the man stood up. Roshaun locked eyes with him as he did so. His height astounded Dairine; meeting this man's eyes for long would give even her father a sore neck.

"You came more quickly than I thought you might," said the man. The voice was like Roshaun's, a light tenor, somewhat roughened by age.

"This promises to be a busy time for us all," Roshaun said, "and it seemed discourteous to keep you waiting any longer than necessary."

Roshaun nodded, and glanced at Dairine. "I would make you known," he said, "to Nelaid ke Seriv am Teliuyve am Meseph am Veliz am Teriaunst am Antev det Nuiiliat; Brother of the Sun, Lord of Wellakh, the Guarantor—"

Roshaun fell suddenly silent, as if not knowing quite what to say next.

"Guarantor that *was*," Nelaid said, looking at Dairine. "It does sound strange, the first time one says it." And now his eyes were on Roshaun again.

Roshaun swallowed. "Father, this is Dhairine ke Khallahan," he said, "wizard."

It's title enough for me, she thought. She gave Nelaid a very slight nod, thinking that between wizards, even if they were royalty, that was gesture enough. *Besides, if I nod too hard, this crown could fall right on the floor.* "I am on errantry," Dairine said, looking up at Nelaid, "and I greet you."

"I greet you also," Roshaun's father said in the Speech. He stepped away from the throne, looked at Roshaun.

"Well, son," he said, "you were not long in donning the Sunstone, as is your right. This only remains to complete the accession." And he glanced at the chair.

Roshaun swallowed again. "I wanted to talk to you about that," he said.

His father tilted his head a little to one side. "I fail to see what could still need discussion," he said.

Roshaun turned to look back down the length of the hall, toward the doors and straight into the light of the Wellakhit sun, still slowly setting. The light caught strangely in the great gem at his throat, washing out its amber fire and leaving it as colorless as water.

"I will not be staying," he said, turning back toward his father. "Errantry takes me elsewhere."

Nelaid nodded, just once, very slowly. "What the Son of the Sun says is, of course, law." But Dairine could hear something else coming. "From the sound of it, however, you came not to ask me what you should do, but to tell me what you had already made up your mind to do. I suspected as much."

"Royal sire," Roshaun said, "I would hardly make such a choice without consulting with the Aethyrs."

It was Roshaun's name for both his people's version of the manual—a small sphere of light into which the wizard gazed—and for the Powers that spoke through it. "The Aethyrs speak to you in a different voice than they do to me," Nelaid said, "which is perfectly normal. But I must question your interpretation of their position."

"Royal sire," Roshaun said, "once you could question that. But you gave up that right when you abdicated as Sunlord in my favor."

"I remain the ranking Senior on Wellakh," Roshaun's father said, "and *that* right of questioning I have not abdicated. You have yet to satisfy me as to how much of this decision is yours."

And he looked at Dairine.

Dairine instantly flushed so hot that she knew she must be clashing horribly with her dress.

"If you assume I've been unduly influenced in my decision, royal sire," Roshaun said, "you're in great error."

"Better believe it," Dairine said softly. "Paying attention to anything *I* say is hardly one of *his* favorite things."

Nelaid gave Dairine a look that was genuinely

amused. "Forgive me, *hev ke Khallahan,* but I have known my son longer than you have." He turned back to Roshaun, the look in his eye more challenging now. "It's the mark of a noble heart to want to help friends in trouble. But when that help distracts you from those you already have a duty to help..." He glanced toward the great barren plain outside, all covered with people.

"Father," Roshaun said, "staying here in obedience to our people's insecurities will solve no problem that faces us now. We must not waste precious time doing the same old things; they will not avail us. I will be protecting our people, regardless of how it looks to them."

"They will not ask you for explanations," Nelaid said. "They will simply watch what you do. And if they do not like your actions, they will keep their counsel...until one of them finds a way to come at you on some visit to the liveside. An energy weapon, a bomb or a knife, an unguarded moment..." Roshaun's father shrugged. "Even you must sleep sometimes. As must I. And your mother."

Roshaun's eyes were on the throne. "I know the fear you've both lived with, all these years," he said. "The knife that almost took you. The bomb that missed you and nearly took the queen. Do you think I'm trying to shirk my turn?"

Dairine could feel the slow burn beginning. "Excuse me," she said to Nelaid, "but in case you haven't heard, your son put his life on the line to fix our Sun while he was on excursus. He saw the problem with it before any of us did. He helped us design the wizardry to deal with it. And when stuff got rough up there, he walked straight into my star wearing not much more than a force field and a smile. That looks like 'brave' to me, so if you're seriously suggesting he doesn't have what it takes to deal with being king here—"

Roshaun's father put up his eyebrows. "You are outspoken," he said.

"Speaking truth to power," Dairine said, "is never 'out.'"

The slightest smile appeared on Nelaid's face. "There are problems associated with this course of action—"

"Royal sire," Roshaun said, "*you* were the one who taught me that sometimes, as wizards, we have to make choices that fly in the face of what looks like common sense. 'Reason is not always everything,' you'd say. There remains that other voice that speaks, sometimes, in accents we don't understand. Or understand perfectly well, and violently disagree with."

"My words exactly," Roshaun's father said. "Unusual to hear you agreeing with them. This would not have been your normal mode...before you went away."

"Nor would it have been your mode to produce so sudden a surprise as your abdication," Roshaun said, "when I left thinking that everything here was going smoothly, and an excursus would do no harm."

"Things change," said the former Sunlord, "as we see." And once again he looked at Dairine. "You arrive for your people's first sight of you as Sunlord, and what do they also see, standing at your side? An alien, garbed in raiment much like that of Wellakhit royalty, wearing some other world's life-color, gemmed like a Guarantor. The rumors are flying already. Does another world have designs on the rule of ours? Either by straightforward conquest, or more intimate means?"

Dairine's eyes went wide as what he meant sank in. "You mean they think that we—that I— *You tell those people that they are completely nuts!* Even if I were old enough to think about stuff like this, which I seriously am not, I have zero interest in being anybody's queen! Especially not *his*—"

And then Dairine stopped short as she saw the peculiar look that had appeared on both Roshaun's and Nelaid's faces.

"Uh," she said then, and blushed again. "Maybe there was a less tactful way I could have put that…"

That small smile reappeared on Nelaid's face. "Well," Nelaid said after a moment, "I perhaps am reassured. But as for our people—"

"Father," Roshaun said, "you taught me that a wizard turns away from the Aethyrs' guidance and his heart's at his peril. Yes, our people may misunderstand either Dhairine's presence here or the fact that I will now immediately leave. For either eventuality, I'm quite prepared. And when we come home from this errand, perhaps they will assassinate me for what they consider a betrayal. It would not be the first time that kind of thing has happened—or the last."

"And, meanwhile, you mean for me to assume the burden of Sunwatch once more, even though I've formally laid it down."

When Roshaun spoke at last, his tone was surprisingly gentle. "You said it yourself, Father," Roshaun said. "What the Son of the Sun commands is law. As a wizard, you know where *your* duties lie. But if I must—"

Nelaid stood there silently for a few moments. "No," he said. "A king's first command should be less painful. I will stand the Watch...though Thahit is once more showing signs of instability."

"That I saw when I returned," Roshaun said. "I examined the star briefly a little time ago, while testing the Stone to see if it interfered with my perceptions. The instability is the one we predicted together before I left."

"What we did not predict was the increased acceleration of the stretching effects in space," Nelaid said. "The sun's instability is increasing accordingly."

"I noted that, Father," Roshaun said. "So while I am gone you must intervene if necessary." He paused. "That said, I should not be taking this into harm's way. I prefer that you keep it for me while I am gone." And Roshaun reached up and started to unfasten the great golden collar around his neck.

Roshaun's father stood silent for a moment, and then made a sidewise gesture with one hand, which Dairine read as "no." "Wizardry is the reality at the heart of the Watch, my king," he said. "I have no need of a mere symbol to do what needs to be done." The tension in the air fell away very abruptly as Roshaun's father spoke. "But the Stone makes you king...so its place is with you. If you young ones fail, it will not matter for long whether the Stone is lost or not. We will all follow you into the dark soon enough."

"And if the star stammers, what of it?" said a voice from the floor.

Startled, the three of them looked down. Spot was regarding Roshaun's father with several eyes.

"Lean times of barren hope
Wait on the composite's daughter,
Sharpening the edge of life."

Spot fell silent. Roshaun and Nelaid exchanged speculative glances.

Dairine felt like swearing. "Couldn't you have waited half an hour?" she said under her breath, and looked up at Roshaun and his father. "Would you two hold that thought?" She felt down toward where the memo pad should have been, in the pocket of her cargo pants... then remembered that there was no pocket there anymore, not to mention no pants. She let out an annoyed breath. "Spot—"

"What?"

"The notepad!"

"In your claudication, along with everything else that was in your pockets."

"Thanks." She reached sideways, pushed her hand into the empty air, and groped around, coming up with the pad and a pen.

Roshaun's father was looking at Roshaun in mild confusion. "When one has manual access, even in alien idioms," he said, "can one not usually take notes by—"

Dairine looked up from her scribbling to throw

Roshaun's father a look that should have singed even a Sun King around the edges. "Everything changes— isn't that what you were just saying? You were right. So don't rub it in."

The two Wellakhi looked at Dairine with exactly matching expressions of superior amusement, then turned back toward each other. Nelaid said, "Where will you go now?"

"Dhairine's associate comes of a species of sentient, wizardly computing devices," Roshaun said. "Mobiles, they call themselves. Both their reasoning power and their wizardry are tremendous, according to the Aethyrs. We go to consult with them on ways to attack the expansion. Meanwhile, the people outside should be told that I am gone on their business—and the universe's. I will come back as soon as I can."

Roshaun's father held his son's eye for a few moments, then bowed slightly to him. "As the king commands," he said. He glanced at Dairine as she finished with her scribbling, nodded to her. *"Dai stihó,"* he said, and with a soft clap of displaced air, he vanished.

Roshaun let out a breath and turned back toward the doors. "Come on," he said.

Dairine turned, too—and then stopped, hearing footsteps. She paused, looked over her shoulder.

Coming toward them was a woman—not as tall as Roshaun's father, but so beautiful that the sight of her made Dairine simply stop where she was. She wore the Wellakhit long overtunic and soft trousers, but in flowing hazy blue; and her hair was the original of

Roshaun's, except longer and fairer, and so feathery light that it seemed to float around her as she came toward them. Dairine was immediately devoured by a desire to have hair like that, even though taking care of it would leave her with no time for a social life, and buying the necessary amount of shampoo would destroy her college fund. "Uh," she said, "Roshaun—"

He had already brushed past her, hurrying. Dairine had never seen Roshaun hurry before. He went straight to the woman, reached out, and took both her outstretched hands and pressed them against his forehead.

The woman smiled and pushed Roshaun a little away. "Are you taller?" she said.

"Motherrrrr...!" Roshaun said.

She smiled past Roshaun at Dairine. "Roshaun *tekeh*," she said. "What about your friend?"

"Ah," Roshaun said. He let go of his mother's hands and glanced over at Dairine.

She smiled, too, and headed over to them, immediately impressed by anyone who could make Roshaun sound like he wanted to roll his eyes. Roshaun looked at Dairine as he put an arm around his mother and said, "I would make you known to Miril am Miril dev ir Nuiiliat, the Sister of the Sun, the Lady of the Lands of Wellakh. Mother, this is Dhairine ke Khallahan."

Her smile was so friendly and kind that Dairine was tempted to simply say, "Hi, Roshaun's mom." But for the moment she did what Roshaun had done, and took the hand held out to her, pressing it to her forehead.

"You're very welcome, young wizard," Lady Miril

said in the Speech. "And you also, sir," she said to Spot, who was peering out from behind Dairine. "I heard you say you were in a hurry, Roshaun, so I won't keep you."

"You heard all that?" Dairine said.

"If the queen of Wellakh doesn't keep her ears open," Lady Miril said, "things deteriorate...especially around this one and his father." She hugged Roshaun a little harder. Roshaun squirmed, but only slightly.

"There was a little...uh..."

"Friction?" said Lady Miril. "Always. These two stalk about in all directions doing good...and then hardly have a kind word for each other. If there's a way for either of them to rub the other one the wrong way, he'll find it. And in recent days the intensity of the game has increased somewhat."

"Mother," Roshaun said, looking at her with a surprised expression, "you saw all this coming..."

"It hardly takes a wizard to tell what's going on with your royal sire, my son," said Lady Miril, "when you've known him since *he* was just a badly behaved prince." She grinned. "And as for *you*—"

Roshaun actually blushed. Lady Miril, though, went quite sober. "But the weariness has been growing on your father, Roshaun. And then while you were away, there was another attempt..."

Roshaun looked at his mother...and then the expression on his face went very strange.

"That was meant for me, was it not?" he said.

"I believe so," said his mother.

"That was why you wanted me to go on the excursus," Roshaun said softly. "You wanted me out of the way, on Earth."

"The thought of a vigorous new power in charge of the planet would annoy some people," Lady Miril said, glancing at Dairine. "They prefer the status quo to an unknown."

"And then," Roshaun said, "Father was caught up in an attack meant for me..." He turned a shade that even for him was pale. "And now... what I just did—"

Was the most idiotic thing I could possibly have done, Dairine heard Roshaun think. *I have thrown my father straight back into the situation from which he thought he had finally been freed. I have—*

Roshaun disentangled himself from Lady Miril. "Mother—" He held a hand out to one side. In it, blinding, appeared the little globe of white fire that was his manual. He slipped his other hand into it, feeling around for something. "We should go."

"No, royal son," said Lady Miril, and the fire-globe vanished. "Not in here. If you will be king in name, you must be king in action as well, or you leave your father in greater danger than before. A king does not sneak away. If he leaves, he does so where his people can see him."

Roshaun looked over at Dairine.

"We can teleport, if you like," he said.

"I don't mind the walk," Dairine said after a moment. "I can use it to compose myself."

Lady Miril flashed Dairine an amused glance. "When will you be back, Roshaun?"

He paused. "I am not sure. Father has told you about the expansion..."

She looked grave. "Yes," she said. "Go do what you must. We'll wait. Dhairine—"

Dairine took the Lady's hand again. "Go well," Lady Miril said.

She turned away.

Roshaun headed for the door; Dairine went with him. About halfway down to the doors, she said, "I can't wait to get out of these clothes."

"The way you did before?" Roshaun said. "That was entertaining. And informative."

Now what the heck is that *supposed to mean?!* Dairine thought.

"Probably not what you think," Roshaun said. "But when you do resume your usual guise..." He reached out toward her as they went, and very casually tapped the cabochon emerald at Dairine's throat.

"Not that," he said. "That I think you should keep. It becomes you."

"Uh, okay," Dairine said, and blushed again, she hardly knew why. "It's just—I'm hard on jewelry. It gets busted, or..."

The expression on his face was so strange that she said, "All right, sure, I'll keep it."

"Good," Roshaun said. "Meanwhile—"

They were at the doors. Roshaun stepped through them. Dairine hung back, waiting. Out beyond the mountain of the palace, all across the plain, the two million Wellakhit people still stood, their quiet now more hushed than before because of the great height;

and before them, near the slender rail at the highest terrace's edge, stood Roshaun's father.

Roshaun went directly to Nelaid and stood beside him at the edge of the terrace. Dairine watched Nelaid's face, set and proud, as he turned it toward his son. After a few moments, Roshaun stretched out a hand.

His father took it. They stood there in the view of that great assemblage, and slowly an uncertain murmur went up at that gesture that Dairine guessed suggested more a joint kingship than one vesting solely in one party or the other.

"You told them?" Roshaun said.

"I did," said Nelaid.

"Then by your leave, royal father," Roshaun said, "I go. And, Father, I am sorry."

"My son," Nelaid said, "the Aethyrs go with you."

And carefully, as if he wasn't sure how to do it in front of all these people, Nelaid embraced his son. The sound from the crowd swelled, still confused, but somehow approving.

Roshaun let his father go. "I have to attach this to a substrate," he said, as he produced his manual again and reached into it, pulling out the compressed darkness that was the subsidized worldgate.

"Go ahead, son."

As Roshaun made his way back toward the wall near the doors, Dairine saw Nelaid throw her a look that was much less stiff than his regard had been earlier. She bowed her head to him again, not too far for fear of what the tiara would do, and then turned to join Roshaun, with Spot spidering along behind her.

"You were going to have some coordinates for me?" Roshaun said.

"Here," Spot said.

Roshaun flung the darkness of the worldgate up against the wall; it spread out into a black circle a few meters wide. "One thing," Dairine said, as Spot fed the temporospatial coordinates of the Motherboard World to the worldgate wizardry.

"Yes?"

"Something you said back there," Dairine said, as the worldgate's vacuum-warding subroutine snapped to life. "'When *we* come home from this errand'?"

"It was a slip of the tongue," Roshaun said after a moment.

"And therefore not true?" Dairine said.

Roshaun wouldn't answer.

Dairine smiled and led the way through the gate.

Collateral Damage

NITA LOOKED AROUND HER as they materialized inside the vast space of the Crossings Worldgating Facility. It was night there; as usual after sunset, the vast, remote ceiling had apparently vanished, and the milky turbulence of the upper atmosphere had cleared, letting the extravagant night sky of Rirhath B show through.

Automatically Nita did the first thing you do in the Crossings when appearing out of nowhere: She looked down to check whether the transport surface they were all standing on was "dedicated" or not. Fortunately, it wasn't. "Come on, guys," Nita said, "everybody out of the zone."

Filif followed Nita over the line as Kit and Ponch and Ronan were crossing over in a slightly different direction. Ponch bounded past them, lolloping off down the wide central corridor of this part of the Crossings. "Don't run!" Nita called after him, concerned that he would go crashing into some unsuspecting alien; but there wasn't much point. They were easily a quarter mile from the nearest other beings who were catching late (or early) gates to their destinations. Ponch galloped along, oblivious, tail wagging, and no one paid him any attention.

Nita looked at her watch as Sker'ret poured past her, heading for one of the many bluesteel information kiosks that rose ten or twelve feet from the floor at intervals all along the length of the concourse. *It really is later than we've usually been in here before,* Nita thought. To her watch, she said, "Crossings time, please?"

The face of the watch restructured itself to show her the thirty-three-hour Crossings day. *It's nearly twenty-nine o'clock,* Nita thought. *Probably no surprise that traffic's a little down.*

Ronan had stopped just the other side of the line and was standing there staring up at the vast starry darkness overhead. Rirhath's neighborhood of space was full of variable stars that slowly but visibly shrank and swelled while you watched. "It's like they're breathing," Ronan said.

Beside him, Kit nodded. "You haven't been here before?" Kit said.

"Once," Ronan said. "It wasn't anything like this then."

Kit smiled. "The daytime view's interesting, though I always wonder what'd happen to all that levitating stained glass up at ceiling level if they had a power failure. This is a lot less tense."

He looked after Ponch as Nita and Filif came over

to them. "You know what he's after," Nita said, looking after Ponch.

Kit shrugged. "Give him a moment to run," he said. "When he comes back we'll get down to business." Then he yawned.

"You and me both," Nita said, rubbing her eyes. "It's getting late back home. We ought to think about where we'll stop for the night."

"Wherever Ponch leads us," Ronan said. "My passenger'll stand guard while we're sleeping. Everybody's got their pup tents with them, so they'll be comfortable enough."

"And I've got my cell phone," Nita said. "If my dad needs to get in touch, he won't have any trouble." She sighed. "I still wish we could sleep at home...I'm getting nervous about what's going on there."

"Going back and forth wouldn't be smart," Ronan said. "For one thing, it'd make us a lot easier to track. Might as well just send the Lone One an invitation to follow us straight to wherever it is we're going."

"Yeah, I know." Nita knew he was right; she just hated to admit it.

Sker'ret was reared up against the nearby kiosk, using numerous upper legs to work its controls. Nita went over to him and looked over a couple of his topmost shoulders. Below the kiosk's translucent surface, in which Sker'ret's topmost two pairs of legs were partially embedded, several layers of patches of light flowed with characters in the Speech. "Find what you're looking for?" she said.

Sker'ret curved a couple of eyes backward to meet hers. "Not yet," he said.

He's never this terse. What's going on? She rested a hand on that beautiful candy-glazed metallic-purple carapace, just behind the head segment. "Sker', are you okay?"

He sagged a little. "Not entirely." He turned some eyes up to gaze at the deep red charactery now running up and down the kiosk-pillar's length.

"If you need help—"

"Not at the moment. But thank you." Sker'ret curved back another couple of eyes toward her. "What about Ponch?"

Down the concourse Nita could see the shiny black shape wandering along toward them, still wagging his tail. "I'll see if he's ready to start work," she said.

Kit was standing there with his arms folded, shaking his head, watching Ponch head toward them. *You were trying to overhear what he was smelling,* Nita said privately. *Any luck?*

Kit gave her a resigned look. *Motor oil,* he said. *Cocoa.*

Motor oil? Nita turned to look up the concourse at Ponch again; he had paused to sniff at another of the information kiosks. *I guess for him those smells symbolize what Ronan and the Champion are after?*

That's my guess, Kit said. *He thinks he's on the right track. All we can do is let him get on with it.*

Ponch came ambling over to Kit, looked up at him, and nosed his hand. *I'm hungry!*

Ronan came back to them and looked down at Ponch. "So when are you going to get started?"

Ponch gave Ronan a slightly scornful look. *I've been working ever since we got here. But I'll need a little more time to sort the scents out. For the time being, you two just talk among yourselves.*

What amused Nita was that he was looking only at Ronan while he said it. Ronan looked a little taken aback.

Ponch turned his back on him. *And while I work on the scent-sorting,* he said to Kit, wagging his tail, *we might as well get something to eat!*

"I don't know," Kit said. "Maybe it's not good for some people to be full of food when they're supposed to be really sharp and heading out on the trail."

Ponch gave Kit a very cool look. *Oh, I get it. Deprive me and I'll function better? Let's see how that works.* He sat down. *Hmm, I feel strangely weak...* Ponch fell over on one side with his tongue hanging out one side of his mouth; one eye looked pitifully at Kit. *Can't... seem to... move...*

Kit looked over at Nita. "Blackmail," Kit said.

Nita shrugged.

"Oh, all right," Kit said. "Come on, let's see what we can find."

Ponch sprang to his feet, spun around in three fast, tight circles where he stood, and then shot off down the concourse. Kit jogged after him. Behind them, ostentatiously by himself, Ronan strolled away.

Filif came up next to Nita, also looking after them, but mostly at Ronan. "And to think that the One's Champion is hiding in there."

"One version of it," Nita said. "An avatar, I guess

we'd say, sort of a splinter of the whole Defender...as much as could fit inside a human being, anyhow." She reached out to readjust Filif's baseball cap. "The concept doesn't seem to surprise you much."

"Why should it? The One's Champion does that kind of thing all the time, the Wind says. Seems like It loves to dress up."

Nita grinned. "Well, you haven't seen it the way we have," she said. "It lived at Tom and Carl's for a long time, disguised as a bird." She rubbed one ear thoughtfully. "It had some issues then, too. Kind of a temper..."

She could feel Filif's amusement. "Such was the Defender's way with us, as well. It was the Great Tree, the Star-Reacher, that first caught the Wind in its branches and shared the sound of it with us." Filif turned most of his eye-berries to look down the other end of the concourse, and upward toward the vast and splendid Rirhait sky. "Before that, the Wind was just another noise. After that, it became the sound of words and wizardry, the power to change our world..."

Nita glanced around them. "Fil, did you see where Sker'ret went?"

"Uh, no." Filif rotated in place. "He was working at that kiosk."

"We can always message him," Nita said. "Come on, let's see what they're up to."

The two of them headed in the direction that Kit and Ponch had gone. The Crossings might have been quieter than usual, but Nita didn't mind that, since it meant that you had less chance of being run over by aliens and their luggage while rubbernecking. The place was nearly half the size of the island of Manhattan, and besides the actual worldgates—set into the floor all down the length of the concourse, as their entry gating area had been—it was also full of endless haphazardly stacked modular bluesteel "cubes" containing shops, lounges, living areas, food courts, and every other kind of facility necessary to cater to the needs of the thousands of species that used the Crossings as a vital transportation link among several major galactic and transgalactic civilizations. Even at a "quiet" time like this, there were any number of fascinating beings to look at as they wandered from place to place, gazing into the windows of stores or restaurants. *Though not as many as usual...,* Nita thought.

"Is that Kit coming back?" Filif said to Nita. "Who's he with?"

Nita peered down the concourse. "Doesn't look like him." She took another look. "But they're human." There were three people there, heading in their direction—two boys and a girl, Nita thought.

"Other wizards," she said to Filif, as they got closer and it became plain that the approaching three were Earth-human and not some other variety. One of the boys, with shaggy fair hair, was wearing dark pants and a matching dark sweater that might have been a school uniform; the other one, a dark-haired kid, was in jeans and a windbreaker, close enough to what Kit was wearing and close enough to his height that Nita could see why Filif might have made the error. The girl, who had short brown hair, was wearing what seemed to be a short, richly patterned silk kimono over jeans and low-heeled boots, a look that Nita admired as soon as she saw it.

The newcomers were a hundred feet or so away from Nita and Filif when Kit and Ponch appeared from one of an array of cubicles over to the left. *Over here,* Nita said silently to Kit. *We've got company.*

Ponch came bouncing up to Nita, who reached down to ruffle up his ears. "So how was it?" she said.

We didn't even go to a restaurant, Ponch said, in profound disappointment, throwing a reproachful look over his shoulder at Kit. *He just went to a machine and put words from his manual in it and food came out. But there was only one blue thing. That was hardly enough. Look at me! You can see my ribs.*

"Later," Kit said. "We need to find Ronan and Sker'ret. And talk to these guys, I think."

"*Dai stihó!*" the girl said, as they got close.

"*Dai,*" Nita and Kit and Filif said more or less in unison.

"You're just up from the Moon?" said the boy in the school uniform, in a broad Australian accent. "Is the gate still open there?"

"It was a few minutes ago," Kit said.

"Great," said the boy. "We're heading back."

"Where've you been?" Nita said. "If it's not private."

The second boy shook his head. "Edge of the Local Group," he said. "Over by IC 1613."

"How are things there?" Nita said.

The first boy looked grim. "That galaxy was always kind of thin and spread out to begin with," he said.

"But it's a lot thinner now. You know the Katahn empire there?"

Nita and Kit both shook their heads. Filif said, "I know of it. How does it fare?"

"Badly. Its systems are being pushed away from each other so fast that the empire's falling apart," said the boy in the jeans. "The big crowd of blue-white stars in the middle of that galaxy is being ripped up; the whole thing could turn into a blazar."

Nita sucked in her breath. The boy shook his head. "We're going back to get some help. There are a few really young kids back on the Moon right now. Might be we can get together enough raw power to slow down the expansion."

"Even if we can't do that right away, we should be able to keep the blazar from igniting," the girl said.

"We think," said the Aussie-sounding boy.

All of them trailed off. They looked terrified, but determined. Nita thought, *And that's how we look to them, I'll bet.*

"Good luck," Kit said.

"If there is such a thing," said the girl. Her look was defiant. "But we're not going to wait to find out. Come on. *Dai.*"

The three of them waved and went back the way Nita's and Kit's group had come.

Nita turned to watch them go as Ronan came out of another of the cubicle shops over on the right and rejoined them. "So," he said, "the big gut here finish stuffing himself?"

Ponch gave Ronan a dry look. *I wouldn't talk if I*

were you, he said. *That greaseball hamburger you were eating was nearly strong enough to drown out the scent of what we're tracking.*

"Which you've finally got nailed down?" Kit said.

The scent's faint, Ponch said, *but I can find the way from here, or at least get us headed in the right direction. How do you want to go?*

"Using a fixed gate would be better right now," Ronan said.

Then I can show you the way in my head, Ponch said to Kit.

"And I can use the manual to convert those into co-ordinates the Crossings gating system can use," Kit said. "But we'll need to go talk to the station staff to get them to allocate us a gate."

"Yeah. Let's message Sker'ret."

I can smell where he is, Ponch said. *This way.*

Ponch galloped off down the concourse toward the intersection where the secondary concourse wing met the major one they were in. Just past the spot where the two wings met rose an open structure of blue-green metal, looking like a cross between an office cubicle and a set of monkey bars. Around it a number of Rirhait people were gathered, making a noise like a lawn mower having an argument with a rock it had found hiding in the grass.

Sker'ret was there, the front half of him reared up off the floor as he worked at one of the subsidiary kiosk-columns that made up the body of the structure. The column had extruded a control console covered with patches of embedded light, which Sker'ret was tapping at with great speed. Three of the gathered Rirhait were looking over one or another set of his shoulders; two others were rushing around the cubicle as if they were looking for something. With a wizard's ear, Nita could hear Sker'ret saying to one of the Rirhait looking over his shoulder, "See, this is all you need to do. It's easier than you think. If you just make sure that the equations for the hypersphere balance have the same asymptotic expansion variables laid in—"

He looked up as Nita and Kit and Filif and Ronan stepped up to the cubicle. "Oh," Sker'ret said.

"We're about ready," Kit said. "Can you finish up here?"

"I'm trying," Sker'ret said. He cocked about three eyes each back at the two other Rirhait who were looking over his shoulders. "So are we clear about this, sibs? This is going to hold you just fine for the meantime."

"I'm not sure exactly where to go after that, though," said one of the Rirhait who was watching whatever he was doing at the console. She sounded nervous.

"What about the spin foam variables?" asked the other Rirhait.

Sker'ret reached out some spare legs to the column on the other side of him. It extruded another floating keyboard structure toward him, which he poked until it displayed the keying pattern he wanted, and started tapping on while still typing into the first one. "You do it like this," he said. "Let the software handle the brane issues; it's built for that. Ignore the zonotope and the polar sine relationships. All you have to do is intuit the way the spin foam variables are sliding, and add about a radian and a half—"

"You following this?" Kit said to Nita under his breath.

"You kidding?" Nita muttered. "It's math, Kit, but not as we know it."

"—and then you pull in the last twenty sets of figures from the leech-lattice version of the hypersphere-packing readings, paying special attention to the kissing number. Then you just massage the string density quotient—"

Sker'ret was too intent on simultaneous input at both consoles to notice the sudden frantic wreathing of eyes of all the Rirhait surrounding him, and the way the two who had been pacing now froze in place with all their eyes pointing over Sker'ret's shoulders. "And that'll hold you for the next two standard periods at least."

"Good," said another Rirhait voice from behind Sker'ret...and now it was Sker'ret's turn to freeze. All his eyes held quite still, looking at what he had been keying in...and then very slowly one of them curled up and around to look behind him.

The Stationmaster of the Crossings, a Rirhait somewhat bigger than Sker'ret and of a lighter, more silvery-blue shade, poured into the cubicle and arranged himself among and over some of its interlocking rails and bars, peering with various eyes at the keypads where Sker'ret had been working. "So you've changed your mind," he said. "I'm glad you've come to your senses. We need you here."

Nita wasn't sure how someone so smooth-carapaced could seem to bristle, but as Sker'ret curved some more of his eyes around in the Stationmaster's direction, he was managing it. "Unfortunately, you're wrong," Sker'ret said. "I haven't changed my mind."

"What?" The Stationmaster pointed all his eyes at once at Sker'ret. The other Rirhait around him all pulled their eyes in close to their bodies.

"You need me more where I'm going," Sker'ret said. "I've spent all the time I can here. This fix will deal with the problem at hand...and now we're going to head out."

"Are you insane?" the Stationmaster said. "*Look* at this place!"

Nita looked. She couldn't see anything wrong with it, except that it did seem much emptier than usual.

Sker'ret glanced around with various eyes. "This is only a symptom," said Sker'ret, "of what's coming. And no one with all their brains in place wastes time treating symptoms. A cure's what's needed...and that's what we're dealing with now."

The Stationmaster flowed a little closer to Sker'ret and did something that Nita found briefly alarming: It reared up and grasped Sker'ret's front end with some of those many little clawed legs. "Listen to me, broodling," the Stationmaster said. "What's happening out there is far too big for any species to cure. The world is changing! And there's nothing we can do. How do you seriously expect to keep *space* from expanding?"

"But wizards—"

"If wizards could have stopped it, they'd have done that already," the Stationmaster said. "We've just got to teach our mechanisms to handle the new distances and vectors in the long term...or all this is going to come to a halt, and with it the transport and commerce of three galaxies!" More of the Stationmaster's legs waved around them at the travelers of many species who were hurrying by, ignoring them.

"Your sibs have better sense," the Stationmaster said. "They're not running off on some fool's errand at a critical time. But you've been hard to reason with lately." The Stationmaster glared with many eyes past Sker'ret at the gaggle of humans and others who were uncomfortably watching all this unfold, and one eye stared straight at Nita. "Something to do with the company you've been keeping."

Nita went very hot and opened her mouth. Before she could say anything, Sker'ret shook off his ancestor's forelegs and bent every eye on him. "I'll thank you not to malign wizards of goodwill and friends of mine," he said. "And as for the long term, there'll be no long term for anyone or *anything* if we don't move to alter what's happening."

"And so you'll go off and abandon the place to which you owe the most responsibility."

"We can't turn inward now!" Sker'ret nearly shouted. "This is no time to try to find ways to dig our own burrow deeper! Turning outward to solve the bigger problem is the only way for us to save ourselves!"

"I have been Master here for nearly two hundred

circuits of our sun," the Stationmaster said, very quietly. "And it's amusing to hear someone barely out of his fifth decade claim that he understands better than I how to handle the threat that—"

"You don't understand a *tenth* of what you think you do!" Sker'ret said. "You're too scared to raise an eye or three to peer past the obvious conclusions. And your job description has changed, but you haven't even noticed—even though the truth's staring you in the head and waving all its eyes at you. You saw the Station's stats! Gating across the three major galaxies is down almost thirty percent! *Everyone*'s turning inward, from fear, and that's just what our old Enemy wants! To drive us apart, each into his own burrow, to keep us away from the interaction that keeps us in touch with the Prime Mover and makes us one—"

"I don't have time for metaphysics right now," the Stationmaster said. "I need to keep this place running. If you're going to forget where your real place is and go running off Mover-knows-where, there's nothing I can do to stop you. But you're jeopardizing your positions here. *All* of them."

There was an unnervingly final sound to that. Nita swallowed, waiting to see what Sker'ret would do.

He disentangled himself from the support framework and dropped back to the horizontal position. "Perhaps I am," he said. "But at least, when we succeed in what we're doing, there'll still *be* a place for my replacement to have a position at. And a place for my sibs to learn whether you value them as you do me."

All his eyes were fixed on all his ancestor's. There was a terrible silence. Then slowly, one after one, the Stationmaster turned those eyes away.

Sker'ret didn't flinch. "We need a gate," he said after a moment.

"The one-seventies are all idle," said the Stationmaster, in a tone of voice that made Nita wonder how she'd ever thought it sounded rude *before*. "Use one of them. And don't let us delay you."

He turned and swept off down the far side of the concourse. With reluctant backward looks, Sker'ret's sibs went pouring after him. A few seconds later, only Nita, Kit, Filif, Ponch, and Ronan stood there.

"Wow," Kit said softly.

Sker'ret glanced over at Nita with some of his eyes; the rest of them were still on his esteemed ancestor and his sibs as they hurried away across the shining floor.

Nita shook her head as Sker'ret flowed out of the cubicle structure, and hunkered down beside him as he paused, still looking down the concourse. She rested one hand on the carapace-segment just behind his head. "What I said about our basement," she said, "I meant it."

"Thank you," Sker'ret said, and the strange eyes that Nita had previously had so much trouble reading now seemed full of gratitude and weariness. "But everything is still all wrong."

"Wrong how?"

Sker'ret paused. "None of that sounded like what my ancestor would say," he said at last. "You don't get to be Stationmaster of the Crossings by saying how things can't be fixed. You find ways to fix things, no matter *what* it takes. 'Broken' isn't an option. And the bigger the problem, the more committed you are to fixing it." Sker'ret shook his head, and the ripple of it went all the way down his body. "That's the kind of thing he would always say to me. And all of a sudden, to hear him sound like he did just now—" Sker'ret sounded confused. "He'd given up. He didn't sound... like *him*, somehow."

Kit looked at Nita. "Tom warned us," he said, "that there would be changes because of the way space was stretching. Ethical changes, personality shifts."

Everyone looked uncomfortable. "It's going to get worse," Nita said. "We've just got to get on with what we're doing. Though it really is freaky." She glanced at Kit. "You see any adult human wizards here while you were on your own? I didn't."

Kit shook his head. "Sker', where are the one-seventies?"

"Hang a right, thirty stads down on your left," Sker'ret said. "It's one of the bigger clusters."

"Let's go," Nita said.

Their group left the cubicle and followed Sker'ret as he led the way around the corner and down yet another of those seemingly endless, shining white corridors, all the gate hexes and squares lining either side of it alight...and many of them empty. For someone who knew the Crossings as well as Nita did, the effect was unnerving.

"This way." Sker'ret turned off into a large circular area, maybe a quarter mile across, that budded off the transverse concourse. The area was completely surfaced with gate hexes, nested fairly closely together, outlined in many different colors depending on the species intended to use them.

"Here we are," Sker'ret said. He led them over to the large gate at the center of the hex grouping, went to its kiosk-column, reared up against it, and tapped his uppermost legs against it. The column extruded a console like the ones he had been working with at the central resource station.

The embedded outline of the largest hex came alive with a clear fierce blue. Sker'ret turned to Kit. "What have you got for me?"

Kit looked at Ponch. Nita could feel something of the communication between them; it was like watching someone whisper to someone else, while not being able to hear what they were saying...and, still, at one remove, it smelled of cocoa and motor oil. *Weird*, she thought, as Kit turned to Sker'ret.

"I'm not sure I can handle this keyboard," he said.

"Just speak it to me in the Speech," Sker'ret said. "I can do the input."

Kit recited a long string of words, numbers, and variable statements to Sker'ret. Sker'ret's little end-of-leg claws danced over the keypad.

"Done," Sker'ret said. "Everybody into the zone, please. Thirty seconds to the transit."

He pushed the keypad away from him; it vanished into the column. Sker'ret headed into the middle of the biggest hex, and they all followed. Nita was half amused, half scared to see how everybody put themselves as far into the middle of the hex as they could, so that at the end of the exercise three humans, a dog, a centipede, and a Christmas tree all stood back to back, facing outward against whatever might come at them.

"Twenty," Sker'ret said. "Ten."

Nita looked around her at a section of the Crossings that had no one in it but them, no one at all. It was unnerving.

"Five."

Her heart was pounding. She glanced over at Kit.

"Zero—"

Everything went dark.

Nita had to blink a couple of times to get used to the darkness. There was air, at least—Crossings gateways had a vacuum-guard on them, so they wouldn't dump you out into an inimical or absent atmosphere without warning. As usual, she looked up first at the sky.

There wasn't one.

They stood on a small, arid, empty world, and Nita had known it was empty the moment they came out of nowhere. The lack of life has a specific feel to which any wizard past Ordeal quickly becomes sensitive, a sensation of something missing that ought to be there, but isn't, like a pulled tooth. Above them, there should have been stars.

But there weren't. Nita tried to make sense of what she was seeing as she looked up. It was like when you stare into the dark for a long time and start imagining that the dark itself is moving. But this movement was real. It was as if the darkness was heaving with small shapes, no bigger than grains of rice—but all darker even than the blackness where they grew.

Nita had a sudden thought of the mealworms she'd once found all through a bag of bad flour—heaving, rustling against each other, like a live thing that was also a lot of little live things. The darkness of space above them stirred and heaved with little darknesses. They were *there*. And Nita very much did not want to think what they would start to be like when they were bigger.

She swallowed, fighting the thought of being sick, which wouldn't have helped. Before this, space might have been inimical, bitterly cold, airless, arid, but it was at least clean. Suddenly that innocent, unself-conscious deadliness had been taken from it. Something was trying to squirm through the crevices of reality and fill that calm dark emptiness, void of everything but stars, with something heavier than starstuff, darker than the longest night, and horribly, mindlessly alive... with no interest in any other kind of life except squeezing it out, pushing all the native life more and more apart, filling everything so full with itself that there was no room for anything else. This was what the dark-matter expansion looked like, up close and personal. But the dark matter, innocent enough in itself, had had something added to it... something terrible.

She looked over at Kit: His expression was as shocked and horrified as hers must have been. She wondered how all the wizards there were could possibly stop such a thing. *And we don't even* have *all the wizards there are. Old age and experience can beat*

youth and power every time, Dad always says. Now all
we've got is youth and power. Is it going to be enough?
And what if it isn't?

Kit put out a hand and said a few words in the
Speech. A moment later, a small bright spark of wizard-
fire materialized above his hand. Nita followed suit,
telling hers to hover over one shoulder and just behind
her. Around them, the others brought light about as
well—Sker'ret's carapace came alive with it, and all of
Filif's berries blazed. Ronan took that clip-on ballpoint
pen out of his pocket and gave it a shake. A moment
later he was holding the Spear of Light in its full
form—the seven-foot Spearshaft glowing softly, the
head of the Spear wreathing itself in a chilly white-
golden flame.

Kit was looking up into the darkness, and to Nita's
eye, he looked faintly unwell. "That has to be the
creepiest thing I've ever seen," he said.

Ronan stood leaning on the Spear, his free hand
resting on his hip, his shadow lying pooled black
behind him from the Spear's radiance. It might have
seemed a casual stance at first. But as Ronan gazed up
into that unhealthy, seething dark, Nita started to sense
how tightly he was controlling himself, like someone
working hard not to run away. His face was very still,
though, and Nita for the first time actually saw someone else look out of Ronan's eyes. The expression was
one of recognition coupled with a very controlled
anger. The one who looked out had seen something
like this before.

She went over to him. "Something familiar about this?" she said.

Ronan nodded. "From a long, long time back," he said. "When the Lone One first revealed that new thing it had invented, entropy, this was one of the early side effects."

"And the Champion stopped it?" Kit said, coming over with Ponch to join them.

Ronan shook his head. "No. It's weird, but when the Pullulus first began to occur, it was the Lone Power Itself that stopped it."

Nita found that bizarre. "Something too dangerous for even It to manage?"

Ronan shook his head. "I used to think I knew My brother's mind," said the Champion with Ronan's voice, "but that issue was never clear to Me or any of the other Powers. Whatever, this perversion of dark matter hasn't been seen since. To see it again now... I find that troubling."

"Troubling" didn't come close to describing Nita's feelings. "I am really not wild about the idea of sleeping here," Nita said. She looked down at Ponch. "Couldn't you walk us a little way, just enough to get us out of here?"

I'm tired, Ponch said. And he lay down and put his head down on his paws, though Nita saw him watching the sky with an expression of concern.

Nita let out an annoyed breath. "Look, we've got our pup tents," Kit said. "We'll be comfortable enough for a few hours."

Nita nodded. "Yeah," she said. "Right." *No point in making a scene about it. I'll cope.*

Sker'ret and Filif came over to them, getting out their pup-tent interfaces. Sker'ret reared up on his rearmost legs, hung the silvery rod of the spell interface on the empty air, and pulled on the little string of characters in the Speech that hung down from the rod. A subtle shimmer of wizardry a few feet wide followed it down, like a roller shade following its pull cord. Sker'ret "fastened" down the spell-surface that acted as gateway to the room-sized pocket of space, waggled a few eyes at Nita and Kit, and poured himself inside, vanishing. Past him, Filif was doing the same; he slid in through his own doorway and was gone.

Nita let out a long breath. "Ronan?" she said.

He shook his head. "I'm okay," he said. "My partner's got energy to spare. We'll stand guard."

Nita set up her own pup tent, then glanced at that awful unstarred sky again. For some time now she had been getting into the habit of trusting her hunches, and her hunch right now was to be worried. *What's going on back home?* she thought. *What's going on with Daddy? And Tom and Carl? And Dairine, what's she getting into? Is she under a sky like this someplace?*

And is she as freaked out as I am?

Nita stepped into her pup tent and looked around, checking out the space that had become her home away from home while she and Kit had been away before. Everything was as it should be. There were a few pieces of spare furniture from home—a TV table and a spare desk chair, along with a beat-up old sofa that had been down in the basement until her dad had it recovered and suggested she move it into the pup tent; over the back of the sofa, a multicolored wool throw that her mom had crocheted a few years back; off to one side, some boxes of dry snacks and cereal, some six-packs of fruit drinks and mineral water. A pile of books to read at bedtime, some notebooks and assorted school supplies. It all should have been very comforting...except it wasn't. She couldn't get rid of the image of the darkness outside.

Then suddenly Nita got angry. *I may be freaked, but I'm not going to just roll over and let the fear run the way I act!* She turned around and put her head out through the interface again, staring defiantly up at that evil sky. Above her, the dark Pullulus seethed and heaved against itself, blocking away the stars. Looking at it a second time didn't make it any easier. *It probably isn't ever going to be easy,* Nita thought. *And I don't care.*

She glanced to one side and saw Kit leaning out through his own pup-tent interface. Past him, Ronan stood leaning on the Spear, looking up at the darkness. He, too, turned his gaze away from it now, looking at Nita.

"You, too, huh?" Kit said.

Nita looked at him for a moment, then gave him a quick, angry smile, and vanished back into her own space...feeling, once again, not quite so alone.

High-Value Target

DAIRINE BECAME CONSCIOUS THAT she was lying curled up on a chill, smooth surface. She then became conscious that she had been *un*conscious, and had no idea for how long. *Ohmygosh, the shields!* she thought. But as she took an involuntary breath, she realized that the force field protecting her and Roshaun was running exactly as it should. Otherwise, the two of them would have been freezing cold, not to mention smothering in a next-to-nothing hydrogen atmosphere.

She opened her eyes and blinked to get focus. The only thing to be seen at the moment was the ground on which she lay: almost perfectly smooth and flat, shining like a polished floor, softly dappled with subdued shades of gold and rust underneath the slick surface. *Well, we're where we ought to be*, Dairine thought. *But how come every time I arrive here, I do it flat on my face?*

Dairine found that she had her arms wrapped around Spot. *You okay?* she said silently.

No problems.

Good. She pushed him carefully away from her onto the planet's surface and rolled over onto her stomach. Then she immediately wished she hadn't; her stomach rebelled. Dairine lay there and started to retch, thoroughly miserable. *It's not fair! I thought I was done with this kind of thing. I didn't think a subsidized worldgate would act this way.* But the tremendous difference between the vectors and accelerations of Wellakh and this extremely distant world were too much for humanoid bodies to take no matter how sophisticated or powerful the worldgate was.

Dairine was distracted from the sickness, though, by an upscaling sound in the back of her mind—a muted roar of life lived at a three-quarter beat, rushing, as quick and strong as a waterfall in spate. *I'm back in circuit with the Motherboard!* It was an astonishing sensation, after having become used over time to the faint rumble of trinary data that was normally all that reached Dairine down her linkage to the mobiles' world.

She also realized that her clothes had changed again. *What happened to that dress?* Dairine said.

I replaced it with your normal clothes while in transit, Spot said.

Okay. However, Dairine put a hand up to her throat and found that big emerald still there; she smiled slightly. *Good call. Come on.*

She levered herself up on her hands and knees and

looked around, holding still again because her stomach was still roiling. "Roshaun?"

He had come down on the surface behind her, sprawled; now he lifted his head, and winced. "That was not," Roshaun said, "the usual sort of transit."

"Nope. You all right? Besides your injured dignity, I mean."

Roshaun rolled over and slowly sat up, grimacing— then looked ashen all of a sudden, and had to put his head down on his knees. Normally such a sudden show of vulnerability in Roshaun would have delighted Dairine, except that she was too busy keeping herself from throwing up. *I am not going to barf a second before he does,* she thought, breathing deeply.

Roshaun, however, did not throw up. Very slowly he straightened again, looking up and around . . . and then let out a long breath of wonder. Dairine got up on her knees, looking up at the vista she remembered so well.

It was worth looking at, even in the daytime. Halfway up the sky from the high and strangely distant-seeming horizon was a small, dull red star, so dim that you could look at it directly. But beyond the planet's sun, undimmed by it, standing high and spreading across half the sky, was the delicate shimmer of a barred-spiral galaxy, the wide-flung arms richly gemmed in the soft golden gleam of an immensely old stellar population. Roshaun sat looking up at that still splendor for a good while before he stood up.

"Transits by subsidized gate are normally instantaneous," Roshaun said, still looking up at the distant glory. "We seemed to be in that one for…quite a long time. How long?"

Dairine glanced at her watch. It said eight thirty, but she'd forgotten to set it to handle gating-transit time, and now its second hand wasn't moving. "I've got to reconfigure this thing," she said. "I'll get a reading off Spot and let you know in a while."

"How far from your own world is this one?"

"At least forty trillion light-years," Dairine said. "Maybe more, but I've never done the math. I don't know about you, but when I start getting into the trillions, I find that forty and forty-five look pretty much alike."

Roshaun stared at her in shock. "Then we are over our universe's event horizon," he said softly. "That galaxy there…and the one we're in now…would have intrinsic velocities faster than light. As far as our home galaxy is concerned, this place doesn't even exist."

"You got it," Dairine said. "And for people here, *our* galaxy doesn't exist. Except they know it does, because I came from there." She stood up cautiously. Despite the size of the planet, the gravity here was less than that of Earth; the effect was like being on Mars, and left you light enough to bounce if you weren't careful. Roshaun looked around at the curious surface—slick as glass and dappled with faint drifts of color buried under the perfectly level surface. Here and there across the surface were scattered various sharp cone shapes. "Volcanic," Roshaun said.

"Yeah," Dairine said. "The volcanoes laid down the surface structure, all these layers of silicon and trace elements. It goes down for miles; the whole place is one big computer chip. But it's a lot quieter now than I remember it." "Quieter" had more than one meaning, for the place to which she and Roshaun had transited had been the birthplace of the mobile species, the scene of the end of her Ordeal, and the site of a battle that had cratered or reduced to slag a deal of the surrounding real estate. Those craters remained, as did glass heaped and humped by the terrible forces that had melted it and spattered it for miles around. Elsewhere, the surface looked much as it had when she had first arrived—like the surface of a gigantic billiard ball, except where the cones of the ancient volcanoes pointed at the sky. And it was as empty. Dairine looked around in vain for any sign of a welcoming committee.

Roshaun had turned his attention to the planet's star. "There's something odd about the primary's flare pattern."

"Wouldn't be surprised," Dairine said. "I chucked a black hole into it."

Roshaun put his eyebrows up. "Stars in your neighborhood seem to have a rough time of it."

"If ours acts weird, talk to Nita," Dairine said, rather annoyed. "First time it went out was on *her* watch."

Roshaun slipped out of the gauzy overrobe he had been wearing on Wellakh and folded it up. "You know quite well the Isolate was to blame," he said, reaching sideways for access to the space pocket in which he stored things while on the road. He stuffed his formal overrobe into the claudication's opening, then came out with that oversized T-shirt of Carmela's again, and slipped into it. "That brief snuffing may be the cause of your star's recent instability."

Dairine got up, too. "Well, I still want to know why, when the Sun was talking to us, I couldn't understand what it was saying, even though we were all working in the Speech."

Roshaun shook his head. "The situations we have been dealing with have been unusual for all of us," he said. "And you were under considerable strain. If you—"

"Are you saying I couldn't cope with the stress?" Dairine said. "I seem to remember that *you*—"

Then she stopped, seeing his expression. "Sorry," Dairine said, turning away. "Sorry. Why do I have to bite you every time you say something that might be useful?"

Very quietly, Roshaun said, "When you find out, do let me know. It's information I might find useful as well."

Dairine let out a breath and looked around. "But where *is* everybody? I don't get it; this is where I saw them last."

She turned, scanning that impossibly distant horizon. In all that huge space, nothing moved. Dairine let out a long breath and got ready to drop to her knees and get in closer circuit with the Motherboard, to send a message she hadn't thought she of all people would have had to send: *Hey, guys, I'm here. Anybody home?*

"Wait," Roshaun said. "What is that?"

Dairine turned to look. A single small shape came

steadily toward them across the pale, pink-glazed surface of the world, light from the whirlpool of stars glancing off its shiny shell. It was apparently just a hemisphere about half a meter wide, scooting along the floor of the world like a windup toy—the impression made that much stronger because of the movement of all the little legs around its outer edges. The dome was a pale translucent white, striated in cross section with thin bands and layers of many colors. And it glowed as if between some of the layers a faint light burned, illuminating the layers above and below like moonlight through stained glass.

Dairine grinned and took off at a trot toward the little scurrying shape, being careful about the gravity. Shortly the leading edge of the bubble of air she took with her "ran over" the little approaching dome; and the instant it did, the dome began to decelerate, looking at her with many-lensed eyes that bubbled out in a breath's time on its forward surface.

"With?" it said in the Speech, and then burst out laughing.

Dairine skidded to a stop, laughing, too, at the reminder of the first thing this mobile, or any other, had said to her. She reached down, picked him up, and swung him around. "*Gigo!*"

"As always," the mobile said, wiggling his legs a little, and exuding the same innocent pleasure that had been his specialty since he was born. "Dairine, it's good to have you back in the flesh!"

"Sorry it took so long," she said, feeling guilty. "It

wasn't easy to come, right after my Ordeal. There was a lot to do. And then my power levels changed..."

"We know," Gigo said. "But you had business to do closer to home. And not even at power levels like your first ones would it be easy for a wizard to come all this way out to the Edge of Things, especially just to be social! It doesn't matter. We knew you'd come back when you could."

She hugged Gigo again. "You always were good at understanding," Dairine said, putting him down. "Look, I brought a friend. Roshaun—"

Roshaun slipped into Dairine's air bubble and paused to gaze down at the mobile. "We know him very well," Gigo said. "We looked at him through you a long time ago. Sunlord, you're welcome."

Roshaun bowed. "An honor, Designate," he said. "And well met on our common journey."

"You are, indeed," Gigo said. "And here is our oldest colleague."

Spot came ambling along. Gigo stepped over to him, and the two of them paused, shell to laptop case, silent for a moment while they communed. *"Dataaaaaa...,"* Spot said under his breath.

"The breath of life," Gigo said. "We'll be trading a lot more of that. Dairine, come on, there's much to do."

"Yeah," she said, and glanced around. "Where *is* everybody?"

Gigo looked around as if confused. "Where is—" And then he laughed. "Oh, they wouldn't have come *here*! This is the birthplace, where we began. We try to keep it as it was, the way you do with this one—" And the undersurface of the ground under their feet abruptly flashed out of translucence into imagery, coming alive with a vast glowing image of the surface of the Sea of Tranquillity, and the place where the first lunar module had landed. The four of them seemed to stand in the middle of one corrugation of a single immense boot-print pressed into the powdery dust.

Dairine broke up laughing. "Wow!" she said, turning right around to see how far the imagery effect went; it flooded straight out to the horizon. "What have you guys been *doing* to this place?"

"Remaking it in our image," Gigo said. "Though we're still working out just what that is."

"Okay. Where do we go from here?"

"Oh, we don't have to *go* anywhere," Gigo said. The boot-print flickered out, to be replaced by a sudden tide of multicolored light that rushed away in all directions, tracing a myriad of glowing lines and curves under the glassy surface—the outlines of geometrical figures, and deeper down the three-dimensional shapes of solids; spheres and cubes and hypercubes, interlocking, interacting in sizzling bursts of light that were also words and characters in the Speech.

Roshaun looked out across the spreading plain of light and let out another long breath of astonishment. "This is all one great spell diagram," he said, as the patterning fled toward the horizons, and past them. "The whole planet!"

Gigo grew a ball-jointed handling arm and gestured

off toward one side. There, amid the lines of light, an empty circle grew: a gating nexus. "If you'll stand over here—"

Dairine and Roshaun and Spot made their way over, stepped over the boundary, and stood inside. "At least this worldgating won't make me feel like the last one," she said to Gigo.

"Almost certainly not," Gigo said.

And to Dairine's astonishment, the circle started to slide across the vast spell diagram as a mobile inclusion, skating across it the way a drop of water scoots across a hot frying pan. The rest of the spell slid and slipped around it, letting the circle pass. Slowly it began to accelerate, and the spell diagram around them poured past more and more quickly until it was one great multicolored blur.

Dairine kept wanting to brace herself against something as the acceleration increased, but there was nothing to hold on to—and there didn't seem to be any need to brace. Though the glowing spell diagram landscape slid more and more quickly past, she and Roshaun and Spot and Gigo might have been standing perfectly still in the middle of the plain. "Are you guys messing around with *inertia* somehow?" Dairine said to Gigo.

She got the sense that Gigo was grinning. "For transits like this," he said, "we temporarily rewrite the kernel that manages local gravity and mass in our solar system. It's no big deal."

"Oh, listen to you," Dairine said, and snickered. " 'No big deal.' "

"They certainly take after you," Roshaun said.

"I'd like to think it's mutual," Dairine said. Certainly for a while after she'd come back from her Ordeal, she'd often awakened in the middle of the night and not been quite certain whether she was human or machine anymore—mortal creature or living manual. To find herself looking at her bedroom ceiling, and not this remote and spectacular sky, had sometimes come as a shock to a mind still filled with the glowing afterimages of spells being built faster than any human being could think. Now here was the concrete reality behind the images, spreading itself out before her—a world of true computer wizards, already evolved far past anything she would have had the brains to create, and still evolving at speeds Dairine couldn't grasp, mired as she was in the kind of thoughtspeed mandated by a brain made of carbon compounds and water. *Any comparison between the mobiles and me has got to be flattering. Or it will be later, assuming we can all figure out something to help us* have *there be a later.*

Ahead of the transit circle, something poked up above the horizon. At first Dairine thought it was more volcanoes. But these shapes were more regular than volcanoes, far more pointed, and much too tall. As the transit circle shot toward them, Dairine realized that she was looking at huge needlelike towers, all of the same glossy silicon as the planet's surface. No tower on Earth could have been so tall; only the low gravity here made such buildings possible... along with a little magic. The towers glittered where the setting red sun's light caught them, high up, and every one was etched with the white fire of wizardry in endless moving patterns of words in the Speech and symbols from spell diagrams.

The place was one huge wizardry endlessly in progress, the typical shimmer of a working spell wavering around every tower like a halo of pale fire. The whole vast interlinked structure hummed with a faint vibration, its own version of the silence that leaned in around a wizardry as you said the words of the spell in the Speech. But here, Dairine knew, the words were being spoken by the planet's interlinked machine intelligences faster than any noncomputer being could utter them. Working in "quicklife" time, thousands of times faster than any Earthbound computer, the intricacy of the mobiles' spells would be far beyond anything a human wizard could ever live long enough to construct. At the thought, Dairine's heart leaped; it was the first time she'd dared to feel real hope in their present situation. *If anybody can help us find a way to stop the darkness,* she thought, *it's these guys.*

The towers just kept rearing up and up, and time and time again Dairine had to readjust her sense of scale. Part of the problem was the planet's size; it was bigger than Earth, and the more distant look of the horizon played tricks on her. But as the transit circle drew closer to the towers, and their bases proved to be as wide as the base of the Empire State Building but their peaks more than four times as tall, Dairine gave up trying to work out from moment to moment how big things were. *Just really, really big,* she thought. *My guys have been busy!*

As she looked ahead and the transit circle started slowing down, it seemed to Dairine that the ground at the feet of the towers was darker than elsewhere. They got closer, and the effect started to look strangely granular—

And then Dairine saw what was causing it, and her mouth went dry. The diagram was exactly as it had been all the way across the planet's surface. The difference here was that it was obscured by the bodies of shifting mobiles—thousands of them; hundreds of thousands of them. *Maybe millions...*

The transit circle slowed; the obscuring shapes became more distinct as they approached the edge of the central ring of towers. Crowded around the towers' bases were many shapes that Dairine had invented—mobiles with all kinds of manipulating devices and oculars, sporting locomotors of every kind, from legs to wheels to treads. But there were also countless new shapes more involved and outré than anything she could have thought of. The transit circle slipped between two of the towers, heading for the center of the mile-wide ring of spires. The waiting mobiles concentrated in that great space drew aside to let it pass, a great crowd of tall slim shapes like trees of glass, low broad mobiles like domes or cylinders, all glittering with reflected wizard-fire.

"Just *look* at all of you," Dairine said to Gigo, astonished.

"You said that we should make more of ourselves to share the world with," Gigo said. "So, after you left, we did."

She shook her head. "I wouldn't have thought you could find enough energy to do all this."

"We've found other ways to draw power since you went away," Gigo said. "We found out how to sink wizardly conduits into alternate spaces empty of anything but physical energy. Now we have power that never runs out, and we've passed the conduit technology back to the Powers That Be."

The tremendous crowd of mobiles gathered close around the transit circle. Dairine couldn't see past the first few layers of surrounding mobiles, but through her contact with the surface she could feel the building wave of emotion running back and forth through the substrate that connected them all. The mobiles were as afraid of the building darkness as she was; they had seen it growing for what seemed like far longer. They were as angry as she was about what that darkness was doing. But they were also filled with resolve, and a strange joyful certainty of success that had roots in nothing but the fact that Dairine was there. "Welcome!" they all shouted, with voices, or silently, through the Motherboard: "Welcome, Mother, welcome, Creator, welcome here, *welcome home!*"

Dairine started to fill up with tears, and didn't care. Out here on the fringes of this universe's life, at the edge of the longest night of all, the mobiles she had created had made themselves into a lighthouse in the dark—the most distant home of wizardry, and possibly the most powerful. She scrubbed her eyes dry and stood up straight.

Beside her, Roshaun looked out across the tremendous crowd. *And here I was telling you how to behave like a monarch,* he said silently. *Perhaps I spoke out of turn.*

Familiar shapes pressed in out of the crowd toward her and Roshaun and Spot and Gigo—mobiles Dairine had designed herself, seen born from the planet's crust, and named. Tall mobiles and short ones, fat round ones and low flat ones all crowded around. Some she knew instantly, from a distance. One was a tall gangly design that had always reminded her of a stork.

"Beanpole!" she yelled, and grabbed him... and then the shorter mobile behind him, all arms and lenses. "Hex! Oh, and Pinout, look at you!" And behind Pinout came Loop and Sulu and Storm and Truman and Augusta, String and Strikeout and Drive and Buffer and Peek and Poke... a crowd of mobiles through whom Dairine made her way, hugging them one after another until she felt like her front was one big bruise. Last of all came one of the smallest and plainest of the mobile models, just a dome with legs. It stood in front of Dairine, looking up almost shyly. It was Logo.

Dairine picked him up and hugged Logo with her eyes squeezed shut. The sight of him brought her Ordeal back in unusual clarity—a long, cold, nerveracking time full of impromptu bologna sandwiches and the gleam of that red sun on the pale glass of the plain, the glitter of the plain as it shattered under the upward-heaving bodies of the newborn mobiles, the darkness that fell over them all as the Lone Power arrived to interfere in yet another species' Choice. But the darkness had a completely different feel to it now.

She put him down after a moment. "You're okay," Dairine said.

"And so are you," said Logo. "I was worried. You all by yourself, back on that little world, with nothing around you but slowlife."

Dairine smiled. "It's all right," she said. "Slowlife has a good side." She glanced over at Roshaun, and then looked around for a place to sit as the transit circle faded into the smooth glassy surface.

Immediately next to her, and so suddenly that it made Dairine jump, the ground grew a chair. Dairine bumped into Roshaun; he steadied her. "*That* was interesting," he said, examining the chair, a sleek one-piece construction with a Danish-modern look to it.

"No kidding," Dairine said, getting her balance back and bending over to have a closer look at the chair. It was banded with the usual striations of the planetary subsurface, and these had many faint layers of glow between them, like the mobiles. She glanced over at Gigo. "Does the world usually do this kind of thing since you started working on it?"

"Normally it requires more provocation," Gigo said as Dairine sat down on the chair. "We've tailored it from the first to be responsive to desire. But until recently, you had to elucidate the desire first. These days the substrate's been anticipating us."

"The power increase," Roshaun said.

"That's right. We're still mastering it. Here comes the imaging team—"

Several mobiles who'd been standing around now moved off to one side or another, and about twenty others, of all shapes and sizes, appeared scattered among them.

"Like any other wizards, we all have specialties," Gigo said. "But some of us enjoy working in teams, and the imaging team is one of the oldest. They started work shortly after you left; now there are more than eighty thousand of them scattered around the planet. These are the team leaders: Cam, Mikhail, Strontium, Bunny—"

"It's great to meet all of you," Dairine said. "What have you been looking at?"

"Everything," said Cam.

Roshaun raised his eyebrows, looking skeptical. "That must take up a great deal of your time."

Dairine just grinned. "You don't get it, Roshaun," she said. "They don't just mean all kinds of things, or everything they have time for. They mean *everything.*"

"The more we became able to see," Logo said, "the more we realized how we could be most useful. We decided we could store all the knowledge in the physical universe if we could just see it, find the places where it's stored, learn how to read what's written in every kind of information storage—everything from the heart on out. That's what we do here, out at the edge. That's our purpose."

Dairine could only shake her head at the size of the

vision. "Guys," she said after a moment, "you make me proud."

"That is our other purpose," Beanpole said. "Our first one."

Delight and embarrassment left Dairine briefly speechless. Roshaun eyed her, amused. "Cousin," he said, "would the technologies make any sense to me?"

"Some might," said Strontium, a low, domelike mobile whose whole surface was a pattern of lenses and mechanical eyes. "One is an in-matter viewing routine that lets us look out of the heart of any 'light-matter' object from an atom to a star if we know its coordinates."

"What about the dark matter?" Roshaun said.

"Long ago we tried using it for the same purposes," Beanpole said. "Why not make use of something there's so much of? But it couldn't be spoken to until recently. Now something has spoken a word to it that we never could. Now it's alive...but also hostile to life. It won't stop its expansion until it's destroyed every living thing, across the worlds."

"Our local wizards tried to stop it," Dairine said, "and couldn't."

"We tried, too," Gigo said. "We enacted a few local reversals, but the effect always reasserted itself more quickly every time. We realized we were teaching the dark matter how to expand faster, so we stopped wasting time with the symptoms and started hunting for the cause."

"And now that *you're* here," Gigo said to Dairine, "we'll shortly find it."

Dairine swallowed as she looked around at them all, gazing at her in such certainty. They scared her worse than Roshaun's people had—for they were all expecting the Mother of their Species to come up with the good idea that would save the universe.

"Let's take this one step at a time," Dairine said. "Or start with a smaller problem first, and warm up. Spot—"

"I am *not* the problem," Spot said. "I'm the solution."

Spot sounded more alive than he had until now. Beanpole looked at Dairine. "You've been in circuit with the Motherboard for only a little while," he said, "and already you're hearing us more clearly. As for Spot, we've been reprogramming him ever since he got here."

"I asked for it," Spot said to Dairine. "It was time for an upgrade. The ones you've been giving me have been all right; you've been doing the best you can. But there was something missing."

"And something extra," Beanpole said. "He's been carrying data he hasn't been able to process."

"What?" Dairine said. "Where'd it come from?"

"Spot's been in contact with an avatar of the Defender," Hex said. "For some time, information seems to have been passing between him and the power inside your colleague Ronan that couldn't have been parsed or detected by slowlife ... not even slowlife as talented as our mother." He bowed to Dairine, projecting an air of embarrassment. "And Spot hasn't had the routines to parse it, either."

"Hex, listen," Dairine said, "it's no big deal. Life's all the time sending *me* messages I can't read." She flicked just a second's glance at Roshaun, who she was starting to think was yet another of those messages.

"I'm glad to hear you say that," Logo said, "because you, too, are carrying information of this kind."

Dairine's mouth dropped open. "*What?*"

"The One's Champion has also used you as a courier," Beanpole said. "For what, we can't tell as yet; we must get you more securely into circuit with the Motherboard."

What's he stuck inside me? Dairine wondered, starting to feel twitchy. "You guys can help us get at this data and make sense of it?"

"Yes," Gigo said.

"Good," Dairine said. "Then let's do it."

Roshaun looked dubious. "You would think that the other Powers would simply communicate all of what they knew to the Winged Defender, so that straightforward action could be taken."

Dairine shook her head. "Security," she said.

Beanpole swayed from side to side in a gesture of agreement. "To give all the information in the clear to any one being," he said to Roshaun, "would ensure that the Lone One would know all about it in a matter of days. But if you split it up and give only parts of it to those who need to know, and let them pursue the material separately…"

"Everyone gets together and completes the puzzle," Dairine said. "And if one of us is betrayed somehow, the rest of the information has a chance of staying safe." Nita's recent run-in with a wizard who had been overshadowed by the Lone One had left Dairine badly shaken, for until then, the idea that wizards were absolutely to be trusted had seemed something that you could always depend on. But life wasn't as simple as it had once seemed.

"What we're doing here is safe as well," Beanpole said. "The One's Champion was here briefly in the direct mode during your Ordeal and our Choice. It's still here, integrated into the Motherboard in a format like an avatar, but less covert. It has the same power to protect us from being overheard as Ronan's version of the Defender does. We can pursue our search for the Instrumentality without fear."

"Okay," Dairine said. "How are you going to get what you need from Spot?"

"They've already got it," Spot said. Dairine's eyes widened a little at the sound of his voice. It sounded even more alive than when he'd last spoken.

"The two of you needed to be here physically to make the transfer safely," Logo said. "Now we can finish our preparations. We have to lay your personal information into the finding spell we've been constructing; that data has changed significantly since you came here first, and there have been other alterations." He glanced at Spot, who hunched down a little as if the attention somehow unnerved him. "Brother, come with us and we'll get you up to full speed again. Mother—"

They all bowed to her. Dairine rolled her eyes. "Guys," she said, "give me a break. We're all just wizards together, here."

"Of course," said Gigo and Logo and Beanpole together...but they were humoring her. The three of them and Spot vanished into the crowd of mobiles, who now mostly settled down onto the surface and sat quietly.

The stillness was an illusion. Dairine felt the tempo of their communication with and through the Motherboard increasing by the moment. "You look concerned," Roshaun said from behind her.

Dairine scowled over her shoulder at him. "The whole universe is in danger," she said, "and we're not sure how to save it, assuming it *can* be saved. One of the Powers That Be has stuffed secret messages into my brain without telling me. And a friend of mine who happens to be my wizard's manual is being reprogrammed with software that even these guys haven't had time to beta test! Wow, Roshaun, why would I need to be concerned?"

Roshaun glanced at the ground. Another chair grew up for him, a slight distance from Dairine's. He lowered himself into it, stretching his legs out with a sigh. "Sarcasm," he said. "Amusing, if ineffective." He leaned back, looking up at the golden glow of the rising barred-spiral galaxy, reached under his baggy T-shirt, and came out with a lollipop.

"At least if the universe does end in the next month," Dairine muttered, "your teeth won't have had time to rot."

Roshaun raised his eyebrows and produced another lollipop, which he held out to her.

"How many of those things do you have?" Dairine said.

"Not nearly enough," Roshaun said.

Dairine sighed and took it. "Fine, we'll rot together."

She stuck the lollipop in her mouth and worked on it quietly for a few minutes; it was one of the fudgy ones that she preferred. The neighboring galaxy rose slowly behind the spires of the mobiles' city while the two of them watched, and the stately, silent immensity of its going started to settle and calm Dairine's mind the way the rising of the Moon did at home. Before her eyes, something endlessly bigger and older than she was going about its ancient business as usual. The thought came to Dairine after some moments that no matter what the abnormal expansion might do to the universe, even though all life might be destroyed, somehow, someday, there would be another awakening. It might take uncountable years, but the Life that wizards served was just too permanent, too tenacious, too wily. It would outlast its enemy, no matter how long it took. And suddenly Dairine got a flicker-glimpse of a new morning somewhere, somewhen—dew on long grass, and low sunlight turning it all to diamonds; an overturned game board, the pieces scattered in the fresh wet green; and hands reaching down to pick the pieces up and put the game back in order again—

The image fled. Dairine shook her head, uncertain where it had come from.

"I have seen that, too," Roshaun said after a moment.

Dairine looked at him sidewise. "You've been hearing me think?"

He tilted his head in the odd way that Wellakhit used for "yes."

"That doesn't bother you?"

Roshaun just gazed up at the rising galaxy.

"It can mean," Dairine said, unable to leave it alone, "that wizards are getting—"

"Too close?" He still didn't look at her, but Dairine felt that he was still, somehow, considering her very closely. "How close is too close? Neither of us thinking of doing anything...inappropriate."

"Huh," Dairine said. She moved the lollipop from right to left in her mouth, and then from left to right again, and finally said, "I don't know how 'inappropriate' looks to your people."

"You should read the manual more," Roshaun said.

"Seemed simpler to ask you."

"And possibly more embarrassing."

"Maybe I just like yanking your chain," Dairine said, "as much as you like yanking mine."

Roshaun's expression was bemused. "The idiom is peculiar," he said after a few moments, "except insofar as it implies we're linked."

Dairine stayed quiet.

"My father's concerns about the two of us," Roshaun said, "I take as an indication of other things that were going on with him right then. Wellakhit are not moved to seek unionbond with another until at least a third of the way along in our life span. I am nowhere near that, and you, if I'm right, would be only about a sixth of a way along, as your people reckon time."

Dairine did the multiplication. "Sounds about right," she said. "You do have the idea of being 'just good friends?'"

He gave her a sidewise look. "For so high and honorable an estate," Roshaun said, "'just' seems a poor modifier to choose."

Crunch! went the lollipop Roshaun was working on, and Dairine flinched.

"I *really* wish you wouldn't do that," she said.

"You are always hearing trouble before it happens," Roshaun said. "Some might say it was a sign of a lack of faith in the benevolence of the universe. Or of dysfunction."

Dairine glared at him. "You keep this up, I'll give you a dysfunction where you'll have trouble finding it again," she muttered.

"Now there you have it," Roshaun said. "All this aggressiveness! I wonder about you sometimes."

You wonder about me! Dairine thought.

Yes, Roshaun said in the back of her head.

Dairine saw that Roshaun was wearing a brooding look. "And what's the matter with *you*?" she said.

Roshaun let out an annoyed breath. "My father," he said at last. "My business with him did not go as I thought it would."

"What? You expected him to just roll over and agree with whatever you told him?"

"On the contrary," Roshaun said. "I expected a great fight with storming and shouting. Then everything would have been over with, and in a short time we would have been set at rights with one another again. But this—this calm complaisance—" Roshaun shook his head. "It sounded nothing like the way he usually does. It troubles me."

"Well, *I* was sure troubled," Dairine said, "and if that was him being *calm*—"

Roshaun laughed. "And you thought I was so lucky to have a wizard for a parent."

"Is it possible for me to admit you might have been right *without* you rubbing it in?" Dairine said.

Roshaun gazed out into the darkness as if giving a strange new concept some thought. "Perhaps," he said. "Next time I'll try."

They leaned back in their chairs again and looked at the silently rising galaxy. "Forgive us," said a voice down on the ground between their feet, "but we're ready for you now."

They both looked down. Logo was there, and his back was roiling with Speech charactery, a brilliantly blending muddle of symbols and figures. Dairine looked down at the shifting patterns chasing themselves across Logo's hide and suddenly, unreasonably, found them threatening. She swallowed. "What do you need us to do?" she said, and got up.

"We'll be setting up the diagram out here," Logo said. "You'll want to check it, of course, to make sure that your personal information is complete and correct."

Logo trundled out into the very center of the huge open area inside the circle of towers. The mobiles all around drew back and left the great space empty; under Dairine's and Roshaun's feet, the surface went dark, and that darkness ran straight up the surrounding towers and extinguished their fire.

Dairine could feel the jolt of power that passed between Logo and the surface. From the low dome of his back, a multilobed diagram far more complex and more densely interlaced than anything Dairine had seen so far raced out across to the towers and up them. Light in many colors burned bright and dim through the pattern as it established itself, the color and brightness of every line and curve signaling the relative importance of the part of the spell involved.

Dairine gulped at the immensity of it. "Wow," she said. "Even you guys couldn't have built this whole wizardry just now!"

"No," Logo said. "We had help. You'll see." He sprouted an arm and waved it across the expanse of the wizardry. Three relatively dark patches had been left open in the diagram, each of them a many-sided polygon with a minimum of inscribed words in the Speech inside. "There are your spots," Logo said. "Yours over there, Dairine. Roshaun, yours there."

The two spots in question were perhaps ten meters apart. Dairine went to hers and stood in it; the diagram around her started to glow brighter as she took her place. She knelt down, found the wizard's knot that marked the beginning and ending of her name in the Speech, and began to trace the many-branched curve of it right around the circle.

Spot scurried out of the crowd of mobiles to settle himself in the third, smaller dark patch that had opened up. "I'll be storing the proceedings," he said, "so that if you need to refer to them later, you'll have everything handy."

"Okay," she said, turning a little to get a better view of the next part of her name. "How're you feeling?"

Spot paused. "Different," he said.

He's not the only one, Dairine thought. She traced along one section of the long sequence of Speech-characters, which made up the description of her that was crucial to a working wizardry. Some of its elements spoke more of the machine than the human. She'd seen those growing slowly since her Ordeal, and during her affiliation with Spot, but today some of them were crowding the strictly human qualities somewhat. "You feel better?" Dairine said to Spot.

"I think so," Spot said. "Clearer, anyway."

"Good," she said, and turned to Roshaun. "You ready for it?"

"Yes," Roshaun said, and looked down at her with an amused expression. "Always assuming you don't need time to compose yourself because you have been panicked by the sheer size of the impending wizardry. Even I am impressed."

Dairine smiled a half smile. "Yeah, I'll just bet you are," she said.

Most of the mobiles who had gathered to see their arrival had now crowded back out of the space, but not because they weren't participating. Underneath every mobile Dairine could see, a small circle of power was flaring—each one's own name and a power-conduit linking it to the central wizardry. Logo, Gigo, Beanpole, and Hex made their way out into the center of the master spell diagram, where similar circles flared under each of them. They were followed by the rest of the core imaging team, who arranged themselves around the inner four at the vertices of a hexagon.

"We are nearly ready," said Beanpole.

"But one question," Logo said. He turned toward Roshaun. "What's that you bear?"

Roshaun looked around him in confusion. "What— Oh, this," he said, looking down at the great stone around his neck. "It's a token of my office as Sunlord."

"Its structure is unusual; it needs to be a separate part of the spell," Beanpole said.

Roshaun raised his eyebrows, and lifted the great torc from his throat. "If you need a description of its physical properties—"

"There," said Beanpole, indicating a newly appearing empty spot in the wizardry, just to one side of Roshaun. A "container" for the collar bloomed there in the surface—a hollow sphere of pale filigree fire, constructed of numerous long phrases in the Speech all knitted together and burning. Roshaun went to the glowing sphere and looked it over carefully, tracing several of the longer curves of Speech with one finger. Finally he slipped the collar into the sphere. It hung there, gleaming in the white fire, turning slightly.

"Is the description accurate?" Hex said.

"So far as I can tell," Roshaun said, making his way back to his own circle.

"Very well," Logo said, and looked out toward Dairine, Spot, and Roshaun. "Does the ground suit?"

It was one of several traditional queries for a wizard

proposing a potentially dangerous solution to a problem. Dairine looked at Roshaun, who tilted his head "yes," and then at Spot. "Yes," he said.

"On the Powers' business, all ground suits," Dairine said. "Let's do Their work, and the One's."

A rustle of tension and expectation went around the huge circle. "All right," Gigo said. "If you two would get into circuit with the Motherboard? Skin to skin, to begin with."

Dairine sat down cross-legged in the middle of her spell diagram, and put her hands flat down on the cool surface on either side of her. The sudden jolt of power, of connectedness to everyone around her, took her completely by surprise. She wobbled as she looked back at herself through thousands of other eyes. Then she heard a voice she hadn't directly heard until now, a rumble in the bones.

You've come back, the Motherboard said to Dairine. *You've come home!*

Yes, Dairine said, feeling a little embarrassed, as if she'd been out late and hadn't let her mom know beforehand.

And you're much more than you were, the Motherboard said.

Now Dairine started to feel the faint discomfort of someone being praised for something they haven't actually earned. *Uh—*

But you are, the Motherboard said. *No need to dissemble. I may be a mother, but you are* mine. *And you know that we never feel like we're enough for our chil-*

dren, whose job is to surpass us. Ours is simply to make sure they work hard enough at it that they feel they've earned it when it happens.

There was a smile in the voice that Dairine would never have suspected. She grinned, too. *You think we got the job done?*

Without any possible question, the Motherboard said. *Now let's take on the next one.*

"Okay," she said, glancing up and over at Roshaun.

He had been looking a little blank; now he broke out of it, looked over at Dairine. "She is . . . quite something," he said after a moment, sounding strangely out of breath.

"You haven't seen anything yet," Dairine said.

This wizardry must take place in two parts, the Motherboard said. *We must first extract the information that our mother is carrying. After that, the implementation's hers to direct: We'll merely assist.*

A wave of agreement went around the vast assemblage. *Ready?* the Motherboard said to Dairine.

Go, Dairine said.

The power started to build. Dairine felt "taps" from this world into other universes open up, spilling unimaginable amounts of force into the wizardry. Time began to stretch as the mobiles' perception of what was happening swamped her own. Dairine started to see herself as the mobiles did—a life-form seemingly frozen in time, and as a spell diagram, tidily compartmentalized. The combined intention of the Motherboard and the mobiles sought down through her structure and focused on one of those compartments, an obscurely glowing area easily lost among other, brighter ones surrounding it in Dairine's mind—

That compartment grew until every intricacy of its contents was made plain in a delicate lacework spattering of pale light, like dark-side cities seen from space. The mobiles and the Motherboard spent what seemed like a long time examining the compartment and the data inside it. Finally, the Motherboard spoke. *This is the information the Defender left,* she said. *It can't be decrypted without breaking the container open.*

Right, Dairine said. For the moment, she was part mobile, and could act at their speed. She reached out a hand. In this darkness all spangled with light, a hand of light reached out, laced fingers through the webwork of darkness surrounding the data, and pulled. It came away in her hand like a fistful of cobwebs. The data burst out of prison like a storm of silver bees—

The mobiles threw a net of Speech-words around them. The light of the data ran down the strands of the net, particles shifting, moving themselves into a different order. Then everything went dark again.

Logo's voice seemed to come from somewhere far off. *And now the information Spot was holding,* he said. Distantly, Dairine saw another container's contents trying to flee into the darkness—then being netted and contained, as her data had been.

The world came back. Dairine took a few breaths, stood up and stretched. It felt like she'd been sitting in the same place for an hour, though she knew it had been only a matter of seconds.

Before her, spread out in a new dark area that had opened up a couple of meters away, was a single long line of characters in the Speech. Dairine read them slowly.

"They're coordinates," she said then. "But not to a place. To a *person*. This'll tell us who has the Instrumentality—the thing that'll save the universe—"

"*If* we can find it in time," Roshaun said. "And work out how to use it."

"Let's go," Dairine said. "You guys ready?"

Show us what to do, said the Motherboard and the mobiles together.

"We need an imaging routine," Dairine said, and knelt down in her circle again, sitting back on her heels. She put a hand down on the surface again, getting back into more direct contact with the Motherboard. In her mind a series of possible imaging routines presented themselves. *Close-range out-of-atom, long-range out-of-atom—*

That one looks about right, Dairine thought. She glanced down at the set of coordinates burning just under the surface before her.

Light blasted out and away from her through the surface, curving and twining away in all directions as long sentences in the Speech etched themselves under it in living fire. She had a peculiar sense that someone else was in the spell with her. Not the Motherboard, not the mobiles, not Spot or Roshaun: nothing living—or at least not with the usual kind of life. All around her, the mobiles glowed more brightly by the moment as the spell drew on the Motherboard's manual functions and showed Dairine what to say.

The feeling of the sheer power running through her astonished Dairine. *I'd forgotten it could be like this…* The throb of it ran up her arms and into her brain; she stood up slowly, let it build. *If it wasn't for how desperate all this is, I could really enjoy this.*

And she *was* enjoying it. There was no use pretending otherwise. Dairine started to speak the words in the Speech that were the search coordinates. The sound of them going out of her was like thunder. They shook her from side to side as she spoke them, streaking out into the structure of the wizardry to build its fire higher, second by second.

Across the diagram, Roshaun knelt at his focus point, his expression full of the terror and exaltation of the power that was suddenly his by virtue of his connection to the wizardry and the Motherboard. Dairine couldn't remember ever having seen so naked and open an expression on his face before. Past him, in its container, the Sunstone blazed the orange-gold of Wellakh's star.

You okay? Dairine said silently.

He lifted his eyes to hers. The look slammed into Dairine with force that felt like it should have knocked her down. The world whited out. It was as if the two of them stood in Earth's Sun again, working the spell that drained off the excess energy which would have made the Sun flare up and roast the side of Earth facing toward it. But this time the roiling sea of power above which they stood was partly the Motherboard, and partly Dairine—or, rather, the surface of Dairine's mind as Roshaun saw it.

From Roshaun, Dairine got the sense of someone standing on a narrow bridge over what looked like untameable chaos and fury paired with infinite power. That power was speaking to him, too, tempting him to get a little closer to the edge. *Don't get any ideas!* Dairine said silently.

The answer was a strange low garbled roar, one she instantly recognized, since it had shocked her so when first she'd heard it. *The Sun said something, and I didn't understand.* But now it was Roshaun saying something in the Speech, and once again Dairine wasn't getting it. *Impossible. Everything understands the Speech!*

She shook her head. *No time for it now,* she thought. *It's some weirdness to do with him; we'll figure it out later.* The rest of the Speech was working just fine; the spell lay before her, ready to implement.

Dairine took a breath and said the single word in the Speech that is the shorthand for the wizard's knot, the "go" word of the spell.

Everything went dark. Then images began to superimpose themselves on the darkness, blotting out even the viewer's sense of being at the center of a point of view, so that Dairine felt more like a bodiless presence than an observer. She saw the strange slick cloud of some atom's shell, from the inside, an undersky fuzzy with probabilities. The "sky" rushed toward her, blew past her like fog, leaving her gazing out on interstitial space alive with the neon ripples of "strong force" between a seemingly infinite latticework of atoms. Another few breaths, and the view was a solid mass of chains of molecules, writhing among one another like a nest of snakes. Another blurring outward rush, and reddish lightning rattled and sizzled everywhere, whip-cracking down the length of strange bumpy textures like a child's blocks strung on rope. Another rush, and everything went milky and crystalline, with a faint strange movement going on outside the surface of the crystal.

One last blur of fog descended, and the image resolved itself into a peculiar view seen through eyes that fringed every object with brilliant rainbows of color. It was a landscape, all in flat dark reds, the sky black with heat; and finally there was a point of view associated with it. *This is it,* Dairine said, exultant. *This is what the world looks like for the person who's got the Instrumentality. Now all we need to find is* where *they are.*

The envisioning routine backed out several steps farther. A smallish, ocean-girdled planet circled a giant white sun, the fourth of its eight planets. Another jump, and the star dwindled down to just one of a drift of thousands in an irregular galaxy's core.

Several long strings of characters in the Speech appeared by that galaxy, tagging it and numerous others around it that were visible only as tiny cloudy whorls or disks.

Okay, Dairine said. *Store that.* And she waited until the data was stored, and then said the word that cut the wizard's knot and dissolved the spell.

The space between the towers reappeared. Slowly the spell diagram faded, leaving only the image of the "found" galaxy, and the outlines of the circles in which all the spell's participants had stood. Dairine let out a long breath. She was a little tired, but nothing like as exhausted as she should have been after such an effort.

"I can't get over that," Dairine said, as Beanpole and Logo and the others made their way over toward her and Roshaun. "It was like the wizardry was helping me, somehow..."

"It's the power-increase effect, the peridexis," Beanpole said. "We've been taking advantage of it, too."

Dairine walked out of her circle to where the image of the tagged galaxy burned just under the surface. She bent down to look at the annotations. "It's close to our own galaxy. At least we won't have any more really big transits to deal with when we get back."

"That's well enough," Roshaun said, settling the torc with the Sunstone about his neck. "We may know where the person with access to the Instrumentality can be found. But if we can't get them to give it to us, or learn how to use it to stop the expansion, this will all have been for nothing."

"I'm not gonna throw our own universe in the trash just yet," Dairine said. She peered down at the tagging characters next to the galaxy. "Good, it's got a New General Catalog number: NGC 5518. It's in Boötes, somewhere." Then she stopped. "What's this?" she said over her shoulder to the mobiles.

Spot came over to her from his own circle, and put out several eyes to examine the word in the Speech that Dairine was indicating. "Enthusiasmic," he said.

Dairine frowned. "You mean enthusiastic."

"It says enthusiasmic," Spot said.

"That's not a word!"

"It is now," said Spot.

Roshaun came to look over Dairine's shoulder. "And what is that word next to it supposed to be?" he said. "Incorporation?" He looked bemused.

"So this is a word that didn't have a meaning until just recently?" Dairine said to Spot. "A word for something new."

"So I believe," Spot said.

Dairine shook her head. "Enthusiasmic incorporation," she said. "Of the hesper—" Then Dairine blinked, and a moment later her eyes widened.

"That's not a word in the Speech," said Gigo, sounding perplexed.

"No," Dairine said. "It's not. But it's a word we know in English. Or part of one." She swallowed. "Enthusiasmic incorporation of the Hesper—"

She hurriedly bent down and picked Spot up. "Quick," she said. "You have to message Nita for me. Or one of the others. I don't care where they are. Just get me one of those guys!"

The ground underneath all their various feet or treads or wheels came alive with the kind of display that would have shown on Spot's screen, had it been open—the apple-without-a-bite imagery of the manual software's Earth-sourced version, rippling bluely under the surface. And then the message, both written in the Speech and seemingly speaking itself into their bones: *Messaging refused. Please try again later.*

"Refused?" Roshaun said.

"They're somewhere where they can't take an incoming communication, because they're scared they might be overheard," Dairine said. She bit her lip.

"Perhaps we should simply go to them," Roshaun said.

"You're exactly right," Dairine said, putting Spot down again. She turned to the mobiles. "Guys, I hate to spell and run, but we've got to find them right away—because if they don't realize what they're dealing with, they're going to mess it up. And if it gets messed up this once, then the whole universe is screwed up forever."

"Even more screwed up than it is at the moment?" Roshaun said.

"You have no idea," Dairine said. "Come on, let's open up a gate and *get going!*"

Active Defense

Kɪᴛ ᴄᴀᴍᴇ ʜᴀʟꜰ ᴀᴡᴀᴋᴇ to the sound of something bumping on the floor, very fast, and something jingling. He opened one eye.

Dim light—the wizard-light he'd left hovering near the ceiling in case he needed to get up in the middle of the night—showed him Ponch, sitting by where the door of the pup tent would be when Kit spoke it open. Ponch was scratching behind his collar, turning it around and around as he scratched.

It wasn't as if Kit didn't hear this jingling nearly every day. What had awakened him was the utter silence into which the sound fell: a silence devoid of the little creaks and breathing noises that every house made, of wind or rain or weather outside the house... and of the normal world in which it all existed. Kit lay there for several moments just listening to that barren stillness. There was nothing but vacuum and cold outside. *Well, that's all there is on the Moon, too,* Kit thought. But the Moon was different. It was within sight of home. And it didn't have that roiling, growing darkness above it, shutting out the stars.

Kit felt around for the zipper of his sleeping bag and pulled it down, sitting up and rubbing his eyes. His pup tent was sparsely furnished compared to Nita's. Besides his sleeping bag and some essential toiletries, mostly it seemed to contain dog food. "*You* can starve when you have to," his mother had said to him, "but your pet won't understand why his meals are late, whether he can talk or not! So you make sure your dog always eats before you do. And whether you do or not." And when Kit's mother finished with it, the "short wall" of Kit's pup tent was half obscured by a stack of cans and bags about four feet high, not to mention five or six big bottles of watercooler water. His own supplies seemed meager by comparison— mostly beef jerky and fruit jerky and trail bars, and one or two of the kinds of cereal he didn't mind eating straight from the box, since finding milk while out on errantry was usually a problem.

I have to go out, Ponch said, standing up and shaking himself.

"Okay," Kit said, reaching for his manual. "I'll make you an air bubble."

No, it's all right, Ponch said. *I can take air with me, if I think about it.*

Kit stood up and stretched. *Maybe it's not just our power that's getting boosted,* he thought.

Would you open the door? Ponch said. *I have to go!*

"Okay, just a minute." Kit pulled on his jeans and

had to hunt for his sweatshirt before he found it had somehow managed to get under his sleeping bag.

Kit pulled it on. Ponch had started turning in circles on the pup-tent floor, either in excitement or because he really needed to be out of there. "Okay, okay," Kit said, and reached down for the door's little spell tab, which acted like the pull on a zipper. A long spill of words in the Speech came up on the plain gray wall, showing him details about the outside environment: Some words flashed urgently on and off to remind Kit that there was hard vacuum outside.

Kit just pulled up on the tab. Like a blind going up, the silvery-gray surface of the pup tent gave way to a view of the barren surface of the planetoid where they had camped. Ponch burst out through the interface, galloping away across the surface and bouncing in the lower gravity. Kit watched him go, noting idly that this place wasn't as dusty as the Moon, even though it felt much older.

He went back to the sleeping bag and rooted around for his socks, put them on, and his sneakers, and then picked up his manual. "Bookmark, please?" he said to it.

The manual's pages riffled through to an image of the world to which Ponch had brought them. The world had no name that living beings had ever given it. Nonetheless, it had its own name in the Speech, Metemne, and the manual showed its location, well out toward the edge of a small irregular galaxy some hundreds of thousands of light-years past the Local Group. *A long way from home…*

Kit paged through the manual to his routines for vacuum management, found the one that he'd been using on the Moon, and spoke the words that would activate his personal bubble. Then he stepped out through the pup-tent door onto the rough dark gray surface.

Except for the position of the planet's little star, now high in the sky, nothing had changed; the dark shifting and swarming of the Pullulus continued. *I didn't think I could hate something just because of the way it looked,* Kit thought, *but I think I hate that. Maybe because I feel so much like it hates me.*

Kit glanced off to his left. There was a little rise off in that direction, and he could see the soft slow wreathing of the fire about the head of the Spear of Light, jutting up from behind a massive boulder at the top of the rise. Ronan was still on guard, or if he wasn't, the Defender in him was. *It has to be weird,* Kit thought, *to have something, someone, like that, sharing brain space with you. But at least He's on our side. I think...*

Kit sighed. Once it hadn't been so complicated. If someone was a wizard, they were on your side, on the right side. But these days, the mere exercise of wizardry wasn't a guarantee. You found yourself wondering about people's motives all the time. And if you didn't know them well, you started to be less certain about turning your back on them in a tight situation.

And there were other issues on his mind. Ronan and Nita had been close in ways that Nita was too shy to discuss. Now Nita was feeling twitchy about Ronan, and Kit kept wondering why. *Oh, it wasn't anything serious with them. I know that.*

At least, I think *I know that…*

From around the shoulder of that rise, Ponch came galloping back and skidded to a stop in front of Kit. *Okay, let's go for a walk!*

Kit laughed and went off after his dog, taking it easy at first to make sure he had the hang of the local gravity. It was heavier than the Moon's, so that you could run without completely bouncing off the surface if you were careful. Passing the rise where Ronan still sat, Kit had a long look around the surface of Metemne and decided that it wasn't someplace he would come back to for a holiday. The planet wasn't much more than a bumpy rock pile. Whether there had even been water here in the planet's earliest days was a question Kit couldn't answer just by looking.

He crouched down and put a hand on a largish boulder that sat off to one side. From the beginning of his practice of wizardry, Kit had always been good at hearing what was going on with objects that most people would have considered inanimate. Now he let his mind go a little unfocused, and waited.

…no one here, the stone said eventually. *For a long time…*

It wasn't that it actually spoke; that took a different kind of life. But the impression was plain. "Did anyone ever live here?" Kit said.

Never. It would have been nice, the boulder said. *There was an atmosphere…and water. But nothing ever got started.*

"I'm sorry," Kit said.

We can't all have what we want, I suppose, the boulder said, and fell silent.

Slowly Kit got up and dusted off his hands as Ponch came running along from behind a nearby outcropping of gray stone.

There's nothing here, Ponch said. *Come on, let's play!*

"I wouldn't say *nothing,*" Kit said, glancing down at the boulder. "No people, maybe." He walked off to have a look around the outcropping, and Ponch trotted along beside him.

Then it's nowhere important.

"I guess it's easy to think that," Kit said. "There's so much life around, we start taking it for granted that any planet'll get some in time." He shook his head. "Trouble is, once life does show up, before you know it, the Lone One's turned up, too, and it's running around messing up the Choices of every species It finds."

It didn't mess up ours, Ponch said.

Kit raised his eyebrows. "I keep meaning to get the details on that," he said, as they walked around the outcropping together. "Though it must have gone the usual way, since there's no Choice without wizards, and there are dog wizards, Rhiow tells me..."

Ponch's expression was eloquent of skepticism. *Oh, well, if you're going to believe things* cats *say about dogs...*

Kit got a sense that he was poised above a dangerous abyss. "Uh," he said, "okay, maybe I should ask someone who knows about it firsthand."

Ponch woofed; it was a dog laugh, of sorts. He

picked up a rock in his mouth, shook it from side to side as if to make sure it was dead, and came bouncing over to Kit to put it in his hand. *We have wizards, yeah. But as for the Choice, I just know what everybody's mom tells them when they're still drinking milk.*

Kit took the rock and spent a while trying to get the dog slobber off it. "So educate me," he said.

Oh, it's the usual thing, Ponch said. *There was us, and the Ones, and we ruled the world. And then the Bad Thing came and said, I can make it better for you. But we said, How? We have the Ones. We live with them, and hunt with them, and run around with them, and they give us whatever we need, and everything's fine. So the Bad Thing went away. The end . . . So throw the rock!*

Kit blinked, and threw the rock well away from the outcropping, across the bare gritty plain. Ponch tore off across the planet's surface after it, leaving little scoots of gravel hanging up in the vacuum in a trail behind him. *If that's his idea of "the usual thing,"* Kit thought, *then all the Choices I've run into now have been real unusual.* In fact, Ponch's version of his species' Choice didn't sound much like a choice at all. *And he didn't sound very interested in talking about it.*

He watched Ponch pounce on the rock, pick it up, shake it around, and lose it because of shaking it too hard; he went bounding across the surface again to get it back. *Then again,* Kit thought, *there are some species that're in really close relationships with each other, and their Choices are interrelated. Why shouldn't the dogs'*

Choice be involved with the human one? It makes a kind of sense.

Ponch skidded to a stop in front of Kit, dropping the rock in front of him. *Again!*

"Yeah, sure," Kit said. He picked up the rock and threw it. Ponch went bouncing off after it. *Boy, he's really into it this morning. Needs to dump some stress, I guess.*

Kit had to grin at himself then. *Oh, great. Now you're doing psychoanalysis on your dog.*

But still... There'd been an overly casual quality to the way Ponch had been talking about the canine Choice. *As if there was something about it he didn't want to be thinking about. Almost as if he was trying to distract himself.*

Ponch came bounding and plunging back with his rock, and dropped it in front of Kit once more. *Again!*

"Uh, no, I think we've done enough of that."

Why? Is it time for something? Ponch looked a little crestfallen.

"Probably," Kit said, fervently hoping that this was true. But he had to smile; Ponch's sense of time was weak, except when mealtimes were concerned. "Let's have a look here." He got out his manual and flipped its cover open to show the front page, which he'd set to show him the date and time. "See, it says here—"

Then his jaw dropped.

762.3? How did that *happen? Crap!*

Kit slapped the manual shut, turned around, and started back toward the pup-tent accesses. "Come on," he said, "we're running really late! We have to get Neets up."

Ponch began to jump up and down with excitement as they went; in the low gravity, he was able to jump up to a height where his head was level with Kit's. *How come?*

"Because it's a lot later than it should be!" Kit started doing the astronaut-bounce that was the only way to hurry in this kind of gravity without falling on your face. "And I don't know how it got that way. Come on!"

Nita stood in front of the mirror over the chest of drawers in her bedroom, staring anxiously at her face. *I was right,* she thought, utterly exasperated, as she pushed her bangs aside to get a closer look. *It is a zit.*

She let out a breath, then. *Trouble is, this isn't real. I'm asleep. And what am I wasting my time dreaming about? Zits!* Nita shook her head. *I can't believe that the other day I actually thought this was a big deal.*

Nonetheless, the place where the pimple was coming up still stung. Nita found herself torn between the eternal choices: Squeeze it, which always grossed her out and sometimes left a mark? Or do a wizardry on it? Or just let it be, and go through the next couple of days feeling like a leper?

She shrugged. *It's a dream. There may not be a pimple at all. Just leave it alone... We've got more important things to think about.*

Nita turned away from the mirror and found herself not in her bedroom at all, but out on the surface of

Metemne. This sort of abrupt transition was normal for lucid dreaming, and Nita had learned over time to let these experiences take her where they wanted to.

Reluctantly, she looked up into the sky, knowing what she was about to see, and instead saw ... nothing. There was no sign of the Pullulus, but neither was there any sign of the stars, or interstellar space, or even the little planet's sun. The effect was like being in a closed, windowless room with the lights off. Nita didn't much care for it ... for inside the "room" with her she could hear slow, steady breathing.

She held very still, trying not to panic. The breathing stayed steady and slow; it was as if something slept nearby, something very big. She became concerned that she might wake it up. Then it occurred to her that this was the problem. Whatever was asleep, it *needed* to wake up.

"Hello?" she said, and her voice sounded as if she actually was inside a small room, like her bedroom with the door shut—but a bare unfurnished bedroom, an empty place in which her voice echoed. "Hey! Can you hear me? Wake up!"

No answer. Nita looked around. There was nothing in any direction but the barren, gritty surface of the planet. *That breathing,* she thought, *that's the Pullulus.* To her surprise, the idea didn't upset her: The sound of it frightened her a lot less than the way it looked. And after a few moments, the heavy-breathing sound started to seem slightly comic, like someone pretending to be asleep so you'd go away.

Nita rolled her eyes. "Oh, come on," she said to the

darkness in the Speech. "Are you going to just leave me talking to myself here? Say something!"

It won't answer you, said a voice from somewhere nearby. *There is only one to whom it will answer, and that one's not here.*

She looked around to see who'd spoken. There wasn't anyone to be seen. But from off to one side, there had to be a light shining, because suddenly Nita had a shadow.

Nita stared down at it. The shadow was a double one, as if the light sources producing it were in slightly different positions. She looked toward where the light should have been coming from. But there was nothing there but more barren rock and grit.

Nita looked down again. The shadow was fuzzy-edged, as if thrown by a candle, and the flickering continued. She scuffed at it curiously with one sneaker, then looked around. "Well," she said, "I'm on errantry, and I greet you. Wherever you are..."

Everywhere, the voice said, *for quite a while now.*

There were all kinds of potentialities and forces running around in the universe that could truthfully say something like that. "You're one of the Powers?" Nita said. "Ronan? Is that you? Or your buddy?"

She caught a distinct feeling of surprise from whatever she was talking to. *You are thinking of one of the Great Intervenors,* it said, *the Light's own designated Defender. No, I would not be anything so exalted.*

She looked at the two fuzzy shadows lying out across the grit of Metemne. "You're a dual-state being of some kind," Nita said. "Like a twychild."

Nothing like that. Was that a breath of wistfulness behind the thought? *But something old... and something new.*

Nita remembered her mother telling her an old poem and showing her the sixpence that an English friend had sent her to put in her shoe the day she married Nita's dad. "Are you by any chance blue?"

The being was amused. *No. But often borrowed.*

"How come I can't see you?" Nita said.

But you can, the being said. Her shadows flickered more energetically.

"That's my shape," Nita said. "Not yours."

But all the shape I have is the one wizards give me, the being said.

Her shadow writhed and flickered against the dusty ground, and as if inside it, Nita caught a glimpse of a number of images melting one into another: something with wings, and then a long twining shape, like a faint light in the shadow—almost the shape of two snakes curling and sliding past each other, so that Nita was reminded of a caduceus. *Matter, and the power to do things to matter,* she thought. *The idea, and the thing you say or do to make it happen—*

"You're wizardry," Nita whispered. "Wizardry itself."

Not quite. I'm peridexis: the combined effect of the words of the Speech and the power that lives within it. But without the ones who speak the words and decide how to use the power, there's no wizardry. It always takes at least three...

"So you're the 'power surge' we've been getting,"

Nita said to the bright shapes in the shadow. "But also sort of the soul of the spell…"

Of every spell, yes. And to a certain extent, the manual.

"Wow," Nita said. "It's a shame you're not usually this talkative."

This isn't a usual sort of time, said the voice of the peridexic effect. *Now more than ever, wizards need their spells to give them some extra help.*

"It's going to surprise a lot of people that you're conscious," Nita said. As she spoke, she was studying the light submerged in her shadow. Curious, Nita got down on one knee to touch her shadow with a couple of fingers, and found that she could actually put her hand down into it. The bright shapes rose to meet her, and she felt the slight jolt of power as they did, as if she'd touched the poles of a battery with wet fingers.

Not many will notice, the peridexis said. *Those who might be bothered by the concept of the living spell won't hear my voice.*

Nita nodded. "Doesn't bother me," she said, glancing up again at the strangely empty sky. "But what about the Pullulus? 'It won't answer,' you said. That was what the Senior Wizards were trying to get it to do, wasn't it?"

Yes. But they were the wrong ones to speak to the Pullulus, and didn't know the word that needed to be said.

"So who's the right one to do the speaking?" Nita said. "And what's the word?"

Without warning, she found herself kneeling by the chain-link fence across the parking lot from her high school's main doors. Nita got up and dusted her hand off. It was gray with the dust from the worn-in pathway that ran along the fence, the place where kids leaned during lunch hours and "off" periods when they couldn't leave school property, but were intent on getting as far from school as possible. Over to one side, as far down that path as she could get without being on the sidewalk that led out the parking lot's gate, was the lanky, thin form of Della Cantrell.

Del was a transfer from the high school over in Oceanside. There were all kinds of stories about the transfer, since almost no one had been willing to get close enough to her to find out what was really going on. One set of rumors claimed that her folks had moved here, to what was a less expensive suburb of the county, because her dad's business had failed. There were whispers of some kind of vague white-collar wrongdoing—extortion, embezzlement, no one knew what. Others said that Del herself was the problem, that she'd been causing trouble at her old high school and they'd thrown her out. The rumors about what *that* trouble might have been were even worse than the ones about Della's dad.

Nita had started to be infuriated by the whispering campaign when she'd first seen the very pretty, very lonely looking girl sitting all by herself in her history class during her first week at Nita's school—hardly glancing up, interacting exclusively with the teacher, plainly nervous about looking anybody else in the face. That feeling Nita knew all too well from the time before she'd become a wizard, the time when she'd first come to understand it was unlikely that anything she did to her clothes or her hair would ever change the way the other kids saw her—as a nerd—and every passing day had left her more hopeless and angry about it. Now, far more certain of herself and far less concerned with what most of her classmates thought of her, Nita was in a better position to feel concern for anyone else caught in the same trap. As soon as that class had finished, she'd gone over and introduced herself.

This had not been without its penalties, for Nita knew the whispering would start about *her* within minutes. The most popular kids in school saw her simply as a bottom feeder, a geek with so few friends that she'd purposely befriend a newcomer and outcast so that she'd have someone to be more normal than. *Let them think that*, Nita had thought. *When I'm dealing with them, I have to do right by them ... but, otherwise, after we all graduate in a few years, with luck I'll never see most of these people again.*

"Hey, Del," Nita said, wandering over to where Della was leaning against the chain-link fence.

"Hey," Della said, not turning her head. She was looking over past the school, down toward the parking lot, which was almost empty at this time of day. The juniors and seniors who had cars had pretty much all pulled out half an hour before.

"You okay?" Nita said.

Della turned her head, looked at Nita slowly. Though the look was unsmiling, over time Nita had come to know that it wasn't actually hostile. This was just the way Della defended herself from people, refusing to reveal anything they could use against her; usually the flatness of the look was enough to scare them off.

"You look depressed," Nita said, and leaned against the fence as well.

Della sighed and looked away. "The news is all so bad," she said. "Nothing but bombs and fighting and security alerts everywhere. The world's coming apart all around us, and everything else on TV besides the news is just dumb, and my brother's really getting on my nerves."

Her voice was surprisingly resigned and bored. "You've got a sister," Della said. "What do you do when you feel like killing her?"

"Try to get her to go to some other planet," Nita said.

Della smiled a rather bitter smile. "Have much luck with that?"

"Not as much as I'd like," Nita said. "But sometimes she gets the hint."

They leaned there in a companionable silence for a few moments. A teacher came out one of the side doors of the school carrying a briefcase and an armful of books, and headed for his car. "I hate just lurking around here," Della said, watching the teacher get into the car and start it up, "but lurking around home is worse. There's nowhere to hide; even when I'm in my room, I know my mom and dad are just waiting for me to come out so they can look at me that way they do, like there's something I'm supposed to do to make everything turn out all right." And Della manufactured a sort of creepily threatening cross between a scowl and a smile. The expression looked to Nita so much like something that would normally appear on a cartoon character that she had to laugh.

Della snickered, too, then. "See, not even you take me seriously," she said, and pushed the long curly blond hair out of her eyes. "Come on, give me a hint: What am I supposed to be doing to make it all right? What is it They want?"

Nita's eyes widened. She looked more closely at Della, but Del's face was unrevealing. "I'm not sure," Nita said.

"But you're supposed to know," Della said, gazing across at the school doors as if she was intent on not meeting Nita's eyes. "You're the one who's been left in charge. You're supposed to have all the answers. Help me out here!"

Nita looked thoughtfully at Della, looked hard. The wind blew the hair across Della's face again. Annoyed, she lifted a hand to push it aside.

Not a hand. A claw—

Nita's eyes widened. Then she started violently as something she couldn't see struck her in the side of the head. She flinched and flung her right hand up, and the lightning-bolt charm with a particularly aggressive "blaster" spell bound into it glinted on her charm bracelet in the late-afternoon sunlight. Nita opened her mouth to say the twenty-third word of the spell and turn the force-blast loose against the thing that had hit her; and as she did, Della pressed herself back against the fence, the darkness that surrounded the claw shimmering up around her, abolishing the blond hair, the face—

Something came down over Nita's mouth, so that she couldn't speak. Something else stuck itself in her ear. Nita's eyes narrowed; she started to simply think the twenty-third word of the force-blast spell instead of saying it. It was a long one. Light twined around it, paired serpents of fire—

Don't do it!

And abruptly the thing in her ear was a tongue, one she knew entirely too well.

Ewwwww, Nita thought, opening her eyes. Kit stood at the head of the couch, looking down at her anxiously; he'd just removed his hand from her mouth. Ponch, meanwhile, had finished washing her ear and was now enthusiastically working on her face.

"Thanks for not blasting me," Kit said.

"Good thing you moved fast, 'cause I didn't know it was you," Nita said, pushing Ponch away. "Did I oversleep? It's morning already?"

"It's not just morning. It's *Monday* morning."

"*What?*" Nita's eyes went wide. She sat straight up, or tried to; as usual, the crocheted throw had wrapped itself around her like a cocoon. "It can't be! We were only gone—oh, four or five hours, there was the stuff on the Moon—and then we did the transit, and we slept here, yeah, but it should still only be—"

"*Normally* it should still only be," Kit said. He looked at Ponch.

Ponch looked guilty. *I brought us straight here . . .*

"But it took longer than usual," Nita said, struggling to get out from under the throw. "Ponch, don't worry! It wasn't your fault. It's got to be the expansion—it's throwing everything off."

"Tell that to your dad," Kit said, sounding rather grim. "I get to do it with *mine* in a minute. Or if my luck runs out, with my mama."

Nita swallowed. Her dad—who knew if he'd been trying to reach her? And if he had, why hadn't her phone gone off? *Tom and Carl did the wizardry on it,* she thought, *it should be okay!* But if wizardry wasn't behaving correctly in some of the places they were going— And then again she saw it, the shimmer of a hand that was a claw, and eyes that willingly blinded themselves behind a sheen of darkness—

She covered her face with her hands and tried to pull everything together so that it made some kind of sense. *This may take a while . . .* "Okay," she said to Kit, pushing her hair back, "give me a minute or two to kick my brains into shape. What's everybody else doing?"

"Getting up," Kit said, "like they had a choice." He glanced in Ponch's direction with a slightly exasperated look. "I kept him out of here as long as I could. But Ponch had himself a good time with everyone else first. Don't even ask what he tried to do to Filif."

Ponch, who had spent the past few moments investigating everything in Nita's pup tent that he could stick his nose into or under, now bounded back wearing an expression of complete innocence. *I wasn't really going to do that!* he said. *It was just kind of funny for a moment...*

Kit gave Nita a skeptical look. "Let me get the humorist out of here," he said. "You want something to eat before we go?"

"I'll grab something," Nita said. "You go ahead."

Kit and Ponch went out. Nita finally managed to get completely free of the throw. She got up, folded the throw and chucked it over the back of the sofa, then pulled on jeans and sneakers and a soft shirt, shrugged into the vest-with-too-many-pockets that she'd brought along, and started going through the pockets in search of a candy bar. *Sugar,* she thought, *I really need some sugar.* Nita turned up, in rapid succession, a wad of shredded facial tissues, an empty gum packet, a clear plastic mint box with one lone mint left rattling around in it, an extremely sticky ice-cream wrapper, and, finally, a slightly squashed chocolate-and-peanut bar. She unwrapped it and ate it in three bites. *Hand. Claw. An eye goes dark—*

Nita crumpled up the wrapper of the candy bar and shoved it in yet another pocket. Making notes on what she'd seen was going to have to wait, but at least she wasn't likely to forget *that* image in a hurry. She went fishing among the pockets for her cell phone, and finally turned it up.

Nita hit the "dial" button and waited. The somewhat altered dial tone of a cell phone running wizardly routines came on, and then cut out...and Nita broke out in a sweat. *Oh, please don't let this be broken. This really needs to work right now—*

"Hello?"

"Daddy!" Nita said. "It didn't ring."

"It rang here," her father said, "which I've been waiting for it to do *for four days*! You said you were going to keep in touch—"

Nita could understand how annoyed and upset he sounded; she was annoyed herself. "Dad, I'm sorry, but for once it's not our fault," she said. "For us it's just been eight hours or so since we left. It looks like the dark-matter expansion is screwing up our transit times."

"Well, that's just great," her dad said. "Is this going to keep happening?"

"I don't know," Nita said, and rolled her eyes. *I wish somebody would ask me a question I know the answer to.* "I'll call you as often as I can, but if time's running weirdly for us, I don't want to wake you up in the middle of the night and worry you even more."

"I'll take my chances with that," Nita's dad said. "Has anything bad happened? Are you all safe?"

"We're fine," Nita said. "We're just getting up . . . we had a few hours' sleep. Not as much as I would've liked."

"Well, I didn't get as much last night as *I'd* have liked, either."

Nita made an unhappy face. "Daddy, what time is it for you?"

"It's twenty-five after six."

"Did you have a bad time in the shop today?"

"Why?" Just as it had sounded like he was calming down a little, her dad sounded angry all over again.

Nita's eyebrows went up. "Uh, you just sound... really on edge."

She heard her dad take a long breath and let it out again. "Not that I wouldn't have reason to be," he said, "what with what's going on with you, and the way everything else is here at the moment...but—" He paused. "Yes, you'd be right to say that I've been feeling the strain a little more than I usually would."

Nita swallowed. "Us, too," she said. "I'm sorry. That's all I wanted to say, I guess. I'm sorry all this is happening this way."

"It's hardly your fault," her dad said after a moment. "And I shouldn't have snapped at you. I'm sorry, too. But I'm really relieved to hear from you."

Nita had to admit that the relief was mutual. Her dad's matter-of-fact groundedness was one of the things she'd come to count on to help keep her on course when everything else in her life seemed to be going to pieces. "Look," Nita said, "I'll call as often as I can. But we may get to places where it won't be safe to do that. When that happens..."

There was a silence at the other end. *I wish I could see his face,* Nita thought, feeling a little nervous. "I'll try to give you advance warning," she said. "But I may not be able to. When we get where we're going, we may have to operate undercover for a while." She swallowed. "And if wizardry starts acting up, too, the phone connection might just stop working until we fix what's broken." *Until. Just keep thinking "until."*

"You're telling me that I'm just going to have to tough this one out," her dad said.

"We all are, Daddy."

He sighed. "Well, if that's all we can do, I guess we may as well get on with it," her dad said. "Speaking of 'all': Have you heard anything from Dairine? I haven't heard from her, either."

"Nothing so far," Nita said.

"Okay. Well, if you do, tell her to get in touch."

"I will."

"I know that tone of voice," her dad said. "You've got something to do. Go do it, sweetie."

"Okay, Daddy. Love you."

"Love you, too, kidlet. Go kick old What's-Its-Face around the block for me." There, at least, was a flash of her dad's normal humor.

"First thing on the list, Dad. Talk to you later."

"Bye-bye."

Nita hit the hang-up button and stared at the phone. Finally she shoved it into one of the vest's many pockets, then reached sideways into her otherspace pocket and pulled out her manual. "You need to be a *lot* smaller," she said. Obediently the manual reduced itself to the size of a pocket notebook, and Nita shoved it in another of the vest's pockets. As she did, she glanced down at the lightning-bolt charm on her bracelet, the slight glow around it showing that it was still undischarged. As she did so, she got a sudden flash of that image of intertwining light.

"You stopped me the second time, didn't you," Nita said.

Yes, the peridexis said. It sounded almost abashed. *You were in transit between states of consciousness, and possibly unready to decide whether to destroy another wizard.*

Nita laughed. "*'Possibly'?* No kidding. Thanks." Then she glanced sidewise, though she wasn't quite sure what she was glancing at. "You're not going to make a habit of that, are you?"

I have no such ability when you're fully volitional, the peridexis said. *And in transitional states, only as a fail-safe.*

"Okay," Nita said. She touched the bubble-charm that was shorthand for her personal air-handling spell; it came alive around her, and she stepped out the door and pulled the tab that collapsed the entry to the pup tent.

She was left holding nothing but the tab, like the pull of a zipper; she tucked it into her pocket. Kit ambled over to her, tucking his manual out of the way, while Ponch ran around with the wizardly leash flapping along behind him. Sker'ret wandered after him in a casual way, pausing every now and then to pick up a rock, turn it over in his front "handling" mandibles, and eat it.

"Did you talk to your dad?" Kit asked.

Nita nodded. "He sounded really messed up," she said.

Kit gave her a sympathetic look. "He's not the only one," he said. "You should have heard my mama."

"She go ballistic?"

"Suborbital at least." Kit sighed. "But eventually she

realized that it wasn't just me being thoughtless...and there really wasn't anything I could do."

"Yeah." Nita sighed. She glanced over at Filif, who stood off to one side with his branches lifted up, all the eye-berries looking up at the darkness. "We should get moving. The sooner we find what we're looking for, the sooner we can get back home and sort out the parents. Where'd Ronan go?"

"He's still there behind his hill," Kit said.

"Okay," Nita said. "You go collect Ponch and Sker'ret." She went off in the direction of the little rise.

Filif was on her way. "You get some rooting done?" Nita said as she went by.

"A little," he said, turning various berries toward her. "But it's hard, without a star."

"Tell me about it," Nita said, grabbing a few of his fronds and tugging them affectionately. "Hang in there. We'll get you out of here shortly."

She went on around the rise. Ronan had just stood up and was stretching; he looked around and raised his eyebrows. "Are we ready?"

"Just about," Nita said. "You feel okay?"

"Not a bother on me," Ronan said.

"I'll assume that's Irish for 'yes.'" Nita glanced down the rise, where Sker'ret was munching on a last few rocks while Kit caught up with Ponch. "Everything's been happening so fast, I've hardly had a chance to talk to you."

"Everybody's been busy," Ronan said, leaning the Spear against the front of him and shoving his hands into his pockets.

"How are things back home?"

"Pretty much as usual," Ronan said. "With a few changes. Your friend Tualha? She gave up being a bard when they made her Queen of the Cats. Now she's having kittens."

"Wow," Nita said. "But she was so little..."

"Cats grow up faster than we do," Ronan said. "They've got a real short latency, which is why you don't see any of their Seniors here. Anyway, not even an emergency like this is going to make the Powers That Be put an oracular in Tualha's situation on active duty. The kittens come first."

That made sense to Nita, but it also made her nervous. "If the cat Seniors aren't on the job right now," she said, "who's handling the worldgates on Earth? That's their specialty."

"There are some very new feline wizards, just past Ordeal, who're taking up the slack," said Ronan, though it wasn't quite Ronan. Something else shivered around the edges of his voice, a sense of more power, more age. "It's as if they were born just in time for this."

Nita sighed. "One less thing to worry about," she said. "But I feel sorry for them, being pitched straight into the middle of all this trouble."

Ronan shrugged. "Not much we can do," he said, and turned away from the Spear to see what Kit was doing. Nita reflexively reached out to stop the Spear from falling over, and then saw that it just kept on leaning against nothing in exactly the same way it had been leaning against Ronan, the fire wreathing undisturbed about that bitterly sharp blade.

It has a mind of its own, said that other voice. *Though maybe "mind" is the wrong word. The kind of consciousness a virtue has isn't much like the human kind.*

Kit had caught Ponch and was checking the leash-spell, the blue-fire glow of it stretching thin and bright between his hands as he checked its wizardry to make sure that it was intact and working correctly. "Something on your mind?" Ronan said, turning back to Nita.

"I don't know," Nita said. "I guess..." She wasn't sure whether she wanted to say what was on her mind, then shrugged as well. "You two are doing okay, aren't you?"

Ronan's smile got a bit sardonic. "Told you she'd ask," he said.

His situation's hardly unique, the Defender said. *Various of the Powers have living avatars for one reason or another.*

"Though the rest are all a lot older," Ronan said. "Apparently it's unusual for someone so young to be able to cope so well." He made an ironic face.

Nita raised her eyebrows. *Why didn't I see this coming? If there's anything Ronan was going to be good at, it'd be coping.* "So you're telling me there's nothing for me to be worrying about," Nita said, "for either of you."

There was a pause. Ronan looked briefly flummoxed. *You're worried about me?* said the Defender.

"It can't be easy being... what you are... and having to live inside a human being," Nita said. "Especially now, when so many things aren't working the way they should."

For a moment Ronan's face looked as if neither of the two beings living behind it knew how to respond. Finally, Ronan dropped his gaze. *Of course my kind of power suffers from being wrapped up in flesh*, the One's Champion said. *But it's inside physicality that the great Game's played.* He looked up again, met Nita's eyes, and for all the age and power in the voice that spoke, the eyes were strangely young, and there was an odd glint of excitement in them. *It's like chess*, the Defender said. *It doesn't matter that you could stand up and turn the board over. That wouldn't be winning. The only way that matters to win the game is from inside. So*—he shrugged—*we put up with the limitations, because there's no other way to win. Not having access to our full power, yes, it's frustrating. And if we break out before we're scheduled to, we pay the price.*

"But for the time being, you're okay," Nita said.

Yes, said the Defender. *And I thank you very much for asking.* It sounded bemused.

Nita nodded. She looked down from the rise and saw that all the pup-tent accesses were gone now, and Kit and Ponch were standing with Sker'ret and Filif. "Looks like we're ready," she said.

Ronan reached out and grasped the Spear. "Let's go."

They bounced down to where the others were waiting. Ponch was jumping around, the line of light between him and Kit stretching and shrinking to accommodate him. "Why should you be so nervous?" Sker'ret was saying. "It went just fine the last time."

"Except that we lost four days getting here," Kit said. "And that wasn't nearly as long a jump as this one's going to be."

He glanced down at Ponch, whose bouncing went on uninterrupted. *It'll be all right,* Ponch said. *I know where we're going. Come on, let's go!*

"Maybe I'm just feeling paranoid today," Kit said, not quite glancing up at the Pullulus, "but I think we should be in physical contact when we go." He reached his spare hand out to Filif, who wound a few fronds around it; Sker'ret took hold of some fronds as well from behind Filif, and held a rear handling-claw up.

Nita glanced at Ronan. He shook his head. "I think I'd sooner keep a hand free," he said, lifting the Spear.

Oh great. I get to hold his hand. Nita swallowed, took Sker'ret's claw with one of hers, and with the other, took Ronan's free hand. It was sweating.

She smiled slightly. "All set," she said to Kit.

Kit looked down at Ponch. "Okay," he said.

Ponch took a step forward; they all followed, and the gray surface of Metemne vanished behind them.

Darkness. For a couple of breaths, that line of light between Ponch and Kit was the only thing Nita could see as they all moved forward together. When she glanced nervously over her shoulder, she couldn't even see the Spear, though she could still feel Ronan's hand in hers. There was a surface of some kind under their feet, but Nita couldn't see it, couldn't even feel it. The sensation was most peculiar.

"Is it usually like this?" Nita said to Kit—or tried to say. But when she spoke, there was no sound.

Sometimes it is, Kit said silently. *Sorry, I should have warned you.*

It's as if there's no air, Filif said.

I'm not sure there is, Kit said. *What's weird is that whether there is or not, you don't feel like breathing.*

How much longer? Sker'ret said. He sounded somewhat unnerved.

Ponch? Kit said.

Not long.

They kept walking. Nita found herself having to count paces by how her legs moved, since when she put her feet down, she couldn't really feel anything. *Twelve. Thirteen. Fourteen. This is so weird! Fifteen. Sixteen.*

The count went past twenty, and still there was nothing but that darkness. Past thirty, and nothing. Nita was having to resist the urge to start singing or whistling, partly because she knew she wouldn't hear anything, which would just make her feel creepier. And it wouldn't take much to start imagining the Pullulus infesting this darkness, pressing closer, pushing in—

Nita swallowed and went back to concentrating on counting paces. *Forty. Forty-one. Forty-two. Forty-three…*

She blinked, not sure whether she was really seeing a dim gleam of light far ahead, or whether she was hallucinating it. *No, it's there, all right,* Nita thought. *But what is that?* The light seemed faintly greenish; as they walked, the green color seemed to get stronger. *Fifty. Fifty-one. Fifty-two—*

The source of the light quickly grew closer, as if they were moving far faster than a walk. The light began to distinguish itself into shades and patterns; tall dark pillar shapes rose up within it, casting long shadows across the greenness. And then the light swept around them and closed up behind, sealing the darkness outside....

Nita let go of Ronan's hand, wiping the sweat off against her vest, and stood there gazing up and around her. The dark shapes were huge trees, hundreds of feet high, as broad in the trunk as sequoias, but with broad leaves rather than needles. They towered above the little group, vast branches overhanging the green grass at their feet, and moving shadows from sunlight far above patterned the grass as a slight wind stirred the branches. At the head of the group, Ponch was bouncing up and down excitedly. Kit, looking chagrined, let go of the wizardly leash. "I can't believe this," he muttered. "Go on..."

Nita saw Filif and Sker'ret and Ronan looking around them in confusion. Ponch ran barking off across the green lawn under the trees...

...and from high up in the branches, thousands upon thousands of gray shapes came boiling down the tree trunks.

Ronan stepped hurriedly past Nita with the Spear of Light. Thin tongues of white fire coiled and curled around the Spear's head, and the starsteel of the head itself burned silver-white as if the spearhead had just come out of the forge again, while Ronan hefted it in one hand, ready to throw.

But the squirrels paid no attention whatsoever. Their attention was all on Ponch. The ones behind Ponch ran after him, and the ones in front of him ran away from him and up the trees again as he started to chase them.

Ronan lowered the Spear. "Uh," he said. "I don't think this is where we're headed..."

"Absolutely not. Sorry about this," Kit said, sounding exasperated. "And welcome to dog heaven. This is one of the first places Ponch made; he seems to need to use this as a first stop..."

Let him get it out of his system, the Defender said.

"Not that it looks like we have any choice," Ronan said. He shouldered the Spear again, which began to quiet down, the uneasy flame about the blade pulling itself in and going quiet.

Nita walked up across the perfect, manicured lawn to join Sker'ret and Filif. Sker'ret's eyes were looking in all directions at once, as usual. Filif was standing there with all his eye-berries glowing blue, gazing up into the pale blue sky beyond the branches.

"Kit told me about this," Sker'ret said, "but he understated the strangeness somewhat."

"More than somewhat," Nita said. "It's like a movie set. All perfect. If you're a dog..."

Ponch was running back toward them now, surrounded by waves of squirrels. He and the squirrels dodged off to the left, past several of the really large trees, and briefly went out of sight.

Kit and Ronan came over to join them. Ponch ran out from behind the trees and back to Kit, the squirrels hanging back a little. As he came, Filif leaned away from Ponch a little, pulling his branches in. "You're not going to try to water me again, are you?"

It was a joke, Ponch said, sounding somewhat pained.

"Good," Filif said, with some force.

"And I think we've had about enough of the joke stuff for the time being," Kit said, sounding unusually severe. "I thought we agreed earlier that we'd come here *afterward*?"

There was something here I needed, Ponch said. *I can't find the way by myself.*

Nita blinked at that. "But you said you knew where we were going."

I do. This is how. Ponch looked up.

Everyone else looked up, too, rather confused. Nita craned her neck back to follow Ponch's glance, and was surprised when, all by itself, down the largest of the trees a single squirrel came running. It was white.

The squirrel ran down the bole of the tree onto the ground, and there sat up in the middle of the perfect green grass and looked at all of them. Ronan suddenly started to laugh.

Now I understand, said the Defender through him. *It's an embodiment, a way to perceive the trail as an active entity rather than as something passive. Very sophisticated.*

And fun. Hurry up and put the leash on! Ponch said, while the white squirrel sat there completely still, its little dark eyes moving across them, one by one. Nita met its eyes and was briefly transfixed, perceiving it somewhat as Ponch might have. It was shorthand for a twisting trail made up of a complex of many virtual scents, all braiding and corkscrewing through a peculiar skewed landscape that might have meant time and space as a dog saw them...or as Ponch did, and he wasn't just any dog anymore.

Kit got Ponch to sit down beside him, and fastened the "collar" end of the wizardly leash around his neck again. Nita and Sker'ret and Filif and Ronan all arranged themselves behind Kit, holding hands or claws or fronds as they'd done before.

The white squirrel's eyes met Ponch's. Ponch leaped forward. Just a few lengths ahead of him, the squirrel ran across the grass, then jumped into a sudden darkness that leaped forward to surround them all.

They ran. Ahead of them in the dark, like a white streak through the blackness, the squirrel ran. Ponch tore after it. Kit ran after him, or was dragged. All the rest of them were dragged along as well, and a breath later the darkness vanished—

—to leave them running over something that cracked and glowed. Nita looked down and gasped as the heat struck up at her, burning through her sneakers. They were running over lava, under a dull red sky in which hung a single huge planet, banded in eye-vibrating greens and blues. The lava churned and flowed, hot and sluggish, and as two smaller bodies like moons came cruising across the fierce hot sky, Nita glanced to one side and saw how the lava humped toward the new moons' pull in strange swollen tides—

A second later, the darkness fell again, and the heat and the burning light were gone, and they were racing through the dark, faster now. The white squirrel bounded away in front of Ponch, and Ponch tore after him, and the darkness fell away behind them like the sides of a tunnel until they were all out in a new light, cooler. A blue-green sky stretched over a dusty violet wasteland without a single feature—not a tree or a plant or a rock to be seen anywhere, only the wind blowing a pinkish stinging dust past them, with clouds of more pink, blowing sand airbrushed against the sky's distant lavender-tinged horizon. The cold began to bite, the air smelled strange, but Nita had no time to get more than a whiff of it before the darkness closed around them all again—

—to break and leave them running across a wasteland of snow, huge mountains uprearing in the background, but closer to hand, the hard-packed snow sculpted into ridge after knife-sharp ridge, imitating the mountain range behind. They plunged and slid down the broad side of one of the ridges, the squirrel almost lost against the whiteness, but Ponch running right behind it, fast and sure, not losing the trail. Then up the far side of the little valley, sliding, trying to get purchase on the snow. The white squirrel leaped, and Ponch leaped, and the darkness folded down around them all again—

Ponch ran, his speed increasing so that it became more and more difficult to grasp the details of one universe before they were into the darkness again, and out into the next world.

The "squirrel" hardly had that shape anymore. It was a line of light, streaking ahead of them, zigzagging, jumping upward, bouncing down, world to darkness to world again; energy getting ready to discharge as soon as it reached its goal. And that had to be soon. *We've come so far,* Nita thought. *Not even Ponch can keep this up for much longer.* They were flickering from world to world now at least once a second, so quickly that Nita was tempted to close her eyes to keep the flicker from disorienting her. She concentrated on just breathing, because otherwise she would start thinking about the growing pain in her legs, and if she did that, she'd have to stop.

Flicker. Flicker. Flicker. Nita's lungs burned. The pain was beginning to force itself through her concentration. *Just run. Just run. Just keep running—*

—and then suddenly she tripped over Sker'ret, who'd stopped, and fell on top of him; and from behind Nita, Ronan fell on top of her.

The air went out of her lungs, leaving Nita unable even to say "Ow!" Within a second or so Ronan got up off her, and Nita could just lie there for a moment, feeling her legs—or wishing she couldn't feel them.

Underneath her, something hard and edgy moved, or tried to. "Nita," a muffled voice said in the Speech, "could you please get off me before we accidentally become more than just good friends?"

Nita opened her eyes at that, partly in alarm. She wasn't entirely sure what Sker'ret meant, but she didn't intend to find out. "Sorry," she said, and disentangled herself from him as best she could. It was kind of like having fallen into a closetful of coat hangers, but finally she managed to get herself and her clothes undone from all those jointy pointy legs of his, and carefully stood up to have a look around.

The ground of the dimly lit clearing where they'd wound up was strangely soft underfoot. All around them was a great silence, broken only by a faint rushing sound a long way off. Nita glanced toward Kit, who was removing the wizardly leash from Ponch, and then looked around.

Trees, was her first impression. *Trees as far as the eye can see. But they're so weird!* The trees were many-trunked, their branches reaching down half the time to root themselves in the ground again. Other branches and trunks reached higher, but almost immediately got involved and snarled up with the wrestling, shoving trunks and branches of other nearby trees, so that the upper canopy was as much wood as leafage. It made Nita think of a many-arched roof trying to grow into a cathedral, but strangling itself in grappling loops and buttresses, and having to break away each time in some new direction—then getting tangled and strangled all over again. Little light pierced such a canopy, but what did was blinding. Here and there the strife between the upthrusting, furiously contending branches had let a crack of the high sky show. This burned whiter-hot than the daytime sky above the Crossings, an unbearable glare that seared the skins of the trees through which it tore. Like multiple fiery spearshafts, that light struck down through the branch-ceilings, scarring the nearby growth to a scabrous black and plunging like white knives into the squelching surface below. Slowly, softly, the spongy peat-black stuff underfoot bubbled where the light bored into it, as if something there boiled.

Kit sniffed the air. "Motor oil," he said. Nita caught the scent he meant, and looked over at one of the closer patches on the bumpy, root-tangled surface, where brown-black tar came oozing up through the ground, slicked over with what was probably crude oil. It gave off the scent Ponch had been tracking.

The rushing sound was slowly getting louder. The effect was like walking toward a waterfall, except that none of them was walking. The sound made it seem as if the waterfall was coming toward them.

And then, in the distance, Nita saw the shadowy shapes moving slowly among the giant, broken-backed trees, in several lines, one after the other, somber, dark, steadily approaching. Slowly she started hearing more than just that rushing noise as the shapes got closer. She heard a low humming or singing sound, and other noises that made her hair stand on end: anguished cries and sobbings that got louder as the marching shapes drew nearer. The crunch and creak of breaking wood told Nita that they were breaking the trees as they came, tearing down branches, ripping away every scrap of brush and undergrowth.

The shrieks echoing along the path of the approaching creatures became louder every moment, and Nita had to force herself to stand still and keep silent, concentrating on not panicking as she heard the trees wailing in anguish as their branches were bitten away. Onward came the softly singing column, leaving everything that had stood in its immediate path now bare except for the spongy ground underfoot. Off the creatures went and out of sight, bearing with them branches like banners, oozing strange sap; and behind them the trees moaned low, and more sap fell and trickled onto the soft ground, pooling like tears.

Filif stirred in silent horror. "And you're sure this is the place we were looking for?" he said.

Ponch stood up again, gazing at the indistinct, moving shapes with interest. *This is the place.*

"What are they?" Nita whispered. "I can't see."

"I think we should keep that mutual," Kit said.

Nita nodded and reached down to her charm bracelet for the ready-to-implement invisibility spell, taking hold of the fabric of the spell and whispering its last word in the Speech. She felt the faint itch on her skin that told her it had taken hold, and around her the others all winked out of sight as well.

Best we keep any comments mind-to-mind for the time being, Ronan said.

Silently the others agreed. They all moved carefully forward: not just to avoid making any sound that would be noticed by the creatures they were stalking, but because everybody was using different kinds of invisibility, and this made it all too easy for people to bang into one another.

Something light tickled Nita in the kidneys. She whirled, but there was nothing there, which meant what she'd felt was one of Filif's fronds. *Sorry, Fil.*

My fault, I was too close— What?

Sorry, it was me, Sker'ret's ratchety mind-voice said.

Nita let out a little breath of laughter as she softly

skirted around the vast intertwined trunk of one great tree. She put out a hand, touched it—

The tree shuddered. Nita snatched back her hand, shocked, and then laid it against the tree again, much more gently. *What's the matter?* she said to it silently in the Speech. *Don't be afraid, I'm not going to hurt you.*

But it *was* afraid. It was in absolute terror. It was holding itself still in utter dread, frightened to speak to Nita, frightened to do anything at all. It was afraid of something far worse than the merely physical destruction Nita had seen. Finally she took her hand away and moved off, rubbing the hand nervously, as if the tree's anguish was something that could cling to her like sweat.

What? Kit said, catching some leakage of what she felt.

It reminds me of the way the trees were in the Central Park in that other Manhattan, she said, *when we were out on Ordeal. That same kind of dumb fear. They wouldn't respond to the Speech.*

Come on.

Softly they made their way closer to the long lines of dark creatures weaving their way among the tree-trunks. Nita could just barely hear the soft footsteps of the others around her, and the slight rustling noise that Sker'ret and Filif made when they moved. She came up behind one particularly large tree and, without touching it, peered around it at the twisting pathway running between it and other large trees a few yards away.

Her nose wrinkled at the strange smell that hung in the air. *It's almost like coffee,* Nita thought, as one of the shadowy shapes came around the huge tree that blocked the pathway, *but more bitter, a little burnt, as if it—*

One of the shapes came around the tree and drifted toward her, almost without a sound—and Nita lost the thread of her thought completely, utterly shocked. A great, shining, dark-glossed almond-shaped body, held up at a diagonal on legs that were longer at the front than in the back; eight black legs, jointed three times each, the back edges of them razor-sharp; up high, a blunt wedge of a head with great dark mirror-shade eyes. Huge claws, hinged at the front top of the body shell, even sharper than the legs, held the squirming, dripping branches torn from some tree.

Nita stood frozen as the creature walked delicately past her. A few seconds later another one passed, and another, in what seemed an endless line. They came in all sizes, but even the smallest of them was the size of a big car. The larger ones, the creatures with the longest claws and heaviest armor, were more the size of vans or small trucks. They went on along the path, some of them making a low soft hum as they went, three or four notes repeated one after another. They weren't words; if they were, Nita would have been able to understand them as Speech. Unnerved, Nita began to back away very slowly and softly as the long parade continued. The image from her dream was on her mind now: Della's expression suddenly buried behind a glossy unrevealing eye, a claw coming up to brush blond hair away. *Whatever it means, I have to find out.*

At last the final dark-shelled creature went past Nita and out of sight beyond the trees down the path. Nita let out a long breath of relief, but couldn't get rid of the profound unease that had been troubling her since she first touched the tree. *There's something really bad going on here*, she thought. *And we don't have much time to find out what.*

Without warning, from behind her she heard a different kind of humming sound, getting louder by the second. Nita turned quickly to see what was making it—

She had just time enough to jump back as a claw huger than any of the ones on the parading creatures came snapping straight at her face. She jumped back again in shock, grabbing for her charm bracelet, and the creature followed, snapping at her again. *It sees me! But how?*

The huge shelled creature lunged at Nita, its claws snapping as she dodged around the tree, doing her best to stay out of its way while she dumped the invisibility spell, which could interfere with what she was about to do. Then she said the short phrase of a basic defense spell, the single spell she probably knew better than any other in the world, because it had been the first one she'd ever done. As the creature followed her and its great down-reaching claws stabbed at Nita again, she saw the claws skid away from the spell. Nita hurriedly held up her hands and spoke the words of the blast spell that she'd been ready to use on whatever had been attacking her in her dream. In a blaze of glowing green-white fire, the force-blast wizardry jumped away from her outstretched hands. The creature vanished in it, leaving her staggering backward. *Wow. Who'd have thought it'd have a kick like that. It must be the power boost.*

The fire faded down as Nita straightened up, relieved. *So much for that. I hate having to use so final a spell on anything, but—*

—and then she gasped and backed up fast, as the creature came right at her through the fading light of the wizardry. Its armor was shattered and cracked, but it was still making that awful, bone-rattling hum that now escalated into a roar. Those huge claws reached out for her. One of them struck at her shield-spell, and this time the claw didn't skid aside. It burst right through.

Nita backed up and blasted the creature again. From behind her, Kit, also visible again, came up and did the same. His blasting spell was built differently from Nita's, and this one knocked the thing back against the nearest tree...but only for a second. The creature recovered its footing and came at them again, the huge claws reaching out.

Down! someone said from behind them, and the word was as much wizardry as order: Nita's and Kit's muscles took control of them and flung them down hard on the soft, oozing ground. Nita just managed to turn her head as she went down, and so was able to see the furious fire of the Spear of Light streak over her and Kit and into the huge chitin-mailed form. The ferocity of the light left her briefly blind; she could only hear, and what she heard was a roar like the wind shouting in rage, followed by a silent wave of white-hot force that made Nita throw her arms up around her head to shield it. Then, nothing but silence.

Nita looked up, blinking and still half blinded, and

pushed herself up to her knees. She and Kit were both covered with a dusty, scorched-smelling powder that was still sifting down through the air from where the attacking creature had been. Behind her, Ronan put out his hand, and the Spear flew back to his grip.

Filif and Sker'ret and Ponch came up behind him as Kit and Nita helped each other up. "I think we need to get out of here right away now," Ronan said, "and go somewhere quiet for a think."

"Boy, are *you* ever on," Kit said.

Nita brushed herself off, looking at the vanishing tail end of the column of creatures, and listening to the faint sound of the sobbing trees behind them. "Bugs," Nita said softly, and the hair stood up on the back of her neck. "Giant bugs…"

Hurriedly, the six of them vanished.

Operational Pause

"THE WORLD'S CALLED RASHAH," Kit said.

They sat on a transparent sheet of hardened space a couple of thousand miles above the planet's surface, gazing down. The world turned sluggishly under them, its seemingly endless expanses of green and blue-green and brown stretching far to either side of a narrow, profoundly deep sea. Hovering a few feet above the wizardly surface where they sat, and surrounded by five intent wizards and a dog, Sker'ret's implementation of the manual—a spherical holographic display like a particularly high-tech crystal ball—was showing them a slowly turning, annotated version of the planet.

Filif leaned past Kit, all his eye-berries on one side trained on the image as it rotated. Kit glanced over at him, concerned, for though Filif now looked fairly steady, he had been trembling all over when they first made it up into space. "You feeling better?" Kit said.

Filif rustled impatiently. "The initial shock's passed,"

he said. "Those plants aren't sentient the way my people are. But they're still in great pain." His thought turned dark with anger. "The Kindler of Wildfires has plainly made this place Its own."

There seemed no way to argue with that, for over the image of Rashah in Kit's manual, and across it in Sker'ret's view of his own, a string of boldface characters burned in the Speech. They said, *"ARESH-HAV,"* an acronym for a much longer phrase, and one rarely seen because few worlds were so completely dominated by the Lone Power to qualify for its use. "Aresh-hav" implied "lost"—a place almost as much lost to hope as to the powers of darkness, and presumed to be beyond redemption until the Powers That Be should intervene directly. The term also implied that the intervention might possibly be fatal for the world's inhabitants, if the Lone One could not be otherwise dislodged.

Kit turned in his manual to the page that held the breakdown of the planet's physical characteristics. Rashah was the fourth world out from its sun, at about the same distance Jupiter would have been in Earth's solar system. The other three planets were much too close to Rashah's ferocious blue-white O-type star for even Life's endless inventiveness to do much with. Those worlds weren't much more than little scorched Moon-sized rocks, their sunsides repeatedly slagged down by flare activity. Rashah at least had been distant enough from its star, Sek, to keep its atmosphere through the flares; afterward, the plant life that had come to cover the world had slowly exhaled enough gases to breed a greenhouse effect, which allowed other life to evolve there—though not much of it. Millions of years had produced a planet where the vast march of the ruthlessly struggling rain forest was broken only by tar pits thousands of miles wide, slicked over with lakes of oozing oil—the last remnant of far more ancient forests killed by solar flares and transformed by heat and dead weight over thousands of millennia. Rashah's turbulent weather was as unforgiving as its sun: Summers hot enough to melt Earth's polar caps alternated with winters that were simply one long, supremely violent hurricane.

Most of the living species on that planet were plants. There were a very few flying and creeping species with no intelligence to speak of, and of these, only the ravenous "topflyers" were tough enough to survive Sek's awful burning light for long. These infested the uppermost levels of the rain forest that covered the two great continents of the world, eating one another and anything else foolish enough to venture up or out into the terrible fire of day.

"It looks like everything else living here except those topflyers stays undercover if it wants to keep on living," Nita said, looking up from her own manual. "Even the one intelligent species..."

She turned a couple of pages, and Sker'ret's display shifted to match hers, showing them a closely annotated image of one of the giant bugs. "They call themselves the Yaldiv," Nita said, "though they're such a hive species, I'm not sure that the concept of them 'calling themselves' anything is right. According to this, they've got kind of a common undermind or sub-conscious, so they may just think of themselves as one body with a lot of moving parts." She shook her head. "Not a 'them': an 'it.' "

Kit, glancing over at Nita's manual, pointed at large blue-glowing patches that appeared here and there on the pages. "What the heck are those?"

Nita shook her head again. "Some of the species background information is blocked," she said. She laid her finger on one patch, which came alive with the words in the Speech, "Data in abeyance." Another lined-out passage, when she touched it, said, "Data withheld."

"Withheld by whom?" Sker'ret said. "Or what?"

Nita looked over at Ronan. *Such redacted notations,* the Defender said through him, *mean that some other Power is interfering with the exchange of information.*

"And you can just guess which one," Kit said softly. "Darryl did say—"

Kit saw Nita swallow. "That we shouldn't hang around any longer than we have to," she said. "So let's get down there and find out what the Instrumentality is, and what we have to do to get it and make it work for us."

Filif rustled all his branches and looked rather challengingly at Ronan. "I don't suppose you could be a little more forthcoming now about any details you've received from your sources."

I don't have anything new to share with you, the One's Champion said through Ronan. *The other Powers seem to think we've been given enough information to find the Instrumentality without any further input.*

"I hate that," Kit said, though without any particular force. "You know? I really hate it when They trust us so completely."

Ronan looked nonplussed. *You're all we have to work with,* said the One's Champion. *And you've always produced the result before.* Suddenly Ronan grinned; it was a sour look. "See, this is your reward for not letting the Lone One defeat you a long time ago."

"You wouldn't think it was so funny if you knew what Its idea of defeat usually looks like," Kit said. "And I still wish the Powers thought we were a little more clueless. We might get things done faster."

But not as effectively, the Champion said.

"Yeah, well," Nita said, sounding uncomfortable. She turned her attention back to her manual, and when her gaze was turned away, Kit sneaked a concerned look at her. Nita had been as unnerved as Filif when they'd first gotten up here, and to Kit's eye, she still looked pale. "Probably we should start with the cities," Nita said. "There are two city-hives on the bigger of the two continents, kind of like giant anthills. They're a few hundred miles apart. They've been fighting each other, on and off, for"—Nita looked at the numbers on the timeline indicator that shone on the page, and squinted in disbelief—"*millions* of years?"

"They must really be enjoying it," Sker'ret said dryly, "to keep the war going so long."

"I don't know if *enjoy* would be the right word," Nita said, turning another page. "Each side sees the other as a terrible threat." She glanced at Sker'ret. "Just think about it. If each of the Yaldiv cities always saw itself as the only being in the world—and then all of a sudden another one turned up, one that thought of *itself* as the only being in the world—"

"Then both sides have a great reason to panic," Ronan said. "And an excuse to wipe the other side out."

"It looks like somebody might already have had a run at that," Kit said, turning a page in his own manual. "Have you looked at the background radiation numbers for this place?"

Nita looked surprised. "I thought maybe those were so high because we're so close to the star."

Kit shook his head, looking increasingly grim. "Oh, yeah, the atmosphere's real ionized, but that's not going to account for the plutonium residue all over the place." He pointed at the manual page. "Look here. And over there—"

Filif shook all over, a horrified shudder. "Someone here was using *atomics*?" he said. "The Kindler must have driven them completely insane."

"It's a popular kind of crazy," Kit said. "Unfortunately."

"You'll be telling me next that they burn their hydrocarbons!"

"Uh, no," Kit said. "But it looks like there was a more developed civilization here once...a *real* long time ago. There's nothing left now. It's been completely degraded."

"Were the creatures here part of that civilization?" Sker'ret said to Nita. "Or are they a successor species?"

Nita shook her head. "No way to tell. Almost all the rest of the history section is blocked out. 'Data withheld.'"

"And here's something else that's kind of nasty," Ronan said, glancing back at the group. He had been looking off into the distance, the way Irish wizards did when consulting their memory-based version of the manual. "All these creatures've got a significant, aware fraction of the Lone Power as part of their souls."

Nita turned a horrified look on him. "Are you saying that the whole Yaldiv *species* is overshadowed?"

It's rather worse than that, the One's Champion said. *And rather more permanent. They're all avatars.*

Everyone stared at Ronan. "*All* of them are mortal versions of the Lone One?" Sker'ret said. "How's that possible? Such a multiple embodiment would require immense power."

Which It has, said the Champion. *But, yes, even for one of us, this kind of power outlay would be significant. My guess is that this culture has either been owned for so long that this kind of avataric presence has simply seeped into the species' nature over millennia... or else the manifestation is something new, a test bed for something the Lone Power is planning.*

"Probably a good reason for the world's history to be blocked," Filif said, "at least from the Lone One's point of view. It would be a fair guess that we'd have a better idea where to start looking for the Instrumentality if we knew more about when this process started, and what this world has been through."

Ronan ran his hands through his hair and looked

harried. "All right," he said. "Where do we go from here? We've got to figure out what the Instrumentality is, and where it is...and what to do about it. While walking around in the middle of a war zone full of giant bugs who can see us even when we're invisible."

"And just how did that happen?" Nita said to Ronan. "And how was that thing able to get through my shield-spell?"

"The Lone One can break a working wizardry when it's directly present," Ronan said. "It was party to wizardry's creation, so It can easily interfere, if It's got a local foothold in a willing soul. That's what avatars are all about. They can be worked through a lot more effectively than the merely overshadowed."

"But did that avatar recognize us as wizards?" Kit said.

Possibly not, said the Champion. *Avatars don't have to be conscious of their status.*

"With such creatures about, it's a shame there's nowhere quieter to do our reconnaissance," Filif said. "Say, the other continent."

Ponch had been lying and looking down with a brooding expression at Rashah as the planet rotated in seeming serenity beneath them. *But what we're look-ing for is down where I brought you out,* he said. *Why go elsewhere? We'd just be wasting our time.*

"That being something we don't have a lot of," Nita said. "So let's get busy." She glanced over at Ronan. "I do want to call my dad in a little bit, though, to make sure what day it is back home. Is it going to be safe?"

I can cover you, the Defender said. *But putting forth*

power as a cloak is itself a detectable usage, if anyone's looking for such. So keep it short.

Nita nodded. "But as for the Instrumentality," she said, "what do we do when we find it? Just take it? What if it's something that belongs to the Yaldiv? What if they don't want to let us have it? Or they won't tell us how it works?"

"One thing at a time," Sker'ret said. "We've got to go down there and do some research." He was looking through his own manual. "I can set up short-range transits for us from here to the surface in such a way that they ought to be undetectable. You'll want to look over my shoulder to make sure I don't miss anything," Sker'ret said to Ronan. "But what then? We're going to have to walk some places. We're going to have to go into the Yaldiv cities and pass unnoticed. And as you say, the usual invisibility doesn't seem to be enough. These creatures, the warrior-foragers anyway, have a better-than-usual sense of smell, as well as what looks like an innate sensitivity to force fields. Merely visual disguises aren't going to do the job."

Filif suddenly shook every frond he owned, and all his berries blazed. "Well, it's plain that there's no such thing as coincidence," he said. "Have a look at this."

A moment later, Kit found himself looking at another Nita. He glanced over at the original one. Her jaw had dropped.

"How does it look?" Filif said. And, bizarrely, his voice sounded like Nita's.

"Wow!" Kit said.

"Does it feel right?" Filif said. He held out an arm.

Kit pinched it experimentally. "Yeah…"

"Does it smell right?"

"I wouldn't answer that if I were you," Nita said. She got up and went over to Filif, looking at him up close and very carefully. "It's almost like a mirror," she said.

"It's a *mochteroof*," Filif said.

The word was plainly in the Speech, but Kit had never heard it used before. "Some kind of seeming?" he said.

"About halfway between a seeming and a full shape-change," Filif said…and once again the voice was Nita's. "It's less likely to leave you with the side effects that a complete change would. Yet it looks and feels solid. It'll pass all the common sensory tests—touch, smell, taste."

Kit was impressed. "When'd you start work on this?"

"When I started to realize I didn't want to look, sound, or smell too much like a vegetable," Filif said, "in a world full of herbivores."

Nita suddenly looked embarrassed. "Uh. Sorry. We, uh—"

"Don't apologize!" Filif said. "I found soon enough that plants on your world aren't like they are on mine. And I got caught up on my research and discovered you were built to eat the way you do. Just look at your teeth! Anyway, when Roshaun and Sker'ret and I started going out visiting places with Dairine, I built myself a wizardry that was mostly a strictly visual illusion. It worked well enough when we first went to the mall, but it failed when I got distracted. So afterward I took the work I'd done and used it to construct something more robust—an overlay that wasn't as taxing as a full shape-change but could still cope with being touched, and would react properly to all the other senses."

Nita leaned close to Filif and pushed his/her bangs aside to stare at his/her forehead. "What?" Kit said.

"He's even got my zit!" Nita said, straightening up. She sounded rueful but impressed. "You've really been working hard on this, Fil."

"I noticed you looking at it," Filif said, "and inserted it. The image self-updates when you do that. Otherwise, it just runs true to your last memory of a given template. Here, look at this."

And suddenly the other-Nita turned into Carmela.

Kit made an exaggerated choking noise and fell over. "Oh, no," he said. "Not her, not here! No way."

"What's the matter?" Filif said, sounding confused. "Did I get something wrong?"

Nita snickered. "No," she said, and got up to stretch. "I'd say you got it just right." She looked at Kit in amusement. "No wonder 'Mela spends so much time bugging you! You give her these huge reactions. If you didn't make such a fuss, she wouldn't have nearly so much fun."

Kit rolled his eyes. Filif went back to being a tree again, and Ronan, too, stood up and had a stretch. "All right," he said. "So all we need to do now is decide where to start looking for the Instrumentality."

Kit looked up at Ronan. "You saw where Ponch

brought us out. I think we should have some faith in his talent, and start our work near there. One of the cities isn't too far from our landing site."

"We'll have a lot less trouble getting lost in the crowd where there are a lot more Yaldiv," Nita said. She touched Sker'ret's rotating globe with one finger. The view of the planet in her own manual and in the larger display expanded to show the cities' locations. "Yup, that's the bigger of the two cities."

"So all we have to do now is tailor versions of Filif's *mochteroof* for ourselves," Sker'ret said.

Ronan nodded slowly. "Right you are," he said. "And since it looks like the Yaldiv are diurnal—a lot of them go out of the city to work in the forest in the daytime, then come back when it starts to get dark—when they do, we'll go back in with them."

"Makes sense," Sker'ret said. "We'll need someplace near our target city to use as a base, though, somewhere to put up the pup tents. A cave or something similar."

"My very thought," Ronan said. "I'll go see what I can find. Back in a tick."

He vanished.

Nita stood looking down at the planet's surface, while off to one side Sker'ret started laying down his short-transit routines, a lacy filigree of glowing lines embedded in the invisible surface they stood on. Kit wandered over to Nita. "You okay now?" he said.

"Huh? Oh, yeah. I got past it." She folded her arms, hugging her manual to her. "It's just...Ronan. Sometimes he sounds so normal."

"Sometimes," Kit said.

"But then without warning he gets edgy again."

"So? Where he's concerned, so do you," Kit said.

Nita looked at him. "What?"

Kit shrugged. "You should see your face sometimes. It's a real 'You get on my nerves but I can't take my eyes off you' kind of look."

Nita's expression went suddenly exasperated. "There wasn't anything like *that* going on with us," she said.

"But there could have been."

"Like what? He's about a million years older than me!" Nita said.

"Two," Kit said.

"Two million?"

"Two years older than you," Kit said.

Nita looked less exasperated and more befuddled. "Your point being...?"

Kit took a breath. "You kissed him," Kit said.

Nita briefly looked shocked. Then she rolled her eyes. "That was *all* I did."

"I know that!"

"Yeah? And how, exactly?"

This, by itself, was almost enough to stop Kit cold. Wizards who worked closely together sometimes overheard things going on in each other's heads that hadn't been specifically "sent" by the other party. It was an occupational hazard... and a sign of their closeness. *But this is as far as I've ever gotten along this line with her,* Kit thought, miserable, *and if I give up now, I may never have the guts to bring it up again! Or the time—*

He opened his mouth. "Look, never mind, I can guess," Nita muttered, and turned away. "Anyway, you know it's true. And it just *happened.* It was just— He was— I don't know. So vulnerable right then. You see how he is usually! Ronan being vulnerable—it's kind of an attention-getter."

She really did sound embarrassed. *Back out of this slowly while you can,* said some unusually nervous part of Kit's brain.

"But I do feel a little better about him generally," Nita said. "If I was feeling a little paranoid about him, maybe it was left over from the last time someone I trusted was being overshadowed by the Lone One. It's not like Ronan can be overshadowed while he's got the One's Champion inside him."

"As far as we know," Kit said. "But a lot of things aren't working the way they usually do."

"Oh, don't *you* get paranoid now," Nita said. "Remember how it was with Ronan before, when he just wanted the Champion to fall asleep or go away? Now at least the two of them seem to be working together. We ought to be really grateful, because we're all going to need that."

"Yeah, I guess." Kit let out a long breath, feeling relieved. But Nita glanced back at him, and the smile she was wearing was distinctly odd. "What?" Kit said.

"Uh, nothing serious," Nita said. The smile started to turn into a grin. "I was just thinking about Carmela."

"Filif got a little too close to the original there," Kit said, passing a hand over his eyes.

Nita snickered. "Not that. I was thinking that when we get back, somebody'd better make sure she knows exactly what she's getting into."

"With what? Ronan?"

"Yeah."

Kit raised his eyebrows. "You mean we should *tell* her that being hot on Ronan is actually being hot on both a cranky Celto-Goth hottie and a Senior Power-That-Is who spent most of the past ten years living on Earth and wearing a macaw costume?"

Nita looked at him.

"Nah," Kit said at last. "Let's not say anything. Let's just let it play out." And then Kit broke up laughing.

Nita's look grew annoyed. "You're *enjoying* the idea," she said.

"Oh yeah!" Kit managed to say. It took a while to get control of his laughter.

"If she realizes that you're letting her walk into this without a warning just for your own amusement," Nita said, "the universe being destroyed is going to come as a *relief.*"

Kit wiped his eyes, forcibly smothering the last few laughs. "Look," he said, "when we get back, if he hangs around for very long, Ronan'll have to tell her. Assuming she doesn't figure it out herself, somehow. She's been figuring out entirely too much lately."

Nita suddenly looked concerned. "You don't think she's going to pull a late-onset Ordeal on us?"

Kit shook his head. "She's too old. But even if she *is* getting good with the Speech, you won't find me complaining. I'd rather have her the way she is than like my other sister."

"Oh, please," Nita said. "Helena and your 'deal with the devil.' What a laugh."

"I can't believe she could even *think* I'd do something like that. You live with somebody all your life and then—" Kit threw his hands in the air, let them fall again, a helpless gesture.

Ronan appeared off to one side of their hardened-space platform. "I've got just the thing," he said, coming over to them. "There's a big stony outcrop a couple of miles from the end of the tunnels of the biggest city."

"So what did you find?" Nita said. "Caves?"

Ronan nodded. "A big bubble cavern with no connection to the city tunnels," he said. "But there's plenty of room there for all our pup tents, and no surface access of any size; no one's going to come sneaking up on us." He glanced over at Nita. "You want to call your dad now?"

"Yeah," Nita said, and got out her phone. "Feed the cave coordinates to our manuals, huh?"

"And to me," Sker'ret said. "I'll want them for the short-term transits."

Ronan headed over to where Sker'ret was working with Filif on the spell diagrams. As Nita dialed her phone, Ponch got up from where he'd been lying and ambled over to Kit, his tail swinging idly.

We're going now? he said.

"Yup," Kit said.

Good. I'm hungry!

Kit reached down to scratch behind Ponch's ears. "It's all about dinner or playing or sleep with you, isn't it?" he said.

Not all, Ponch said in a slightly hurt tone of voice. *There* are *other things. Sometimes it's about squirrels.*

"Oh, great," Nita said under her breath. "What now?"

Kit glanced over at her. Nita gave him another of those exasperated looks and hit the button that started up her cell's speakerphone function.

At the other end—the other end of the galaxy, or the universe, for all Kit knew—the phone was ringing. And ringing, and ringing, and ringing...

"Nobody's home," Nita muttered. She started dialing again.

"Maybe your dad's at work?" Kit said.

"I sure hope so," Nita said. "Not that I'm sure what time it is there."

But when the call started to go through, that number, too, just kept ringing. After a few rings someone picked up. Kit saw Nita's expression go a little less scared. "Hi, this is Harry Callahan—"

"Daddy! What time is it? I thought you'd be—"

"—at Callahan's Florists," said her dad's voice. "Unfortunately there's no one available in the shop to take your call right now. Our normal business hours are 8:00 A.M. to 5:30 P.M. Monday through Friday—"

Nita hung up. "Okay," she said. "His cell phone—"

She dialed again. But this time all she got was a different recorded message, a digital one. "The party you are dialing is not available at this time. Please try again later—"

Nita hung up again, starting to look upset. "This makes no sense," she said.

"You could try getting hold of Dairine," Kit said. "Maybe she's heard something."

Nita nodded, pulled her manual out, and opened the back cover, where she kept her messaging routines. "Dairine Callahan," she said to the manual.

The back page blanked. Then a single phrase in the Speech came up out of the whiteness: "Recipient is out of ambit or in transit, and is not available. Record a message for delivery when ambit or transit status changes?"

Nita rolled her eyes. "Yeah, Dair, it's me," she said. "Have you heard anything from Dad? Call me back in the book as soon as you can. End message."

The page flickered, spelled the message out in the Speech, and then blanked it. "Saved for delayed send."

"Thanks," Nita said. "Now get me Tom Swale or Carl Romeo, and flag it urgent."

The back page blanked. Then a single phrase came up: "Messaging in abeyance."

" 'In abeyance'?" Nita said. "What's *that* mean?"

"And not even any 'Try again later,'" Kit muttered. "What's going *on* back there?"

Nita shook her head, closed her manual, and picked up her phone again. She punched in the number for Tom's house, hit the speakerphone function. Once again the dialing tone tinkled through its usual sequence, followed by a long silence.

Nita almost hung up, but at last the phone at the other end started ringing. And it rang, and rang, and rang...

She let out a long breath, hung up.

"Maybe they're out somewhere," Kit said.

"Why do I not believe it's that simple?" Nita covered her eyes with one hand. "They always have a wizardry that forwards calls from wizards to their cells," she said, looking up. "And they're hardly ever *both* not there—"

"They were last week," Kit said, "and you know what *that* was about." He was trying hard to sound calm, but he wasn't sure how well it was working.

Nita rubbed her face. "Look," she said. "I'm really freaked now. I'm not going to be any good here until I check on things back home and make sure my dad's okay. It won't take me long."

But we just got here! was the first thing Kit wanted to say. He resisted the urge.

"Look, I know what you're thinking," Nita said. "I don't care. What good am I going to be for anything if I'm not sure what's going on with my dad?! And, Kit, what if we *did* just have another of those big time lags? If it's all of a sudden five days later, we'd better find out about it *now*—because if Dairine and I have to go back and cover for ourselves before school starts making trouble for my dad..."

She looked furious and frustrated. Kit let out a long breath, because she was right. "Okay," Kit said. "But how're you going to do this?"

Sker'ret had finished conferring with Filif, and now

came toddling over to them. "You could always send a fetch back home to see what's going on," Sker'ret said.

Nita thought about that, then shook her head. "No way," she said. "It's not just about what *I* need to see. If my dad's upset already, dealing with a transparent version of me that can't get solid when he needs a hug isn't going to do him any good at all."

"Ponch can't take you," Kit said. "We're going to need him here. And even if we didn't, you'd run into the same time lag problem all over again."

"I'll do a direct gating," Nita said. "The only reason we needed Ponch to get here was because we didn't know where we were going. Now that we've got the coordinates for Rashah, I can gate straight in and out." She glanced at Ronan. "You can cover for that, too?"

I can, said the Champion, sounding uneasy, *but we need to keep this kind of thing to a minimum.*

"For once the spell won't have to be terribly complex," Nita said. "We've all got the power now to push gatings through just by brute force, rather than finesse."

"I can coach you on how to compensate for any equivalent lag," Sker'ret said, "now that we know how much of it we're dealing with. In fact, it'd make sense to take that information back to the Crossings—it'll help my sibs keep things running there for a little longer." He glanced over at Kit and Ronan and Filif. "Can you spare me? I won't be gone any longer than Nita is."

"While we're still just doing our first on-the-ground surveys," Kit said, "sure. And it makes sense for you to go out at the same time as Neets." He glanced over at Ronan. "It means you'll have only one transit to cover, instead of two."

"Let's get ready for it, then," Sker'ret said. "I'll get the gating set up." He scuttled away in the darkness to start altering one of the transit circles.

"I'll check your spelling," Filif said, going after him.

Nita watched them go, then glanced back at Kit. "You're annoyed at me," she said.

Kit gave Nita a look, hoping she wasn't going to force him to answer. She returned the look, in spades. Finally Kit said, "Not annoyed. But you're holding out on me. It's not just your dad, is it? It's Tom and Carl, too. Isn't it?"

For a long moment, Nita didn't say anything. Then she sighed. "Look, I know we had to run with the information that Ronan and the Champion gave us. But I still feel like we've run out on our Seniors, and they probably got worried about us when they came looking for us and couldn't find us anywhere."

"You're not going to tell them anything—"

"Of course I'm not going to tell them anything! But they just need to know we're okay."

She was quiet for a moment.

"And that's still not all of it," Kit said.

Once again, and for a much longer time, Nita said nothing.

"Look," Kit said, "don't say anything if you don't want to; I guess it's not really important—"

"You're eavesdropping on my brains again," Nita said.

Her tone was resigned. "No," Kit said, and blushed. "I just overheard— You know how it is. More a feeling than a thought."

"Yeah," Nita said. "I know how it is."

The look she gave him left Kit embarrassed enough to want to glance away; but he didn't. "A feeling is *all* it is," Nita said. "I wish I had something more concrete to go on than a hunch! But that's all I've got. There's something back that way that needs doing, and I have to go there and find out what it is, and do it. And I hate acting like being on Rashah is freaking me out enough to make me immediately run away!"

"I know that's not it," Kit said.

"Do you?" said Nita.

Now it was Kit's turn to pause. *Is it smart to tell her how seriously scared I am?* he thought. *Is it going to make her feel worse?*

"Yeah, I do," Kit said at last. "I don't want to spend a minute more here than I have to. But I don't have any hunches, and you do. So get out of here and do what you have to. And do one thing for me?"

"Sure."

"Call my mom when you get there? Let her know we're okay."

"Yeah," Nita said. "No problem."

They turned back to the others. "We're done here," Sker'ret said. "Filif's checked everything over, and we've got the coordinates for the cave. We'll meet you there when we're finished."

"Then you two go on," Kit said. "We won't do anything too exciting until you get back."

"Why do I have serious doubts about that?" Nita said. But she smiled, even though the smile was wan. "Look, if Dairine turns up before we get back—"

"I'll fill her in."

Nita went over to where Sker'ret was standing in one of the spell diagrams. "You ready?" she said to Ronan.

He lifted the Spear of Light. "Go," he said.

The Spear flared into life. Nita and Sker'ret began to speak in the Speech together. Under their feet, the spell diagram came alive with light—the spoken words chasing their way around the circle, knotting in the wizard's knot, then blazing up too blindingly to let a viewer see individual characters.

Nita and Sker'ret vanished. As they did, Kit once again caught what he'd "overheard" before, that strange feeling of fear combined with Nita's sense of something that absolutely had to be done. And mixed with it, bizarrely, he could hear a sort of buzzing sound, sharp and abrupt, repeating again and again. Kit frowned. *Now where've I heard that sound before? If I didn't know better, I'd think it was somebody using some kind of energy weapon . . .*

He didn't hear anything further. *Weird,* Kit thought. *Never mind.* To Filif, who was now standing over Sker'ret's short-term transit spell diagrams, he said, "How's everything look?"

"Perfect."

Ponch, sitting there looking down at the planet, now stood up again and shook himself all over. *Are we going finding again?*

"Pretty soon," Kit said. "But we should get to the cave so you can have some dinner first."

Ponch began to jump up and down excitedly. "Okay, okay, do it over here," he said, leading Kit to one of the transit circles Sker'ret had set up. Nearby, Ronan and Filif each stepped into one of the others. Ronan glanced over at him. "Ready?"

"Ready."

They vanished.

The darkness and silence of the cave was total, and the air was absolutely still, except for the gentle wavering of the heat they felt rising from the surface on which they stood. The stifling air was slightly tainted with an oily smell that reminded Kit of the last time the repairmen had to be called in to deal with the furnace at home.

Very slowly Ronan allowed the Spear of Light to show itself in a faint ghostly glimmer of blade, while Filif's eye-berries glowed at their softest. Kit spoke the words of his small wizard-light spell and pushed it loose into the air, where the tiny spark of it hung and made a dim green-blue glow. Around them on all sides, the cavern stretched out, vast, empty, the distant walls glittering faintly. The floor was curved slightly upward toward the far walls, so that the four of them seemed to be standing in the middle of a huge, pale, shallow bowl. In such low light, the ceiling was invisible.

There's nothing here, the Champion said after a moment. *We're safe enough.*

Kit let his light get about as bright as a hundred-watt bulb, and the Spear flared up into its full glory;

Ronan let the shaft of the Spear sink into the stone of the floor and fasten itself there. Filif's berries paled down. They could now see the ceiling, at least a hundred feet above them, maybe more. A bristling of tiny thin stalactites, probably the result of many centuries of trickling water, hung from it like a coarse, thick fur. Here and there the floor was bumpy with little walnut-sized lumps of dripped-down mineral salts, which crunched underfoot when Kit experimentally stepped on them.

"Was this area volcanic once?" Filif said.

"Could have been," Kit said. "I think the magma underneath burped out a big gas bubble...then it all got pushed up toward the surface. The gas got out, the water got in..."

"Not too much of it," Ronan said, "fortunately for us. Otherwise, there might be other ways in." He looked around, satisfied.

Kit nodded and reached into his otherspace pocket for the pup-tent interface. He hung it in the air and pulled the door down. Ponch dashed through it. "Back in a minute," Kit said.

He went after Ponch, popped open a can of dog food, and emptied it into one of the waiting bowls. Then he poured some water into another dish from an open bottle. Ponch turned in a few happy circles and then began noisily and happily eating. Kit rooted around in the piles of supplies for one of the prepackaged sandwiches his mother had left for him, unwrapped it, and took a moment to stuff it into his face.

Then he stepped out through the interface with the second half of the sandwich.

Ronan had vanished into his own pup tent. Filif stood off to one side, looking down at the bright circle of another transport spell, which was now etching itself in burning lines into the stone. "Sker'ret gave me a compacted version of the transport routine," Filif said, "for transfers from here to the outer surface." He brought up his own implementation of the wizard's manual, which manifested itself as a sort of fog that clung about his branches. In that fog Kit could see a schematic of the immediate neighborhood of the planet's surface, with the main city-hive marked on it.

"There's a main trail from the city-hive that passes not too far from here," Filif said. "We can make our way easily enough to it from our transit point. Since these creatures are so scent-sensitive, we should put the outside end of the transit wizardry in a little loop that leads from the path and goes back to it, so that it won't be obvious to any Yaldiv stumbling on it that our trail goes only so far and stops."

"It'll look as if we just wandered off the main path a little and then right back again," Kit said. "Great." He ruffled up Filif's branches a little, affectionately. Filif was such a hardworking wizard, so self-effacing, but so good at what he did, that Kit was coming to admire him immensely. "You hungry? You should get yourself something."

"I'll root in a while," Filif said. "I want to make sure this is in order first. And this—"

A couple of Filif's branch-fronds reached inward to touch each other, then parted again. Between them stretched a thin filament of green wizardly fire, the most delicate possible chain of characters in the Speech. As Filif stretched the chain out, it became more and more complex, like a single strand of spiderweb becoming the whole web, then a complex of webs in three dimensions, building a shape in the air. Filif drifted backward from where he had originally been standing, and the green-fire construct stayed anchored in the air and grew upward and outward, becoming more and more complex every minute. It resolved into the big oval shape of a Yaldiv's body, spreading outward into the legs and the claws, the light then filling the innards of the shape as it sketched itself on the air. Shortly the shape of a complete Yaldiv hung there, resting lightly on its walking claws, towering over Filif and Kit. Filif let go of the filament of wizardry, and the spell stood on its own. He drifted around it, looking it over.

Kit followed, also examining it. He was impressed by the way the many, many sentences in the Speech interwove to produce the result. The *mochteroof* was woven all around a wizardly "virtual copy" of the Yaldiv's whole body. "I took the template from the Yaldiv that Ronan had to blast," Filif said. "Poor creature, it had little enough time to serve Life, even as crookedly as it did. Now it will serve it another way." He stood back from his work, admiring it. "If, as in some other hive cultures, the warriors here have additional status, this may offer us an extra layer of protection. Or enable us to go places where the workers cannot."

"I hope it doesn't also get us in some kind of trouble we can't anticipate," Kit muttered. "I wish the manual functions weren't so messed up here. We don't know as much about these people as we need to."

"We have no choice, though," Filif said, "do we? We're going to have to take the chance."

"No argument," Kit said. "Should I try it on?"

"I was hoping you would ask."

Kit took another look at the wizardry, seeing the spot near the back of the virtual Yaldiv where the user was meant to step in and shrug the new body around him like a coat. Carefully, he stepped into the center of the weave.

The whole thing blazed up with power and pressed in on Kit like a second skin... then vanished. He stood there tremendously confused for a moment: the *mochteroof* seemed to have simply vanished. Kit held up a hand—

—and saw the shadow of one of those huge, sharp-edged claws come up in front of his face. It was so odd and sudden that he jumped; the claw jerked. "Wow," he said, and turned around. "This is cool. And I still feel like me."

Ronan had come out of his pup tent and was heading over to fetch the Spear. He looked over at Kit with interest. Ponch, who had come out of Kit's tent a little before, now started dancing around Kit and barking joyously, as if this was intensely funny. *You're a giant bug!* Ponch said. *You even smell like one!*

"I'll take that as a compliment," Kit said, and was astonished at the bizarre humming and crunching noises that came out of him instead of words. He looked over at Filif, and was aware of the dark mirror-shade eyes that he was "seeing" through, though it was his own form of vision that prevailed.

"You can use the Yaldiv sensorium anytime you need to," Filif said, drifting around again to check that the *mochteroof* was working correctly. "You can scent and see either in your own mode exclusively, or as they do, or both at once. The Yaldiv see mostly as heat; a lot of the visible spectrum is lost on them. Scent comes through the legs, and they don't go in much for tactile information, as far as I can tell. Taste is in the mandibles."

"And wizardry?" Kit said.

"Won't be impaired," Filif said. "Your portable claudication is exactly where it would normally be, as are your preprepared wizardries. You can do whatever you would normally—"

The sudden *bang!* of displaced air was astonishingly loud in this small space, and was followed by an abrupt shower of a sort of flaky rain, as many of the tiny damp mineral-drop stalactites from the ceiling came pattering down onto the floor. Kit whirled around with a disrupter spell in his hands—a little core of compressed wizardry burning hot and ready to fire—and was only briefly surprised by the huge claw-shadows that seemed to enclose the hands holding the spell. Out beyond the shadows of the *mochteroof*, Ronan had snatched the Spear up out of the stone floor and was standing there with it flaming in one hand, ready to throw. Filif's berries were suddenly burning a disconcerting dark color that Kit had never seen before. But then Kit let out a breath and waved his hands and their shadow-claws apart, dismissing the spell, at the sight of the two figures standing there, one shorter than him, one much taller.

Dairine and Roshaun looked up around them at the interior of the cave. Dairine's hands were also holding some spell that fizzed and glittered as whitely blinding as a Fourth of July sparkler. Roshaun was holding ready in one hand what might have been a meter-long gilded rod, except for the hot, orange-golden, sunlike light that writhed and coiled inside it. Down on the floor between them, Spot crouched, glowing a soft and dangerous blue.

Then Dairine and Roshaun and Spot (extruding a few eyes to do the job) all stared at Kit. Dairine actually squinted at him, and it took some moments before she finally grinned. "Hey," Dairine said. "On you, that looks good."

Kit laughed. He pulled one of the tags of the Speech that was hanging down inside the *mochteroof*, and it fell away.

"How'd you find us so fast?" Ronan said. "We didn't even know we were coming here until a little while ago."

"I got Nita's message when we popped out of transit on our way in," Dairine said. "She left a pointer to the new coordinates, and forwarded it to the transits Sker'ret built for you. But where'd she go?"

"Home," Kit said. "Have you heard anything from your dad?"

Dairine shook her head. "I was going to call," she said. "Why? Neets tried and couldn't get through?"

"Yeah," Kit said. "Nothing."

"Then I won't bother right now," Dairine said. "We've got bigger fish to fry."

Roshaun looked briefly nonplussed. "Is this the time to be thinking about food?" he said.

"If you'd had as little to eat as I have today, it sure would be," Dairine said, "and if you ask me, Ponch has the right idea, because despite all the hoopla back at your big fancy royal palace, the one thing that *didn't* put in an appearance was a buffet. So forgive me." She reached into her otherspace pocket and started feeling around in it. "But we found out what we're supposed to be looking for."

"The Instrumentality?" Kit said.

"What is it?" Ronan said.

Dairine came up with a trail-mix bar and started unwrapping it. "Not a what," she said. "A who."

Ronan and Filif and Kit all stared at one another.

Dairine gave Ronan a cockeyed look as she bit into the trail-mix bar. "And it's funny that not even *you* know," she said, munching, "since your passenger was carrying the information. But then, not even *He* knew. Did you?" she said to the Champion.

I've often worked as a courier before, the One's Champion said. *"Messenger" is one of the most basic parts of my job description. But I've never before carried a message I didn't* know *I was carrying.*

"First time for everything," Dairine said, having another bite. "Ronan, around the time you stopped by our house, part of that message got loaded into Spot, and you never even knew it was happening. We couldn't get at it until we got to the mobiles' world. They put some info from the Defender's presence in the mobiles' world together with that information, decoded it..."

She smiled. Beside her, Roshaun sat down on the floor, cross-legged, with his usual effortless grace.

"The Instrumentality," Dairine said, "is the Hesper."

At that, Ronan looked up sharply.

"Or *a* Hesper," Dairine said. "There's not much difference at this point, since there's never been one before, and there may be more later...if this works out."

Kit shook his head. "What's a Hesper?"

"It's a made-up word," Dairine said. "We don't have an English equivalent to the word in the Speech. You know any of the old names for the Lone One before It fell?"

Kit thought a moment, hearing an echo of the word in an old memory. "Hesperus?" he said. "Is that in Greek mythology?"

"Yes and no," Dairine said. "But *you* know." She looked at Ronan, or rather, at his interior colleague. " 'The morning and the evening star,' they used to call the Lone Power, before there was that disagreement at the beginning of things. Then the 'star' fell."

"Phosphorus and Hesperus," said Ronan. "The Greeks didn't know the morning and evening stars were the same planet, so they had two different names. Some people started using 'Hesperus' as the name for the Lone One before It fell."

Dairine nodded. "That's the closest word we've got

for what we're looking for. What's about to happen," she said, "is the emergence of a 'bright' version of the Lone Power."

Kit's mouth fell open. *"Here?"*

"Looks like," Dairine said. "All we have to do now is figure out who it is, where it is, and how to help it."

"But the Pullulus," Kit said.

Dairine gave Kit an exasperated look. "Don't you get it?" Dairine said. "That's not even *slightly* important compared to this! I think the Powers are trying to tell us that doing the right thing about the Hesper will save the universe, too. The Hesper's a lot more important...and we've got exactly one chance to get this right. If we *do*—"

She stood there and waved her hands in the air. Kit realized that he was seeing a historic thing happen: Words had just failed Dairine.

The thought scared Kit almost worse than the Pullulus did.

Friendly Fire

THEY CAME OUT INTO the dimmed light of evening at the Crossings, and Nita let out the breath she'd been holding since Sker'ret's transit spell started to work. At a time when wizardry was acting peculiarly, any successful gating was a triumph.

Beside her, Sker'ret hadn't moved off the transit pad. He was looking around him with all his eyes, every one pointed in a different direction. "Did you hear something?" he said.

"No," Nita said. And then that struck her as strange. Nita walked off the gating pad and stepped out to where the hexagon of the enclosure met the corridor. She looked up and down the length of that bright, shining space...

...and shivered.

"This is really weird," Nita said.

Very quietly, Sker'ret came up beside her and looked

up and down the broad corridor. There was no one to be seen, absolutely no one at all.

"Okay," Nita said, thinking aloud, and glancing over at the nearest information standard, which was showing its default display of Crossings time. "It's the middle of the night…"

"The middle of a Crossings night," Sker'ret said, "doesn't look like this. Somewhere in fifteen or twenty thousand worlds, it's always the middle of the day for somebody. Somebody is always passing through."

Nita shivered again. "You did say when we left that the reduced traffic was a symptom of something that was going to get worse."

"Yes." Sker'ret sounded unnerved. "But not *this* much worse, not this fast. And there's still…"

He trailed off.

The feeling of alarm in him was suddenly very pronounced. *Still what?* Nita said silently. She felt oddly unwilling to make the silence around them seem any louder by speaking into it.

Something wrong, Sker'ret said. He turned and flowed back to the information column by the gate cluster's transit pad, rearing up against it to trigger the extension of its command-and-control console. Sker'ret brought up a display on the floating console and tapped at the control pad beside it. The display brought up a number of paragraphs in the dot-patterns and acute angles of Rirhait, but the bar graph beside the figures and annotations told Nita enough about what was going on here. *That's showing recent transits through the Crossings?* she said.

In the last three standard days, Sker'ret said. The bar graph showed the number of travelers passing through the Crossings' worldgates in a standard hour. Every bar was shorter than the one before. Then, in the last standard day, there was a brief shallow spike in both incoming and outgoing transits, after which all of them stopped completely. *No one's come through for some hours,* Sker'ret said. *Absolutely no one.*

They stood there looking at each other in silence. Then Nita said, *You don't think that's possible, do you?*

Sker'ret looked back toward the corridor with several of his eyes. *I want to have a look at the central management station,* he said. *And I want to find out where my esteemed ancestor is!*

Come on, Nita said silently.

Walking through this emptiness, with the gating-information standards silently changing minutes on their digital readouts all down the concourse, felt to Nita just like it would have felt to walk down a street in Manhattan that had no one in it at all. She found herself staring into every gating-cluster alcove that they passed, but there were no people anywhere: not the briefest glimpse of a tentacle, not a glimmer of an alien eye. Down the corridor, Nita could just make out a portion of the shining rack that was part of the Stationmaster's office. Normally there would have been people passing by it in all directions, making their way to one gate or another. Now the rack stood there all by itself, and Nita and Sker'ret made their way toward it, through the silence, through the emptiness—

Nita's eyes went wide; without actually hearing anything, she felt a sound go blasting past her ear. *"Sker'!"* she cried, and threw herself on top of him, knocking him down flat against the floor.

And then the actual sound came, and a blast of energy just above her head—a moment too late, for Nita had just said that fourteenth word in the Speech, and her personal shield-spell had gone up around her and down to the ground on either side, covering Sker'ret as well. *It'd better work right this time!* she thought furiously, and felt around in the back of her head for that shadowy presence that she was now expecting to find, half double serpent of light, half backbone of wizardry. *Are you there?*

Here, the peridexic effect said. Nita could instantly feel the extra flow of power go rushing through her into the spell. Several more energy bolts splattered into the shield, gnawed at it, and splashed away.

You carrying anything offensive? Nita said to Sker'ret.

His eyes thrashed around underneath Nita. She levered herself up a little to let him squeeze them out to either side. *Absolutely,* Sker'ret said, sounding grim. *Roll off and I'll bring my shields up. Where's the fire coming from?*

She peered down the corridor. It was hard to see through the eye-burning brightness of the blaster fire, but Nita could just make out a number of tall, thin shadows down that way, leaning out from behind various outward-projecting kiosks to fire, then ducking back again. *I think they're a lot farther down this corridor, past your ancestor's office.*

Right. Roll now!

Nita rolled off Sker'ret to his left, and felt the bump on her side as his own shield came up and pushed her sideways. She scrambled to her feet as several more energy bolts hit her shield, then reached down to her charm bracelet, grabbed the charm that looked like a lightning bolt, and said the single word in the Speech that released the wizardry's "safety."

Instantly a shape of light formed in the air in front of her: a long slender stock, tapering down to an almost needlelike point. It was one of numerous wizardly versions of a blaster, this one being nothing more than a portable linear accelerator that pushed a thin stream of charged particles as close to lightspeed as they could go, and then (this being, after all, magic) just a little faster. The effects of being struck by a beam from the accelerator tended to be noticeable, and unfortunate, for the target. Nita grabbed the accelerator out of the air with the intention of making its use very unfortunate for someone in a big hurry if they didn't stop shooting at her.

Okay, let's see how loud I can be now, she thought, unnerved but excited, as she stood up in the midst of all that blaster fire. There are phrases every wizard knows he or she may have to use in the line of work, and doesn't really want to. But most wizards nonetheless *dream* of using them, just once or twice, under the right circumstances...and this was Nita's first chance to use this one.

"In Life's name," she shouted in the Speech, while the energy blasts kept striking her shield, "and for Its sake, I advise you that I am here on the business of the Powers That Be! Your actions toward me, and through me, toward Them, will determine the continuation or revocation of your present status. *Be warned by me, and desist!*"

Slowly, the blaster fire stopped.

Just as slowly, Nita started to grin—

—and all at once the blaster fire started up again, twice as ferociously this time, so that the multiple impacts against her shield made Nita stagger.

"Oh, really," she said under her breath as she got her balance back and made sure of her shield's integrity. "Sorry, guys, you blew it."

Both angry and sad, she chose her first target with care—one of those thin shadows standing behind a particularly aggressive stream of energy blasts—aimed, and fired. Away down the corridor, across the central intersection of the Crossings, that source of the blaster fire failed. "Sorry," Nita said under her breath, meaning it, though not hesitating to immediately choose another target. She fired again. "Sorry."

Beside her, Sker'ret made his way down toward the central intersection. The closer he got, the more blaster fire hit his shield. It turned a fierce glowing red, mirroring itself in Sker'ret's shiny carapace—and every bolt that hit it bounced instantly and directly back in the direction from which it had come. Any unshielded being standing in the same place after having shot at him suddenly found itself on the receiving end of a boosted version of whatever it had fired. Nita followed Sker'ret, not hurrying, choosing her targets with regret and great care. The fire from in front of them began to lessen, but now Nita felt some fire hitting her shield from behind. She turned and started walking backward, aiming carefully at more of those thin shadow-shapes who leaned out from behind cover farther down the corridor. "They're behind us, too, Sker'!" she called. "How are we planning to get out of here? I don't want to get cut off."

"I'm not going anywhere till I find out who these people are, and get them out of here somehow!" Sker'ret called back, making steadily for the intersection. "I'll open you a gate and get you home."

"Not the slightest chance!" Nita said, coming abreast of him. "If you think I'm gonna leave you here in the middle of a firefight, you're nuts."

They paused together just before coming out into the open intersection. The central control structure was just within sight. Nita had half expected to see the Stationmaster's body hanging there in the rack, but it was mercifully empty. Nita swallowed. "Okay," she said, "you ready?"

"Let's go."

They ran out across the intersection together. As Nita had expected, both their shields immediately lit up with crossfire from both sides. They ducked into the control structure, and Nita got down behind some of the control surfaces while choosing more potential targets. Sker'ret's shield kept up its active-defense role, and the rate of fire dwindled—but not nearly as much as Nita would have liked it to.

She popped up, aimed at a shadow that was getting

too close for her comfort; it went down. Her stomach turned. While Nita hadn't been able to clearly see the results of her own fire, self-defense had been easier. "Sker'," she said, "what now?!"

"Give me a minute," Sker'ret said. "I'm making this up as I go along." He pulled himself up into the racking, enough to tap briefly at the main control console. The rate of fire at them increased, and Nita popped up once more, sighted on yet another shadow—they were getting bolder, getting closer, no matter how many of them she, or Sker'ret's shield, took out. She fired again, and once again her stomach wrenched. *I hate this,* Nita thought. *But I'd hate it more if the weapon* stopped *doing that.*

All around them, the blaster fire continued, but the impacts on both their personal shields abruptly ceased. Nita looked around and saw that a larger force field had sprung up around the central control structure. This one was invisible, but its hemisphere was clearly defined by the bright splatter of frustrated energy hitting the outside of it.

"That'll give us a few minutes," Sker'ret said.

"A *few*?" Nita said, alarmed.

"The console shield will cope with this level of fire all right," Sker'ret said, sounding very grim indeed, "but how long do you think it's going to stay like this? Whoever those people are, they plainly intend to take the Crossings by force. When they find they don't have enough force, they'll bring up some more. I give us maybe five minutes. By then I should be able to find out why the Crossings' own defense systems haven't come up, and either I can get them up again or...do something else." His voice went perfectly flat in a way that Nita had never heard before. "But you need to keep them off my back. Stick some of your power into the shield, give it a boost. Here are the schematics—"

A glowing diagram full of lines and curves and weird symbols appeared in the air in front of Nita. She gulped; not even knowledge of the Speech could turn you into a rocket scientist between one breath and the next. "Sker', I'm a wizard, not an engineer!"

Sker'ret pointed an eye at the diagram. "Right there," he said. "Energy conduit. Put whatever spare power you've got right into that."

Nita let out a breath and started to think of how to hook a power-feed wizardry into the energy conduit. In the back of her mind, instantly, the peridexis showed her the spell. Nita hurriedly spoke the words, and a few seconds later felt the built-up power inside her flowing into the shield. "Okay," she said to Sker'ret, "I've boosted it maybe five hundred percent."

"Let's hope that's enough," Sker'ret said.

Down at the far end of the Main Concourse, Nita could see more clearly the shadowy figures that kept darting out of cover to fire at them. The shapes were tall and angular, and very thin; it was hard to tell their bodies from the weapons they were carrying. "It's like being attacked by a bunch of praying mantises," Nita muttered. "What *are* those things?"

Sker'ret chanced a glance up through the blaster fire. "Sort of tall, skinny creatures?" he said. "What color?"

Nita peered at them. "Red," she said. "No, kind of purple. Magenta, I guess."

"How many heads?"

Nita couldn't tell. *If I could stick a lens into the shield,* she thought.

She felt the peridexis once again suggesting the wizardry that was necessary, needing only her approval. *Okay,* she thought, and started to say the words in the Speech, except it was almost as if they said themselves, leaping out of her as if they, too, were weapons. The force field in front of her suddenly went sharp and clear, as if Nita were looking through binoculars. *I could get really used to this,* she thought, grim but also triumphant. *Is it like this when you're really a Senior out on errantry? Does the power just flow to you on demand?*

She got a view of what she was supposed to be looking at. "Just one head," she said to Sker'ret, whose handling claws were still tapping frantically at the console. "What's the matter?"

"They've taken the defense systems completely offline," Sker'ret growled. Nita was startled. She'd never heard him sound so furious before. "Sabotage. Or an inside job, and somebody on our own staff betrayed us." He hissed. "Never mind now. Just one head? Those are Tawalf."

"Never heard of them."

"I wish I never had," Sker'ret said. "They're a very…mercantile people. They'd buy anybody from anybody, and sell anybody to anybody, if the price was right. Looks like someone on our staff decided that our security was merchandise." He growled again. "The

Tawalf sell themselves, too. They make some of the best mercenaries in this part of the galaxy."

"Looks like somebody went out and bought them in bulk," Nita said, as more and more of the Tawalf came into sight, every one of them armed with at least a blaster, and every one of them firing at the shield surrounding the rack. "Can you turn the defense systems on again?"

Sker'ret waved his upper body from side to side, his version of a human shaking his head. "There are a couple of things I still need to try," he said. "But there's no other information on what happened here. Everything's been left on auto, and no station staff have logged in since that last transit spike."

"So you don't know where your ancestor is."

"Or any of my sibs."

"You don't think that these guys could have—"

"They could have done a lot of things," Sker'ret said, sounding grimmer every moment. "What's that?"

The pace of fire against the shields had started to step up again: Nita was having trouble seeing through it, there were so many impacts now. "They're covering for something," she said. *I need better visibility!* she thought.

Once again the wizardry constructed itself in her head, ready to go. *Yes!* Nita thought, and just briefly the shield cleared in front of her, showing her, far down the concourse, a very large, very heavy piece of machinery being floated out from a place of concealment.

"Uh-oh," Nita said. "They're rolling out the big guns. What about those defense systems?"

"I can't get them up again!" Sker'ret whacked the console in frustration with most of his forward legs. "Now I wish I remembered some of the things about their basic programming that my ancestor kept on boring me with."

"Forget it," Nita said. "We've got other problems!"

The lens in her shield gave her a much better view of that piece of machinery as it came drifting toward them, being guided with some kind of remote by a Tawalf who was dashing from the cover of one kiosk to the next. The weapon had a muzzle of impressive size, and some kind of massive generating apparatus hooked to the back of it. *Can we stop that?* she said silently to the peridexic effect.

There was no immediate answer.

This in itself was answer enough for Nita, and a flush of pure fear ran straight through her. Apparently, there were limits to what even the present power boost for wizards could do—or what she could do with it.

"Make or break, Sker'!" Nita said over Sker'ret's shoulders. "We've gotta make a choice in about a minute. Run for it, or make a stand." *And if we do, I have this feeling it'll be a* last *stand.*

"If we run," Sker'ret said, "this place will be lost to us and won by those Tawalf. They, and whoever is behind them, will have free run of my planet, and this whole part of the galaxy. Since whether they know it or not they're doing the Lone One's business—" He growled again. "No way I'm leaving them here! I will not let the Lone Power have the Crossings."

"But what can you do?"

"The one thing they're sure I don't want to do under any circumstances," Sker'ret said. "And therefore the one thing they didn't sabotage completely enough to keep me out."

He reached sideways and hit a control that caused another small console to appear from nowhere. This tiny console had some very large, alarming-looking Rirhait characters glowing on it. Nita looked at it and swallowed hard again. "Self-destruct?"

"At least," Sker'ret said, suddenly sounding worried, "I don't *think* they sabotaged it that completely."

Sker'ret started speaking urgently to the console in the Speech, while hammering on the keypad beneath it with what seemed every available foreleg. Nita was keeping power flowing to the central structure's own shield, but she couldn't keep her eyes away from Sker'ret. "Sker'ret, you *live* here!" she said. "You're going to blow up your own *home*?"

"Believe me, there've been some times I've wanted to," Sker'ret said. "I just never thought it was going to look like this when I got my chance."

He kept working furiously at the console. Finally, the display on it changed. "All right," Sker'ret said. "I think I can make this work."

Nita looked at that slowly oncoming weapon, and gulped. "Give me ten seconds first," she said.

Sker'ret swiveled almost all his eyes at her except for the one that was watching the self-destruct console. "What? Why?"

Nita ignored him and shut her eyes for a moment. *What kind of energy are those things using?* she thought.

The peridexis gave her the answer as if it were the manual itself, laying it out in graphics and the Speech with blinding speed. Nita scanned the diagram it showed her. *It's fusion,* she thought. *And there are ways to damp that down. If you just mess with the magnetic bottle a little—*

Nita shivered. Once upon a time, the Lone Power had done something similar to the Earth's Sun. And then she smiled just slightly. To turn Its own trick against It, but with just a little extra twist—

That fusion reaction right there, Nita said to the peridexis, *let's snuff it.*

There is a high probability that the smothered reaction will interact unfavorably with matter in the immediate vicinity.

Will our shield hold?

Yes.

Then let's start getting unfavorable!

Nita started speaking the words of the spell, feeling the power build. This wizardry felt less like a thrown weapon than a squeezing fist—like a gauntlet into which she'd thrust her own hand, pressing the power of the mobile weapon's tightly controlled fusion reaction into a smaller and smaller space. The reaction wasn't built to take such punishment. It started to strangle. Nita held the pressure, squeezed tighter, feeling the hot bright little light in her "hand" burning her, but nonetheless starting to go out, fading, failing—

The magnetic bottling around the little fusion fire inside the weapon, responding to the fusion's own loss of energy, lost its balance and stepped down to match it.

Nita smiled and quickly opened her hand.

Every Tawalf anywhere near the mobile weapon turned to stare at the slow, threatening glow of light beginning to burn through the weapon's metallic fabric. Suspecting what was coming, Nita hastily told the control structure's force field to go opaque itself. Almost the last glimpse she got was of Tawalf scattering in every possible direction. Then came the sudden blinding burst of repressed starfire as the magnetic bottle in the mobile weapon failed.

The force field was opaque to light, but not noise or vibration. From outside came a roar, and the floor under Nita and Sker'ret rocked: Things crashed and clattered all around them. After a few seconds the ruckus started to die down. Nita let the "gauntlet" of wizardry vanish, and let the control console's shield go transparent again.

Outside was a billowing cloud of smoke and dust, slowly dispersing. There were no Tawalf to be seen.

Sker'ret's eyes were staring in all directions, except for the one that was still trained on the self-destruct console, ready to guide the four or five legs that were poised over it. "Do you think—"

Nita, too, peered in all directions. "I don't see any of them here."

Sker'ret stretched his mandibles apart in what Nita knew he was using to approximate a human grin. "Hey!" he said, holding up a foreclaw.

Nita held up a hand, too, and had to keep it there until it stung; high-fiving a giant centipede can take a while. "Not bad," Sker'ret said when he was done. "We should apply to get that one named after you. 'Callahan's Unfavorable Instigation,' or something like that."

Nita grinned. Having a spell named after you was beyond an honor: It suggested that the wizardry was both unique to your way of thinking and useful in a way that no one else had thought of before. "It can wait," she said. "Let's make sure the place is secure."

Sker'ret glanced over his consoles, looking annoyed. "My scan facility's down."

Nita reached for her otherspace pocket to get her manual. "I'll do a detector spell. At least now we have a specific life sign to scan for. We can—" She blinked. "Sker', GET DOWN!"

The intuition hadn't even come as not-hearing that time: It was as if it bypassed Nita's brain and went straight to her muscles. She threw herself on top of Sker'ret again and took him out of the line of fire, and once more she got her personal shield up just in time— a good thing, as the control console's shield was suddenly struggling under the onslaught of several fusion beams like the one that would have come out of the first mobile weapon if Nita hadn't destroyed it.

"They've got two more of them!" Nita shouted over the noise. "No, make that three! One behind us, two on either side, they came out of one of the crosscorridors farther down. And they're *bigger* ones!" The three sets of beams now crisscrossed relentlessly over them.

Oh, God, Nita thought. *I can't do more than one of the "unfavorable" wizardries at a time, and while I'm doing that, the other big guns are going to blow the main shield away.* Even now she could start to see places where the cubicle's shield was dimpling inward, no matter how much wizardry Nita poured into it through the peridexis. "Sker', we can't stay here, the shield's giving! We've got to do a personal gating out of here to somewhere else. Hang on!"

Sker'ret's eyes waved in wild distress. *"No!* There's too much energy in the air around us! It'll derange your wizardry, and you'll come out at your transit point as half a thwat of powdered Nita!"

I wonder how much a thwat is? Nita thought, scowling in terrified fury. *Thanks so much, mister hunch. Was that why I was in such a hurry to get here? Did I have an appointment to* die?

No answer came from the peridexis. Nita was getting more angry than scared. *It's not supposed to end like this!* she thought. *If I'm going to die, it should be right in the middle of things, not out at the edge! And not until I know my universe is safe.*

But suddenly this seemed untrue. Suddenly Nita began to understand the feeling she'd read about in books, but never really understood: the feeling that it was genuinely all over, that nothing further could be done...except to go out as well as you could. For a moment, the realization froze her rigid.

But only for a moment. *I'm on Their business,* Nita thought. *And I am going to go out doing Their business. I've been through this before. I've been ready to go. It's just that now...now it's going to happen for real.*

"I'm gonna stop feeding power to the main shield, and feed it to ours, instead," Nita said. "You ready?"

"For what? *Nita!*"

Nita stood up and turned to face the weapon that had come up behind them and was now the closest. The dimples in the main shield grew deeper and deeper as she watched. In a moment one of the weapons would punch through and it would be all over. Nita lifted her hands in the air, spread them out to either side, and said silently to the peridexis, *All right. Let's go. You know what I need—*

She closed her eyes. Perfectly clear in her inner vision hung and burned the words in the Speech that gave the Powers That Be the authorization to take the last thing you had, your life, and make the best possible use of it. You were, of course, allowed to make suggestions. *Take everything I have,* Nita said silently, *and clear all these creatures and weapons out of here so Sker'ret can do what he has to do to keep the Lone One from getting the Crossings.* For just a second she thought sadly of Kit: There would be no way to tell him what she was having to do, no way to say good-bye— Nita squeezed her eyes tightly shut, and opened her mouth to say the first word of the wizardry, the first word of the last spell she would ever recite—

And then her eyes flew open at a sound she had not expected. A soft strange hum, scaling up, getting louder. *Where have I heard that before?* she thought. *Sker'?*

Right in front of her, the bigger mobile weapon that was trained on them shuddered, strained itself apart, and blew up.

Nita hit the floor. *This is getting to be a habit!* she thought, as the breath went out of her with a *whoof!*—

but as soon as she could, she struggled up, pushing herself free from a tangle of Sker'ret's legs, and stared out to see what had happened. *How come I didn't hear that one coming? What in the—*

That hum scaled up again behind her. "Uh-oh," Nita said, and once again went flat on top of Sker'ret. Behind them, the second weapon shuddered itself apart and destroyed itself in a huge blast of noise and fire.

"You really *do* want to become more than just good friends, don't you?" Sker'ret said from underneath her, sounding rather squashed. "I don't know how I'm going to explain this to my ancestor, assuming we ever find him."

Nita put her head up, trying to see what was happening to the mobile weapons. That hum started to scale up once more. Again she ducked, and from much farther behind came yet another explosion. *Are they malfunctioning? Or is someone else doing that? Are they on our side? And what if they're not?*

"And don't I get to throw myself on *you* sometimes?" Sker'ret said. "People will think you don't believe I can take care of myself."

"Sker'ret," Nita said, "will you please just put a sock in it?" Cautiously, she peered around, trying to see through all the smoke.

Sker'ret put some eyes up, too. "I don't wear socks," he said.

"Just as well," Nita said. "You'd bankrupt yourself." Through the smoke of the second mobile weapon's explosion, Nita could just see something moving. *Oh, great,* she thought. *What did I do with the accelerator? Is it another of those—*

But whatever was coming, it didn't move like a Tawalf. Though it was still mostly hidden by the smoke of the last weapon's destruction, Nita could see that it went on just two legs. Nita spoke the words of the spell that made the accelerator remanifest itself, then put it against her shoulder, sighted—

It's a humanoid, Nita thought, as the figure came to-ward them through the smoke. *What's that hanging off its head? Humanoids don't usually have tentacles there. And it doesn't look like it's armed.*

It wasn't a very big humanoid, either. It was only a little taller than Nita. As it came through the smoke, she could have sworn that it was actually human—the skin color was one of the possible ones, the eyes and other features seemed all to be in the right places, and the clothes— *Jeez, will you look at those,* Nita thought at the sight of the cropped black T-shirt, the cargo pants in a truly eye-jangling hot-pink-and-green floral print, and the strappy, high pink boots. And the "ten-tacle" wasn't a tentacle at all, but, hanging down in front of one shoulder, a single long, thick, dark—

—*braid?*

Nita's mouth dropped open as the girl came all the way out of the smoke. She had a light backpack-purse on her back, some kind of holster hanging at one hip, and a wicked grin on her face.

Nita shut her mouth, and opened it again.

"Carmela?" she said, in sort of a strangled squeak. "*Carmela?*"

She came striding over to them. "Hey," 'Mela said, "I'm glad to see you, too." And she peered at Nita curiously. "Why're you so red? You have *got* to start remembering the sunscreen, Neets; you're going to die of skin cancer or something."

Nita laughed weakly at the stinging feel of her face, burned by the overloading shields. She looked up and down the corridor to the smoking wreckage of the remaining three fusion weapons...and the walls and other structures that had been between them and Carmela. "How the heck did you do that?" Nita said.

Carmela smiled. From the holster, the kind that beauticians carry their hair dryers in, she pulled out a foot-long object that seemed to combine the features of a curling iron and an eggbeater. The beaters throbbed faintly with a threatening glow, like the one that had come from the first mobile weapon just before Nita blew it up.

Nita blinked. "That's the thing you got off the alien shopping channel?" she said. "But that was just a laser dissociator—"

" 'Was,' " Carmela said. She grinned again. "I sent away for the free upgrade."

Sker'ret clambered out of the control console's rack and flowed over to the two of them. "And there's my favorite bunch of legs!" Carmela said, and hunkered down to Sker'ret's level. As he came up beside her, she reached out and yanked a couple of his eyes in a friendly way. "Hey there, cute-as-a-bug," she said. "You okay? You look a little scorched around the edges."

Sker'ret simply stared. After a moment, he said, "This is...unexpected!"

Carmela produced a pout. "You're not glad to see me!"

"Oh, glad, *absolutely* glad, but you shouldn't be—"

"Why?" Carmela said. "*Why* shouldn't I? Really, why do you guys all think you have to be wizards to save the universe? You people get so *grabby* sometimes."

Nita blinked. *Did I say I thought the weird quotient in my life was going to start rising? Remind me to keep my mouth shut after this.* "Forgive me if I take a moment to see where the people who were shooting at us are now," Nita said, and got out her manual.

"Sure." Carmela looked around her, admiring the architecture through the general destruction. "Hey, nice ceiling. Or is it really a ceiling?"

"What's left of it," Sker'ret said, since a lot of the ceiling was now on the floor.

Nita turned to her detector spells, found a favorite all-purpose one with a good range, and read it, inserting the name in the Speech for the Tawalf species, and the energy signature of the big fusion weapons. The silence of a working spell settled around her, while in the back of her mind she could sense the peridexic effect waiting to see if she needed extra power. *Hey,* Nita said silently, *thanks for what you did back there.*

You *did that. As for the rest—* Did it actually sound a little shy? *It was my pleasure. And also a pleasure to see a spell I haven't seen done quite that way before. That's one for the book.*

Nita smiled as the wizardry completed. Closing her

eyes, in her mind she could see a swarm of little sparks, like thirty or forty bright bees, all seemingly orbiting one another in a tight swarm down one end of the main cross-corridor. There were no other Tawalf life signs present in the Crossings, and no further live-fusion signatures.

Nita opened her eyes. "Not many of them left," she said. "They're all down at the left-hand end of that corridor." She pointed. "I think they're trying to get out."

"That they won't do," Sker'ret said. "I've cut power to all the gates, and instructed the master gating matrices to refuse any incoming gating. Let's go have a word with the Tawalf and find out where my ancestor and sibs are."

Or if *they are,* Nita thought. Suddenly, she felt very tired. "And you turned off the self-destruct?"

"No," Sker'ret said. He reached up to the self-destruct console and pulled off what Nita had at first thought was a small protruding piece of the monitor panel. As he detached it, the little slick black piece of metal or plastic came alive with the same frozen figures that shone on the main monitor. Sker'ret opened his mandibles and swallowed it.

Nita's eyes went wide. "Uh, feeling like a snack?"

"Not *that* much like one," Sker'ret said. "This way it can't be lost or taken from me, and if I have to destroy it, that option's only a stomach or two away. Let's go deal with the survivors."

Nita climbed out of the rack while lifting the accelerator wizardry carefully to keep it from interfering with the local matter. As the three of them walked down the corridor, detouring around blasted pieces of Crossings and remnants of the destroyed fusion weapons, Nita put her free hand up to her face and found herself dripping with sweat and covered with dust. " 'Mela," she said, wiping some of the sweat away, "how in the worlds did you *get* here?"

Carmela was ambling along on the other side of Sker'ret, gazing in idle interest at the general destruction. "Well, when you left, the TV and the DVD player were still in sync with Spot," she said. "While I was changing channels, I found where the two of them were storing the coordinates of all the places you were passing through. And since I didn't feel like just sitting around after you guys utterly *ditched* me, I started using the TV's browser to look up where you'd been. There's a lot there about the Crossings. I thought, 'Hey, I could go there! I know the address now.' And the TV showed me how—"

"The TV *showed* you?"

"It's real helpful," Carmela said, "when it's not being bossed around by the remote. Come to think of it, it's been a lot more talkative the past few days."

"And it made you a worldgate," Sker'ret said, sounding bemused.

"It put it in the closet in my room," Carmela said. She smiled sunnily. "I told Kit I wanted a magic closet! And now I've got one."

"Oh, boy," Nita said, imagining what Kit's reaction to this was going to be.

"I was going to do some shopping," Carmela said,

glancing around her regretfully at the trashed and blasted shops. "But when I got here, I heard all this noise, so I ran down this way. And what do I find but all these skinny purple aliens running around shooting at everything! Some of them started shooting at me, too. That was *not* very friendly of them." Her tone of voice might have been used to describe the antics of unruly toddlers. "I told them to stop. They wouldn't. And then after that, I saw them shooting at *you*. I thought maybe Kit was here, too, so—" She shrugged. "Nobody gets to blow up my baby brother while I have anything to say about it. Or his best friend! So I took steps."

"Uh," Nita said, and could think of absolutely nothing else to say.

"Where is he, by the way?" Carmela said.

This is not a place where I want to be overheard discussing what's really going on. "Uh, there's another planet where we're doing some work."

"Great," Carmela said. "When we're done here, let's go."

"Ah," Sker'ret said. "Carmela, the situation there is—"

"'Mela," Nita said simultaneously, "look, we're really grateful that you got here when you did, but—"

Carmela gave the two of them what Nita's mom used to refer to as "an old-fashioned look." "Yeah, right, don't even bother, you two," Carmela said. "I can hear it already. Blah blah blah for your own safety, blah blah blah don't know what you're getting into, blah blah blah *forget it,* Neets!" Her voice was casual, even cheerful, but she hefted the curling iron in a very meaningful way. "It's really a good thing Kit didn't void the warranty on this thing when he was putting the safety on it," she said. "But it doesn't matter, because I figured out how to get the safety off...and then how to get the upgrade. I can figure out most things, given time. Juanita Louise, you take me home and it'll take me about ten minutes to figure out where you went...and I'll be right back. How much time can you spare to waste dragging me back home over and over?"

Nita's mouth dropped open again. "*Who told you about 'Louise'?*"

Carmela grinned.

"Did Kit tell you? *I'll kill him!*"

Carmela laughed. "Kit doesn't tell me anything." Her look got, if possible, more wicked. "*That's* gonna change."

Sker'ret was staring at them both in good-natured confusion. "Look," Nita said. "'Mela, there's something you need to know about where we're going. You're not real big on bugs—"

"Oh, I've heard this one before," she said, and snickered, reaching down to yank in an affectionate way on some of Sker'ret's eyes. "It won't work, Neets."

"No, listen to me. These are not cute bugs. These are *big* bugs! They"—it had taken her a while to come to terms with some of the things she'd seen about the Yaldiv in their précis in the manual. Now she simply said, "They eat each other, and anything else that's alive enough. They'll eat us, given half a chance! And we have to make sure that they do *not* know we're there under any circumstances."

"Kit's there?" Carmela said. "And Ponch?"

"Yeah."

"And my favorite Christmas tree?"

"Yeah."

"And Dairine and Roshaun?"

"They might be there by now—"

"And *Ronan*?"

"Uh," Nita said.

"That sounded like a yes," Carmela said, and smiled a supremely predatory smile. "Let's go."

Nita rubbed her face, finding more dirt and more sweat... and a final annoying sting that told her her zit was still in residence. She sighed.

"Okay," Nita said. "You can come with us! But I have to get back to Earth first. That was what this trip was all about."

"You go right ahead," Carmela said. "Sker'ret and I will tidy up here."

Sker'ret looked up at Carmela, confused.

Carmela looked around at the burned and broken wreckage all over the place. "Sker'," Carmela said, "Just think of all the stuff here you can eat!"

Most of Sker'ret's eyes went very wide.

"It wasn't allowed before," Sker'ret said in a hushed tone, like someone suddenly presented with a landscape full of infinite possibilities. "I mean, I'm station staff, and we have to control our habits where Crossings property is concerned. My ancestor would—"

"Your not-so-illustrious ancestor," Carmela said, disapproving, "isn't here, is he?" She glanced around. "So don't sweat it. If I were you, I'd just tuck in now; later on you can blame the mess on the purple guys. Assuming there *is* a later." She glanced over at Nita. "I gather from the TV that that's the problem? End of the world, everything's on the table, a million-to-one chance of fixing it all?"

"Quadrillion," Nita said, not wanting to later be caught in an understatement.

Carmela spun her curling iron around on what could have been mistaken for a hanging loop, and shoved it into its holster. "Sounds good," she said. "Let's go deal with it. I've got nothing here but solutions."

They paused halfway down the corridor. Far down, at the end of it, Nita could see a lot of tall, thin, purple shapes crowded together. "Think we should put the shields back up?" she said.

"We won't need them," Sker'ret said. "I've put a damping field over this whole wing. No energy weapon will work. But the damper won't bother wizardries."

"You mean I can't use my curling iron?" Carmela said, and produced a pout.

"'Mela," Nita said, "you won't need it. If I'm reading these guys' physical attributes correctly, you could break one of them in half like a pencil. They're on the fragile side."

"It's why they like these big weapons so much," Sker'ret said, sounding annoyed as he eyed the damage behind them. "I have a feeling that when I get at the system logs, the damping fields will have been the first things shut down."

The three of them walked toward the crowd of Tawalf, in step, taking their time. The crowd clustered closer together as they approached. As the three of them got closer, Nita looked at the Tawalf and found herself feeling strangely sorry for them. *They look kind of helpless and pitiful,* she thought, *without their big fancy weapons. Which is good for me, since now I have to make sure I'm not influenced by the fact that they would have blown me away without a second thought.*

Sker'ret and Nita stopped; Carmela did, too, stepping a little away to watch what they did. The Tawalf glared at them.

"We are on errantry, and we greet you," Sker'ret said.

"Not that you particularly *merit* greeting," Nita said.

"And, additionally," Sker'ret said, "I represent the constituted authority of the Crossings, an independent political entity of Rirhath B. I inform you that you are now to be placed in Crossings custody for a number of local and planetary infractions. You have the right to send to your homeworld through our independent travelers' representative—when we manage to locate it—for whatever legal assistance you require. Meanwhile, we have the right to require of you all pertinent details concerning your presence here, your actions while here, and information concerning those of our station staff who were involved in attempting to prevent your access."

There was a long silence. Then one of the Tawalf said, "There weren't any."

Knowledge of the Speech made the words understandable, but the sense was still ambiguous. "Weren't any *what*?" Sker'ret said.

"Attempts to prevent our access," the Tawalf said.

"Where are the station staff?" Nita said.

The Tawalf who had spoken looked at Nita scornfully, and then threw a strange look at Carmela. *Maybe it's the pants,* Nita thought. They certainly made *her* eyes vibrate when she looked at them.

"We don't know," the Tawalf said.

"Somehow I doubt that," Nita said.

"They ran off somewhere," said another Tawalf, looking sullen—insofar as it was possible to look sullen with such expressionless eyes, like polished pebbles. "Probably hiding elsewhere on the planet."

Nita glanced at Sker'ret. *What do you think?*

I don't know what to think. It doesn't seem in character. But then my ancestor wasn't behaving as usual when I saw him last, either.

"Where did you people come in from?" Sker'ret said. "Who sent you?"

None of them would answer.

"Oh, come on," Sker'ret said. "No Tawalf does something unless *valuta*'s changed hands. You didn't just turn up here with a pile of heavy weapons because you felt like it!"

The Tawalf glowered at him. "We've been bought once," one of them said. "We can't break our contracts."

"And saying anything would be breaking them."

Nita frowned. "You don't *have* to say anything," she said.

They all glared at her now, and Nita hoped her bluff wasn't about to be called. Wizardries designed to get into people's minds and take out information forcibly were almost as hard on the wizard as they were on the victim. *But we have to get this place secure and running before we move on.*

You have the power if you need it, the peridexis said in the back of her mind.

I know I do. But I really don't know if I want it for this… Yet it seemed to Nita that she might have no choice, and time was flying.

The Tawalf who had spoken first had been watching Nita. Now it laughed, a nasty ratchety sound. "You won't do it," it said. "Wizards! Everybody knows you were always weaklings, afraid to lose your power by using it the wrong way. And now, after all these centuries of being so nicey-nice, you're losing it anyway! So you're finished running things in this universe! And *your* people are through running this place," it said to Sker'ret, "and controlling all the wealth and power that flows through here. It's up to the smart ones and the strong ones now to take what they want."

"What *we* want," said another of the Tawalf.

The rest of the crowd behind them started to join in that nasty snickering noise. Nita's fingers clenched on the accelerator in anger.

"I dislike this necessity," Sker'ret said. "But if psychotropic spelling is required to restore the Crossings to its normal function—"

"Sker', let me," Nita said. "I don't like it, either, but maybe I have a way to—"

"Guys," Carmela said. "Wait a sec."

Nita and Sker'ret looked at her.

"You get more honey with flies," Carmela said, and then paused. "Wait a minute, that's not how it goes. Never mind. Here—"

She reached over her back into the little bag she was wearing, and felt around. The Tawalf watched her with some curiosity.

Then one of them, the one who had spoken first, made a strange sniffing noise—and so did its second-in-command. The two of them stared at Carmela with a sudden total concentration that made Nita raise the accelerator and get ready to fire.

Carmela withdrew something from her bag. It was thin and black, a long slim rectangle with a glint of gold at the ends. She held it up where all the Tawalf could see it.

"I have here," she said in very clear and New York–accented Speech, "a *new* bar of Valrhona Caraïbe Single-Estate Grand Cru."

Nita looked in astonishment from Carmela to the Tawalf. Their eyes, already prominent enough, actually started to bug out of their heads. "Very aromatic," Carmela said, waving the chocolate bar under her nose. "Long in the mouth . . . nice overflavors of candied orange and smoky vanilla . . . maybe just a hint of cappuccino." She waved it at them. "Sorry, guys, help me out here. I don't know where your nose or whatever you smell with is. Are."

The two foremost Tawalf each reached out a tentative, spindly magenta foreleg. Carmela waved the chocolate bar cautiously under each one.

The first Tawalf made a grab for it, but not quickly enough. Carmela had already snatched the bar back, and Nita had the accelerator trained on his head.

"Ah, ah, ah," Carmela said. "Hasty hasty. This is yours...all yours...for a price." She glanced sideways at Nita.

"Information," Nita said. "You heard what we asked you."

"Oh, they're going to have to tell you a lot more than just what you asked them," Carmela said, waving the chocolate gently under her nose and gazing thoughtfully at the Tawalf. "You're going to answer *all* this nice Rirhait's questions, aren't you, boys? Or girls. Or whatever. And when you've done that, you can form yourselves a little syndicate, and I'll give that syndicate free title to...*this.*"

She held up the chocolate bar.

Every single Tawalf stared at it. Nita and Sker'ret spared each other one sidewise glance.

"We can't!" squeaked one of the Tawalf in the back.

"Our contracts!" moaned another.

"Oh, come on," Carmela said. "Your 'contracts'! Like you expect me to believe that somebody actually paid you *this* much to come in here and take this place over? I really doubt it." She snickered. "If someone had given the whole bunch of you the value of even *half* of this, you'd be the highest-paid mercenaries the universe ever saw!" Carmela waved the chocolate bar in the Tawalf's direction again.

They swayed toward it as if it had the gravitation of a micro–black hole. Nita raised the accelerator again. The Tawalf saw the look in her eye and swayed back. "But no one's paid you anything like that much," Carmela said. "So just think. You cooperate with my friends here, and I'm sure they'll do what they can to see to it that the authorities here treat you fairly. And afterward, when you've paid your debt to society, or whatever your species pays its debts to, on the day they let you all go, they give you ... *this.*"

There was a long, long silence.

Then the Tawalf leader said, "No."

Nita and Sker'ret gave each other another glance at the sound of the scratchy muttering that started to go up from behind the leader.

"Oh, my," Carmela said. "That's too bad. Just think what you all could have had!" She glanced past the Tawalf leader to the others behind him. "But just because he got stubborn ... well. Now I'm just going to have to do ... this."

She moved the chocolate bar to her left hand ... and very, very slowly, moved her right hand toward it. Carmela took hold of the outer black paper wrapper between finger and thumb ... and ever so gently started to pull on the paper, as if to unwrap it.

"*No!*" at least half the Tawalf screeched. And the second-in-command shouted, "You'll ruin it!"

"Right here in front of you," Carmela said. "While you watch...and with the *greatest* possible pleasure." She smiled ever so sweetly. "I'm going to pull the wrapping off, and shred it. I'm going to rip off the foil and crumple it up into a little ball. And then I'm going to take the unspeakably valuable stuff inside...and I am going to break it up into those nice little squares... and I am going to eat...it...*all*."

The leader of the Tawalf began to whimper. His second-in-command exchanged meaningful glances with the others.

"The information," Carmela said.

The noise level among the Tawalf began to increase.

"You can have a moment to think," Carmela said, and turned away. Nita and Sker'ret stayed as they were, facing the increasingly shaken Tawalf, though Sker'ret turned a few of his eyes toward Carmela.

"And without even laying a finger on them," Nita said under her breath. "I'm impressed."

"Yeah, well, it's just the usual problem with aliens and chocolate," Carmela said, very amused. "Is it a collectible, or a controlled substance? Or both? And whichever way the species sees it, it's always worth a lot more in the original packaging."

"This is cruel," Sker'ret said. His tone, like Nita's, was one of reluctant admiration. "I'm not sure you're not speeding up entropy somewhat."

"I'd say they had it coming," Carmela said, "since they seem to have done a fair amount of speeding it up around here themselves."

The muttering among the Tawalf got louder. Nita,

watching the leader and his second-in-command as their subordinates pressed in around them, got the idea that greed, fear, and peer pressure were operating among the aliens in entirely too human a manner. Finally, the noise began to die down a little. Nita glanced at Sker'ret.

"Well?" Sker'ret said.

The Tawalf leader's voice, when he spoke, was surprisingly small. "All right," he said. "We'll tell you what you want to know. If we have your word as wizards that you will comply with the agreement as it's been presented."

"Oh, yeah, all of a sudden the nicey-niceness of wizards becomes a *good* thing," Nita said, though not so far under her breath that she couldn't be heard.

The look that Sker'ret flashed her was equally ironic, but they were of the same mind. "In the Powers' names, and the Name of That which They serve," Sker'ret said, "and as the Crossings' legal representative present, I give my word."

Carmela carefully handed Sker'ret the chocolate bar. "Don't crease the paper!" she said, as he delicately took it in a forward handling-claw. "So. All you guys behave now," she said to the Tawalf. "If you don't, I'll hear about it, and I'll refuse to relinquish title."

There was a lot of broken-spirited muttering from the Tawalf. "I'm going to transfer you to a secure holding facility," Sker'ret said, moving over to the nearest gate-cluster standard and tapping at it so that it extruded its own control console. "We'll be along to see that you have nourishment shortly, and to start your questioning. Everyone into the zone, please."

A pad came alive, glowing red. The Tawalf spidered their way onto it and huddled there. A moment later they vanished.

Nita and Sker'ret looked at each other. Nita let out a long breath. She could hear the tiny multiple hiss as Sker'ret pushed a sigh out of the little spiracles all down the length of his body.

"You should get on home to do what you need to," he said. "I'll pop a gate open for you now."

Nita looked around her, concerned. "Are you going to be able to manage here?"

"I'll call the planetary authorities," Sker'ret said. "They'll send me plenty of staff until I can get the systems back up again, and get a clearer sense of what happened here. The logs should help me figure it out. And assuming that my ancestor is all right—"

He fell silent.

"I'm sure he is," Nita said. "He's too mean to—" She stopped herself. "I mean—"

"I know," Sker'ret said, amused. "Go find out where your own ancestor is. I'll meet you here afterward, and we can go back together."

"Yeah," Nita said.

She turned to Carmela. "One thing before I go," Nita said. "Are your pop and mom okay?"

"They're just fine," Carmela said.

"Do they know you've left?"

"Sure. I left them a note on the fridge, the way Kit does."

Nita was uncertain what the Rodriguezes' response to *that* was going to be, but right now she had other concerns. "Look, I don't think I'm going to have to be gone long. Are you sure you're going to be okay here?"

"Haven't I been okay so far?" Carmela said.

Even in her present stressed-out condition, Nita had to grin. "Just possibly you have," she said. "Keep an eye on him, okay? Help him out however you can."

"Now, you know I live to do just that," Carmela said.

"Got a gate for you," Sker'ret said, training one eye on Nita while another one gazed at the red-lit hexagon of one of the pads in the nearest cluster. "There's that spot out at the far end of your backyard that's seen a lot of traffic—"

"Perfect," Nita said. She headed for the pad.

"Better lose the accelerator," Sker'ret said. "If anybody in your neighborhood's sensitive enough to see the wizardry, they might talk."

Nita nodded, tossed the accelerator up into the air, snapped her fingers at it; the spell resolved itself into its component words in the Speech, a long tangled drift of words and symbols that hung wavering in the air like glowing weeds in water. Nita snagged the spell, wrapped it back around the charm on her charm bracelet that usually held it, and made sure it had sunk into the charm's matrix again before she stepped across the boundary line into the gating hex. "Go," she said. "I'll be back soon."

Sker'ret hit a control on his console, and Nita vanished.

Acceptable Losses

THE CAVE IN THE outcropping on Rashah had become a busy place. The fifth of seven Yaldiv-shaped *mochteroofs* stood on the floor on its delicate walking-legs, at the center of a circle of bright floating wizard-lights. All the *mochteroof*'s underlying spell structures were exposed, a wire-frame of wizardry. Filif was looking it over, checking all the fine details to make sure everything was in place. The other four *mochteroofs* stood complete—images of giant bugs all still and shining, each one waiting for a wizard to step into it and bring it to life. Off to one side of the circle of lights, Dairine and Kit and Roshaun and Ronan and Ponch sat or sprawled on blankets or pads from the pup tents, waiting for Filif to finish.

"Each one of these is going to have to be a little different," Filif said, drifting around the *mochteroof* and poking the occasional frond into it here and there to test its disguise routines. "After all, if we all looked exactly identical, that could provoke as much attention as all of us just walking around in our own shapes."

Dairine smiled. Filif was fussing, and typically for him, he seemed not to have noticed that no one was paying much attention. But Dairine didn't think he minded. Also typically of him, he had understood about the Hesper more quickly than any of them, even Ronan. Ronan was having problems, and Dairine was getting increasingly tempted to kick him, except that it wouldn't have helped.

Then again, maybe it's not just Ronan, she thought. *His invisible friend may have reason to feel odd about all this, too...*

"Fil?" Dairine said. "How much longer, do you think?"

"Perhaps twenty minutes," Filif said, poking another frond into the *mochteroof.* "Planet dusk is coming. When it does, we'll be ready for it."

"'Enthusiasmic,'" Ronan said, shaking his head. "You sure it didn't say 'enthusiastic'?"

Dairine glanced over at Spot. Spot grew some legs and toddled over to where Ronan sat cross-legged with the Spear across his lap. The mobile flipped his screen open and showed Ronan the word that had appeared under the surface of the mobiles' world.

"See," Dairine said. "It's got the root word for a spirit, not just a mortal soul but one that's a lot more powerful. One that can confer immortality on its vessel, once it gets properly seated." She shook her head. "And 'incorporation,' over there—it doesn't have anything to do with industry. There's the 'ensoulment' root, but with that procedural suffix. It's not something that's finished with; it's an ongoing process."

"One that could get derailed," Kit said.

"We'd better hope not," said Spot.

"But think of it," Roshaun said. "A new Power, never seen before. Not just a redeemed version of the Isolate, but something truly new. A version of the Lone Power *that never fell.*"

He crumpled up the wrapper of the fifth or sixth of Dairine's trail-mix bars, and tossed it away. Dairine smiled half a smile. He had been eating more or less constantly since they got here: first a lot of his own food, and then (without having asked permission) one after another of Dairine's trail-mix bars. She was putting up with it because he seemed distracted, but also because she had used this opportunity to push off on him a lot of the bars with dried cranberries in them, which she hated.

"This moment has been a very long time coming," said the Champion after a few moments. "If the embodiment survives long enough to come to Its full power, then the universe is truly changed."

"*If* it does," Kit said. "But no wonder the Pullulus is happening now. If It knows about this, the Lone Power must be completely freaked. A completely new Power is coming into the game. One that's going to be the Lone One's very own dedicated enemy..."

Ponch lifted his head, and his tail banged against the floor. *I told you I smelled something brand-new!* he said. *That's part of what I was following.*

If *It knows,* the Champion said. *Great efforts have been made to keep It from discovering all the details. Or any of the other Powers, for that matter. If, as seems to be the case, the efforts to keep the secret have been successful... then our job is to make sure that the ensoulment goes through without a hitch.*

"All we have to do now is find out *who's* going to be the Hesper," Kit said. "Get to it, and find out what we have to do to help it."

"Probably get it past being physical, and out the other side," Dairine said. "The soul inside the Yaldiv body might belong to a new Power, but all its strength's going to be trapped inside, useless, until it gets clear about who and what it is. It's got to make the connection to the part of it that lives where the other real Powers do, outside of time. And there's no telling what *that's* going to look like."

"Probably like a bomb going off," Kit muttered, and threw Ronan a slightly amused look. The area on the mobiles' world where the Champion had exited its former, merely physical form had looked like a war zone afterward. "This neighborhood may not be the safest place to be."

"Who cares?" Dairine said. "It's what we've got to do!"

Ronan nodded. "But the odd thing," he said, "is that this seems such an *unlikely* place for this to happen. I mean, a major power for good turns up incarnated in somebody from *this* species? They're all supposed to be 'lost.'"

"Then this is the very best place for that Power to do it," Kit said.

Dairine's eyebrows went up. All the others, except for Filif, busy with the sixth *mochteroof,* looked at Kit. He looked a little abashed by all the sudden attention. "Well, think about it," he said. "If the Lone Power thinks that it owns this planet and everyone on it, thinks It has a foothold in every living soul—"

Roshaun's eyes were suddenly alight; Dairine suspected his thoughts had been trending in the same direction. "Then It will be far less suspicious of what happens here," Roshaun said. "It will perhaps hardly be suspicious at all. And more—" He reached into one of the pockets of those baggy trousers of his and came up with a lollipop. Dairine rolled her eyes. "What if the Isolate *has* had some whisper of news that this event was about to happen somewhere in our space-time?"

Crunch! went the lollipop. Dairine winced. "And not Itself being sure of the location, the Isolate would desire above everything that no one else, most especially wizards, should find out where the Hesper's embodiment *was* to happen. If they did, they might be able to help it." His expression went grimly amused.

"So It creates this big distraction," Kit said.

"This diversionary tactic," Roshaun said. He waved the shattered lollipop on its stick in a little circle that indicated their whole home universe being pushed apart by the dark matter of the Pullulus. "So that no wizard has time to waste following up any rumors that *they* might hear."

"And the Lone Power's looking all over the place for the Hesper," Kit said. He was starting to grin. "But It doesn't know that Its plan's already backfired. The Hesper's about to manifest right under Its nose."

"In one of the places It thinks It doesn't have to worry about," Dairine said. And she grinned. "You think the Powers That Be read Sherlock Holmes?"

To hide something in such plain sight, the Champion said, and Dairine was oddly excited by the amusement in its voice as Ronan looked over at her. *The One is such a gambler.*

Something about the Champion's tone made Kit begin to wonder. Had the other Powers That Be been kept away from here on purpose, to make sure that the secret was kept? *Don't make a fuss,* he could just hear the profound silences of the heavens whispering among themselves; *don't act as if anything's going on there. Wait for the ones to get there who won't attract undue attention, who can do the job without raising the alarm. Or at least not until it's too late—*

"Just one more to do now," Filif said from the work area in the middle of the cave. "The *mochteroof* for Ponch. Then we're ready."

Dairine turned to Ponch, who was lying on the floor with his feet in the air. "While we were back on the mobiles' world," she said, "I saw things here, just for a moment, as if I were inside the Hesper itself. I guess those 'personal' coordinates will have changed now—if it's a member of this species, it has to move around—but its other characteristics will be the same. Spot should be able to pass that set of coordinates to you. If you can read it your way, as smell instead of sight—"

I can do that, Ponch said.

Filif stepped back from his work, looking over the shining row of mock Yaldiv. "That's it," he said. "There are spares for Nita and Sker'ret when they get back; I've left them a note in each one on how to use them if they want to follow us. And the advice that possibly they should wait until we get back."

"Fil," Dairine said, "you're a smart guy. Let's suit up."

Everyone got up and went to the *mochteroofs* that Filif had labeled for them. Dairine watched for a moment as Kit fastened Ponch into his. It was a goofy moment: The dog vanished, a large gleaming green-blue Yaldiv suddenly became real, and then started spinning around and around in the middle of the floor, trying to catch a tail that wasn't there.

Half in and half out of his own *mochteroof,* Kit sighed. "Let him get it out of his system," he said.

They all helped one another get into the shape-change routines. Dairine slipped into hers, held up her hands, and wriggled the fingers; the huge claws clashed. Behind her, Roshaun came over to examine the wizardry. "Elegantly built," he said. "Filif is an artist."

"Yeah," Dairine said. For the moment she wasn't so much paying attention to the artistry of the spell as she was to Kit, off on one side, and Ronan, off on the other, as each got into his own *mochteroof.* They were both looking at Dairine and Roshaun, and both of them were trying not to look like that was what they were doing.

I see it, Roshaun said.

Dairine made an annoyed face as she put Spot down. Filif had built a virtual shelf inside the *mochteroof* for him, so that Dairine could keep him close to eye level and still have her hands free. *The problem is,* she said silently, *there isn't a word for what we've got. Whatever that is.*

"Friendship" might possibly suffice as a description, Roshaun said.

But it seemed insufficient. *You know what I mean,* Dairine said. *And no one ever believes that's all it is. Everybody starts trying right away to put their own labels on it. And then they run into the age thing.*

Roshaun turned away to check his own *mochteroof*'s status. *And then start thinking the worst.*

Whether there's even the slightest evidence...

They both fell into an annoyed silence.

Filif—no longer a tree but a Yaldiv—glanced over at Ronan. "Are we clear outside?"

"No one's within half a mile," he said.

"Then let's go," Kit said.

They all filed onto the transit diagram that Sker'ret had left for them...

...and stepped out into the green light of day.

At least that was the way the *mochteroofs* rendered the infrared component of what Yaldiv daylight filtered down between the wrestling, striving trees. Dairine saw that the space between those trees defined a slightly meandering loop of pathway, broader than the one they'd first approached; this, in turn, flowed into the bigger path that would lead to their destination. Ronan glanced from one side to the other, the Champion in him making sure that no Yaldiv was in any position to see that they had appeared from nothing. Then he stepped aside to let Ponch and Kit lead the way.

The surface was fairly level even on the minor path. Once they reached the major one, it was easy walking. This was good, because within minutes they saw coming down the path toward them what Dairine was suddenly less than eager to get close to—a group of Yaldiv, some of them bearing leaves torn from the trees.

The wizardry is functioning correctly, Spot said. *There should be no problems.*

Dairine really hoped that was true. Kit and Ponch kept right on going, and the Yaldiv who approached them suddenly all moved to either side of the path. As Kit came up close to the foremost Yaldiv, they lifted their claws to him as he passed, even those who were carrying leaves in them.

"The Great One be gracious to these," said the foremost Yaldiv.

Dairine could see that Kit wasn't sure what the right response should be. He lifted his claws but didn't say anything. On he went, with Ponch in tow, and the others followed him.

Soon they came to another group of Yaldiv, all smaller than their *mochteroofs. Workers, I think,* Dairine said silently. These, too, lifted their claws to Kit as he and the others approached. "The Great One be gracious to these."

Once again Kit lifted his claws and passed by. *No personal pronouns, I'll bet,* she heard Ronan say. *"This" and "these," not "me" or "you."*

Ahead of their group, Dairine could see some bigger Yaldiv coming, warriors. She watched a further group of workers reacting to them, and saw that the warriors simply lifted their claws and walked on. *So far, so good,* Dairine thought. *Let's see what happens when they meet us.*

The warriors drew closer. Kit didn't do anything right away, waiting for them to give him a lead. When they were perhaps five meters distant, the lead warrior looked at Kit and held its claws up in a slightly different way, crosswise instead of vertical. Kit held his claws up the same way as they passed. "May these do the One's will," said the lead warrior.

"May these do the One's will also," Kit said, and went by. Dairine started to relax as they went on, meeting more groups of workers and warriors. *It's not going badly so far,* she said silently to Spot. *I just hope they're able to communicate in more than these rote phrases. Otherwise, we're going to have a lot of trouble telling the Hesper why we're here.*

They walked on, examining their surroundings. It was hard to see much terrain through the trees, but they got a sense that they were approaching the city-hive as the path they were walking was joined by more paths from either side. The main path broadened out, and the traffic on it increased considerably, until they were all lifting their claws every ten seconds or so to salute some new band of workers or warriors.

This place could give you cramps in the arms pretty quick, Kit said. He was managing not only his own claws but Ponch's as well, and he sounded a little uncomfortable.

Maybe we won't have to do it inside, Filif said.

Dairine looked ahead. Over the bodies of the many Yaldiv who were now sharing the path with them, she could see the forest around them thinning slightly. Beyond it, the trees, no longer so gnarled and tangled, were starting to be replaced by bigger-trunked ones, darker-colored, leafless—perhaps stripped of their leaves by the depredations of thousands of Yaldiv. But then, as the trees lining the path began to give way to a much more open area, Dairine saw that she had been mistaken. As the line of Yaldiv immediately ahead of their group poured out from the narrow path into a space easily a mile wide, she found herself looking up and up at a structure she could hardly make sense of. A roughly conical central tower speared upward out of a wide, dark, shining surface in a random patchwork of beiges, reds, and rose colors. Hundreds of feet high it rose, toward a forest ceiling far higher and less claustrophobic than the one under which they'd been traveling until now. Close around the central tower, several smaller towers rose from the dark surface, which Dairine could now see and smell was tar—an immense pool of the stuff, all slicked with rainbowy oil. It was a city of paper, at least above ground; probably it had been built of the chewed leaves that they had seen the workers tearing off, and dyed with the unfortunate trees' sappy blood.

Across the lake of tar and oil a number of causeways had been built; they were made of stones and rubble underneath, and paved with more of the chewed-leaf paper. Kit led the way in the wake of many, many more Yaldiv who were making their way toward the city in the fading light of day's end. At the end of the causeway was a great tunnel guarded by warriors, and even from halfway across the causeway, Dairine could see the words written above it in the Yaldiv language.

THE COMMORANCY IS ONE
THE COMMORANCY IS ALL

It seemed like weeks since she'd first heard the word. *Commorancy.* A home, a place inside the walls—

Every Yaldiv who approached the door was stopped, and there was an exchange of some kind between the entering Yaldiv and the guards. Other warriors were entering the tunnel in front of them, and Dairine watched to see what they did. They raised their claws crosswise in the same kind of greeting as had been used on the outer path. But at this distance, she couldn't hear what they were saying. She hoped Kit could.

Kit came up to the warriors and saluted them. Before he could speak, Dairine heard two of the warriors chorus, "Within or without?"

"Within, absolutely," Kit said.

The warriors stared at him briefly, their little scent-detecting antennae working. Then one of them waved him past. "Pass, and go about the Great One's business."

They walked through the guarded door. As they went, Dairine saw Ronan elbow Kit warningly with one foreleg. *Don't get cute!*

Strikes me that the one thing it'd be smart not to lose around here is your sense of humor, Kit said.

They followed Kit in, and for a good while simply walked around and tried to get a feeling for the size and structure of the place. Dairine quickly realized that, on a first visit, this was going to be impossible. It was too complex. Tunnels led into tunnels, into archways and galleries; ramps led up and down between levels, up into the spire and down into dug-out galleries and arcades beneath ground level. *We'd better not get lost,* Dairine said silently.

I am saving everything we see and all the paths we walk to memory, Spot said. *Even if manual functions are not able to build us a more complex map, at least we will know where we've been, if not always where we're going.*

At least Filif was right, Kit said, also sounding relieved. *You don't have to do the claw thing in here.*

Probably there's not a great deal of room for it everywhere, Roshaun said. *And these people seem quite rigid, very regimented . . . so what can't be done everywhere inside isn't done at all.*

Regimented is right, Dairine said as they walked. *Look at all the rules.*

Darkness had fallen as soon as they'd entered, but there was no need for artificial light: The Yaldiv saw by heat, and so everything glowed, or seemed to, more or less brightly. The walls were no exception. In infrared, their rough-paper patterning showed up every change in texture. But what also showed was a never-ending flow of words and phrases and instructions and diktats written on the tunnel walls in scent, and woven into the structure of them, mile after mile of papier-mâché bas-relief. Some of them were quite beautiful, even graceful... but the sentiments expressed made Dairine even uneasier than she'd been to begin with. *The Commorancy is the world. The world is the Commorancy's. Everyone should be like us. Everyone will be like us. All who will not are the enemy. Whoever is not with us is against us.* There were hundreds of other mottoes and maxims, but they all came down to the same thing: The only purposes of the Yaldiv were to build the city greater or dig it deeper, to make more Yaldiv, to kill their enemies... and by doing all these things, to honor the Great One.

Three guesses who that is, Dairine said silently.

We don't need to guess, Ronan said. Dairine couldn't see much of his expression, but the tone of his thought was more than usually angry, even for Ronan.

It's all too familiar. It was the Champion's thought this time, and though it, too, was angry, there was something challenging about the emotion. *All too often I've seen this kind of thing, in other shapes and styles. The places where a species' Choice has gone wrong and we've lost the fight.*

But you keep coming back, Kit said as they kept walking deeper into the spire.

Someone has to, said the Champion. *Someone has to go down to the souls in prison, down in the dark, and try to bring them the fire—even just a spark of it, enough to light a candle and find the door. No matter how many times they've rejected it, no matter how many times It catches you sneaking in and chucks you out, we have to keep trying—*

Through Ponch's *mochteroof,* Dairine could see his head suddenly go up. *Do you smell that?* he said.

Dairine sniffed. It wasn't so much a smell he was describing but a change in the air, and the Yaldiv senses in the *mochteroof* immediately knew what it meant. *The guards have sealed up the door-tunnels for the night,* she said. *Unless we gate out, we're stuck in here.*

That's no problem, Filif said. *Even in here we should be able to find somewhere private long enough to gate.*

But then something else started to happen. The workers and warriors, and the more slender Yaldiv whom Dairine had also started to spot in the tunnels, now all paused where they were. After a second, they all began to head in the same direction, deeper into the city.

Kit and Ronan and Filif and Dairine and Roshaun all looked at one another. *When in Rome,* Ronan said.

They turned and followed the others. The tunnels, like the paths out in the forest, widened as they went in deeper. Soon the group was hemmed in by other Yaldiv, pressing against them, starting to hum a chorus of sounds deeper and more rhythmic than the ones heard outside. Carried along by the wave of Yaldiv, the wizards were swept into higher-ceilinged spaces, wider hallways and colonnades—and finally through a tunnel opening into the biggest space of all.

It's like one of those skyscraper hotel atriums, Dairine thought. The hollow space speared upward into what was probably the highest reaches of the city-hive. In the vast open space, thousands of Yaldiv were already crowded together, and still more were crowding in.

Kit plainly didn't mean to be caught in the middle of them all, which was an idea Dairine approved of. He and Ronan started pushing and forcing their way closer to one of the farther walls of the great space. The other Yaldiv, workers mostly, let them pass. Shortly they found themselves close to the wall across from the tunnel by which they'd entered. The space was somewhat bowl-like, like their cavern. By being near the wall, they were slightly higher than most of the other Yaldiv. They turned to look out across the tremendous gathering . . . and saw what they had not been able to see before because of the crush and press of Yaldiv bodies.

The space was shaped more like an ellipse than anything else. At what would have been the farthest focus of the ellipse, on a dais maybe a hundred feet in diameter, lay a huge and swollen form, glowing with heat. Dairine instantly knew what it was from her earlier look at the species précis in Spot. It wasn't a Queen; it was a King.

The original carapace of a Yaldiv body was now almost the smallest thing about it. The organic structures inside that carapace had long outgrown it, burst out of it, pushed it up and away; the whole original sloughed-off body, now split in two, clung to the top of the much-enlarged thorax like a little shriveled pair of wings. Down near the floor of the dais, the head of the King was almost invisible in the shadow of its vast bulk. The mirror-shade eyes were two tiny dots nearly lost in the upswelling of the vast, puffy body.

Near the head, on each side of it, stood a line of slender Yaldiv, smaller and lighter than the warriors. *Handmaidens,* Dairine thought, watching them come and go. She'd had a chance to check Spot earlier for some of the details on Yaldiv physiology, and immediately thereafter she'd really wished she hadn't. These handmaidens, though, weren't doing any of the things that had grossed her out. They were bowing before the head, feeding it, then moving away again. But Dairine found that this grossed her out differently—the mindless, endless munching of the mouth-mandibles as the handmaidens put food into it, bowed, moved away. She gulped and quickly turned her attention elsewhere.

It was hard. This whole gigantic space seemed to direct one's eye back to the swollen thing lying at the heart of it, the apparition before which, as if before some indolent living idol, the whole mighty congregation of Yaldiv lay bowed down in abject worship. *And of course I'm anthropomorphizing,* Dairine thought. *It's not like your toenails or your spleen worship the rest of you. These guys don't even see themselves as separate from the King.* But the air was thick with feelings, and she was having trouble keeping her own reactions in order.

This was a problem that recently had been getting worse for her. *Is this Roshaun's fault somehow?* Dairine wondered. *Or something to do with Spot?* Whatever the cause, the feeling of sheer evil that flowed off the King, and was reflected back to it by its worshippers, was horrifying to Dairine, and familiar. She'd felt it before, on the mobiles' world, during her Ordeal. This was the sentiment behind the terrible gloating laughter she had kept hearing back then—the amusement of the Lone Power, darkly entertained by the pitiful struggles of mortal life in the universe in which It went from door to door selling Its invention, Death, to the unwary. But here there was something different about the silent laughter. There was a sense of smugness. *There's nothing more to do here,* It seemed to be saying. *Everything is just the way I want it. Now all there is to do with eternity is take it easy and enjoy what I've accomplished.*

It's not the whole Lone Power at all, Dairine thought. *It's an avatar, like all the others. Maybe a more aware one. But, otherwise, it may not have a lot of autonomy.*

A warrior with strange glowing patterns laid out on its carapace came forward and was joined by several others. It abased itself before the dais, along with its compatriots. The King never gave it even a glance, as far as Dairine could tell. *Though whether it can move at all is the next question,* she thought.

The crowd began slowly to press toward the dais. "The day is done! Let the Arch-votary speak!" a Yaldiv said, lifting up its forelegs. Others began to chime in: "Let the Arch-votary tell us the Great One's will for tomorrow!"

More and more Yaldiv began to chant together: "Speak! Tell us the Great One's will! Speak!" This went on until the warrior with the glowing patterns on its shell, the Arch-votary, lifted its own forelegs.

The assemblage swiftly became quiet.

"All praise to the One!" the Arch-votary said.

"All praise to the One, the Great One, the King, the Lord of All, the Master of Creation!" said all the gathered Yaldiv together. They all bowed to the swollen mass on the dais. It annoyed Dairine, but she bowed, too, as Ronan and Kit and everyone else was doing.

"Let the sacred story be told!" said the Arch-votary.

"Let it be told," the immense crowd whispered in awe.

"In the beginning was the One," said the Arch-votary. "And all things were well. But then, from outside, came Another. That Other said to the One, 'Your way is wrong, and this other way is right; bow down to me and admit your wrongness!'"

"Down with the Other! Death to the Other!" the crowd answered.

"And the One rose up and said, 'Evil Other, old shadow-ghost that haunts the ancient darkness, you have no right to question my creation or my will! I will never bow down to you.'"

"Never!" the crowd cried. "The One is all! These are in the One, and no Other!"

"And the Other spoke in pride, saying, 'If you will even now bow down and admit your wrongness, you shall be forgiven!' And the One spurned this craven word. Then the Other spoke in threat, saying, 'If you do not bow, you shall be punished and driven out!'"

"The One must not bow! The Other is evil, the Other is outside!" chanted the crowd.

"But the Other could not frighten the One, or move It from Its purpose!" said the Arch-votary. "And when it realized this, the Other came with its minions and made everlasting war on the One. But it could not prevail. And while these are Its faithful servants, the evil Other can never prevail, not until worlds' end and beyond!"

"Praise to the One! We will always be loyal! We will fight the Other until the ends of the worlds!" cried the crowd, and bowed down before the King.

Dairine kept doing what everyone else was doing. But she was both infuriated and disgusted. *It takes the truth and twists It around to serve Its own purposes. But It doesn't take any more of the truth than It absolutely has to . . . because truth's essentially good, and It hates it for that.*

"Now the One in our King gives commands for the next stage in the new war against the Other's minions in our world," said the Arch-votary. "Tomorrow a great force of warriors will be sent to intercept marauding warriors who are coming to attack our hive and devour us and our children. By bringing them the gift of death, we will turn their evil to good. By ending their miserable lives, we bring them peace, inside us, inside the King."

"Glory to the great King! Glory to the One in the King!" the crowd shouted.

"The One in our King commands that we allow the attackers to cross the Great Ravine," the Arch-votary said. "When enough of them arrive on our side, we will attack and destroy them. Their flesh will feed our King, and be the beginning of thousands of new children. Those children will grow into mighty warriors and fertile handmaidens, who will labor until their breath fails them for the destruction of the Other!"

"Let the Other be destroyed forever!" the crowd cried in anger and joy. "Death to the enemy of the One!"

"Go now and prepare the Other's death," said the Arch-votary, "and the glory of the One!"

"We go for the One's glory!" cried the assembled masses.

The warriors stepped away from the dais, leaving that huge bloated shape lying there tended unendingly by its handmaidens. The assembled Yaldiv began streaming out the many entrances to the heart of the hive.

So there you have it, Dairine thought. *Not just a declaration of war on the other hive, but on all the other "Others" in the universe, everything that's not the Lone Power's . . . or the Lone Power Itself.*

What now? she heard Filif say to Kit.

We follow everybody out, I guess, Kit said. *Ponch, did you scent anything we're looking for while they were all in here?*

I got something, Ponch said. *The scent was familiar.* He sounded uncertain, though.

Which tunnel did they go out?

I think—Ponch sniffed the air for a moment—*I think that one.* Ponch indicated one of about ten tunnels off to their right. *I'll be more certain when I get closer to it.*

Okay...let's go.

As the crowd in front of them lessened, the wizards started heading in the direction of that tunnel: first Kit, with Ponch close behind him, then Ronan, Filif, and Roshaun and, bringing up the rear, Dairine.

So now what? Ronan said.

Well, Kit said, *we can spend some more time looking around here. If Spot's saving data to help us find what we're looking for, we should get some more.*

You won't need that much more, Ponch said. *I should be able to bring you to where we can find what we're after.*

Assuming, Filif said, *that the one Ponch is tracking is located in a place warriors are allowed to go.*

So far, that's been everywhere, Kit said. But his tone of thought suddenly sounded strained. Dairine looked ahead to see what the problem was.

Until now, there'd been only intermittent traffic through the doorway for which they'd been heading. Now, though, there was no traffic there at all. That doorway was completely blocked by warriors with the same kind of markings that the Arch-votary had worn. And between the group of wizards and the door, the Arch-votary itself stood and waited, watching them.

Suggestions? Roshaun said.

Just play it cool, Kit said.

They walked in line up to the Arch-votary. Kit stopped. Dairine, watching him, broke out in a sweat. The Arch-votary lifted those huge claws, but the gesture was not immediately threatening. It was more like the gesture it had used when calling the assembly to order. "This one is commanded to bring these before the King," the Arch-votary said.

Oh, God, it knows! Dairine thought, and sweated harder. Kit merely said, "These obey the command."

The Arch-votary led them across the rapidly clearing hall toward the dais. Dairine was having trouble looking at it steadily. The closer she got, the more she felt that vast glowing mass on top of it was somehow sucking her toward it—sucking her attention into it, maybe even sucking out her will. But then the thought occurred to her that the sensation might have something to do with the *mochteroof*. *And I'm still me in here,* she told herself fiercely. *No refugee from a dime-store ant farm is going to make me forget that!*

The feeling of ebbing will backed down a little bit, but as they got closer, Dairine found she had to expend more effort to stave it off. *If we don't have to be here too long, I'll be okay. But if it knows what we are—*

"The warriors are brought to you according to your command, Great One," said the Arch-votary.

Dairine watched Kit to see what he would do. He bowed, as the Arch-votary had done, and Dairine and all the others followed suit.

For a long moment, no one said anything. Then the King spoke.

"You are minions of the Other," he said.

There was something about the voice that Dairine instantly found repulsive. The voice was very slow and rich, very deep; and somehow it hardly sounded conscious—as if it was not a living thing but a very expensive answering machine or voice-mail program.

"We are servants of the One," Kit said.

Inside the *mochteroof*, Dairine smiled.

"Your appearance is that of servants of the Great One," the King said. "You have the scent of Yaldiv, and the look of Yaldiv. But your souls betray you. They smell of the Other."

Dairine broke out in a sweat again, and glanced ever so briefly in Roshaun's direction. Kit said nothing, just met what he could see of those tiny, empty black eyes.

"What is the Great One's will with these?" the Arch-votary said.

Here it comes, Dairine thought silently to Spot. *Get something ready.* Slowly, inside the *mochteroof,* she reached sideways into her otherspace pocket and felt around for one of the more deadly wizardries she had at hand.

Then, in the silence, the King laughed.

Dairine actually had to suppress the desire to retch, for the sound was truly revolting. It was full of the casual amusement of someone who has you completely in his power, and can do anything he likes with you. "Let them go about my business as they have done," the King said. "They have no power here."

Dairine's eyes went wide.

The laughter began again, sounding even more self-assured and unconcerned. "Many other such minions are traveling among the worlds in these days," said the King. "They seek to undo the great gift of the greatest and final Death. They cannot undo it. Now that Death is coming, inescapable, for them all." The King chuckled as if at a particularly nasty joke. "They have no power to stop it—least of all here, where my strength is most strong."

The Arch-votary, bowing, looked completely puzzled by all this. "To what labor shall they be put, Great One?" it said.

"They labor already," said the King, his voice lazily, wickedly amused. "They labor to no purpose. And when their labor comes to an end, and the gift of Death comes to them all—very soon now—they will know that all their work, from the first to the last, has been in vain."

It laughed again. Dairine gritted her teeth. "Let them go, Arch-votary. Whatever they do here, they will be doing my business. And it will amuse me to watch them doing it."

The Arch-votary bowed down. Much against her will, Dairine bowed along with Kit and Roshaun and the others. "The Great One bids you go about Its business," the Arch-votary said, and then turned away and ignored them.

Kit glanced at Ronan; then the two of them turned away from the dais and started to make their way across the vast hall. The others followed, and Dairine came last of all, heartily wishing she had an excuse to blow King Bug up. *It'd mess everything up, of course.*

Our chances of doing what we came here to do would become about zero. But, boy, it'd be so much fun.

None of the others said a word as they made their way across the hall. As they approached the tunnel for which they'd originally been heading, the warriors who had been standing guard over it moved away.

Silently the wizards headed into the tunnel. Dairine was alert for whatever trap might be on the far side, but there was none. As Kit led them around a curve into the next tunnel, lined with many more tunnel exits and a number of chambers, all Dairine saw before them was the normal steady traffic of Yaldiv, going and coming about the Great One's business.

We should find somewhere quiet, Kit said at last, *get out of here, and figure out what to do next.*

No argument, Ronan said. To Dairine's ear they both sounded as if they'd been in a fight that they felt they'd lost, and couldn't figure out why.

Ahead, Dairine saw Kit turn a corner into another tunnel. Behind him, Ponch paused, looking back, then went after Kit.

And then something unexpected happened to Dairine, something as literally shocking as when she'd brushed up against an exposed wire in the Christmas tree lights the year before last. One of the chambers they passed had a long line of Yaldiv waiting outside, and another line going out. *More of these handmaidens,* Dairine thought, glancing in as they passed. *Getting food for King Bug.* She was beginning to recognize the slender look of the handmaidens, the smaller foreclaws. One handmaiden in the incoming line, as Dairine looked in, turned to glance out at the Yaldiv "warriors" passing in the corridor.

As she met that Yaldiv's eyes, a jolt went straight through Dairine like that shock from the Christmas lights. She knew those eyes. On the mobiles' world, she had looked out through them. And she saw herself looking out of them now.

Hastily Dairine glanced away. But it was too late; she had seen the Yaldiv's reaction. It was one of recognition... and then alarm. Those eyes had not seen the *mochteroof,* the Yaldiv shape. They had seen what lay under it. *They had seen Dairine.*

In front of her, Roshaun felt Dairine's shock. *What is it? What's the matter?*

Don't stop. We're in trouble. Just keep going!

They headed down the tunnel at the same steady pace. Dairine reached into her otherspace pocket and got out the wizardry she'd been prepared to use earlier to give them time to escape. She was hoping even now that she wouldn't have to use it. Time stops were expensive in terms of energy, even in the present circumstances. *But I'll use it if I have to,* she thought. The spell burned cold and ready in her hand, a rigid lattice of frozen time variables, all set to let go. Every moment she expected the shout from behind: "The Other! The minions of the Other are here! After them! Kill them!"

But the shout never came. Everything around them went on exactly as it had. Dairine hugged Spot to her and kept walking, too, terrified, and moment by moment increasingly confused. *She saw me. Why isn't anything happening?*

Greatly daring, Dairine glanced behind her. The lines were still there, Yaldiv going in, Yaldiv going out. And in the doorway, a single Yaldiv, looking after them—

Dairine looked away before she could meet those eyes again. All the same, they were looking at her. The Yaldiv watched them go, silent, still. Then it vanished again.

Dairine hurried after the others, eager to get someplace where they could talk. Things were going terribly wrong...

...but possibly, just possibly, in the right kind of way.

Nita appeared among the trees at the far end of her backyard. For a long moment she just stood there, getting her breath. It wasn't that the transit from the Crossings put you through much in the way of physical difficulties. It was just that, now that she was here, she was almost afraid to go into the house and see what she would find.

She took a deep breath and walked out from among the trees. Nita fished around in the pockets of her vest to find her house keys, but as she got close enough to the backyard gate to see the driveway, she saw her dad's car there. The sight both reassured and scared her. *If he was home before, why wasn't he answering the phone?*

She ran up the steps to the back door, got her keys out, and bumped the screen door aside with one hip to keep it open while she unlocked the inside door.

"Dad?" she said, walking into the kitchen. It was clean; no one had eaten any meals here recently. "Daddy?"

She went into the dining room. The table was clean; it was almost as if no one had been here for a while.

She turned her head, hearing the TV in the living room. "Daddy?" she said, going in. The living room was tidy; the newspapers, usually left in a casual heap, were stacked neatly by her dad's easy chair.

"—Tension continues to build in the Caucasus as the government of Ossetia maintains its hard-line stance against the paramilitary group that claims to have stolen between ten and twelve kilograms of weapons-grade plutonium," the TV said. Nita saw several different shots of men in military uniforms rushing around— *Some kind of SWAT team,* she thought. "—rumors of a nuclear briefcase weapon, and has threatened to sell the material to terrorist organizations in the area—"

Nita swallowed, and picked up the remote to change channels. But even on the nonnews channels, she kept running into screens that said NEWS BULLETIN or SPE-CIAL REPORT. Even the main cartoon channel had a news crawl running along the bottom of its screen. *Are the network people crazy?* Nita thought, annoyed. *Don't they realize how scared little kids are going to get when they see that? Do they think that just because they watch cartoons, they can't read?* She changed the channel again, finding herself looking at another BULLETIN screen. *What the heck's going on around here?*

But she knew. It was the local effect of the Pullulus, which Tom and Carl had predicted: people being pushed further and further away from one another. She threw the remote down on the hassock by her dad's chair. "Daddy?"

And then Nita jumped nearly out of her skin, because he was right behind her; she'd been so preoccupied with the TV that she hadn't even heard him. She grabbed her dad and hugged him, hard, and said, "What were you *doing* there?"

"I live here," her dad said. "This is my house. And yours, when you have time to get home to it." He hugged her back, looking over her shoulder. "I didn't expect you to come home just to watch TV, though."

"I didn't," Nita said. "Daddy, where *were* you? I was worried sick! I tried to call you, and I couldn't reach you on the cell phone, and you weren't in the shop, and you weren't at home—" She was almost babbling, and she didn't care. "I started thinking maybe you'd been in an accident—or, or—"

Her dad kissed Nita on the forehead and hugged her harder. "What is it they say," he said, "about living long enough to worry your children? Guess I've done at least that." He held her away from him. "I had to be out of the shop this afternoon," he said. "I had to take Mike to the hospital."

Nita stared at him. "What's the matter with Mike?"

Her dad laughed a little, though the sound was rueful. "He had an allergic reaction to some lilies," he said. "He swelled up in the most incredible hives. He couldn't see to work, or even get himself to the hospital; I had to drive him."

"Is he going to be okay?"

"Yeah, they pumped him full of antihistamines and

cortisone," her dad said. "He'll be all right in a couple of days. Meantime, I have to handle the shop by myself and make the deliveries, so the place'll be closed while I'm gone. It's no big deal."

"But your cell phone—"

"Oh, that," her dad said. "Everybody's been having trouble with their phones the past day or so. We had another of your solar flares. Didn't Roshaun say we might get some more of those after he and Dairine and the others fixed the Sun?"

"Oh my gosh," Nita said. "I forgot. So much has been happening, and I thought—" She sighed. "Never mind."

"It's a pity you weren't here last night," her dad said. "We had a really nice aurora. You'd have loved it."

An aurora, she thought. *When did I last have time to look at the sky for fun?* "Daddy," she said, "this is going to sound really strange, but what day is today?"

"It's May the eighth," her dad said.

"Oh, no!" Nita said. "We have to be back at school on Monday; that's as much time as Mr. Millman could get us! What if we can't, what if..."

Her dad sighed and sat down in his easy chair, though he didn't lean back. He looked at Nita, concerned, and then glanced at the TV. It was still discussing wars and rumors of wars. "I know this sounds unlike me," he said, "but don't worry about that right now. How are you doing with what you left to do?"

"It's too early to say," Nita said. "But things are really messed up."

"Yeah," said her dad. He threw another glance at the

TV. "The news is so bad right now." He shook his head. "Let's not get into it. Sweetie, you should get back there and concentrate on your job."

"But what about you?" she said. Sker'ret's ancestor was on her mind, and Dairine had left a précis in the manual about her meeting with Roshaun's family. All Nita could think of at the moment was her father, alone in an empty house at a bad time.

"I'm doing okay," he said, looking her in the eye. "Don't distract yourself. I can cope."

"But—"

"Honey, things here may be going to hell in a hand-basket," he said, "but after what you've told me, I know *why*. So when I feel awful, at least I'm privileged to know what's causing it. For the meantime, you let me worry about this planet, and I'll let you worry about all the others. If what you're doing works, we'll all have less to worry about here." He smiled, though the smile was pained. "Dairine's all right?"

"As far as I know."

"Good," her dad said.

"I have to call Kit's mama and pop and tell them that he's okay, too."

"I can do that for you," her dad said. "I need to talk to them anyway. In case the school decides to give us any trouble, we're going to want to present a united front."

"Okay," she said. "I have to go check in real quick with Tom and Carl. As soon as I've done that, I'll be going back."

"Have you got enough stuff in your pup tent?" her dad said.

"Loads," Nita said. "I'll come back if I need anything."

"Okay," her father said. He looked at the TV, picked up the remote, and very pointedly turned off the TV. "At times like this," he said, "you can pay too much attention to the news. Either they'll blow up the world, or they won't. Meantime, our job is to get on with life."

"I think you're right," Nita said. "Daddy..."

She went to him and hugged him again. He hugged her back, hard. "You be careful," he said. "But do what you have to. Don't worry about me."

She looked up at him. "I'm going to anyway," Nita said. "But I *will* do what I have to."

"Good," her dad said, and pushed her gently away. "Don't worry about the phones. Get in touch when you can, or just leave me messages on the answering machine. Okay?"

"Okay."

"Then I'll see you later." He smooched her on the top of her head, and went into the kitchen, and outside.

"Bye-bye," Nita said.

Standing there in the living room, she heard her dad start the car up and back out of the driveway. Everything was suddenly very quiet.

Hurriedly, Nita headed out the back door, locked it, and set out on the short walk to Tom and Carl's.

She hadn't had to ring the doorbell more than once before the door opened. Tom peered out at her. "Oh, hi, Nita. How're you doing?"

He looked so perfectly normal that she could have wept. "Oh, wow, it's great to see you!"

"It's always good to see you, too," Tom said. He stood in the doorway and looked at her quizzically.

This conversation somehow wasn't going quite the way Nita had imagined it. "Where's Carl?"

"At work. Where else would he be?"

That calm reply ran a chill down Nita's spine. *Wrong, this is all wrong.*

"Uh," she said. "Yeah. Listen, I thought I should touch base about where we've been."

Tom raised his eyebrows. "School, I thought," he said. "Spring break would have ended, I don't know, last week sometime?"

Nita opened her mouth and closed it again.

"Listen," Tom said, "I'd love to chat, but I'm on a deadline. I've got to get this article to the magazine by Friday."

Magazine? What's going on *with him?*

"Tom," Nita said. "Uh, this is kind of important. Do you have guests or something?" She leaned a little past him to try to see into the house.

"Guests? No, I'm just working." His tone was polite, but a little cool now.

Nita was beyond understanding what was going on. "Okay, I won't keep you. But this is an errantry matter."

He blinked at her, actually blinked. "Errantry?"

Then he laughed. "Oh, wow, you had me going there for a minute. I remember how serious we used to be about those role-playing games. Wizardry. Spells. The magic Speech that everything understands. It's great that you still like thinking about that kind of thing even when you're in junior high."

Nita stood there absolutely speechless. Tom's laugh was kind, but he wasn't playacting.

We'll lose our wizardry, he'd told her himself. *All of us.* And also, *Wizardry does not live in the unwilling heart... or the heart that's come to believe that it's impossible.*

Nita had to give it one more try. "Tom," she said, "the universe is tearing itself apart, and we've been out trying to repair it. I just didn't want you to worry about where we were."

He sighed. "You've been listening to the news, too, huh?" he said. "It's enough to make anyone want to take their second childhood early." He glanced over his shoulder. "Look, sweetie, I have to get back to work. Was there anything else? Anything serious, I mean. How's your dad?"

"He's fine," Nita said. Her heart was breaking, and there was no way she could take time to deal with it now. "Uh, where are Annie and Monty?"

"Carl had to drop them off at the groomer's this morning," Tom said. "Their fur was getting out of hand again. You can stop in and play with them later if you like."

"Okay," Nita said. She knew it was irrational to try to prolong the conversation, but she desperately wanted to. *What am I going to tell Kit? This is so awful. And we're really on our own now.* "Do you mind if I go around back and see how the fish are doing?" she said.

"Sure. Anything else? I have to get back to this."

She looked into Tom's eyes, desperate to find there the one thing she wanted to see, but it wasn't there. "Nope," she said. "Thanks."

"Come back anytime," Tom said. "Best to your dad." And he shut the door.

Nita stood on the doorstep feeling utterly shattered, bereft in a way she hadn't felt since her mother died. The bottom had fallen out of her world again, and this time what had gone out from under her was something that had seemed too solid, too important, ever to go away. Not even just wizardry itself, but the memory of having *been* a wizard, party to the most basic glories and tragedies of the universe, was now suddenly reduced in Tom—her role model, in some ways her hero, a figure of power and competence—to a cute memory of some kind of friendly "let's pretend." The thought was almost too painful to bear.

But bearing pain, and learning how to deal with the weight of it, was something at which Nita had been getting a lot of practice lately. She went down the front steps and around on the little path that ran down the side of the house to the backyard.

It was tidy as always. Across the lawn, near the back wall, was the koi pond. Carl had spent considerable time rebuilding it over last summer, widening the edge of the pond so there was a place to sit while he fed the fish.

Nita wandered over to it, looking toward the sliding doors at the back of the house. They were closed; it was still chilly for the time of year. From inside, just very faintly, she heard the machine-gun fast clicking of Tom's computer keyboard. For a long time she and Kit had teased Tom about his typing speed, claiming that it almost certainly had something to do with his wizardry. *Apparently not.*

Nita sat down on the pond's edge and gazed into the water. It was clear enough, but the bottom needed to be cleaned; a lot of leaves had gotten into it over the winter. Lily pads hid about half the surface. *The koi are probably under there,* Nita thought. *Carl used a wizardry to keep the water warm enough for them to stay active in the winter. But if that's stopped working, they're probably real sleepy now.*

She let out a long, unhappy breath. There was no point in her spending any more time here. She should get back to the Crossings, and then to Rashah, and get on with work. But Nita couldn't bring herself to move just yet. Walking away from this house, where there was suddenly no wizardry, was going to hurt. She would delay that pain for just a little longer.

As she looked down into the pond, an old memory stirred. She felt around in her pockets, looking for a penny, but couldn't find anything but a dime. Nita gazed at her reflection in the water for some moments, waiting, hoping, but no fish came up to look at her. Finally Nita dropped the dime into the water.

The tiny *plunk!* sounded loud in the silence. Nothing happened. She let out a long breath. *It's like everything that's happened was a dream.*

And what if it was? What if it was all a game—noth-ing but a fantasy?

That terrible thought hung echoing in her mind. Nita shivered. *I wouldn't want to live in a world where what I am isn't real anymore!* she thought. *A world with no room in it for wizards—what kind of place would that be?*

Very slowly, a drift of white and orange came up to the surface of the dark water. The koi looked at her, blank-eyed, almost with a sad expression—

—and spat the dime back at her. It hit Nita in the chest, surprisingly hard. The koi eyed her with an annoyed expression. "Boy, are *you* people ever slow learners," it said. "I thought we told you *no throwing money on our living room floor!* Seriously..."

Another koi, bigger and more silvery, with bright scales like coins scattered here and there down its body, drifted up beside the first. Nita was practically gasping with relief. "You're still you!" she said. "You haven't lost wizardry!"

"We've got less to lose," the marmalade koi said. "Or more. Humans are always sort of in the middle when it comes to magic; they're always trying to talk themselves out of it."

"They're always trying to talk themselves out of *whatever* power they're given," said the koi with the mirror-scales. "Just listen to them! Whatever happens to humans is always somebody else's fault. It's almost, pardon the phrase, magical."

"But the magic's going away, all the same," Nita said softly.

A third koi, one of the calico-patterned ones, drifted up to the surface. *"Night falls,"* it said,

> *"and all things*
> *Go too silent for me; my*
> *Heart's chill with starfall."*

Nita sighed. The sentiment sounded as sad and full of foreboding as she felt. "Do you guys do anything *but* that?" she said.

The calico koi gave her a look. "Everybody's a critic," it said. "You prefer sapphics? Those are hard."

"You want *hard*," said the mirror-scaled koi, scoffing, "you want sonnets. Sonnets are *tough*—"

Nita rolled her eyes. "I meant, do you do anything besides predict the future," she said.

The calico koi gave her a morose look. "We're talking to *you*, aren't we?"

"Not a lot of future to predict at the moment, anyway," said the marmalade koi. "Normally there are billions of branchings from one second to the next. Right now, though..."

"Everything's started to look like mushroom clouds," the mirror-scaled koi said.

Nita thought of her dream: of Della, brushing her hair aside. *The news is so bad.* She shivered in the chill. "But there's something else," she said. "It's darker than usual on the far side of the Moon."

"You saw that, too?" said the calico koi. "'And the moon is no dream.' Interesting."

Nita swallowed. "Was it real?" she said. "Is that really going to happen?"

The koi all looked at her with eyes that were unusually unrevealing, even for fish. "Depends," said the calico koi.

"On whether you can make it happen," said the mirror-scaled koi.

"And whether it's a good idea," said the marmalade koi.

Nita grimaced. "And here I was thinking maybe it was you guys I really came back here to see," she said. "A lot of help *you* are."

"But we are," said the calico koi. "We're just not supposed to do it *directly*. That's not part of being oracular. Our job is to make you think."

"It takes some doing sometimes," said the mirror-scale koi, its expression clearly scornful now.

Nita mulled that over. "So there's still hope?"

"Always hope," said the mirror-scaled koi. "But you can't just sit there and stare at it. You have to do something with it."

She nodded. "I wish there was something I could do for *them*." Nita said, glancing back at the house.

The mirror-scaled koi looked at her with compassion. "Save the world," it said. "And don't get hung up on the details."

"A world of dew," said the mirror-scale koi,

> *"And within every dewdrop*
> *A world of struggle."*

Nita nodded. She was learning to take her time with these utterances. They worked better if you let them unfold slowly than if you tried to crack them open like cracking a nut with a hammer. "I should get back," she said. "You guys take care of yourselves."

The fish bowed to her.

"And take care of them," Nita said, looking back at the house.

"We'll do what we can," the mirror-scaled koi said. "But if anyone's going to fix this, it's going to have to be you."

Nita nodded and got out her manual. A moment later, she was gone.

Regime Change

WHEN NITA REAPPEARED AT the Crossings, she glanced around from the pad where she stood and was astonished. The whole place was crawling with giant centipedes—thousands upon thousands of Rirhait in blue, green, various shades of pink, and more shades of purple than she had known existed. *At least,* she thought, *the place doesn't feel as creepy anymore.*

This far down the side corridor from which she'd originally departed, there wasn't as much damage as there had been nearer the main intersection. Farther up the wide corridor, among the shattered shops and kiosks, some of the damage was being put right in what, for Rirhait, was a fairly straightforward way. They were eating it.

She headed up the corridor, and several Rirhait came flowing along toward Nita. They stopped in front of her, and one of them reared up about half of his body into the air in what Nita had come to recognize as a gesture of respect. "Emissary," he said, "Sker'ret is waiting for you at the central control module."

Nita nodded. "Thank you," she said. "Please tell him I'll be with him in a moment."

They wreathed their eyes at her and flowed away. Nita headed after them, mulling as she went the things the koi had said to her. There was something about the structure of the second haiku that was puzzling her. *Within every dewdrop, a world of struggle.* It was going to take her a while to figure out what that meant. *Not too long, I hope.*

When she got down to the command center, she found it almost completely surrounded by bustling Rirhait. Not actually in the rack but within reach of it, Sker'ret was standing with his eyes pointing in many different directions, giving orders to the Rirhait all around him as fast as they presented themselves. As Nita approached, she saw one eye swivel in her direction. Spotting her, Sker'ret came flowing over to her, almost as if relieved to get away from the other Rirhait.

"Are your people at home all right?" he said.

Nita nodded as she came up by the control center, and leaned against the outer racking. "My dad's okay," she said, "but Tom and Carl—" She shook her head. "They've lost it."

"Your Seniors!" Sker'ret looked at her in horror. "Mover's Name, I didn't think it could start happening so soon."

"Just a check," Nita said. "How long have I been gone?"

Sker'ret looked confused. "Hardly an hour of your

time," he said. "Oh, I see, you're worried about the irregular transit times. Don't be. I've corrected for them—for the moment, at least. When you transit again, if you lose time, it'll be hours, not days."

"But you're going to have to keep correcting—"

"Yes. And it's going to get harder," Sker'ret said. "The Pullulus is affecting our local space now."

"Right," Nita said, looking around at the frantic activity going on around her. "You find out anything more about who was behind our little friends the Tawalf?"

Sker'ret waved some of his upper legs in an I-don't-know gesture. "It doesn't seem to have been the Lone Power, at least not directly. The Tawalf's aggression contract was bought by a crime syndicate somewhere in the Greater Magellanic Cloud. There are two or three species involved, all from economic or political groups that have had disagreements with the Crossings in the past. The Rirhait law-enforcement authorities are following that up."

"Well," Nita said, "that's good." She smiled, a little ruefully. "I guess it's a nice change of pace to be dealing with common crooks."

"But all this is driving me crazy," Sker'ret said. "We have to get back to Rashah! The others—"

"Yes," Carmela's voice said, "the others." She came ambling over from the other side of the command console, and the various Rirhait she passed all reared up in that respect gesture. She smiled. "When do we go?"

Nita looked around her, and then back at Sker'ret. "I don't know about 'we,'" she said after a moment.

"Sker', what's the local situation? Have you got things running again?"

"It's going to take a while," Sker'ret said. "The defense systems still aren't secure enough to make me happy. I want to make sure we're not vulnerable to a second strike. And there's a lot of gating that ought to be passing through here routinely that *hasn't* been. Then there's the emergency traffic—"

Nita was becoming more expert at reading Sker'ret's expressions and body language, and right now he looked as if he felt like tearing a few of his eyes out by the roots. "What about your ancestor?" she said a little more quietly.

"We don't know," Sker'ret said. He held still for a moment, and that, too, struck Nita as something of a danger sign: It was rare for there *not* to be something about Sker'ret that was moving. "When the aliens took him and my sibs prisoner in the initial attack, they shoved them all onto a pad and sent them to a portable gate target somewhere in the Greater Magellanic. The first storming team that went to that planet looking for them didn't find anything. The target had been dismantled and taken somewhere else, possibly through another gate. The law-enforcement people are looking into that, too."

Nita sighed. "Sker', you can't just leave all this and go back to what we were doing. This is where you're needed."

Sker'ret sighed out of all his spiracles, and sagged a little where he stood. "If even just a few of my sibs were here," he said softly.

"But they're not," Carmela said, getting down beside him and rubbing the top of his head segment. "I don't think you have any choice."

"And there are plenty of us working on you-know-what," Nita said.

"Ooh, mystery," Carmela said. "This is more fun every minute."

Sker'ret looked troubled. "I dislike letting the others down—"

"You're not," Nita said. "What you have to do now is not let this whole part of the galaxy down! You can't walk away from this."

"Even though I've been trying to for so long," Sker'ret said, and gave Nita a wry look out of several eyes.

The ironic tone that had come back into his voice reassured Nita. "Well, things are different now," Nita said, "but it looks like when you walked away that last time, *that* was a good idea. If you'd stayed here then, whatever happened to your ancestor and all your sibs could have happened to you, too."

Sker'ret sighed. "We can't ever be sure," he said. "Anyway, here I stay. In the meantime, I can gate the two of you back quickly enough. You'll want to warn Ronan that you're incoming."

He and his partner know, the peridexis said in the back of Nita's mind as Carmela got up to stand beside her. *The One's Champion left a stealth routine in place. You can safely direct-gate straight in.*

"They've got it handled," Nita said. "All we have to do is go."

"Take the closest gate there," Sker'ret said. "I'll send you out."

He turned, then, looking with all his eyes at the bluesteel racking of the Stationmaster's control area. All around, the Rirhait who had been taking Sker'ret's orders drew back a little and watched. "It was just a little hut, once," Sker'ret aid. "A little hut outside a cave."

"It's a lot more than that now," Nita said. "And it's all yours."

Sker'ret shivered in a shiny ripple that ran right down his body, and then he poured himself into the heart of the cubicle and up onto its racking, draping himself across the control structures. He turned his attention to one of the consoles. "The main pad on the far side," Sker'ret said. He looked at Nita and Carmela just briefly with every eye. "Call if you need anything."

"We will," Nita said. "Hold the fort, Sker'."

He wreathed his eyes at her. "And, cousin, *dai stihó.*"

"You go well, too," Nita said. " 'Mela—"

Carmela reached up and tugged at one of Sker'ret's eyes. "Make me proud," she said.

"And as for you, try not to blow up anything that doesn't need it," Sker'ret said.

"Me?" Carmela said, in a tone of dignified but wounded innocence. "When would I ever do *that*?"

Nita took Carmela by the elbow and steered her over to the pad. "Stand in the middle," she said. "If you ever lose your balance in one of these things, you want to make sure you do it inside."

"I would never lose my balance," Carmela said. "I am a paragon of grace and stability."

"Oh, yeah. Who said *that*?"

"Roshaun."

Nita grinned as they positioned themselves in the middle of the pad. "Just wait till Dairine hears," she said.

The de facto Master of the Crossings raised a few forelegs to them. Nita raised a hand. Carmela got out her curling iron and touched a pattern of spots on its side, upon which it started to make a soft and very businesslike humming sound.

Nita threw her a look. Carmela simply smiled. "You never can tell," she said.

They vanished.

Back in the cavern on Rashah, out of their *mochteroofs* again, a very confused and troubled group of wizards sat down under the floating spell-lights to eat something and try to make sense of what had happened.

"It doesn't know why we're here," Ronan said, shaking his head. "It actually doesn't *know*!"

Will we be able to keep it that way? Filif said.

"If we're careful, maybe," said Kit.

"It was really strange," Dairine said. She had broken out another trail-mix bar, one that didn't have cranberries in it—Roshaun was eating the last of those, while wearing one of his more brooding expressions—and she paused to take a drink of one of Nita's favorite lemon sodas, which she'd stolen. "It really did sound as if it was running on automatic. The King may be an avatar of the Lone One, like all Its other people, but You-Know-Who wasn't completely there."

"I felt that, too," Kit said. "But did you feel It sort of...sucking at you? Trying to make you willing to do whatever It said? I did."

And I, said Filif, all his branches and fronds rustling in a shudder.

"As did I," Roshaun said. "Disgusting." He, too, shuddered all over and looked at Kit with a sort of troubled admiration. "Doubtless that is the source of some of Its power over the hive. I wondered that you could find such self-mastery, to stare It in the eye and not flinch."

"Oh, I was flinching, all right," Kit said. "But sometimes you just have to cope. Besides, you were all there. It's different when you have so much backup."

I didn't feel anything, Ponch said. Wagging his tail idly, he came ambling along past Kit, having just finished his own dinner, and put his head over Kit's shoulder. Kit, not missing a beat, moved the bag of pretzels he was eating out from under Ponch's nose and into his other hand. *And there's only one person who can make me do what he says.*

Kit rolled his eyes. "Oh, really? Who would that be?"

Ponch barked and started to bounce around Kit, wagging his tail harder. Kit sighed and gave him a pretzel.

Dairine shook her head. "I can't get past the fact that the King *knew* what we were...and then let us walk away. How come?"

"Perhaps because the situation is exactly as Kit extrapolated it," Roshaun said. "And because this is not a complete avatar of the Isolate. Possibly the species' rigid structure militates against that. Or the Lone One's attention, as Kit also suggested, is elsewhere. Besides which"—Roshaun glanced at Ronan—"we have protection."

It isn't easy to divert such a creature's attention from the truth of what's going on right in front of it, the Champion said, *but it can be done. Still, even with just a partial avatar to deal with, and in my present circumstances, I'm finding it... challenging.*

When she heard that, Dairine's mouth felt suddenly dry. "Which brings us to our next problem," she said. "The Hesper..."

"That was indeed the one we seek?" Roshaun said to Ronan.

Ronan nodded. "It was," he said. "Ponch"—and he reached out to ruffle the dog's ears—"has done effing brilliant work."

Thank you. Got a dog biscuit? Ponch said.

Ronan gave Kit a look. Kit headed for his pup tent, reached inside its door, and came back with the dog biscuit box. He handed Ronan a biscuit, and Ronan gave it to Ponch; loud crunching noises ensued. "Now all we have to do is find out how to make contact with the Hesper," Ronan said. "Assuming we can get to her without raising the alarm."

Spot popped his screen up. "I've been processing the mapping information I stored while we were there," he said, "and coordinating it with the markings on the tunnel walls. Some of them, rather than being mottoes and other propaganda, are labels."

On his screen, and in the middle of the rough circle in which they were all sitting, appeared a three-dimensional map of part of the Yaldiv city-hive. "This is incomplete," Spot said, "but it's possible to extrapolate a lot of structures we didn't actually examine from the tunnel openings we passed, and the road signs on the walls." A small pulsing light appeared in front of one chamber in the diagram. "Here's where you saw the Hesper," Spot said.

Dairine leaned down to look at the label that was flashing on the diagram on Spot's screen. "'Grubbery'?"

"Possibly we would say 'nursery,'" Filif said. "A place where the younger and more fragile members of the species are kept or reared."

"It looks like they reproduce sort of backward from the way hive insects work on Earth," Dairine said, bringing up another display on Spot's screen and scrolling down it, while the main map display remained rotating gently in the air in the midst of them. "Instead of a female with a lot of male mates, they have a 'king' male who visits a sort of harem and fertilizes chosen females. Then they go off to the nurseries, and—"

"Oh, please," Kit said. "Sex stuff." He hid his eyes briefly with one hand. "Aren't we supposed to be protected from this kind of thing?"

"Inside our own species, maybe," Dairine said, unconcerned. "But where other species are involved, I think as soon as we're old enough to ask, we're old enough to find out." She gave Kit a slightly cockeyed look, then glanced away again. There were things she herself was still finding uncomfortable about this particular species' take on reproduction...particularly what happened to the females after the many eggs they bore were fertilized. It brought to mind a particularly vivid sequence from a nature movie she'd seen on one of the educational channels last year—a wasp laying its egg inside some hapless caterpillar, which then went about its business until the day the egg hatched, and the wasp grub started eating its way out. *That times a hundred,* Dairine thought. *Or a thousand. More workers, more warriors for the king. And as for the poor handmaiden, or what's left of her—*

Kit turned to Ronan. "You think you can cover for us again when we go back in?"

The way things are at the moment, I don't see any problem with that, the Champion said.

"Then let's do it in the morning," Dairine said. "The handmaidens don't go out of the hive with the workers and warriors; there'll be a lot fewer Yaldiv to avoid if we want to have a chat with her."

"The question being," Filif said, "what do we say to her, exactly? 'Go well, Hesper, and would you kindly now rise up and save the universe?'"

"Don't ask me," Dairine said, getting up and stretching. "Improvisation seems to be the order of the day, so I'm gonna wing it. Or better still," she said, ambling over to look at her *mochteroof,* "wait for one of you older-and-wiser types to think of something." She threw what was intended to be an annoying look at Roshaun, and turned away.

A few moments later, he came up behind her and looked over her shoulder, pretending to flick a speck of dust off the gleam of the *mochteroof*'s skin. "You are somewhat on edge, are you not?" Roshaun said under his breath.

"Now why would I admit to a thing like that?" Dairine said softly, meeting his reflection's eye. "But since you ask, I haven't been so freaked since we were talking to your dad back on Wellakh. I forget what he said, but you gave him this really dirty look and your stone changed color. I thought maybe you were getting ready to blast him or something and then blame it on my unhealthy alien influence."

Roshaun stared at her. "You saw the Sunstone do *what*?"

Dairine looked at him curiously. "It got clear. While you were talking to your father. You *weren't* going to blast him? I'm glad."

He looked perturbed. "It wouldn't be that I wasn't in something of two minds," he said, "but all the same—"

She turned away. "Tell me about it," she said. "He was getting on my nerves, too."

From behind them Filif said, "This has been a taxing day. We should all root, or rest, or whatever. Tomorrow will almost certainly be more challenging still."

Dairine sighed. "My favorite leafy green vegetable has a point," she said. "I'm gonna turn in."

"And just who are you calling a vegetable?"

" 'Whom,' " Dairine said. "Spot, you coming?"

Stalked sensor-eyes swiveled to follow Dairine. "Shortly. I have a little more analysis to do."

"Okay. Get me up as soon as anything starts to happen. 'Night, guys."

She went into Nita's pup tent and got as comfortable as she could in the sleeping bag—the couch was far too lumpy for her. She left just a thin glow of wizard light outlining the door of the pup-tent interface, spent a few moments punching her sleeping bag's pillow into the right shape, and gratefully lay down and closed her eyes.

But it took her a long time to stop her mind going around and around over the same piece of mental ground. *What do we do next? Is it going to be enough? What if it's not? What's going on at home? And where the heck is Neets? She should be back by now. Whenever "now" is...*

And the next thing she knew, she heard a voice saying from outside, "It does not understand. It does not know."

Dairine sat bolt upright in the sleeping bag, her eyes wide. The voice had been quiet, almost trembling; there had been as much wonder in it as fear. And it had also not been human. Well, these days that was hardly a big deal. But it also hadn't been Sker'ret, or Roshaun, or—

She was out of the pup tent about three seconds later, standing on the warm, gritty stone of the cavern floor and feeling grotty and half conscious in the rumpled clothes she hadn't bothered to take off before bed. Everyone else was standing there looking much the same, give or take a few items of clothing... and also staring in astonishment at an eight-foot-high Yaldiv that was presently walking delicately and a little uncertainly around the *mochteroofs,* feeling them with long slender scenting palps. Wandering around after her was Ponch, wagging his tail and sniffing the back end of her long abdominal shell in a curious way.

"Ponch!" Kit said. He was standing there in pajama bottoms and a beat-up, plaid flannel bathrobe, looking bleary, astonished, and annoyed. "Cut that out!"

Ponch lolloped over to Kit, plainly far too pleased to be troubled by his annoyance. *I found her. Can we keep her?*

Kit rubbed his eyes. "My dog brings home strays," he said in Ronan's general direction. "I should have mentioned. Do you think It noticed?"

Difficult to tell, but I think perhaps not, the One's Champion said from inside Ronan. *Otherwise, I should have noticed. Ponch's way of getting places doesn't seem to register as a transit.*

"I guess we should be relieved," Kit said. "Ponch, promise me you won't go off like that again without telling me first!"

Ponch stood up on his hind legs, putting his feet on Kit's chest. *I didn't do anything bad!* he said, sounding worried and a little perturbed. *You all wanted to see her! And I wanted to see if she smelled like I thought she should have smelled,* Ponch said. *And she did!*

"Yeah, but we also wanted to give her a chance to get used to us—"

I gave her a chance to get used to me! I smelled her, and she smelled me. And then we started talking.

Dairine stifled her laughter. Roshaun, who had come out of his pup tent shortly after Dairine, caught her eye. *You said you were planning to improvise?* he said. *You are going to have to move much faster in the future.*

Dairine turned her attention to the Yaldiv handmaiden. She came around the back of the *mochteroofs* and paused to look at the members of the group one after another, taking them in: a tree with glowing berries, a tall humanoid with flowing blond hair, a tall dark humanoid, a smaller one, and another smaller still; a little machine, a strange creature that wagged at one end and panted at the other. The Yaldiv's scenting palps moved uncertainly.

Somebody really ought to say hello to her, Dairine said. But then the question came up: What did you say to a creature that might never have heard of errantry, or might think it was evil? Yet, buried somewhere inside this creature was the hope of a tremendous power for good. You had to let that power know it was safe to express itself.

Dairine opened her mouth. But the Yaldiv beat her to it, raising her foreclaws in the deferential gesture they'd seen used out on the path the afternoon before. Then the Yaldiv let them fall, as if she couldn't use the normal ceremonial response, and thus the gesture was invalid as well.

"This one saw these," the Yaldiv said. *Those weird pronouns again,* Dairine thought. "When they walked in the tunnel, near Grubbery Fourteen. Though they were not Yaldiv, they had a Yaldiv seeming. They wore it strangely, like a shell during molt, but not-like, as if the shell could be seen through. Their shapes were strange. Their shapes were these shapes—" She pointed one claw at each of them in turn.

Then she glanced up again and met Dairine's eyes, and once again Dairine felt the shock of looking out, looking in, mirrors reflecting in mirrors. "But this one saw that one before," she said to Dairine. "And not within the Commorancy."

Dairine became aware that the "older-and-wiser types" were watching her and expecting *her* to produce some useful result. She took a breath. "Yes," Dairine said. "And this one, also, has seen *that* one before."

"When?"

"Not long ago," Dairine said. "And not from within the Commorancy, either. From within that one."

The Yaldiv stood there shifting uncertainly from leg to leg, a rocking motion. "Yes," she said. "There was a glimpse of strangeness. Other eyes, a world in strange shapes, strange colors. Why are these here?"

Dairine glanced at the others. *Anyone have any suggestions?*

You're the only one of us she knows firsthand, Kit said. *You'd better run with it.*

She turned back to the Yaldiv. "To see this one," Dairine said.

"Why?"

I really need a few moments to think about this! "To tell the story may take a while," Dairine said, "as the story told before the King does."

Dairine saw the shiver that went through the Yaldiv—a shudder that literally shook her on her legs.
It was strange, considering the fervent way all the Yaldiv in the hive had seemed to willingly worship that
bloated shape on the dais. *Maybe— No, don't get ahead
of yourself.* "That one should be at ease," Dairine said,
"and this one will be, too, while the story is told." She
sat down cross-legged on the cavern floor.

Spot came spidering over to Dairine and crouched
down beside her. *Look,* Dairine said silently, *keep an
eye on her bodily functions while I'm talking. If I get
near some dangerous topic, I want some warning.*

All right, Spot said.

Very slowly the Yaldiv lowered herself to the floor,
folding her legs underneath her and resting the huge
claws on the floor at what passed for their elbow joints.
As she did this, the others slowly sat down, too—those
who could. Filif stayed as he was, and while the Yaldiv
was watching them do that, each after his fashion,
Dairine saw Spot put up a transparent display above his
closed lid. *It can't be seen from the other side,* he said.
*Here are indicators for brain activity, general neural fir-
ing, and the rates for all three hearts. But as for what
the readings will* mean…

She was going to have to take her chances with that.
"Tell these of this one's life," Dairine said, hoping she
was getting the pronouns in the right order.

"This one is a Yaldah," the Yaldiv said. It was apparently the female form of the species noun. "The Yaldat
are the mothers of our people. We are the engenderers

of our City's defense. To be a Yaldah is our destiny, and our glory."

This sounds too familiar, Dairine thought. The language was much like some of the stuff she'd read in the mid-twentieth-century unit of last year's history class. *"Destiny." Half the time the word's just code for "what someone else wants you to do without asking any inconvenient questions."* "What does this one do in the City?" Dairine said.

"What most Yaldat do," said their guest, and then she did the first casual thing Dairine had seen any Yaldiv do: She lifted one claw to comb back the scent palps on one side, like someone absently brushing the hair out of her eyes. "Feeding meat to the newly hatched grubs who are past their first food. Cleaning away their leavings and molted-off skins until their shells grow. Yaldat tend the hatchlings until they are large and strong enough to be taken away and trained in their work, or the way of warriors... or vessels."

Vessels was a different word in the Yaldiv language than the simple female form. And the *it* pronoun simply meant that the creature using it was just a thing, of no value except as it contributed to the glory of the Great One.

Dairine opened her mouth to ask another question, but she didn't get the chance. "Now these must tell this one of themselves," the Yaldiv said. "These have come to the City wearing shapes that are not their own. And to mimic a City person's smell—that has been done in the past by invaders from outside, the Others."

"These simply did not wish those in the City to be frightened," Dairine said. "The strangeness of these could make a Yaldiv fear."

"The strangeness does not frighten this one," the Yaldiv said. "It is also—" She stopped.

"Also what?" Dairine said.

The Yaldiv was gazing at the cavern floor with those dark eyes. "Also not the same..."

Dairine glanced at the readouts that Spot was privately showing her. The hearts' rate had increased nearly threefold in the past few minutes. She looked up into those dark eyes again, met them, and held them. "There's no reason to fear," Dairine said.

The pause was so long that Dairine broke out in a sweat, wondering if she'd misstepped. But the Yaldiv looked down at her with eyes that somehow managed to show more than fear. There was anger there, too.

"There's every reason," the Yaldiv said. "For when one says the wrong word, the dangerous word, in the wrong hearing—little time passes between the last breath and the first bite of another's jaws on the meat that was one's body."

"Whatever else these may do," Dairine said, also angry now, "these are *not* going to eat that one." And then a little exasperation crept into her own anger. "And these can't just keep calling that one 'that,'" Dairine said.

The Yaldiv looked at her in complete noncomprehension. "What else would this be called?"

"There is something," Ronan said suddenly, "called a name."

The Yaldiv looked from him back to Dairine. "A name?"

A name, said the one inside Ronan, *is the word by which one calls a creature that is different from all other creatures. A creature that is its own unique self.*

Though as far as mere sound went, there was no difference between Ronan's voice and his guest's, the Yaldiv started up, terribly shocked. She wheeled about swiftly to stare at Ronan, and then began to back away. Bumping into one of the *mochteroofs* stopped her, but still the Yaldiv stared.

"This one also it knows," the Yaldiv said. "This voice...It is Death to hear this voice, this word from beyond the outside! It is worse than Death!" She was shivering. Now she began to crouch down again, her claws uplifted in desperate supplication. "There is no such place as the Outside, nothing but the City and the One who rules it! Let the Great One forgive this unworthy one! It did not mean to speak the evil word; it will be faithful to the Great One's trust—"

Ponch got up from where he'd been sitting watching all this, and trotted over to the Yaldiv. Bizarrely, he started licking the claws that were now lifted up to hide the mirror-shade eyes.

The Yaldiv slowly stopped shivering. Dairine watched her turn her attention to Ponch. Stealing a glance at Spot's display, she saw the heart-rate indicators dropping little by little. The dark eyes looked down into the doggy ones.

"This one is not very like you," she said after a moment, glancing back at Dairine.

"That one is Ponch," Kit said. "Ponch is a dog."

Ponch is my name, the dog said. *That's me. It's good to have a name.*

"Why?"

Because that way people can call you and tell you they want to give you things! He went romping back over to Kit. *Like this!*

Ponch started bouncing around and barking. Dairine resisted the urge to cover her ears. Even though this was a big cavern, the noise was deafening, and it echoed. Kit looked at Dairine in helpless amusement, reached into the dog biscuit box, and got one more biscuit out. "Opportunist," he said. "Ponch! Want a biscuit?"

Oh, boy, oh, boy! Ponch barked, and whirled around in a circle a few times, and then jumped up and snatched the dog biscuit out of Kit's hand. To Dairine's total astonishment, he then ran back and dropped it in front of the Yaldiv.

She looked at it in surprise. "What is that?"

Food! Ponch sat down and looked at the Yaldiv expectantly.

She reached down a claw and prodded the biscuit. "This is meat?" she said.

This? Not even slightly, Ponch said. *But it's nice!*

The Yaldiv looked quizzically at Ponch. Then she reached down, picked up the biscuit, and nibbled at it with a couple of small mandibles.

"It is pleasant," she said. She finished it up, then settled herself down again. Dairine sneaked another look at Spot's readout. *A lot better,* she said to him. *She's calming down now.*

That's what happens when you have a name, Ponch said, and lay down near her, panting a little from all the bouncing and spinning around.

"This one supposes...if there is no harm...then there might be a name." She still sounded very uncertain.

"Is there something the ones in the City say when they call this one to do something?" Kit said.

She glanced up. "They say it is unworthy of notice," the Yaldiv said. "They say it is always the last one to be called." Was that a touch of bitterness?

The last one, Dairine thought. She glanced down at Spot, who was still running analyses of words he had seen on the walls. He showed her a word, in both the Speech and the Yaldiv written language.

"Memeki," Dairine said.

The dark eyes met hers again. "'The last,'" she agreed. "It would not be a strange calling."

"When one has a name," Dairine said, "one's not an *it* anymore. One is called *you.*"

She shivered again. "Another strangeness," Memeki said. "This word also you has heard."

"Sorry," Dairine said. "Not enough explanation. When it speaks of itself, and has a name, it says, 'I.'"

Memeki began to shake harder. Dairine swallowed and kept on going. "Like this. I see you." She pointed first at herself, then at Memeki. "We"—she gestured at the others, then again at Memeki—"see you."

The trembling didn't stop, but Memeki looked at them all, and then down at Ponch, who had rolled over on his back in front of her foreclaws, and now lay there exhibiting his not inconsiderable stomach. "And

I—" She stopped. She lifted her claws, dropped them again.

"This one is afraid," she said, so softly that they could barely hear it. "It knows this word. It never thought anyone else might."

After a moment, Dairine said, "Tell how you know the word."

Slowly Memeki made that palp-grooming gesture again, like pushing hair aside. "Often it wished when it was younger that it could achieve such merit as some of the Yaldat had," she said. "But to serve the Great One personally is not an honor offered to many. And those Yaldat who had achieved such merit, they said it could never happen to this one; for this one was not fair enough to ever attract the King's attention. This one came to believe them, and stopped hoping for more. It was content to serve in the grubbery, giving the young ones food in the less meritorious way. Such was honor enough." She glanced down at Ponch, who was now lying there with his eyes closed.

"Yet there came a night when the City was closed as always," she said. "And this one rested, as all rest when Sek is not in the sky. And in the time of rest, this one heard a voice." She looked again at Ronan, and once again that tremor started to shake her limbs. "The voice was like the second voice that... you used to speak just now. It came from everywhere, and nowhere. It used the words... you use, that this one had never heard before. It said, 'You—'" Again she struggled to get the words out. "'You can be far more than this. You can bring your people out of this place, this life, to something far greater. Will you do it?' "

The Yaldiv's trembling was getting worse. "This one did not know what to answer. But the voice that whispered in the night said, 'The ones who will show you the way will come. They will not be like you. When they come, listen to what they say. One will say the word you need to hear.' "

Memeki went quiet for a moment, looking at them. "The voice made this one frightened," she said. "So many forbidden words... This one went through that next day in terror, thinking that those words might force their way out. For they were strong, and clamored to be spoken. They shouted night and day inside this one until it thought that Death was close to it! But nothing happened."

Memeki still sounded frightened, but now a kind of wonder grew in her voice as well. "Then without warning came the day when what had until then seemed impossible nonetheless did happen. The Great One honored it. Everything was changed. And the rest of the Yaldat said, 'See how merciful the Great One is! Even to such a one, whom all thought would be the last to be chosen, if it ever happened at all.' This one became honored even among the workers and warriors. All those said, 'Here comes another of those who defend us from the evil Others; the mighty ones, the weapons in the Great One's claw!' "

Memeki lifted her claws in a gesture more like the one that the warriors had used to greet one another.

"But it was too late," she said, dropping her claws again. "The words of the voice that spoke in the night, and were now inside this one, began to grow as swiftly as the Great One's favor had. And even the mighty honor the Great One had bestowed on it began to mean little, almost nothing. It began to think that it was"—Memeki paused, then said in a rush—"that it was no one's weapon. That it was for much more than that. That it was"—her voice dropped like that of someone whispering heresy—"that it was itself. That it was an *I*."

Dairine held her breath.

"And that I was for something else entirely," Memeki said. She was breathing like someone who'd run a race, as if she was ready to fall over from the strain of saying so short a word. "And now comes strangeness, yet more strangeness. The eyes that . . . I have seen, which are not Yaldiv." Memeki looked at Dairine. "And the voice that—I know—the one I heard whispering in the night, and that no one else could hear." She got up again, and went over to Ronan.

He sat very still as she approached him, and as the huge claws lifted. Memeki drew very close, peered into his face. Ronan, and the Champion, gazed back.

"Hod the Splendid," said Memeki.

Ronan blinked.

How do you know that name? the Champion said.

"Before, I didn't know what a name was," Memeki said. "Now I know. That word was something the voice whispered to me in the night. Are these, then, also your names? Regent of the Sun, ruler of the third Day and the fourth Heaven, avenger of the Luminaries, Guardian of the Divided Name?"

Ronan nodded very slowly. "Messenger of Messengers," he said, "chief Prince of the Presence, Winged like the Emerald, the Providencer." He raised his eyebrows as he looked up at Memeki. "The creature with those names is within me. We'd say, 'Those are my names.'"

"I thought so," Memeki said. "The voice said that one was to be asked. So now I ask . . . you. What comes next? For my people's sake, I must know. What is the word that must be heard? What must I do to become what the voice says I must?"

Ronan sat there looking stunned. *I don't know,* the Defender said through him. And he looked helplessly at the wizards around him.

"There were other words still," Memeki said. Her sudden eagerness made it sound as if just saying the word *I* out loud had broken a dam somewhere inside her, so that all kinds of things were starting to spill out. "The voice said: 'You are the aeon of Light; you are the Hesper. You must find the way. But without the word spoken, there is no path, only darkness; until it speaks itself, only the abyss.'"

No one said anything.

Memeki kept looking from one of them to the next. Finally Dairine said, "You've asked us hard questions. We don't know the answers. But we'll help you find them."

"It may take a while," Ronan said.

Memeki settled down again, and combed that wayward palp back into place. "I will wait," she said. Then she looked up. "The way we came out of the City... I can go back that same way, before morning? No one will know?"

Ponch opened an eye and looked up at her. *I can take you that way,* he said. *Nobody will know.*

She looked down at him, admiring. *You are very wise.*

Out of the corner of her eye, Dairine caught a glimpse of Kit hiding a smile. "I can rest here meanwhile?" Memeki said. "I am tired. This has been... a day full of strangeness."

"Not just for you," Dairine said, getting up. She went over to Memeki and patted her on the shell. "Rest," she said. "Nothing will happen to you here. We'll take care of you."

The strange eyes dwelled on her. *"Yes,"* Memeki said. *"You will."*

A tremor went through Dairine. The voice had sounded exactly the way Ronan's voice did when the One's Champion used it.

Dairine turned away. After a moment or two, Memeki started to lean a little to one side. Quietly Dairine went over to look at Spot's display. The hearts' rates were dropping quickly; the Yaldiv's neural activity was sliding down almost to nothing.

Dairine straightened, looked at the others as the readings bottomed out. *She's gone out like a light,* Dairine said silently. *It almost looks more like a hibernation state than our kind of sleep.*

Yes, the Champion said. *She'll be that way for some hours, I think. I'll stand guard while you others get back to your rest.*

"You're out of your mind," Kit said. "Who could sleep after that?" He let out a breath, then Ponch's nose came over his shoulder. Kit sighed and reached into the box for one more dog biscuit. "We found her. We've talked to her. She's the one!"

Without any possible doubt, the Champion said.

"But what do we do now?"

Ronan shook his head. "He already said, he didn't know."

"Yeah, right. And a lot of help *you* are!" Dairine said.

"Who, me?"

"No, *him*!" Dairine said. "The Defender!"

We're not omniscient, you know, the One's Champion said, sounding annoyed.

"Oh, sure, you're not. Just immortal and incredibly powerful, which doesn't do us much good if after all this running around, you can't give us a clearer sense of what we're supposed to do!"

Ronan frowned and looked over at Kit. "What is it with these Callahan women," he said, "that they're always after yelling at you and giving you grief?"

"Not always," Kit said, sounding resigned. "Just when it's going to get most on your nerves."

"We yell at you because you're hopeless," Dairine said, and sat down, looking extremely cross. "But I guess it's not your fault this time. And where did all these other names come from all of a sudden? I'd have thought you had enough already, just in our own mythologies."

We pick them up in our travels, the Champion said with a weary and resigned look. *It's an occupational hazard.*

"And it's not like *you* don't have a fair number of names," Ronan added. "Dairine. Dair. Squirt. Runt. Speaker to refrigerated aliens. Botherer of her sister—"

"Deliverer of punches in the nose," Dairine said, looking Ronan in the eye. "Ruthless punisher of those who don't cut her some slack."

"One of those was a little weird," Kit said suddenly. " 'Guardian of the Divided Name'?"

Ronan nodded. "The One's full name."

Roshaun looked perplexed. "Why would that need guarding?"

It doesn't, the Champion said. *You do. From it.*

"But the One is on our side, I would have thought," Filif said. "Or we are on Its..."

That's not the point, the Champion said. *You can't really have any sense of how much raw power is tied up in the One. Physicality can't express it. Nothing can express it; it's not meant to be expressed. It's meant to* be. *If the One wasn't careful about how It manifests Itself inside space and time, everything would all just dissolve.*

"So that even the One's Name in the Speech has to be divided up to keep it safe," Kit said, "like a critical mass."

That's right, said the Champion. *The Name of Names has so much primacy of power over mere created matter that it could change or wipe out whole universes if irresponsibly used. So the Names are leaked into creation only in fragmented form... a little bit here, a little bit there. Even names in less central levels of creation get divided up that way—a bit here, a bit there...*

Dairine let out an annoyed breath. "Yeah, well, if even the One's names are so powerful," she said, "why do *we* have to be running around all the time and cleaning up the messes all over our universe? Why doesn't It just get Its butt in here and take care of things?"

Behind Ronan's eyes, the Champion looked surprised. *What fun would that be?*

"For It?"

For us, the Champion said, sounding as if He was surprised Dairine didn't get it.

She stared at him.

"All right," Filif said, glancing at Dairine as she took a breath. "Memeki knows—for the moment—what she is. But not *who* she is, or what she can do. How can we best assist her? For until she fully becomes the Hesper, and achieves whatever her full power may be, there's no hope that she can do anything about the threat to the rest of our universe."

I have no immediate answers, the Champion said. *She's still only in the middle stages of embodiment. Such a process has to proceed at its own pace.*

"There's not a whole lot of time left for it to proceed *in!*" Dairine said. "The Pullulus is pushing everything apart out there, the structure of space is suffering, whole civilizations are going to pieces—"

"He's right, though," Ronan said.

Dairine stared.

"It took a while for me to come to terms, too," Ronan said. His voice was unusually subdued. "I didn't even know he was in there until Nita recognized him." Dairine was interested to notice that when Ronan had started speaking, he'd been looking at Kit, but suddenly he wasn't looking at him anymore. "And when I found out what was happening, I really hated it." He glanced at Memeki. "She seems to have gotten past that, which is amazing. Different psychologies, I guess. But then there still comes a moment when you have to"—he shrugged—"agree to act together. Not just to passively accept what's happened. How's that going to be for her? Can she do it? Her people's lifestyle seems to revolve around doing what you're told. How fast can she get past *that*? Can she *ever* get past it?"

Dairine shook her head, and looked over at the great sleeping figure. "We'd better hope she can," she said, "and try to figure out some way to hurry her up."

Kit yawned. "Sorry," he said. "I can't help it... I need to at least stretch out for a while, whether I actually get any sleep or not. What do we do in the morning?"

Dairine shrugged. "Take her back. Turn her loose. Wait for something to turn up."

"*Wait?*"

"Something always turns up," Dairine said.

"But not because of the waiting!" Kit muttered.

"And in the meantime," Dairine said, looking over at Ronan, "I think Kit's got the right idea. You're going to keep watch?"

Ronan nodded.

"Then I'm going to try to pick up where I left off," Dairine said. She headed off for her pup tent, glancing over her shoulder. "Spot?"

"I can finish this analysis inside," he said, and got up to follow.

They went back to the pup tent together. *You're a little quiet today,* Dairine said, *even for you. What's bothering you?*

I've been running analyses on more than the syntax of written Yaldic, if that's what you mean.

Yeah, Dairine said, *it is.* She sealed the pup tent and sat down on the floor next to Spot. He crawled into her lap. "You've been really quiet ever since we got here from your people's world. What's going on?"

"My people installed a great deal of new software in me," Spot said. "I've been coming to grips with it. Some of the things they loaded into me were patches for my oracular functions."

"Yeah, I noticed you'd stopped the poetry," Dairine said. "Frankly, it's kind of a relief. The notes were starting to cramp my style."

"I found them troubling, too," Spot said. "The problem seems to have been that the messages from the Powers simply had too much content embedded in them: I wasn't able to process them correctly, so they were coming out truncated. But with the patches, I'm now able to perceive more clearly exactly what it is the Powers and the manual functions are trying to tell me in terms of cloaked content, the kinds of things that were showing as blacked-out in Nita's manual. As a result, I've been able to analyze the present situation a lot more accurately."

"Sounds like good news to me," Dairine said.

"It would be if the results of the analysis weren't so

troubling," Spot said. "We're missing something—both in terms of something we don't know, and something that's not here, something we urgently need. A variable is missing."

"Nita," Dairine said, and let out a breath.

"I think so. Her presence here has become vital. Whatever she went back to Earth to obtain, we've got to have it here very soon, or fail."

Dairine got goose bumps. "And she wasn't sure what she was going back for," Dairine said.

"True. Let's hope that she has it when she arrives; otherwise, all this will have been for nothing. And—"

Spot went silent.

"And?" Dairine said, hugging him a little closer.

"If she doesn't have whatever it is," Spot said, "then there *is* no 'and.'"

Strategic Withdrawal

As Dairine vanished into her pup tent, Kit watched with considerable relief. Dairine could get difficult to deal with when Nita wasn't around to stomp on her. *And just where are you?* he thought, glancing at the walls of the cavern as if Nita might suddenly step through one of them.

Ponch had flopped down beside him and was lying on his back again, though his head was turned so that he was watching Memeki. Kit poked him amiably in the gut. "I thought that was just another ploy to get an extra biscuit," he said under his breath. "I don't often see you giving food away."

She was sad, Ponch said. *She was sad before, too. That's why I brought her. None of the others was sad.*

They headed into the pup tent together. Kit lay down again, and within a few moments Ponch was lying with his head on Kit's chest. Kit sighed. "What was Memeki sad about?" he said.

I don't know, Ponch said. *It felt like something wrong had happened to her. I wanted to make her feel better. I thought maybe if she went for a walk with me, I could take her away from the bad thing that made her sad. But it's still inside her.*

And that's not all, either, Kit thought. He put an arm around Ponch. "Well, you did right," he said. "We're going to try to help her, too."

Good, Ponch said.

Kit breathed out, closed his eyes.

But what if you can't?

Kit sighed again. It was hard when there wasn't even an answer that would make sense to a human. But when it was Ponch involved, sometimes the explanations got more involved rather than less. "It's like this...," he said, and trailed off, wondering where to go from there.

You were saying about the things you couldn't talk about.

I was? Kit thought. *No, I wasn't—*

And another voice spoke, both seemingly at a distance and very close.

"There is a story that every Yaldah knows for a short while," it said. "When she's very new. But knowing the story makes no difference. The ones who know it die, anyway. And speaking it means you die sooner. The wise thing is to forget."

I was asleep, Kit thought. He realized that the weight on his chest was gone. But he also realized that once again he'd slipped into the upper reaches of Ponch's mind, so he lay very still, doing nothing to disturb this state in which he could hear what the dog heard, scent what he scented. Right now, Ponch's world smelled of warm stone, mineral-flake grit, somewhat sweaty or otherwise ripe-smelling humans, various foodstuffs and food wrappings...and the unique scent of a Yaldiv. It was like a more refined version of the crude-oil scent he'd followed here: a hot plastic sort of smell, shifting slightly from moment to moment, with the emotions of the one who spoke.

Why forget? Ponch said. *Remembering things is good.*

"Not when they kill you for it." Memeki's voice sounded weary. "And it was so long ago. Nothing that happened such a long time ago can matter now; things aren't that way anymore."

What way were they? I don't understand.

Her voice went low, as if even here she was afraid she might be overheard. "When we're very young," Memeki said, "the blood inside us speaks for a while. It says that once there wasn't a City, or even a little hive. Once the world was big enough for everyone to walk wherever they wanted. And there wasn't just one King. There were many, and each King had just a few chosen ones. There was always enough to eat, and not so much work to do. And there were no Others." She briefly sounded confused. "Or there were Others who didn't want to kill us. I *said* it was a strange story! Then something happened—"

What?

There was a long pause. "No one is sure," Memeki said. "But in the story, it's as if there was a bigger King who made everything to be built—the sky, the ground—the way our own King tells us how to build a nest and kill the enemy. There were some who built the Everything that way, the story says. That other King was supposed to have shown them how. Then Yaldiv came to live in what that Great One's servants had made. They lived there a long time—"

She broke off suddenly. "But that part of the story makes no sense," Memeki said. "How could anybody build the sky? No one could reach it. It's got to be true, what the Arch-votary says the King tells him—that the old stories are madness and death made real, a way for our enemies to trick us."

I know a story like that, Ponch said. *I don't think it's a trick.*

Silence again. "You don't?"

From Ponch, Kit got a sudden sense of reticence. *If your story is like mine, then there's more to tell.*

"Yes," Memeki said. She sounded subdued. "It's as if when everything's made, another Great One appears: another King. That one went about saying that he knew more things than the first Great One, better ways to live. He said that having so many little kings among the Yaldiv was wrong, and that there should be only one—himself. That would make warriors mightier, he said, and workers stronger, and the vessels more fruitful. The little kings and their consorts said they didn't want his way of living. They started a war with the great King and his vessels. It went on forever. But, finally, the second Great One realized they would never do what he wanted, so he made the sky catch fire.

Small suns like Sek fell from the sky on the little kings, and killed them and all their Yaldiv."

But the story that your people tell each other now says something different, Ponch said.

"It says there was never any war before the War of Now," Memeki said. "The only King that has ever been is our own Great One. And when we win the War of Now against the evil City, then the world will be pure."

Ponch was quiet. Then he spoke again.

Do you want another biscuit?

What? Kit thought. Very slowly and cautiously, so as not to make any noise, he put his hand out beside him. The dog biscuit box was gone. *Why, that sneaky—*

Vague crunching noises came from the cavern, much amplified in Kit's inner hearing by the fact that he was inside the mind of one of the creatures doing the chewing. After a moment, Memeki said, "What happens in your story?" She crunched a little more. "Is there a great war? Do suns fall from the sky?"

No, Ponch said. *There's some singing, but mostly we eat.*

Kit got a sudden glimpse of Memeki's mirror-dark eyes looking down into Ponch's. "Your people's story...is about *food*?"

Later, Ponch said, *yes. But it didn't start that way.* The crunching started up again.

I hadn't thought about this for a long time, Ponch said after a moment. *You tend not to think about it... there's so much to keep you busy. Barking. Running.*

Eating. Doing what the One You're With wants you to do. But that's what we've done for a long time. We promised to take care of Them...

He trailed off. *Kit asked me to tell him the story not long ago,* Ponch said after some more crunching. *It's not the kind of thing you ever think of Them being concerned about: They're even busier than we are. I was so surprised, I told him the puppy version, because I wasn't sure how he would take the other one. We love Them, but humans can be strange sometimes.*

Kit lay there, staring into the darkness, wondering what to make of this. The story seemed to be working its way out of Ponch with the same difficulty as it had worked its way out of Memeki.

It was a very long time ago, Ponch said, *when our parents, the First Ones, realized who they were. They woke up and started singing to the Light in the Sky, and heard others singing back, so that they realized we were all singing the same song. Instead of staying alone, the First Ones started to run together in groups, hunting for food together. It was a hard time. The world was full of things to eat, but catching them was hard. Then many of the things we ate went away, or died, and many of us died, too. Our mothers bore more and more of us. They had to, because so many of us died young.*

There was more crunching from Memeki. "That must have been terrible. What did you do?"

At first, we didn't know what to do. There was a pause while Ponch put his nose into the dog biscuit box, knocked it over, and pawed another one out. *Then some of the First Ones started to think, Maybe we should go away. Maybe there'll be more food somewhere else. So we traveled. We journeyed a long way under the Light in the Sky, and came to a place where there was a little more food. But we found something else there, too. We found Them.*

He was quiet for a moment. *We found them living by themselves,* Ponch said, *in cold places. They wore furs, like us. They denned in caves, the way we did sometimes. They were lonely, the way we were before we found out how to live together. And they were so hungry! And we remembered how that had been for us, too.*

"Did they eat the same things you ate?" Memeki said, sounding dubious.

They did then. Some of us said, "Let's go away from here! There won't be enough for everyone to eat." Others said, "Let's drive them away! Then there will *be enough." And some*—Kit could hear the shadow of a growl stirring at the bottom of Ponch's mind—*some said, "Let's eat* them, *and solve both problems."*

Slowly the growl faded. *But then, when they found different ways to catch things to eat, and we saw them do it and cried because we were hungry, some of the humans did what the First Ones thought was the strangest thing. They gave us some of what they caught! They started sharing, the way we learned to do when we began hunting together. So we took them in, into life as a pack, and showed them the other ways it could be— caring for the pups and watching out for each other, and especially the hunting in a group. They learned fast. And the humans took us in as well, into life with another kind of creature, and showed us how to learn their strange new ways. Like how they made things with their clever paws—sharp teeth that they could throw, so that food was bitten and fell down without the humans actually catching it and biting it themselves. We learned to drive the food into those extra teeth of theirs, and then we shared the kill with them. That became the bargain. We promised we'd help our human packmates find food when they needed it; they helped us with food when we needed it. When the animals that hated our packmates got close to their dens, we shouted to warn them; then they'd bring out the fire that scared those things away. We'd even sit together, after the meal, and sing at the Light together. It was a good time.*

There was a long silence. "If your story is like ours," Memeki said, "the good time ends."

Yes and no, Ponch said. *We always heard voices when the Light in the Sky was full, the thing the humans call the Moon. But there came a Moon when all the First Ones actually heard what the voices were saying. One sounded like the brightness of the Moon: cold, and small, sometimes louder and sometimes very faint and soft. It said, "The time comes for you to choose a new path, in which you may become more than you have been. Wisdom will come to you, and the power that will descend on you in that path is great. The One who made all hunters and all the hunted alike will dwell within you and among you, in your own image. But to enter on that path, you must depart from your old comfortable certainties and walk the new way alone." And then the second voice spoke. It was more like the darkness of the Moon, which is always all around it, trying to drown the brightness out. That voice said, "Greatness, indeed, awaits you, but these naked apes, who in your folly you treat like your own kind, will either turn you into slaves or, after the manner of prey with their proper predators, will come to fear your greatness and kill you. If you do my bidding and kill them first, neither death nor pain will touch you, and this world will be yours forever."*

"So your story has the killing as well," Memeki said.

Almost, Ponch said, sounding somber. *The First Ones drew aside to consider. And when they'd sung the matter over together, to the Voices they said, "We've eaten the same meat as these creatures, and hunted in company with them. Though they're shaped differently from us, we're in-pack with them. We'll do them no harm. Yet neither will we desert them, for without our companionship, they might die." At this, the second Voice laughed, and said, "Fools and weaklings! In repayment of your kindness, the ones you've spared will enslave you indeed. They'll change your bodies and your nature at their whim, until you no longer know yourselves. And since you've chosen to stay in-pack with them, you'll suffer the fate they suffer—death and pain until Time's end." And that Voice faded away into the darkness, where it remains in the dark beyond the Moon, always waiting Its time. Yet when It was silent, then the first Voice spoke, still and small. It said, "You've put your proper Choice aside, but this you did in loyalty's name, and so in Life's. For Life's sake, therefore, some of Its power will still descend to you. In every generation will be whelped among you some of those able to sing the Speech that every creature hears. But no power more will come to you, and no new life, until you once more see before you the path you refused, and set out to walk it alone." Then that Voice was silent as well, and though we've sung to the silver of the Moon from then till now, we haven't heard it again. We live and work and hunt with them as we did before, and we take care of them as we promised we would. They give us what we need, which was always their part of the bargain. So everything is fine.*

Kit lay there, hardly breathing.

"But if everything is fine," Memeki said, "then why do you still sing to the Light?"

There was a pause while Kit heard Ponch nosing one last time, regretfully, in the biscuit box. It was empty. *I don't know*, he said. *It's a habit.*

"It sounds as if there's something you still need to do," Memeki said.

A brief cardboard-scraping noise suggested that Ponch had gotten his nose stuck in the dog biscuit box and, as usual, was having trouble getting it out again. *That sounds strange coming from you*, he said. *You don't even know what* you're *supposed to do next.*

"But if I knew what this thing I needed to do was, I would be doing it. It's far better than what awaits me if life goes on as it's been going." That shiver again—

Kit felt Ponch looking up at her. *Are you all right?*

"Not all right," she said, "no. Tell me again what

you told me when we met—what it's like where you live. Tell me what you do."

From the way the point of view changed, Kit could tell that Ponch had rolled over and was looking at Memeki upside down. *I get up in the morning. I go out and* harnf. Kit's eyebrows went up at Ponch's careful use of the politest Cyene word for dealing with bodily waste. *Then Kit gets up and gives me food. Maybe we go walking before he goes off to school. Afterward I go out to my little house in the middle of my territory and have a nap. Then I get up and check my territory and make sure that everything's all right. I have another nap. Then Kit comes home and we go for a walk, and I run, and he throws the ball for me, and maybe I see a squirrel and chase it. And then Kit gives me food.* Ponch's stomach growled; he rolled over again, looking longingly at the dog biscuit box. *Then he does things he needs to do for school, and I lie and watch him while he does that. And then we go downstairs and he watches the Noisy Box for a while, or he does wizardry, or uses the Quiet Box with the screen that sends him messages. And then we go to sleep, and I lie on his bed and make sure that he's safe. Then we sleep—and in the morning, we get up and do it again.*

Memeki was looking down at Ponch with what the dog could tell was the most profound kind of longing. "This is a life beyond lives that you're living," she said, wistful. "No carrying, no digging, no killing—"

I dig, Ponch said. *I have to put my bones some-where! Otherwise the dogs down the street might get* them. *And I carry things. Balls and sticks, mostly. But only when I want to. And as for the killing—* He sounded a little wistful. *It doesn't happen that often, and only to the really stupid squirrels. I don't usually get to catch the smart ones. I think that's how it's supposed to be, though. You have to send the stupid ones back so they can get it right the next time.*

"But what a wonder to live in a world where there *are* next times," Memeki said. "And to do what you want to do, not always what someone else says you *must*."

You shouldn't have to live a life like that, Ponch said. He was indignant. *It's terrible. Why don't you come home with us! If you like caves, we have a cave under the house where you could stay.*

Uh-oh! Kit thought, and his eyes opened wide in the dark as a series of truly terrible images started spreading themselves out in his mind. He could just imagine what his pop would think about Ponch bringing home a pet giant bug. He remembered his popi's reaction to all the neighbors' dogs howling about nothing on the front lawn. *Boy, once they got Memeki's scent, would they have something to howl about then.*

He was going to have to defuse Ponch's idea as quickly as he could. Kit started to get up. Then he paused, for Memeki was saying, "It sounds wonderful—but I can't leave here."

Why not? They're mean to you! Why should you stay?

Some seconds of silence passed. "Because this is my place," Memeki said. "This is part of realizing that I'm an *I*." There was no more hesitation over the pronoun.

"I'm here to do something. I must do it...as soon as I can work out what it is. But you give me...a feeling that maybe things are not so terrible, if *somewhere* the killing doesn't happen, if somewhere no one listens to every word you say and punishes you for the ones they think are bad. Someone should find a way for that to be the way things are *here*. Someone should do something!"

But why does it have to be you? Ponch said. He was sounding distressed now. *You're good! What if you do something, and then bad things happen to you? That wouldn't be fair!* In Ponch's mind, Kit could just catch sensory echoes of things that had lately come to embody this unfairness for Ponch: the flower scent clinging to Kit's clothes after Nita's mom's funeral, the faint cries of pain trapped in young Darryl's mind during his seemingly endless Ordeal.

"Though it's not fair, it might be right," Memeki said. "If no one ever does anything, nothing will ever get better. Sometimes when I was young, I would go outside the City with the other moltlings, and in the forest we would hear the trees crying." She shivered. "I always thought what the workers did to them was wrong somehow. But the Great One said that the City had to be bigger, so that there could be more warriors to fight the Others, and there was no way for the City to be bigger without the paper that the workers make from the trees. Most Yaldiv didn't care about the trees one way or another. And though their weeping troubled me, I'd never have dared say what *I* thought, because the warriors are always looking for anyone who says the wrong word. There's never enough meat, and they get the first bite of any transgressor."

Memeki shuddered again, but all the same, a new note started to creep into her voice, a sterner tone. "Yet I grew angry. I said to myself, if ever I could do something to stop the trees' pain, I will. And later, after the Honor came upon me, I began to wonder: Would they dare touch me if I spoke now? For I remembered what I'd said, and I could still hear the weeping in my heart, though a Yaldah who's been favored can't leave the City." Memeki rustled a little, a gesture like a sigh. "I was almost ready to speak. Then I turned around and saw Yaldiv in the tunnel who weren't Yaldiv, and the world went strange...Now what I said comes back to me. If what the other Voice inside him says is true"— she glanced over in Ronan's direction—"if I'm truly one who can do something, if things here can be made different—"

Ponch whined once, way down in his throat. *I'm afraid for you. Even when people mean to do good things, bad things happen in the world.*

"They're happening already," Memeki said. "Pretending they're not won't help."

Memeki began to tremble again. Once again, through Ponch, Kit felt the tremor—and another one, something that felt like it was happening under the floor. *Uh-oh!* Kit thought. *Is this place earthquake-prone?*

He started to get up, but the tremor subsided. *I still think you should come home with us,* Ponch said.

"But *this* is home," Memeki said. She still sounded

sad, but there was a touch of affection in her voice. "And if it can be made more like yours..."

They went on arguing, if it was actually an argument. *That little shake was weird,* Kit thought, reaching sideways into the air to retrieve his manual from its otherspace pocket. *The last thing we need right now is to find that we're sitting on some kind of volcanic plug. But if we are, it's better to know about it.*

He opened the manual and paged through it to the marked section that dealt with Rashah's physical structure and characteristics. Kit flipped through to the page that showed mapping references for their present location, then zoomed in on the massive outcropping of rock that concealed the cavern. The schematic on the page shifted to show a wire-frame diagram of the cavern's structure. Kit put out a finger and drew it down the schematic: The image obeyed his gesture and the wire frame changed scale to show the structure of the underlying stone. He studied it carefully, and let out a breath. *Okay, at least there's no lava or anything like that moving around down there. I feel better.*

"...but why can't I?" Memeki was saying. "Why wouldn't it be right to change the way things are? The Great One has been telling everyone what was right for—for *forever*—and nothing's any better! Maybe it's time to try something different! To stand up and decide something different for ourselves, and not wait to be told."

But you might get it wrong!

"Maybe we will. But that's no reason not to *do* anything. Maybe someone else got it wrong, too, did the wrong thing a long time ago. If they did, why shouldn't we fix it? And whether they did or not, what's important is to make it right now. No matter what that takes."

And without waiting for anyone to tell you it's right, Ponch said, very slowly. *Just look to see what went wrong, what needs fixing, and then fix it? All by* yourself?

There was a very long pause. "I think so."

A shiver, a jingle of dog-license tags. *It sounds scary.*

Kit looked over the underground schematic for a moment more before getting ready to put it away. *Interesting,* he thought, seeing that there appeared to be several minor interconnecting caverns underneath the large one. The stone's structure seemed a lot more intricate than he'd thought from Ronan's description—

He felt another tremor, stronger this time. *Okay, just what is that?* Kit thought, glancing down one last time at the schematic. And then he was shocked to see that one of those smaller caverns somehow looked longer than it had a moment ago.

He went cold with fear. *I should have looked at this before!* Kit thought, scrambling to his feet as he stared at the manual. *I knew I should have!* "Life signs, quick!" he said to the manual.

The display shifted focus, and various colored sparks of light appeared in it, some of them haloed to show that they were in a "mitigating" field, which meant one or another of the pup tents. Three Earth-humans, one Earth dog, one Wellakhit humanoid, one Yaldiv female— Kit blinked at the fog of life signs associated with Memeki. But of far more concern were the eight, nine, ten other life signs down there in one of those narrow caverns, and getting closer—

Kit plunged out of his pup tent, shouting, "Incoming!" He also really wanted to shout, "Ronan, how the heck did you *miss* this!"—but it would have been a waste of time. He felt another rumble underfoot as the others burst out of their own pup tents, as Ponch and Memeki looked up in alarm.

"What is it?"

"What's going on?"

"They're digging up from underneath!" Kit said. "It's solid rock underneath there; how are they able to do that?"

Ronan looked completely stricken, but for the moment all he did was point the Spear of Light at the spot on the floor where, slowly, with a noise like a series of muffled gunshots, a thin crack had begun stitching its way across the cavern floor, and the stone to either side of it was humping up in fragmenting slabs.

Dairine looked at Roshaun. Roshaun nodded. "How many?" she said to Kit.

Kit glanced down at the manual. "Nine," he said, "no, ten that I can see."

"Someone's started paying attention," Dairine said, frowning. She reached into the air beside her and came out with what Kit could only think of as a lightning bolt, writhing and jumping in her hand and looking positively eager to be flung at something. "What do you think?"

Roshaun looked over at her, then at Kit. "Once we have stopped this incursion," he said, "I can make sure that no more are able to use that route."

Underfoot, that rumbling got louder. "Okay," Kit said. "Try not to mess up the *mochteroofs!*"

"Leave that with me," Filif said.

And then everything started happening at once. The crack burst open, scattering shattered stone and rock dust in all directions, and Yaldiv warriors started clambering up out of it. The first two vanished in a burst of fire from Ronan's spear, but within a second two more had come up. Dairine came up behind Ronan and threw the blinding bolt she was holding. The second pair of Yaldiv vanished. Then came three more, only one from the spot where the first two had appeared, for the crack kept on stretching and widening across the cavern, making room for more and more of the Yaldiv to enter. A secondary crack split away from the main, still-forming crevasse, toward the *mochteroofs,* and first one, then a second *mochteroof* started to pitch down into it. But Filif was already reaching out fronds to them, and in a glow of dark green light, all the *mochteroofs* together floated up and away from the widening crevasse in the floor. Kit leveled his own weapon and took out one of the next pair of Yaldiv warriors; Ronan destroyed its companion. *Only a few more,* Kit thought. *Only a few—*

But it wasn't only a few. Easily another five or six came clambering up along the length of the crevasse. *They were waiting out of range,* Kit thought, and glanced around the cavern in the beginnings of a panic.

Now what? How are we going to get all this stuff out of here, and Memeki—

And that was another problem, for the next few Yaldiv to come up from under immediately charged at Memeki with claws open. Ponch leaped out from beside her, snarling. *Oh no!* Kit thought, and dashed over toward the two of them with his personal force shield turned up higher than he'd ever had it before, saying the words necessary to fling it well out to either side of him, far enough to cover Ponch and Memeki until he could get to them. He could feel the power flowing out of him and into the shield in tremendous amounts. But as he got close enough to Ponch and the terrified Memeki to seal the shield completely around them, and the Yaldiv warriors began throwing themselves up against the shield, Kit started to wonder whether, even with the augmented energy, he and the others were going to be able to hold their own. *The Yaldiv have been augmented too,* Kit thought. *That's how they were able to tunnel up through the stone—* He concentrated on keeping the warriors away from the crouching handmaiden. "Ronan!" Kit yelled.

Blast after blast from the Spear of Light picked off Yaldiv after Yaldiv, but there always seemed to be more. Any time Ronan flagged, Dairine was there with her pocket thunderbolt. But the Yaldiv kept coming, and more and more of them were piling themselves against Kit's shield, scrabbling at it like mad things, apparently willing to sacrifice themselves for the chance that one of their number might be able to get through. *The Great One's decided it doesn't have to do anything but use these things to wear us down,* Kit thought. *But something's made it wake up all of a sudden. What? We have to find out.*

"Roshaun?" Kit shouted, watching Dairine blast several more Yaldiv to nothing. "This isn't getting us anywhere. Might be smart not to wait!"

"I hear you," Roshaun said. He was standing there, as often, with a little light in his hand, his implementation of the manual. Now he gazed into it and began to speak, and it began to glow more brightly. "This is an argasth-type implementation," he said in the Speech, "requiring a median-level transposition of—"

Down at the far end of the crevasse, something went *BANG!,* the abnormally loud sound of a worldgating in an enclosed space where the air was more than usually well sealed in. Then came another loud report, and another, the sound of some kind of energy weapon. Kit's heart froze as a Yaldiv fell over, and behind it, through the dust and smoke kicked up by the fighting, he could faintly see a human shape glance around her and swing the long, lean shape of a wizardly accelerator up to her shoulder. Kit swallowed hard. Of all the times Nita could have turned up, this was both the best and the worst. She started firing.

"Roshaun?" Kit shouted.

A moment more! the silent answer came back as Roshaun kept reciting the spell. "—from the heliospasm into the following coordinate sets—"

More weapons fire spat from the far end of the crevasse, some kind of plasma blast, every blast perfectly targeted and every one knocking another Yaldiv down. Kit stared over that way, distracted as he wondered whether Nita somehow had two weapons going at once. *No, of course, it's Sker'ret*—and then the claws scrabbling at his shield suddenly seemed significantly closer, as the shield bowed in toward Kit a little. He gulped, and concentrated on pouring more power into it, while more Yaldiv warriors than ever came boiling up out of the crevasse, flinging themselves at Kit's shield. Kit did everything he could to ignore what was going on outside the shield now, a task made easier by the fact that there was nothing to see but the bodies and claws and tearing mandibles of Yaldiv warriors. "Roshaun?!"

There was no answer—and then, between one breath and the next, it was as if a star had fallen into the crevasse. The blinding light struck like fiery arrows through every space around Kit that was not filled with Yaldiv. Their rattling, scratchy roaring was now replaced by a high keening whine as they dropped away from the shield, knocked or blasted off it and down into the light. In the depths of the crevasse, Kit could hear the rumbling and rattling of shattering stone suddenly dwindle to nothing, swallowed up by a sluggish, heavy boiling sound as a blast of heat blew up from below. Kit said the few words in the Speech to re-tune the shield for heat as well as physical impact, and put a hand out to the shaking Memeki.

Ponch got under that hand as well, nuzzling it. *Did we win?*

"I'll let you know in a minute," Kit said. There were no more Yaldiv cries. Slowly, in the silence, the hot light vanished, replaced by a low golden-red glow that, in turn, faded to a sullen red, cooling along with the newly melted stone that now filled the former crevasse.

Kit turned his back on the magma. Its heat was still intense, but not so much so that the shield was needed anymore, so he dissolved it.

"Neets!" Dairine went tearing across the cavern. Beside Kit, Memeki lifted herself up a little to watch her go. Ponch leaped up and shook himself, headed after Dairine.

Across the cavern, Dairine tackled Nita in a hug that nearly knocked her over. Nita, grinning, hugged her back while struggling for balance. "Neets!" Kit shouted as he went after Ponch, doing his best to not look like he was ready to break into a run. "Finally! Where were you?" He paused. "Where's Sker'ret? Who's—"

That other figure, who had transited in with Nita and had been facing the other way, now turned around, waving a hand in front of her face to fan away some of the rock dust still floating in the air.

Kit's mouth dropped open. "What are— Why are— Since when are *you* supposed to be here?"

His sister smiled her sunniest and most infuriating smile at him. "Since I got hold of the manual," Carmela said.

Kit's heart simply froze.

"But this is all just too much for you right now, isn't it?" Carmela said. "Never mind, I'll go talk to someone I'm *much* more interested in. Oh, Ronan..." And she headed away.

Not even if the Lone Power Itself had walked into the cavern right then could Kit have done anything whatever but stand there in shock. *Oh no,* Kit thought. *No, no, no, this is worse than bad, so much worse. What did I do to* deserve *this?*

He turned back to Nita. To his complete astonishment, she was still hugging Dairine. "I was so worried about you."

"I was worrying, too. What about Dad?"

"He's okay."

"Uh, Neets," Kit said.

She glanced over at him, smiling. "Oh, and your pop and mama," Nita said, "they're okay, too, my dad says."

"That wasn't what I was worried about."

Nita gave him a look. "You weren't?"

He looked over at Carmela. "Neets, what *happened* with her?"

Nita's expression was both bemused and appreciative. "She showed up on Rirhath B and blew six kinds of crap out of a bunch of alien invaders," Nita said. "We didn't get too much further into the details: There wasn't time." She paused and looked at Memeki.

Her expression appeared shocked, but somehow not in a way Kit had expected. It was almost as if she was seeing something she'd half expected. She let go of Dairine at last, and pushed her hair back on one side as she looked at the Yaldiv.

"This is Memeki," Kit said.

Nita and Memeki exchanged a glance. "Yes," Nita said slowly, "she is."

Okay, this is getting weird, Kit thought, *but I should be used to that by now.* "We can't stay here long," Kit said. "More of these guys are probably coming; we should find somewhere else to be."

"Okay," Nita said, "but before anything else happens, I really need something to drink. Has she stolen all my sodas yet?"

Dairine looked innocent. "She would have," Kit said, "except I stole some first and stuck them in *my* pup tent."

Nita punched him gratefully in the shoulder. "I knew I could count on you," she said, and headed that way.

Kit watched her go, then turned and let out a long, frustrated breath as he saw Carmela prattling away to Ronan. *This is going to take forever to sort out,* he thought as Ponch came trotting back toward him. *Not that we've got that much forever left.* "You all right?" he said to Ponch.

I'm fine! It's so great that Nita's back!

"No argument," Kit said.

And Carmela! I wondered when she'd get here. I missed her! And everybody else was here, so she needed to be here, too.

Kit rolled his eyes. "Yeah, right." He turned to Memeki. "Memeki, how are you feeling?"

Memeki appeared to be finding it hard to speak. Ponch nosed her. *She was a little nervous at first,* he said, *but I knew you'd save us.*

I wish I'd been that certain, Kit thought. Memeki was watching Filif lower the *mochteroofs* back into place, and Kit saw, to his satisfaction, that at least her trembling had stopped. "I *was* afraid," she said. "But you protected me as you said you would." She sounded troubled. "Yet why did the warriors try to kill me? Has my scent changed? I am one of the Favored; no warrior should dare to touch me."

"I don't know," Kit said. He patted her carapace. "We'll try to find out. Meanwhile, I think we're going to have to get out of here pretty quick. Ponch, stay with her and take care of her, okay?"

I will.

He headed over to where Roshaun and Dairine were talking to Nita. "Roshaun," Kit said, "that was a sweet one."

Roshaun looked startled. " 'Sweet'?"

Kit laughed. "An idiom," he said. "What you did, whatever that was, it was terrific!"

"I did a location-to-location matter transfer," Roshaun said. "It was...surprisingly effective." And he smiled.

"You find a volcano on this planet somewhere?"

"Oh, no. I borrowed some stellar metal from the system primary: iron, mostly." Kit's eyes went wide. "It's a novel technique," Roshaun said, and glanced over at Dairine.

Kit raised his eyebrows. The thought that Dairine had been not only practicing fast-deployment routines for pulling white-hot atmospheric iron out of stars, but also coaching someone else in it, freaked him out slightly. *But then Roshaun's good with stars. Maybe I shouldn't worry.*

In the meantime, there were two other things Kit

was going to have to handle in a hurry, and it took him several moments to figure out which of them he disliked more. He sighed and went over to where Ronan was taking down his pup-tent interface. "Are you okay?" he said.

Ronan nodded, the usual curt gesture.

"Then do you mind telling me what just happened here?" Kit said. "I thought you said the Champion could cover for us!"

"I thought he could, too," Ronan said. "But he's on it again, reinforcing the safeguards that slipped."

"And how long's he going to be able to hold them in place this time?" Kit said. "If they slipped once, they're likely to do it again. It's the Pullulus, isn't it? It's affecting even him now."

Ronan nodded. "Or his presence inside time, inside me. He didn't feel it happening at first, and now he's getting worried."

"*He's* getting worried!" Kit rubbed his face. "So when we get out of here, is he going to be any use to us?" Kit said. "And what about you? What—" The temptation to say, "What good are you without him?" was considerable, but Kit restrained himself. "What's it going to take to get him back into shape?"

"Getting rid of the Pullulus would do it," Ronan said, grim. "And while there *is* one other way, it'd probably take another sixty or seventy years to finesse, so maybe we'd better concentrate on taking care of Memeki."

"That's another problem," Kit said. "*They* sure wanted to take care of her." He looked at the few fragments of Yaldiv warrior that had not been completely vaporized or blasted to other kinds of nothing during the attack. "Someone's realized that she's important. But not important enough that It came Itself."

It's still not here in a completely embodied avatar, the Champion said. *That, I would feel immediately. It remains partly unaware... for the moment.*

Kit held his breath at the sound of the Champion's voice speaking through Ronan. It seemed to have lost a lot of the power he normally heard in it. "I guess we should be grateful," Kit said. "But I don't think it's gonna last. Anyway, have the others all take their pup tents down pronto. We won't stay here a second longer than we have to."

He turned, then, and let out a long, annoyed breath. This couldn't be put off any longer. Off by the former crevasse, Filif and Roshaun were checking over the *mochteroofs,* and Ponch had run over to them and the slender figure who now stood by Filif and was fluffing up his fronds. "Just look at you!" said Carmela. "You wore your hat all the way here!"

"It has become a personality thing," said Filif, reaching up with one frond to adjust his Mets baseball cap. Kit had to smile slightly, as Filif's sense of which part of the cap should face forward tended to change from hour to hour.

Carmela glanced down at Ponch, who was jumping up and down beside her, trying to get her attention. She got down to give him a hug, and started getting her face seriously washed as a result.

In the middle of this, Ponch glanced over at Kit and

gave him a reproachful look. *I can't find any more biscuits,* he said.

"That would be because you and Memeki ate every one you *could* find!" Kit said.

Ponch snorted and went back to slurping Carmela's face. "And in the meantime," Kit said, "I really need Ponch to be concentrating on helping us all get out of here to somewhere safer. So if you can please stop fussing over him—"

Carmela glanced up. "Now, here I am having some quality smooch-time with my favorite doggie," she said, "and *you're* just standing there ruining it. Bear with me while I ask one of these nice people for a spell or something to destroy you with." She glanced around. "Filif! Would you destroy Kit for me, please? You're such a honey. Thanks." And she went back to scratching Ponch behind the ears.

"'Melaaaaa!" Kit said as Filif came up behind Kit.

"If I were you," Filif's nearest fronds said very quietly in Kit's ear, tickling it, "I'd bend in this wind, and not break yourself trying to stand against it." To Carmela, he said, "Destroy him how, exactly?"

"Melted lead?" Carmela said. "Boiling oil? Forget it, those are too retro. Disintegration's big this year..."

Filif stood there looking innocently at the ceiling with all his berries as Carmela started to hit her stride. Kit just shook his head and turned away.

Off by the *mochteroofs,* Memeki stood watching Carmela and Ponch and the rest of them. There was no making anything of a Yaldiv's expressions, but Kit got a sense from Memeki of something much like wistfulness, like a kid who stands off to one side of the playground, knowing he's about to be picked last for a game, as usual. Kit swallowed: He'd been there. But there was something else going on besides that sadness—a strange and growing hope that something different was about to happen. Off across the cavern, as she was taking down her pup tent, Kit saw Nita pause, looking at Memeki, too. She glanced at Kit.

She's terrified, Nita said silently. *And not just for herself. But something else is going on, too. You feel it?*

He nodded as he came up beside Memeki and patted her carapace again. "We'll be ready to go pretty soon," he said, "but you don't have to be by yourself."

"Kit," Memeki said. Kit's mouth dropped open, for it was the first time she'd actually used a name for any of them. "You need not take me anywhere else," she said. "I must go back to the City, for I see I am putting you all in danger. Particularly Ponch."

Kit looked at her thoughtfully, as Ponch, who had left Carmela to follow him, stood up on his hind legs and put his forepaws on her. *We'll stay with you,* he said. *We'll take care of you.*

The wash of fear that Kit caught from Ponch was astonishing: It made him wince. "I see how you do that," Memeki said. "You care for each other. It is so strange. Somehow, though you come from so far away, you are like me. How, I can't say." And then she, too, sat down on the ground, a strange, jerky motion. She twitched. "But there are other reasons. I must return to the grubbery. My time—" She broke off, went silent, like someone distracted by a spasm of pain.

Ronan came up behind Kit and stood there for a moment, just a dark presence that said nothing. Kit glanced at him.

"Ponch is right," he said. "If she's going back to the City, we can't just leave her there and tiptoe away, not after what happened here! We've got to stay with her and keep her safe."

"That's not going to attract any attention, I'll bet," Ronan said. "When someone asks, just what are *we* supposed to be doing hanging around her?"

"We're her guards," Kit said. "The One sent us." His grin was a little grim. "Though what we mean by that won't be what they mean by it, it's still true. And if anyone gives us trouble"—he shrugged—"we play it by ear."

Ronan shook his head. "I hope this works," he said.

Kit did, too. He looked around. "Are we packed up?"

Nita joined them. "All you need to do is take down your pup tent, and we'll be ready to run," she said. "What time is it outside?"

Kit looked at his watch. "About an hour till dawn. So we'll go in half an hour?" He looked around at the others. Roshaun bowed agreement; Filif rustled "yes."

He looked over at Carmela, who was leaning against one of the *mochteroofs*, fiddling with her curling iron. Kit let out another exasperated breath. "Fil," he said, "can you retailor Sker'ret's *mochteroof* for Carmela? And better put some training wheels on it."

"I take your meaning; I'm working on that right

now," Filif said. "Fifteen minutes more will see the work done."

Kit nodded. *Neets,* he said silently, *we really need to talk.*

You're right, she said. *We do.* But she was looking at Memeki.

Ponch looked up at Kit. *And about the biscuits...*

Kit sighed. "Okay, so I hid a box," he said. "Come on."

Sitting cross-legged on the floor of the cavern, Nita drank her soda and watched Filif working over the last remaining *mochteroof,* while Carmela walked around it, kibitzing and apparently offering design tips. Off to one side, Dairine and Roshaun were sitting down and conferring about something. Kit and Ponch had vanished inside Kit's pup tent. By the scarred-over crevasse, Memeki crouched, every now and then shivering a little. And in that shiver, Nita suddenly felt that both their biggest problem and its solution were buried.

She closed her eyes and breathed out, breathed in. The messages that were coming to her—whether as hunches or visions or half-heard whispers—were getting so intense, in this past day or so, that she didn't have to be asleep to have them. *Is this going to be a permanent thing?* she wondered. *Or is this just the peridexic effect working? When all this is over, is it back to business as usual?*

Don't ask me, said the silent voice in the back of her brain. *Nothing about* this *business has been usual.*

She smiled slightly, opened her eyes again. Crouched down on the gritty stone in front of her, Spot looked up at her with two small, stalked, glowing eyes. "So how're you holding up, small stuff?" she said. "You feel better since Dairine took you back home?"

"Much better," Spot said. His voice was clearer than Nita had heard it for some time. Nonetheless, there was a hesitant quality to it.

"You don't sound too sure." She reached out and stroked his case between the eyes.

"There's still much stored data to assimilate," Spot said. "And it will take a long time. But in the short term, I can say that I seem to be more than I was. If I can just work out what to do with it."

Nita laughed, just once, a brief and rueful sound. "That goes for both of us."

"But at least you've come back from Earth with what we need," Spot said. "The word that has to be heard."

Nita gave Spot a look. "I have?" She found this news reassuring coming from Spot, and she needed the reassurance.

He wiggled his eyes at her and trundled back off in Dairine's direction. "Getting a lot more vocal, that wee fella," said the voice from behind her.

Nita cocked an eye up at Ronan, and took another drink of soda. *I wonder if it's contagious,* she thought, catching a glimpse out of the corner of her eye of Kit coming out of his pup tent again. Ponch followed him out, and Kit started to roll up the access and pull it down out of the air.

Across the cavern, Carmela's *mochteroof* skinned

over with the simulacrum of a Yaldiv's golden-green inner shell, but Nita was distracted from this by the unusually edgy feeling practically radiating from Ronan. "How're you holding up?" she said after a moment.

She somehow wasn't surprised to see that he wouldn't quite look at her. "Possibly better than some of us."

"Who?" She was conscious of Kit's gaze in their direction—not hostile, not even trying to look like he was particularly interested. But she knew better.

"Not him," Ronan said, annoyed.

"Oh. Your partner—"

Ronan nodded. "It's okay...He's working to make sure our next move is covered," he said. "But this isn't easy for him. He thought he'd have enough power accessible to make a difference when things started to get rough. And suddenly he doesn't seem to have access to anything like enough."

Nita shook her head. "What can we do?"

"Nothing," Ronan said, sounding bleak.

Nita glanced up at him. "Except maybe hope the problem's working both ways."

Ronan stared at her in confusion. "I took a quick look just now at the manual to see what's been happening since I left," Nita said. "When you guys got hauled in front of the King-avatar, he seemed to be a few words short of a spell. Like the avatar was running on auto."

"Don't count on that lasting long enough to do us any good," Ronan said.

"It may already have done all the good it needs to," Nita said softly, glancing at Memeki. "But think about it. Why shouldn't the Pullulus be having some effect on the Lone Power, too? Or at least Its presence in Its avatars?"

Ronan looked astounded. "But the Pullulus is the Lone Power's own weapon. You'd think It'd make sure It couldn't be affected."

"But the Lone One's power is still the same as the power behind wizardry, isn't it?" Nita said. "Just perverted. It still has to obey wizardry's rules while It's physically present in the universe. And the rules say that the structure of space affects the way wizardry works...and vice versa." She thought a moment. "What if It was willing to risk having less power for the moment, just so long as It got the other result It was playing for?" Nita glanced over at Memeki. "Distracting everybody from knowing that *she* was about to happen."

Ronan was quiet for a moment. "Hope you're right," he said, "because that's all the advantage we've got. As soon as It realizes that some of us *haven't* been distracted...or that she *has* happened, which she hasn't, entirely..."

Nita shook her head. "One thing at a time," she said. "But you didn't exactly answer my question."

Ronan gave Nita one of those looks that was meant to frighten her off the subject. She frowned at him. "Don't even *bother*," she said.

The grim look briefly dissolved into one of those dark, wry smiles. "Never did much good with you, did it?" he said.

"Nope," Nita said. She got up and stretched, almost

too tired to bother getting as annoyed at him as she could have. "Look, Ronan, any chance you could stop being so defensive for a few seconds? Do you seriously think I'm asking how you are as a way of secretly suggesting you're going to screw up in some weird way? I was asking about *how you're feeling.* But since you can't get *that* through your head, just work on getting ever so briefly conscious about your own abilities. Think about what you pulled off on your Ordeal! And then back in Ireland, on the Fields of Tethra—"

"That was then," Ronan said, sounding uneasy. "This is now."

"Spare me," Nita said. "Anybody who can 'take in the Sea' on his first time out, and afterward cope with handling *that* thing"—she glanced at the Spear of Light—"has no business wandering around looking morose and fishing for compliments." Then she had to grin a little bit herself. "Which is probably why the Powers have now sent you the greatest challenge of your life."

Ronan suddenly looked shocked, and glanced around him with a sudden guilty look of someone who's just been found out. "What? What do you—"

Nita looked sidewise to where Carmela, having finished up with another session of fussing over Ponch, was heading toward them. "She's all yours," Nita said, and turned away.

Behind her, Ronan didn't move for a moment or so. Then he collapsed the Spear back into its ballpoint pen disguise and tucked it away inside his jacket. *A wee bit freaked,* he said silently. *More than a wee bit. Not at all cool, or calm, or able to deal, no matter how it looks from outside. Is that what you wanted to hear?*

Nita looked over her shoulder just long enough to flash him a very small smile. *No. But the truth's worth hearing, anyway.* Then she headed over to Memeki.

For a moment she paused just out of reach of Memeki's claws. The mirror-shade eyes looked at Nita thoughtfully.

"You do not have to be afraid of me," Memeki said. "I am nothing to fear."

Nita shook her head. "I had a little scare when we first got here," she said. "It wasn't your fault." Then she put out a hand and laid it on that shining carapace. Memeki shivered a little under her touch. "And as for you being nothing to be afraid of—not for us, maybe. But someone else is scared."

Nita had to hold herself very still as she said that, for the touch had told her something about the reasons for that fear. Inside Memeki, Nita clearly felt a growing power, a core of something like heat or light—like a heart quietly beating, getting stronger. But also inside Memeki were a myriad of tinier glittering points of power, and these were of a darker fire. They scorched the testing mind, cruel as sparks spun up from a fire intent on burning.

"I know now who's afraid," Memeki said. "It's the creature that speaks through the King. *It's my enemy... and my other self.*"

Nita swallowed as she felt the sudden surge of power inside the voice. "And it's inside me," Memeki said. "I never really knew that until now."

Nita hesitated a moment, then nodded. "It's inside all of us, a little."

"But not in the same way," Memeki said. "You understand. In you...it's far less. Inside me—It has me outnumbered. And unless something happens very soon, It will put an end to me."

"Not if you don't let It," Nita said.

Memeki combed that palp down again, that uncertain gesture. "There is no way to stop what's coming!" she said, distressed. "You must know! You can feel them all."

"The eggs," Nita said. "Yes."

"They won't be eggs for long," Memeki said. "Soon they'll hatch, each one of them with its spark of the Great One, the Darkness. They'll belong to It. And when they hatch, they will turn to their mother for food."

Nita shivered, suddenly glimpsing a scene Memeki had seen again and again in the grubbery of the city-hive: the little closed-in cells where the handmaidens, the Favored, were kept and ministered to until their time came...until the eggs hatched inside them, and the grubs within turned outward and began to feast on the flesh that had sheltered them.

"It will happen very soon," Memeki said. "A sunrise more, perhaps two, and I'll be taken to the incubatory inside the grubbery, there to wait my time. When Ponch found me I was spending my last hours in freedom, walking, and working and walking again, fearing what was about to happen—and not knowing how to speak of it, not daring to. Knowing that everything was about to be lost, everything from the time the strange voice spoke to me..." She pulled her claws close to herself.

"But you are the one who knows the way," Memeki said then, looking up again. "You know how it will be. You had a mother..."

Nita held still in pure shock. After a moment she said, "We all had mothers. Well, maybe not Filif, and as for Spot, he—"

"But only your mother did what all *our* mothers do," Memeki said. "Surely you understand! I can hear it in you when you touch me."

Nita went abruptly blind with memory. The moments that followed were full of towering darkness and the sound of rushing waters, and a woman's voice saying, in the face of the Lone Power Itself, "You can do what you like with me, *but not with my daughter!*"

Nita wasn't sure how long she stood there in that remembered darkness. When she could see her surroundings again, she was leaning against Memeki's shell with both hands, and her eyes were stinging. She blinked hard, working to get control of herself. Strangely, the feel of those swarming, furious little sparks of dark fire was helping her a lot. *Not again*, Nita thought. *Not this time. And not* this *mom!*

"She died," Nita said, straightening up. "Yes. She died."

"So you understand how it must be for us, for all the Yaldat...how it will be for me." Memeki shivered again, and Nita noticed that those shivers were getting more frequent. "It's the greatest honor that a Yaldah can achieve. I was called to the King. I became his vessel. Inside me, the eggs grew. Now they're almost ready. The Great One's children will come forth..."

"And kill you," Nita whispered.

"Of course they will. This is the holy Sacrifice; this is Motherhood. What kind of mother would not die for her children?"

Once again the memory of darkness came down on Nita, the darkness inside her mother's cancer-stricken body, and the worse one, much later, on the night Nita went up to her room after the funeral, shut the door, and sat in the dark, completely dead inside. But the shock a few moments ago had left Nita less susceptible to this second one...and she wasn't going to let the pain distract her from the business at hand, especially when it was so plain that the whole Yaldiv species was being jerked around in a way that Nita found so personal. Suddenly everything seemed reflected in everything else—the mirror-eye looking back at her, and the koi's words: *Within every dewdrop, a world of struggle.* And this was it, she realized. The struggles were the same; the answers were the same. This was the key.

"What kind of mother wouldn't die for her kids? *Lots* of kinds!" Nita said. Her own anger surprised her, and at the sound of it, Memeki started back. "Would, sure, but *have* to? Most places it's optional, not mandatory! Not for you, though. Someone's picked out the kind of motherhood that'll hurt the most, the kind you can never enjoy, and talked you into thinking it's all you've got!"

Shock practically radiated from Memeki. "But this is—this is—"

"The way it's always been done?" Nita said. "No, it's *not*! There's another story, isn't there?" And as she said it, she knew it was true, the same way she'd known when to throw herself out of the line of fire back at the Crossings. *But nothing about this business is usual,* she thought, and felt the peridexic effect's amusement in response.

Memeki's shock became even more pronounced. She waved her claws in distress. "How do you know that?" she cried. "You were not— He didn't—" She threw a glance toward Ponch.

She told him, Nita thought. *And that's how I know now. This was part of the information that was blocked in the manuals. But when she told Ponch herself, the peridexic effect got access to the information!* "It doesn't matter right now," Nita said. "Listen to me, Memeki! Once upon a time, mothers here didn't have to do that kind of thing, did they?"

"No! They—" Memeki quieted a little. "No," she said.

"Because there weren't so many eggs?"

Memeki hesitated. "Maybe. I don't know."

"But these days there *are* so many," Nita said. "Too many. And they have no other way to be born. They have to kill you." She was getting angrier every moment. It was another of the Lone Power's favorite gambits—perverting the way Life worked just to spite it. "There might be more to it than that. Never mind that right now. Once, things were different. But now you're called to the King—" Nita thought about that for a moment. "'Called.' They *make* you go to him?"

Memeki put up her claws again in distress. "It is an honor—"

"Yeah, sure," Nita said. "What if you don't want the honor?"

"The warriors make meat of you," Memeki whispered.

"So you have no choice," Nita said.

Memeki was silent. Nita put a hand out to her and felt again the burning storm of angry life inside her, all the new little avatars of the Lone One waiting for their first act in life, which would be to murder someone. Away behind her, she could hear Ponch whimpering, and Kit was picking up on his distress. *Neets*—

I know.

We're just about ready.

Give us a minute. "Memeki," Nita said, "the only reason you're here with us now is because somehow you felt different from all the other Yaldiv, all the other Yaldat."

"That's true," Memeki said.

"And you said you heard a voice speaking to you?"

"The voice that said I could be more," Memeki said, "that all my people could be more."

"Memeki," Nita said, "did you give the voice an answer?"

And inside Memeki, Nita could feel all those little sparks of dark fire suddenly blaze up in shock. From the other core of power working inside her, the small, dim-beating one, there was not the slightest sign of reaction: like someone holding absolutely still lest some shy, trembling thing bolt away.

Memeki was silent.

Neets, we really need to get out of here. Ponch thinks he smells something starting to happen.

Just a minute more! "Memeki!" Nita said.

Memeki looked at Nita. "No," she said. "I never knew what to say."

Nita swallowed. "Memeki," she said, "before, you never had a choice in anything. Now you have one, your very own choice. *Give the voice an answer.*"

Almost too softly to be heard, "But what answer?" Memeki said. "What do I *do*?"

Nita thought of Della in her dream: the claw pushing the hair back, the way Memeki groomed her palp, that nervous gesture. *Come on, give me a hint: What am I supposed to be doing to make everything turn out all right? You're supposed to know what They want, the one who's supposed to have all the answers.*

Her mouth had gone as dry as any desert, but Nita managed to open it, and said, very softly, "I can't tell you."

"But you have to! You know!"

I know the right answer. At least, I know a right answer. And it would be so easy to tell her. But if I did… She couldn't even swallow, she was so scared, for Nita was sure that giving Memeki *any* answer would completely screw everything up. *It's not what Tom or Carl would do. And if I'm being a Senior, it's not what I should do either.*

"*Tell me!*" Memeki pleaded.

"Memeki, if I tell you what to say," Nita said, "*it's not your choice.*"

Behind her, Nita could hear Ponch starting to growl. She forced herself to ignore him.

"And you *have* to choose," Nita said. "If you don't, we'll have come here all this way for nothing. Except to die."

"That is a hard saying!" Memeki said. She sounded hurt and indignant, like someone under unfair pressure.

"Unfortunately, it's also a true one," Nita said. "Wizards tell the truth. Sometimes it's all we've got: One way or another, the words wind up doing the job."

"I need time! Time to think, to decide—"

"There is no time," Nita said. "And this kind of choice won't *need* time. It's done in a flash, in a breath. All you have to do is be willing to finally make it, instead of putting it off!"

Memeki turned away from her.

Nita broke out in a cold sweat. *Oh, please don't let me have messed up!* she thought. *If I've ruined this somehow, if the whole universe is going to go dark because I just said the wrong thing—*

"Nita," Ronan said. "*Now.*"

Her head came right around at the sound of sheer command in his voice—and the unexpected desperation.

"They're coming," he said, and this time it was just Ronan. "He can't hide us anymore. His power's going, and there's another great lot of them coming. Five times as many as last time, maybe more. Something's waking up in the City."

Nita swallowed. *His power's going?!* she thought.

How *long is* ours *going to last?* "Look," she said, "maybe we can help Him. Pass Him some power, or operate His shield routine independently. Can you feed Spot the cloaking spell He was using? At least we can buy ourselves some time."

Ronan frowned, a concentrating look. "I have it," said Spot from across the room. "Working..."

"Everybody into the *mochteroofs!*" Filif said.

There was a wholesale scramble for them. "Ponch," Kit said, "if You-Know-Who can feel our transits now, you're going to have to walk us out of here: It doesn't seem to be able to feel *you.* 'Mela, here, get in—"

Nita stood for a moment more with her hand against Memeki's carapace. Memeki swung herself around toward Nita, looked at her, and once again Nita was briefly dazzled by the reflections: mirror-shade eyes, dewdrops, and, suddenly, another eye looking out at her from one of the reflections—

Nita recoiled in terror as the myriad sparks of dark fire inside Memeki buzzed and jostled against one another with sudden rage. Nita jerked her hand away. "We'll get you back to the grubbery," she said, and turned and ran for her *mochteroof.*

"Ponch, where's the leash?" Kit said.

I have it here.

"Great. Fil—"

"I thought we might wind up needing this kind of transit: I left an open receptor for the leash in all the *mochteroof* spells. Tell me the words for your end of the spell. I can chain them together."

He thinks of everything, Nita thought as she got to her *mochteroof* and put her hands up against it. *He's a better Senior than any of us. Where'd we be without him?* She melted straight through the virtual carapace, into the dim green insides of it. Light outside went monochrome, restating itself as heat and cool rather than light and darkness; the cavern around them blazed like day. Nita found the spell-handles inside that would let her wear the *mochteroof* in automatic mode, like a tight-fitting suit, and spoke the words in the Speech to activate each one. "Don't worry about spoken conversation," Filif said. "It'll stay in-circuit; only wizards will be able to hear it."

Nita nodded. "It's in novice mode; all you have to do is walk," she heard Kit saying to Carmela, who was inside one of the *mochteroofs* now. "Walk the way you usually do . . . Uh, maybe not *that* way, but just—"

"Thank you so much," Carmela said sweetly, "but it's not like this is the entertainment system and I need a little kid to program it for me or anything."

Nita could just hear Kit gritting his teeth. "Ponch," he said. "You ready?"

Always.

"Let's go!"

They all stepped forward, vanishing—

—and came out together in some anonymous City tunnel, strung out along it: Kit and Ponch first, with Nita, Carmela, Ronan, and Memeki close behind them, and Roshaun and Filif and Dairine, with Spot, bringing up the rear. Inside the City, everything was terribly quiet—a heavy, hot, unechoing silence like being in a closed room.

Nita stood still with the others for a moment, listening, and looking around at the strange papery walls with their endless messages: *The Commorancy is all, the Outside is the Enemy, the different is the dangerous.* But clearer than any of the writings was the message that she felt all around her, thousands of point-sources of darkness, inert for the moment but ready to awaken: the avatar-presence of the Lone Power in every single Yaldiv, owning every soul in the City, each one ready and eager to do Its will. *They're bad news,* she could just hear Darryl saying. *Deadly. And I think if you hang around where they are, somebody's going to get killed.*

Nita was trembling with nerves and sheer weariness. Stronger far now than the individual Yaldiv avatars in its pressure against her mind was the sense of one presence that was no longer running on automatic. Nita could sense it right through the walls, a core of burning darkness which was definitely the parent of the sparks of dark fire inside Memeki. *It's not going to wait for matters to take their course,* Nita thought.

She glanced behind her. Through the shell of Filif's *mochteroof,* she could see the dark green light of a locator spell. *It's as Ponch thought,* Filif said, his eye-berries glowing faintly through the *mochteroof*'s illusion-field as he looked at the others. *Our cavern is full of warriors again; they've broken in through a new tunnel. Easily a hundred of them.*

"At least we're not there," Kit said. "And they may waste a little more time thinking we are, and looking for us." He glanced back at Memeki. "So, to the grubbery?"

Nita turned to Memeki. The Yaldah rubbed her foreclaws together, shivering.

"Yes," she said. "If I'm not there when the others wake, they will raise the alarm."

It's raised already! Nita wanted to say, but she restrained herself. *Give her the time to realize the truth. Until it's plain there's no more time left.* "Ponch, you know the way?" Nita said.

Of course. He sounded faintly offended. *We're not very close; if they were waiting for us, I wanted a chance to know about it and go somewhere else. But we're not very far, either.*

"Let's go," Kit said.

Ponch led them down through that tunnel and paused at the end of it; the passage they were in grew broader, and two narrower ones led off left and right. He chose the right-hand one, and Kit followed him.

One after another, cautious, they went after. Nita was listening with all of her for the sound of other claws on the floor of the tunnel but heard nothing. Next to her, Carmela—who had been watching Ronan as she walked—staggered into the right-hand wall and rebounded. Ronan rolled his eyes and looked away.

"'Mela," Nita said under her breath, "you need to stop concentrating on someone else's hottitude and get serious, okay? We are *not* in a safe place here."

"Yeah, okay," Carmela muttered. But she shot Nita

a sly look. "See that? Hung up on my little brother as you unfortunately are, I got you to admit it. He is *utterly* hot."

"I am not—" Nita exhaled in exasperation. "Forget it. As for Ronan—yeah, he has his moments."

"Without a doubt," Carmela said. "And how many of his moments have *you* had?"

Nita gave Carmela an evil look as they turned a corner. "It's possible to be too nosy," she said, "even around people as perfect as Kit and me."

Carmela looked thoughtful. " 'Perfect,' " she said experimentally. " 'Kit.' " Then she shook her head. "Sorry, Neets, one of those words is in the wrong sentence..."

Nita grinned. "As for Ronan, better enjoy him while you can. After this is over there's no guarantee he'll be with us that much longer..."

Nita checked behind them. There was no sign of pursuit, not even any sign of workers. *But all the same,* Nita thought, and reached down to her charm bracelet, making sure her accelerator was recharged, loaded, and ready to go.

And just in case the more techie kinds of spell are the first to fail—Nita reached into her otherspace pocket and pulled out her old standby, yet another in a series of peeled rowan wands soaked in full moonlight. Nita shoved it into the belt of her jeans and sighed. Just the touch of it brought back the feel of her backyard on an early autumn evening as she sat against the trunk of her buddy Liused the rowan tree, discussing the finer points of how most artistically to begin dropping your leaves in the fall...

Nita moved a little faster to catch up with Kit and Ponch and Carmela. The three of them were up near an intersection, pausing while Ponch picked yet another turn, moving right and up a slight incline into a wide and still-empty corridor. Kit was saying, "—don't get how this can possibly have happened. You're too old! And you haven't had anything that looks like an Ordeal."

Carmela looked down at Kit as if from a great height. "Oh, yeah? Well, *you* haven't had you for a little brother all these years. It's felt pretty ordeal-ish to *me!*"

"I don't mean *that* kind of ordeal! Wizardry doesn't just get passed out on street corners to just anybody who comes along!"

"Oh yeah, like I need *this* experience to learn that," Carmela said. "You should hear yourself go on and on about it. Suffer suffer, pain pain, responsibility responsibility." She waved her hands in exaggerated distress, and the *mochteroof*'s claws waved around every which way. "Not like you're not having insane and crazy fun, secretly, *every minute of the day!*"

They came to the next intersection. Ponch paused there a moment, then crowded back against Kit. *Somebody's down there,* Ponch said. *Some workers, I think. Wait a moment, they're going by—*

Ponch peered around the corner. "I can't believe this," Kit muttered, just briefly turning his head to look back toward Carmela. "You're one of us and *you're still clueless!* It could only happen to me. Would you just *please* open the manual and read that first page again, the one with the little block of text on it, you know the one—"

Carmela reached behind her. "Anything to shut you up."

"*The first page!*" Kit said. "The one that says, 'In Life's name, and for Life's sake, I assert that I will use the Art which is Its gift—'"

"—in compliance with FCC regulation part 15, section 209(c), which states that any unwanted RF emissions from an intentional radiator shall not exceed the level of the—"

Openmouthed, Kit stared at Carmela. "*What?*"

"Right here," Carmela said, pushing what she held up against the side of her *mochteroof*. "The first page—"

What Carmela was bracing against the side of her *mochteroof* for Kit to see was a paper booklet, in which the lettering neither moved around nor changed, but held almost bizarrely still.

"I said I found the manual," Carmela said.

Kit stared at the paper booklet.

"*For the TV,*" Carmela said, with the slow distinct delivery of someone speaking in a kindly way to the mentally disadvantaged.

Nita took her hands off the spell-controls for her *mochteroof* and put them over her mouth in a desperate attempt to keep herself from bursting out laughing.

Very slowly, Kit looked up at his sister.

"Have I ever told you how wonderful you are?" he said.

"Not lately," Carmela said, slapping the TV manual shut and stuffing it out of sight. "And boy, had you better start making up for lost time, because I am feeling real unappreciated right now. I show up and shoot the butts off eight million hostile aliens to find out where you are so I can give you a hand, and what do I get from you? *Bupkis!*" She glanced back at Nita. "That's my new word for this week," she said.

Nita took her hands away from her mouth and concentrated on looking completely unconcerned. "Where'd you hear it?" she said.

"The TV. It's alien, I think."

Kit, meanwhile, was grinning in a helpless way and looking up. "Oh, thank you," he said—and not, Nita thought, to Carmela. "Thank you so much."

"A little bit late," Carmela said, "but better than never. Sincere-sounding, anyway." Then abruptly she looked at Kit and said, "Wait a minute. 'One of us'?" And she laughed. "You thought I was talking about a *wizard's* manual? I don't need a wizard's manual. I'm just fine the way I am. You can check that with the Power thingies."

"*Thingies?*" Kit said.

They're gone, Ponch said. *Come on.*

"How close are we?" Dairine said from the end of the line. "I think I hear some action behind us."

Just a few minutes' walk, Ponch said. *Up a level, and then a left turn.*

They followed Ponch up the long ramp to the next level of the city, where a number of corridors came together in a small, central concourse or crossroads, under an arched-over papery dome. Down one of the other corridors, Nita could see shadowy figures moving: *Workers,* she thought. Nonetheless, she was walking more softly now, and she noticed that the others were, too. *They all know that, sooner or later, we're going to wind up walking into a trap.* And, indeed, the one subject none of them had so far discussed was one that in more normal times would have been one of the first to come up: *How are we getting out of here?*

They paused again. Ponch looked around him and chose their way, one of the left-hand passages. The relative dimness of a side corridor shut down around them as they went. *But this is more serious than any of us getting out,* Nita thought. *This is a whole universe's worth of trouble, solved or messed up in one shot . . . and they all know it.* It was a relief to know they realized it. And a strange feeling swelled up in Nita: pride in all of them.

They stopped outside an arched doorway. On the wall to either side of it was written, in the Yaldiv charactery, GRUBBERY 14.

Memeki slipped past Nita, went to the doorway. Inside, in the dimness, nothing moved. Nita could dimly see a central pit area that heaved gently with many, many small, caterpillarish forms . . . every one of them alive, inside, with one of those angry, evil little dark-fire sparks. On the far side of the room, past the main pit, were many smaller archways, each big enough to take a single entering Yaldiv. Many of those were walled up. Nita had already seen from Memeki's mind what happened here, as each Favored Yaldah came to her time, entered, and was immured. The newly emerged grubs would be tenderly carried out by the ministering handmaidens, fed and tended . . . and the empty shell that was all that was left of their mother would be given to a worker to dump into the oily swamp.

Slowly, farther down the corridors, other Yaldiv began to appear: workers mostly, heading toward the door of the Commorancy to make their way out into the world for the day's work. Inside her *mochteroof,* Nita turned to Memeki and waited.

Memeki stood quiet. All of them were looking at her now, but she seemed oblivious to this. Nita waited. *Come on,* she thought, *come on! Just say yes! That's all it needs. Just say—*

"I will not," Memeki said.

They all stared at her.

She stood there with her claws together, in a position that was neither the Yaldah's fearful "averting" gesture or the warrior's threat. There was something strangely serene about it, and she looked over at Ponch and bowed. "I will not go in," she said. "I am no longer of the City. I am the Hes—"

And from the dim silence of the grubbery, the warriors came boiling out.

Once again everything started to happen at once. Nita saw Dairine and Filif and Roshaun drop, inside their *mochteroofs,* come up with strange shapes furred with the power-glow of working wizardries, and start firing at the surrounding warriors. To her own astonishment, Nita was horrified. "No! Look out, you'll hurt Memeki, if you—"

Then the firing stopped. That, too, horrified Nita, because it wasn't due to anything she'd said. From around all of them, the *mochteroofs* abruptly vanished.

There they stood, suddenly unshelled—five humans, one humanoid king, one talking tree, one dog, one computer-being, and a Yaldiv—and harsh claws seized them from every side, snatching away everything they had been holding, including the suddenly revealed Spear of Light from the shocked and swearing Ronan. The breath went right out of Nita, not so much from the horror of two giant bugs each grabbing one of her arms, but because of something much more innately awful. Ever since Nita had begun to practice the Art, the rule had been, "A spell always works." But suddenly it *didn't*.

The warriors began to hustle them all away from the grubbery. There was a certain amount of noise. When Spot was pried out of her arms, Dairine had joined Ronan in struggling hard and yelling words that would have given their dad a heart attack if he'd heard them; and Roshaun was accompanying her in Wellakhit idiom that from the sound of it was nearly as bad. Carmela, to Nita's surprise and relief, was angry, but not terrified; as they were dragged along, she flicked Nita a glance and waggled her eyebrows a couple of times, then glanced toward her curling iron's holster, and shrugged. It was empty.

Damn, Nita thought. She glanced at Kit and Filif, who were being dragged along nearby. As Nita was pulled even with Kit, she met his eye, tried to pass a thought to him, but was astonished to find that even in this moment of crisis, she couldn't hear him think. He just looked at her and shook his head.

As they passed various astonished-looking workers and handmaidens and were hauled downward into the heart of the City, in the back of Nita's mind she could feel the peridexis struggling as desperately as a bird clutched in someone's fist. *What's happened?* she said to it, getting less scared and more angry. *Why isn't anything working?!*

The Lone One's now fully occupying Its avatar here, the peridexis said. *And It's locally damped down every secondary wizardly function.* The peridexis's tone was faint and terrified, like that of a creature watching itself begin to bleed to death.

Nita was astonished. *But that would affect It, too—*

No. The only powers fully functioning here right now are those that have possessed wizardry or the power behind it from their very beginnings.

"Oh *no*," Nita breathed. Yet she still found it impossible to believe. In her mind she felt around for the memory of a self-defense spell she'd come across while reading the manual, had memorized, and had then sworn (as required) that she'd never use unless she thought she was in danger of her life. Nita opened her mouth, started to recite it...

...and couldn't find the words. Or, rather, she knew what they were, but as she whispered the first one, it didn't make sense. It was just a nonsense word. The universe didn't get quiet to listen to it. She said the second word, and the third, and they were nonsense, no power to them, nothing magical at all...

Around her, Nita saw the others struggling as she

had done, trying to get a grip on wizardly weapons or say words that would act as such, but the words all sounded made up and did nothing.

Nita started to despair…then found, to her surprise, that the feeling didn't last. She'd been in a similar situation not so long ago, a place and time in which no solution seemed possible. While there, she'd learned that, sometimes, if you just kept doing whatever you could, something would change in your favor. *And I'm not dead yet,* she thought. *Neither are the others. If I can't think of something, one of them might.*

Down and down the warriors carried them, deeper into the depths of the City. Nita knew in a general way where they were headed, from the précis she'd been looking at earlier; they were close to the King-Yaldiv's great cavernous hall. But more to the point, she could feel that dull glow of evil power and scornful rage at the Commorancy's heart getting stronger every moment as they got closer. *The Lone One's just about ready for us,* she thought. *So we've got only a few minutes to think of something.*

I have no help for you, the peridexic effect said miserably.

Nita blinked. *Wait a minute. If all the second-level uses of wizardry aren't working for us now, then how am I still hearing you?*

I still exist, the peridexic effect said. *I am simply of no use.*

I wouldn't bet on it! Nita said as their Yaldiv escort hauled them around another long curve and pushed them into a wide spherical chamber. Its far door was guarded by another warrior, possibly the biggest one Nita had seen yet. *For the moment, you're keeping me sane.* She gulped, because the memory of that horrible moment of disbelief in Tom and Carl's backyard now rose up in front of her as something she definitely never wanted to experience again. *You're proof that wizardry's been* real, *even if it's not working right now. So just hang in there, because right now I need you!*

The warriors turned the group loose inside the chamber and went to block the door behind them. The ten of them all clustered together in the center of the room, the humanoids rubbing their various bruises. Muttering under her breath, Dairine picked up Spot, who'd been unceremoniously dumped on the floor, and stood looking around her with a ferocious scowl. Ronan threw a furious look at the warrior holding the Spear, and eyed Dairine with a sort of disgruntled admiration. "What *is* it with these Callahan women?" he said to Kit as he tried to flex one strained shoulder back into working order.

Kit shook his head. "You okay?" he said to Dairine.

"Yeah. But Spot's not. He's gone mute, and his eyes and legs are gone."

"Pop his screen," Kit said. "See if you get any manual functions. Roshaun?"

Roshaun opened one cupped hand, the gesture he usually used to bring up the little matrix of light that was his implementation of the manual. But nothing happened. He shook his head at Kit.

"Fil?"

Filif rustled all his branches, *No.*

Nita swallowed. She reached for her otherspace pocket...and couldn't find it. She pulled the rowan wand out of the belt of her jeans, and found it nothing but a peeled white stick. She lifted her charm bracelet, shook it—

But now it was just a bracelet, and the charms jingled harmlessly. A lightning bolt, a circle with the number 26, a little fish, a few other symbols.

Dairine had been tapping at Spot's keyboard. Now she was scowling harder than ever. "No manual," she said. "He's still in there, he can communicate through the software, but that's all. No access to the manual functions. And he can't hear his homeworld, or any of his people." She let out an unhappy breath, closed Spot up again, and went back to hugging him. "We're cut off."

Kit had also been feeling in the air for his pocket; he couldn't find his, either. "Okay," he said, "we're supposed to become useless, now, because we think we're marooned, completely isolated, and totally powerless. Forgive me if I don't feel like cooperating. What *can* we do?" He looked around at them. No one volunteered any thoughts.

The warrior who had been blocking the door before them now moved away from it, and another figure came through.

It was the Arch-votary in its patterned shell. Slowly, it approached, those massive claws raised. Nita held her ground, and saw that the others were doing the same, though Ponch, sticking close to Kit's side, growled softly, and the fur over his shoulders and down his back was bristling.

The Arch-votary stopped, looming up before them. "Evil ones," it said, "enemies of the Great One, come and be judged."

Roshaun lifted his head and gave the Arch-votary an inexpressibly haughty look. "Killed, perhaps," he said. "But your dark Master has neither authority nor right to judge us. Therefore stand away, lackey, and keep silent in the presence of your betters."

And Roshaun swept straight past the Arch-votary, right on through that doorway into the central cavern, leaving the angry and befuddled Yaldiv staring after him. Dairine went straight past it, too, throwing it a dirty and dismissive look, and followed Roshaun. Carmela and Ronan and Filif went after her. After a moment's hesitation, Memeki followed Filif through the doorway, and Ponch, with a glance back at Kit, trotted after her, growling.

Kit and Nita threw each other a glance and headed after Ponch. "Roshaun really comes into his own in situations like this," Kit said under his breath, glancing over his shoulder as the Arch-votary and the warriors followed them in.

"You've got a point," Nita muttered back, "but if it's all the same to you, I don't want to *be* in any more situations like this."

"If we don't get real lucky in the next few minutes," Kit said, "you can relax, because we *won't* be."

They passed through the door, their guards following.

The lower bowl of that huge elliptical cavern was empty except for the warriors who blocked the many other entrances. It was a long walk for the group across that strangely soft, papery surface, and after the first look at the huge swollen shape of the King, Nita started to feel her confidence ebbing away, feeling more like ill-founded bravado every moment. The massive, bloated bag of body that lay there on the dais at one focus of the elliptical bowl, with handmaidens constantly bringing food to its little chewing jaws and going away again, felt to Nita as if it was absolutely heaving with millions of those sparks of angry fire, endlessly being spun off like stars of a dark galaxy from that core of evil at their center, the Lone One's presence in the King. And it was strong, stronger than she'd thought. She could feel it sucking at her will as they got closer, as if it was trying to empty all the thoughts out of her brain, every sense that she was herself, that she was anything but a slave, to do what she was told, to obey orders.

She shook her head. There was something she was supposed to be doing, but she couldn't think what.

Something jabbed her in the side. "Neets!"

Her eyes went wide. Nita realized that she'd been walking toward the dais without even being aware of it. She glanced sideways, and saw Kit looking at her in concern, but ready to elbow her again if necessary. "You there?"

"Yeah, thanks."

"Count inside your head, or sing yourself a song or something."

Nita made a face. "You wouldn't want to hear me sing," she said. "Dair's the school-choir department." But she started reciting a series of primes, and tried not to walk in rhythm.

She managed to keep herself from vaguing out again, but as they got closer and closer to the dais, a straightforward horror of the King itself started to set in. The idea of giant bugs had been a problem for her when she was little, a fear mostly exorcised now, but not entirely. Nita had pretty much come to terms with the claws and shells and fangs of the Yaldiv, but this was different. The flabby, pallid, distended bag of the King's body, swollen, gross, heaving, beating with little veins, made her shudder at the very sight of it—and the closer she got to it, the farther away Nita desperately wanted to be. *I don't want to scream,* she thought, *but if anybody makes me go up to it, makes me touch it— I* really *don't want to scream; it'll just set Dairine off.*

"What a gigantic ugly sack of crap," Dairine said, in a tone of completely clinical interest. "Truly disgusting. And would you look at the wiggly bits! I'll bet it thinks they're so wonderful that everyone ought to bow down to them. Pathetic, isn't it? Don't freeze up, Memeki, it's not worth your time."

Nita gulped again, but at the same time felt strangely reassured; she was certain the remark hadn't been entirely directed at Memeki. She gave Kit a glance and saw him roll his eyes in amusement, even here, even now. A shadow on her left made her look that way: Filif was there, rustling against her, saying nothing, but all those little berry-eyes looked surprisingly serene.

As they got close to the dais, the warriors behind reached out claws to stop them. The King's flesh-buried little eyes peered down at them, black, unreflecting, empty…though not nearly empty enough: Nita could feel the darkness behind them, looking out at them all with cruel recognition.

Roshaun held his head up. "Bright star that was," he said, "dark star that falls, in your downward arc with defiance we greet you. Do your poor worst!"

A few moments' silence passed, and then the King spoke. The voice that came out of it was a shock to Nita, a perfectly human sound, though she had no idea how Filif or Ponch or Memeki might be hearing it. "That will not take much doing," said the Lone Power through Its tool, "for the evil power which the Enemy gave you is now yours no more." Nita wasn't sure how that inhuman face could smile, but somehow it seemed to be managing it.

The King tried to hitch itself forward a little; Nita winced at the long water-bed ripple that this sent up its body. Then the Lone One looked at Memeki through the King. "Here, then, is our little heretic, doomed to die so soon, doing my will as she must, no matter how she desires to do otherwise." It paused. "Though she might still die in my good graces, and so achieve as much salvation as she ever will."

It bent Its gaze on her. "Handmaiden, Favored of the Great One," It said softly, "give up this vain dream of oneness, of being one's own self! Don't you realize this is all an evil plot by the One's enemies? They would drive you away from your own kind, from the right way to think, the right way to be. Come back within the mind that bore you; come back and be one again with those who will always honor what you have done as a mother of your people, a daughter of the Great One, honored by the King."

Nita could feel the power the King was bringing to bear on Memeki. Even she began slowly to feel that it was wrong of any being to resist such honor, that Memeki should forget all about them, save herself, bow down before the King.

Beware! said the peridexis's voice in her head. *Don't let Its shadowy little truth overwhelm the greater one.*

Nita blinked, shook her head slightly as if to clear it. *Thanks,* she said, and the King's influence receded. *But this is just Its usual game, isn't it? The Lone One would really love it if It could not only stop Memeki from being the Hesper, but also break her will before she died.*

Memeki now stood swaying on her many legs, her eyes reflecting nothing but the King as she leaned more and more toward him. "For am I not the One who set your people free from the tyranny of the mighty and evil Force from Outside?" the King was saying. "Do you not owe all your loyalty to the One who stole the tyrant's power despite everything it could do, and so made your world free?"

Memeki swayed, swayed, slowly grew still...then looked up. "Free?" she said. "Yes. You made us free." She was shivering again, and she crouched down as if once again feeling the pangs of the eggs beginning to move inside her. "Free to kill. And free to die."

"But what other freedom is there," the King said,

more softly still, "in this concentration camp of a universe, where all things must happen according to the evil Other's inflexible rules, on threat of some awful eternal punishment? Far better to tell it, 'Not your will, but *mine!*'—and turn your back on the Other's unkept promise that groveling to It will bring you joy. Death comes no matter what the Other does, and so only Death's servants, *my* servants, are truly free! Free to take what they want, to kill what they want, no consequences, no punishment, no limits!"

"Except when the freedom is one *you* don't choose to grant," Memeki said, more loudly this time. She was shaking herself all over, struggling to stand straight again. "You hold out hope with one claw and take it away with the other! I may be weak and doomed soon to die, but I will die as an *I*, not just one more nameless scrap of shell to be thrown out into the sucking mud! No matter how little a time it lasts, I will be what all *these* are"—and she looked around at Kit and Ponch and Nita and the others—"selves unto themselves, and beings that matter to each other! Such a life, even a breath's worth of it, is better than anything you've ever given me!"

Memeki was trembling again, but with passion, with determination, desperate and doomed. She took a step toward the dais, and another, her claws lifted not in that old gesture of submission, but in one more like a warrior's threat. "I will *be* what the Voice said I was, the Hesper, I *will* be the Aeon of Light, the Power that made a different choice from yours. I will be the Star that did not fall, no matter how little a time the light lasts!"

The possessed King tapped a fretful foreclaw on the dais, almost like someone drumming his fingers. It looked past Memeki at Kit and Nita and the others. "Well, they have spoiled you beyond tempting," It said, sounding aggrieved. "What a shame. But this is no great loss, for in a very little while I will nonetheless get a couple of hundred more avatars out of you. Oh, yes," It said, as once again Memeki's legs started to give way under her. Dairine and Roshaun reached out to support her on one side, and Kit and Ronan on the other. Ponch shouldered in between them and started licking Memeki's face. "I have hastened your time considerably; you can feel them preparing to come forth. This should be educational for these 'friends' you're so enamored of."

The King waved away the handmaidens servicing him; they scuttled away into the shadows behind the dais. "And after that, you will have an honor guard to accompany you on your road into the dark from which there is no return. But, no, of course, I forget." It looked around at Nita and Kit and the others. "Obedient to the Other's brainwashing, you have all deluded yourselves into thinking that the darkness is actually light. 'Timeheart.'" It chuckled. "Little consolation that place will be to you, even if you manage to reach it; for there you'll sit outside of time, waiting for the sufferings of everyone you've ever known to end. And I need not do anything further to bring that fate about, for the Pullulus has already doomed all your worlds."

It turned Its head just enough to look over at Carmela, who was standing there with her hands on her hips, looking scornful. "And to your ignorance you've now added folly," the King said, "for you've gone so far as to bring with you someone who doesn't even have any of the Other's vile power. Whatever possessed you to do something so foolishly arrogant, so sheerly *useless*?" Then It laughed. "Well, I suppose that in the long run, probably *I* did. You, alien thing, come over here."

To Nita's absolute horror, Carmela's arms suddenly flopped away from her body, jerking like the arms of a puppet on strings. Carmela wobbled, her balance lost, and her face went slack with shock as she took a step toward those nastily working jaws. Then she scowled, dug in her heels, and stopped again.

"Oh, resistance," the King said. "How amusing. But you have no more power against me than that. Now come here."

Carmela struggled, but it was no use. Nita watched with horror as she put one foot in front of the other, clumsy, stiff—and with each step she was able to resist less, and her face went still and empty. "No!" Kit yelled, and started forward, but the warriors who had been lingering nearby now grabbed him roughly from behind. They did the same with Nita and Roshaun and Ronan when they tried to move.

"This has all been just a game for you, hasn't it?" the King said. "But you see now how wrong you were. Maybe it would be amusing to do to you what we do to the handmaidens. Wall you up in an incubatorium, without food or water, and see how long it takes before you beg to be fed what the grubs are fed. Or perhaps even feed you *to* the grubs. There are always some whose first meal isn't big enough."

There was no sign of struggle left in Carmela, none at all; Nita got just a glimpse of the blank look of her eyes as she stepped closer and closer to the King, as if sleepwalking, helpless. Kit threw himself again in the King's direction, but the warriors held him fast. "No!" he shouted. "Do it to me if you want, not her!"

The King's regard slid in Kit's direction. "We will do it to you soon enough, I think," It said. "But first we will let her bleed a little. Just a nip here...a nip there." It lazily stretched out Its claws. "She will feel every moment of it, but not be able to move a muscle. It should be a learning experience for one so spirited."

Carmela stepped closer, and closer. Another step or two would bring her within range of those cruel claws; they were stretching toward her, one of them would be close enough with the next step to brush her cheek— "NO!" Nita screamed, struggling in the grip of the claws that held her.

"But wait. What might this be that I perceive there?" said the King's soft, oily voice. "A weapon of some kind? And how cunningly hidden under that body-covering. But though you might have been clever about hiding it, it makes no difference if the mind that hid it is helpless to hide its own thoughts. Bring it out."

Carmela stopped, and slowly reached inside the light vest she was wearing, bringing out the curling iron. Very softly the King said, "Perhaps blood would be the wrong approach after all. What delicious irony if one who lives by such a weapon should die by it, and be unable even to—"

The terrible blast of fire in that dim place blinded everybody and knocked them staggering. The force of the explosion shoved Nita into the warrior that was holding her; she found her footing again just before it let go of her and went down, crashing to the floor with a horrible, thin, shrilling scream. An awful singed-hair stink of burning bug came billowing out from the dais through waves of greasy black smoke, and it was some seconds before this cleared enough for Nita to see that the King's entire front half had been blown away. Its rear half was now a smoking, bubbling, sagging bag of grossness, the sight of which made Nita simply bend over double and retch, mutely grateful that the soda she'd drunk was now too far along in her system to come back up. When she straightened up again, she saw through the smoke that Carmela was standing in front of the King's smoking remains with the curling iron in her hand.

"Oops," Carmela said . . . and, very slowly, smiled.

Nita stared around them in utter astonishment. Around them, all the other warriors and even the Archvotary were making that same terrible shrill cry, wavering, desperate, as they fell to the ground and went silent. From the depths of the City to its heights, faintly at first and then more loudly, Nita started to hear that shrilling spreading all through the vast place. Ronan instantly whirled and snatched the Spear of Light out of the claws of the collapsed warrior who'd held it.

Kit ran over to Carmela. When he got to her, he

threw his arms around her and buried his face against her. "You dummy," he said, "you incredible idiot, you stupid—"

"Hey, I love you, too," Carmela said, hugging him back as Nita hurried over.

" 'Mela," she said, "it was *controlling* you! How did you—"

"It wasn't," Carmela said. "It made me jerk a little that first time, but after that I was just playing along. Maybe it's no good with our kind of brain or something?"

Nita didn't think that was likely, but she looked about halfway back at the King, making a face. It was very dead, and the smell seemed to be getting worse rather than better. "Okay," she said. "But what about Memeki?"

They turned toward her. Memeki was hunched on the floor, and her limbs, which had before been flailing as if in distress, were now unnervingly still. Nita went over to her, knelt down by her. "Memeki?"

No answer.

"It's starting to happen to her, isn't it," Kit said.

Nita felt sure it was. She reached sideways, feeling around for her otherspace pocket, and still couldn't feel it.

Huh? she thought. *What's the matter?* she said to the peridexis. *The King's dead, the Lone One should be—*

"Uh," Dairine said, very quietly. "Neets—"

Nita looked up, looked around, unable to see what Dairine's problem was. Then she looked back at the dais.

The charred remnants of the King still lay there, smoking. But within them, slowly drawing upward instead of drifting outward, was a deeper darkness, gathering together and shaping itself into a new form: humanoid enough, but taller than any human, and with a far deeper darkness in the eyes gazing down at them as the shape grew more ominously distinct. Solidifying, clothing itself in a long tunic and booted breeches somewhat like Roshaun's, the young and darkly handsome figure of the Lone Power glanced down and around It, and casually kicked Its way out of the ruin of the King's body like someone kicking his way out of a pair of shucked-off jeans.

The Lone One stepped down from the dais and surveyed the smoking remains of the King. Then It turned around and looked at them. "'Oops'?" It said.

The voice was deep, urbane, and dry. It could almost have been pleasant had Nita not known perfectly well that the pleasantness was never more than a disguise or a trap. What worried her most at the moment was that all Its attention was bent on Carmela. It left the dais and stalked toward them. "'*Oops*'?"

Carmela had sense enough to be unnerved. She took a hasty step backward, then another, as the Lone Power approached. "Sorry," she said.

"I rather doubt it," the Lone One said, "but that will change. Is it possible that you don't know you've made things worse for yourself, not better? Then again, you're new at this. Well, in the short time left to you, here's one lesson for you to learn."

It smiled, and Carmela shrank back. Then her eyes abruptly went wide. A little shriek burst out of her. She spun and, hastily, overhand, threw the curling iron away hard. A mere six feet or so away from her, in mid-air, it blew up.

Everyone jumped back. Nita gulped, and was briefly relieved that Carmela had spent so much of this school year on the pitcher's mound for the school softball team.

"So much for science," the Lone One said. "Though I must confess that why you weren't more susceptible to control is an issue for curiosity."

"Might be that someone here was able to keep you from noticing," Ronan said. Leaning on the Spear of Light, he glowered at the Lone One from under those dark brows of his.

"That seems unlikely," the Lone Power said. "He's got precious little power left in him right now, and he can't draw on the pitiful scrap of power *that's* got left." It glanced dismissively at the Spear, which now simply looked like a spear and nothing else; its flame was gone, and not even the twisting fires that normally lived in its blade were there anymore. "But even more unlikely is the possibility that *she* was able to keep the information to herself...so for the moment we'll file the matter under 'interesting but unimportant.'"

It turned around and looked briefly at the King's remains. "What a shame," the Lone One said. "I'd just gotten this one broken in. But I'll soon grow another. Meantime, I have other business here."

"What are you going to do with us?" Kit said.

"Probably nothing," It said.

"Oh, *sure*!" Dairine said.

"No," the Lone One said, "seriously. Why should I exert myself? Not one of you has enough power to turn lemons into lemonade. And that's not going to change." It strolled over toward the softly growling Ponch. "Not even *he* can get out of here; his abilities, not that I care to try to understand them, are derived from wizardry as well. You're all completely stuck."

It turned Its back on Ponch and wandered over to Memeki. "I admit," It said, "normally just killing you would be my initial impulse. But I'm thinking it would be more fun just to let you all wander around on this planet for the rest of your natural lives, which probably wouldn't be long: There's not much to eat or drink here that your metabolisms are built to handle. But you'd live quite long enough to suffer from some of the things that are going to happen as a result of your failure."

The Lone One came to a halt by Memeki's side, gazing down at her. "And as for the attempted 'Aeon of Light' here," It said, kicking Memeki idly with one booted toe, "the Unfallen One and all the rest of the fancy terminology—well, she's a spent force. She waited a few seconds too long to make up her mind. When I sealed wizardry away, she lost access to the power that would have allowed her to enact her transformation. So, starting in a few minutes, when the grubs hatch and she begins to die, her embodiment will officially have failed... and after that, I won't ever have to worry about the much-waited-for Hesper again, in this or any universe. You *did* know that if an emergent Power's first embodiment fails, both the being inside time and the being outside in timelessness cease to exist?"

Nita glanced over at Kit and the others, miserable. "Oh, good, you knew," the Lone One said, pleased. "That will make your failure hurt lots worse. If a Power hasn't actually been on hand at the creation of a physical universe, the initial successful embodiment is the risk it has to take to insert itself into one. If the Hesper had been smart and stayed outside of so-called reality, in timelessness, I'd have left it completely alone. But once it decided to meddle in what's going on inside physicality, it had to pass this test first, which always eventually attracts my attention, though this time it took a little more tracking down than usual. I've been expecting this move ever since my so-called redemption. The One didn't wait nearly as long as I thought It would. Its mistake."

The Lone One looked down at Memeki, amused, and turned away. "So, no more Hesper. She's about to do what all good mothers on Rashah do—die." It smiled at Nita and Dairine. "Her children will go on to start useful and productive careers as my slaves. And I'll have at least a few aeons' more peace and quiet until the Powers decide to try another stunt like this."

"I doubt it will be anything like that long," Filif said, giving the Lone One a look of massive disapproval out of every berry-eye.

"Oh, I think it will," the Lone One said. "The Powers That Be used up a great deal of energy setting up this project . . . and They hate to waste. Now, of course, I used up a fair amount, too, because I needed to distract all you little wizardly busybodies from noticing what I suspected was happening somewhere or other.

It didn't entirely work—after all, here you are. But all the same, you've done me a favor. Without all of you bringing Rashah to my attention, who knows whether I'd have been alerted to this problem right under my nose in time to do something about it?" It smiled again. "So the other Powers have outsmarted Themselves . . . and it'll be a long time before they feel like trying this again." It gave Filif an amused look. "Life on *your* planet will be so much mulch by then. Actually, it'll be mulch a lot sooner, because even though I don't mind all of you living out your little antlike lives in misery on Rashah, your worlds are going to pay up front for your meddling. Certainly you didn't expect otherwise!"

"So you're just going to let the Pullulus destroy everything," Ronan said bleakly.

"Don't be silly," the Lone One said, sitting down on the dais and crossing Its legs. "If I did that, what would be left to play with? There are billions of years' worth of suffering left in your universe yet. Oh, I'm finished with the Pullulus now. When I withdraw my attention from it, it'll run down in a hurry. While it didn't *completely* do what I wanted it to, it did disrupt or even destroy a good number of civilizations in the populated galaxies. The other Powers will waste far more energy trying to save the maximum number of all those trillions of endangered lives than I ever spent destroying them. So I've won this round on two counts."

Its smile got nastier. "And while They're trying to pick up the pieces elsewhere in the universe, I can amuse myself with raising another King for the Commorancy, and watching all of you run around trying to survive on Rashah. It really is a nice little world. Hundreds of thousands of Yaldiv, every one of them devoted to my service, and every one convinced that all other life is their enemy, and that only I can offer them salvation. I haven't had such a promising species to work with for a long time. Possibly not even since yours." It gave Nita and the other three Earth-humans a look of ironic appreciation. "Once I've got enough of them, and I've given them the right technology, they should be able to overrun a significant portion of this universe. But present pleasures first." It glanced at Roshaun. "One early order of business will be to push the Pullulus in tightly enough around your solar system to flare up Wellakh's star. Your people always do react more hysterically to fire than to ice."

Nita saw Roshaun go pale, but he kept his face stern. He plainly wasn't going to give the Lone One the satisfaction of seeing him express his fear.

"And I can use the same technique on your people, I suppose," It said, looking back at Filif. "'Kindler of Wildfires,' they call me? They won't have seen anything like this. The sunside of your planet will be one big charcoal briquette when I'm done. *Your* little friends," and It frowned at Dairine, "have unfortunately made themselves energy-independent…but we'll see how much good that does them when one or two rogue planets collide with theirs from either side. It'll be just like dropping an egg on concrete. All that tinkly shattering silicon." It glanced over at Kit and Nita and Ronan. "And then, of course, Earth. The Pullulus is doing such a lovely job there already, I won't have to do a single thing but watch. It's closing in on your heliopause already, and people's tempers are getting frayed. Every government on the planet with any weapons worth noticing is already at DEFCON Two, and it's only a matter of hours before the big show begins. A fallen skyscraper or two will be *nothing* compared to what's coming up...and you'll know, for the rest of your short lives, that it was all your fault."

It stretched Its arms above Its head and grinned. Nita gulped.

Kit, though, gave It a blasé look. "Nice gloat," he said.

The Lone One gave him a look. "You're too kind," It said. "But I'm just telling you the truth, which you pretend so to value. And, Kit..." It *tsk-tsk-tsk*ed at him. "Denial, even disguised as humor, suits you so badly. Don't you understand? *You're not getting out this time.* You don't have a scrap of wizardry left to you. And did it occur to you that you might have been a little too secretive about getting here? There's not a wizard anywhere in this universe who either knows where you've gone or is going to be able to do anything about it. Since this is now a no-wizardry zone, manual functions won't be able to find you. And don't think I'm forgetting your multilegged friend at the Crossings," It said, looking over at Nita. "He's got his claws full, too, every one of them."

It sat down on the dais, crossing Its legs and swinging them a little. "So, for the extremely foreseeable future, here you stay. It takes quite a lot of power to exclude wizardry from any space, but with my energy investment withdrawn from ninety-nine percent of the Pullulus now, I have some to spare. I'm perfectly happy to use it making sure that the 'Great Art' is permanently disabled here. And in the meantime—"

On the floor before the dais, Memeki began heaving rhythmically.

The Lone Power laced Its fingers behind Its head and leaned back. "No," It said, "there's no rush at all. Nature is going to take its inevitable course, and we'll all get to watch this particular zero hollow itself out."

Nita stood there frozen with horror as she watched the heaving wrack Memeki more and more terribly. That awful wave of desperation she'd felt in the Crossings rose up to possess her again, and this time it stuck. *This is it, then,* she thought. *Despite all our work, regardless of everything we did, it's all over.*

Behind her, someone moved. Ronan pushed past Nita to stand in front of her and Memeki. "All right," he said, pausing to lean on the Spear again, "I don't know about everybody else here, but I for one think it's time somebody put some manners on you."

The Lone Power burst out laughing at him. "Oh please!" It said. "Just look at you! You and the Toothpick of Virtue. That can't hurt me now: It's absolutely no good for anything without someone who both knows how to use it, and has the strength! Which, as we've seen, you don't."

"You're right," Ronan said. "I don't. But someone else does."

"You know, you missed your calling," the Lone Power said. "Why aren't you in stand-up comedy?

You're just another cage for another spent force! My esteemed 'little brother' might be wearing fewer feathers this time, but you're an even worse embodiment for him than his last one." It turned Its back on Ronan and walked away, chuckling and shaking Its head. "You've only once let him have access to his full power, and never again since. Talk about a hopeless mismatch! But since he had to commit fully to embodying inside you, he's stuck there whether he likes it or not. If he tried to leave you, it'd kill you. And, being a Power of Light"—the Lone One turned, and the sneer in Its voice was so full of scorn that the words almost burned in Nita's ears—"he'd never take that chance."

"No," Ronan said softly. "He wouldn't."

"So you see that for all your big words—"

"But I would!"

Nita's head snapped around.

Ronan leaned back and threw the Spear.

Forged in wizardry by one of the Powers That Be, with another Power as old as wizardry itself bound into the starsteel of the blade, the Spear of Light roared out of Ronan's hand toward the Lone One. The Lone Power casually flung up a hand alive with black lightning to deflect it. But the Spear went nowhere near It. Instead, it swung far around the Lone One's back, roared past him, and headed back.

The breath went out of Nita. *"Ronan!"*

He didn't move, except to look just slightly sideways at Nita: that dark, wry, ironic expression of his, mocking himself now as much as the One whom he was attacking in the least expected way. In that last second, Ronan threw his arms wide—a grandstanding gesture, a casually defiant flash of black against the dim heat of the hive—and the Spear of Light struck him in the chest, and he went down.

"*No!*" screamed the Lone Power, and the whole City shook. Nita stood there wide-eyed and gasping, as stricken as if she'd been the one hit by the Spear. She plunged toward where Ronan lay, bleeding blood and fire. But a breath later, a wave of force blasting away from the light that pooled around him struck Nita and knocked her and all the others flat... even the Lone Power. In that shock wave, the fallen bodies of the Arch-votary and its warriors were scattered across the floor of the central chamber like so many toys, and, with the rebound of the shock wave, a huge form of light gathered itself up around Ronan, swirling, streaming upward. Across the floor, the shape that had been human moments before and had been blasted into a puddle of darkness by that fury of light now began straining upward to reform itself, a blinding blackness throwing itself out in a hundred directions in writhing, raging tendrils and tentacles of shadow.

Nita scrambled to her knees, craning her neck to take in the tremendous form towering over them, armed in light, armored in fire. Once again she understood why, long ago, the first thing such an apparition had to say to the people who saw it was "Fear not." No sane and mortal creature could look on the One's Champion in full manifestation without being afraid that mere fragile reality might start to shred around so terrible a Power for good. The Champion towered up into the heights in what looked to Nita like human form. But in this manifestation, the Defender was not terribly concerned about details such as gender or ornament. Light flared behind It like wings, licking upward like fire, as It stood there burning like a statue cast in lightning, laughing uproariously.

Free! the Champion cried. *Once again, Brother, you've underestimated the tenacity of the One's other weapons. This one in particular! I'm surprised you ever let him in here, but then this splinter of you seriously believed that the first work I did with Ronan was what I came to him for!* It laughed again, delighted. *And though there's only one thing I can do, now—thanks to him, it's the only thing that needs to be done. You've done everything else for us; you yourself triggered the whole cycle of events you most desired to avoid!*

The Champion lifted one arm and pointed what It held at the furiously writhing, growing shape of blackness building before It. A sword like a splinter of sun's core lifted over the Lone One, ready to strike. *So as you interrupted my work once before, now I interrupt yours. And what was trying to happen, now has one last chance.*

That unbearable shard of light reared high, struck down. Another blast of power hit Nita so hard that she staggered, but not because of the impact of any physical force. The words came rushing back right through her as the Speech once again *meant* something. Her charm bracelet blazed; the rowan wand in her belt burned moonfire chill. She glanced around, saw the others scrambling up from where the shock wave had thrown them, regaining their power and their weapons.

The light around them grew less bright. Nita looked up in shock and saw that the dark shape of the Lone One lay writhing on the floor like a nest of shadowy snakes. But the burning form of the Champion was fading, slipping away out of the physical world. *I can't stay any longer inside time,* It said in the depths of Nita's mind, and the others'. *This embodiment ended too soon: I have no more power to spend. Now hurry! It's up to you.*

The light vanished: The Champion was gone. *At least It's broken the Lone One's blockage,* Nita thought. But the Lone One was still there. And were Its dark tentacles getting darker again? She glanced at the still-heaving Memeki, who was trying to get to her feet. Filif and Roshaun and Dairine hurried over to her, getting down to support her, pushing her up. But Nita headed straight past them to Ronan, flinging herself down on her knees beside him. The Spear stood upright in him, burning. Nita reached to pull it out of him, then hesitated as its blade went up in a great flame of furious white fire. *Why? Though maybe it's trying to protect him, maybe if I pulled it out he'd—*

Kit was suddenly there, kneeling across from Nita, staring down at Ronan, the light of the Spear glinting in his eyes. A moment later, Nita became aware of a darkness overshadowing her. She looked up. It was Memeki, with Roshaun and Dairine and Carmela and Filif all around her, helping keep her on her feet.

Memeki's claws trembled as she reached down to Ronan, toward the Spear.

"Memeki, no, don't! He might—"

With a great effort, Ronan opened his eyes. "This," he said. "This is your"—he took an incredibly deep breath. "—made for you. Now you can—"

His eyes closed again, his head fell to one side.

The ground began to shake. *This cannot happen!* said a terrible voice in all their bones, as the Lone Power started to rise again, the serpentine arms reaching out of that pool of darkness now getting more solid, as It exerted every last ounce of force It had left to try to force Its way back into full physicality. *I will not permit—*

But Memeki ignored It. She looked down at Ronan, where he lay silent and bleeding. Then she looked around her at Nita, and Kit, and Roshaun, and Dairine, and Filif, and, finally, at Ponch.

"Yes," she said to him. "My answer is your answer. My answer is yes."

And she reached out and seized the Spear in her claws.

Nita braced herself. But instead of what she expected—a cataclysmic shaking, some great scream of rage or triumph—there fell around them instead a profound stillness, into which all sound swirled down and was swallowed away. In silence, the universe bent close to hear what was going to happen next. In silence, Memeki reared up and yanked the Spear out of Ronan's body. In silence, its fire whipped out of it in a vortex of terrific force and swirled around her, burning, hiding her away.

The City was already dark, but now it grew darker still. At first Nita was afraid that the Lone One was doing something. The darkness around them deepened, but that light at the center of everything swirled out, spiraling away from what had been its center. All that remained within the core of the light was a shell, glowing, transparent as the *mochteroofs*, and inside it a swarm of dark sparks of fire. They swirled and burned and then, all at once, burned fiercely bright, too bright to look at, like the myriad sparks of a fireworks display—

They went out. Around them, the glow of the shell that had been Memeki went out like a blown-out candle flame. Memeki was gone.

But the light itself was not. It fountained up into the heights of the central space of the City, and then down again, sheeting and splashing out, illuminating that whole place and flooding outward, striking the papery walls, pouring through them. At first Nita thought the walls were vanishing, but then she realized that they were simply becoming as transparent as glass under the influence of the power that now imbued them. All around, in every direction, hundreds and thousands of Yaldiv became visible in the deepest structures of the nest. Tens and hundreds more began to pour into the central chamber through its many doors. All the mirrory eyes looked up and inward at the blaze of light as it spun downward and outward from the heights, defining a new shape, a radiant and tremendous form shelled and sheened in light; and the beauty of it, even in the strange alien shape, was nearly unbearable. Nita wanted nothing more than to stand there staring at it, waiting to see what other, more momentous shape it would take when her human senses finally came to grips with it.

The chamber was full of Yaldiv now, thousands of them packed into this space. They and the thousands of others elsewhere in the now-crystalline structure of the City gazed inward or upward at the rainbow-streaming shape above them, all their myriad eyes swimming with a light that seemed to come in more colors than physical existence normally allowed—a spectrum as much of possibility as of mere radiance. The light no longer just lay on the surface of those eyes, but sank into them, dwelled in them. Some of the Yaldiv out there were handmaidens, some of them bearing eggs inside them as Memeki had done; and as Nita saw the brilliant sparks held within the huge shape of the Hesper flare up, so did the sparks within the handmaidens below, flaring into ferocious brilliance, burning clean, dying down again to swirls of rainbow glitter, dark no more—

Her heart went up in a blaze of triumph. *But this is what had to happen. And now all the Yaldiv born and unborn will be her avatars, all the Hesper's children and not the Lone One's!*

Nita looked over at Kit. Off to one side, beside him, Ponch had been standing very still, watching this like a dark and shining statue of a dog. But suddenly his tail started to wag, and then he started barking, and jumping up and down. The barking got louder and louder, a sound of sheer triumph.

The rainbow light shivered and trembled to the sound of Ponch's barking. Burning, glinting, like mirrors in the sun, the eyes of the great shelled shape above them looked down at Ponch, and at the wizards who stood or crouched to look up at Her; and at the one wizard who lay still, even the blood pooled beside him reflecting rainbows now. *I am here*, It said: *I am here at last.*

The tremendous voice shivered in all their bones, as the Lone Power's voice had. It was impossibly ancient, impossibly powerful...and it was Memeki's.

For a few seconds, no one said anything. Then, "Elder sister," Kit said, awestruck, "greeting and honor."

To Nita's astonishment, that great shape bowed to them.

My first work's done, thanks to you, the Hesper said. *I've driven the Lone Power away from here, possibly forever. And I have written a new history in the Yaldiv's bodies: They will find ways to live that mean their lives need not begin in death as well as end in it. So this poor world that my other self maimed so badly will now be healed. And after it, in time, so will many other worlds, one by one.*

"It's going to take a long time," Dairine said.

It will take forever, the Hesper said. *But I have forever now. The past, and the future, the ability to be in time...you gave it to me.*

Her regard dwelled on them all for a moment. *I can*

only stay a little more of your time in this form, the Hesper said. *So new a connection between the physical realms and eternity won't hold for long in this ephemeral place; I must depart. But because you and your worlds have endured such danger for my sake, I've done what I can to repay the debt. For a very little while, I have driven our Enemy out of time. While Its brief exile lasts, It can do no new evil. But what It has already set in train, I can't now halt. I must withdraw into timelessness now and recoup my strength, or risk being unable to embody again for a long while.*

Roshaun bowed to her. "Crowned one," he said, "you owe us no debts. In the paths of errantry, we'll meet again."

The Hesper was already fading. Ponch started barking again. *Don't go away! Don't go—*

Those rainbow-mirror eyes rested briefly on Ponch, and Nita thought she saw affection there. *Make haste to your world,* the Hesper said, looking from Ponch to Kit and Nita and Dairine. *Make haste! They will need you there.*

The light faded, slipped away, as if sunset was happening indoors. Finally they all stood or knelt in twilight, surrounded by many curious Yaldiv who peered down at them and held up their claws in a new gesture.

"Welcome," they said. "Friends of the Daughter of the true Great One, friends of the Queen of Light; *dai stihó,* and well met on the journey!"

Nita and Kit stared at each other. "Too much strange," Nita said, *"just too much!"* She rubbed her eyes. "Hi, guys, good to see you, too. Please bear with us for a moment." She turned her attention back to Ronan. "Fil, quick, give us some light!"

All Filif's berries blazed with wizard-light as Nita reached sideways into her otherspace pocket, found it where it belonged, pulled out her manual, and dumped it on the floor. Its pages riffled wildly as she pulled the rowan wand out of her belt and shook it down once like someone shaking a thermometer: White moonfire ran down it. She looked down at Ronan, put a hand on his chest next to the place where the Spear had gone in—then froze.

She looked up at Kit. "Is he breathing?" she whispered.

Kit looked at her, and very quietly said, "No."

Catastrophic Success

NITA'S EARS ROARED WITH her panic. All she could hear herself thinking was *Oh no, oh no, not this, not now! And is it my fault?*

The idea shook her. "The greatest challenge of your life," she'd said to him. *Why did I say that? Except somehow I knew it was true.* All this while she'd been treating the peridexic effect as if it was something cute, rather than what it was, the manual suddenly inside her head, making what she said truer than usual. And now she could hear her voice saying to Carmela, "Enjoy him while you can. He won't be here for long." *No, oh no, please don't let it be that I* made *this happen—*

Everything inside her started to go cold, and the coldness, a kind of distant, freezing calm, was exactly what was needed. Nita looked down at Ronan, lying there bleeding nothing but blood now, and he seemed as remote to her as something showing on TV while she was paying attention to something else in front of her. "Okay," she said. "I know what to do—"

Kit was looking at her with a shocked sort of expression: Nita assumed it had something to do with her voice, which even to her sounded like it belonged to somebody else. "What? A healing spell?"

Nita shook her head. "No time for that now," she said, glancing down at her manual; its pages stopped riffling. "We have to get back to Earth as fast as we can."

"But the Pullulus! If it's getting closer to Earth, wizardry might not be working right—"

"See if the manual tells you anything about that," Nita said. The page she'd wanted in her manual, containing the spell she'd prepared days earlier, lay there waiting in front of her. "But we have to take the chance. You heard the Hesper! We need to head back *now.*"

"But if you don't heal him—" Kit looked past Nita at her manual, peering down at the details of the spell.

She shook her head again, shoving the rowan wand back into her belt for the moment. "Stasis," she said. "After the little chat we had with Darryl, I thought I'd better have one ready."

"Send me a copy!" Kit said, flipping his manual open.

"Did that already," Nita said. She glanced around them. "Dair, Roshaun, Fil, when this is finished we need to transit back to the Crossings and home from there. A straight-in gating might derange this spell, especially if something *is* going wrong with wizardry back home."

"I will contact Sker'ret," Roshaun said, "and make sure they're ready for us."

"I will set up the transit spell," Filif said. "Will you need further assistance with that one?"

"Shouldn't," Nita said. "Kit?"

He nodded, and together they started to recite in the Speech. The old reassuring fade-out of sound started to set in around them as the words of the Speech seized on the fabric of the universe and started to bend it into a new shape, one that would absolutely freeze time for Ronan. It was a particularly "hard" stasis, its emphasis on completely stopping all activity in a living being, right down to the motions of electrons around their atoms' nuclei.

Okay, Nita thought to the peridexis. *If you've got extra power for me, let's have it.*

Nita's whole mind went up a flare of sheer power that rushed out through her and into the spell with tremendous force, scorching her as it passed. Now Nita started to understand why wizards were so rarely allowed to channel power of this intensity: The "power limit" was a safety valve. Do this often and it would scar the conduits of mind and spirit through which it flowed, leaving the wizard too sensitive to bear wizardry's flow. Even lesser wizardries, afterward, would feel as if your own blood was burning you. *Not my problem right now,* Nita thought. *Right now there's exactly one thing to concentrate on—*

The first long passage of the spell was done. Nita paused, taking a long breath as she got ready for the second passage. Even the simplest and most temporary stasis spell wouldn't operate until you correctly described the physical object it was meant to freeze, and this one was neither simple nor particularly temporary. The lockdown was always the worst part of the work. *But if I can't handle this now, I'll never be able to.*

She caught Kit's eye: He nodded. Ronan's name in the Speech was already laid into the spell. Nita looked across the burning pattern the spell made in her mind, expecting to see the reality of what was going on with Ronan, probably a swirl of pain and shock.

But there wasn't any pain, and the emotional context she sensed was very far indeed from shock. It was utterly serene. And off in the distance, getting more distant by the moment, Nita caught sight of a growing glow of light.

Oh, no, you don't! she shouted inwardly. *Not that way! You don't get to do that right now! Kit!*

I can't get at him! He won't listen, he's not—

Typical, Nita said, furious. *Ronan!*

She poured more power into the spell. *Don't let me down now,* she said silently to the peridexis. *Now's when I need it! Come on, let me have whatever you've got.*

The new access of power burst through her with terrific force, leaping away from her across the spell diagram and past her and Kit to the dwindling figure that stood silhouetted against the faraway light. Nita hung on, though the scorching at the back of her mind got worse and worse. *No—you—don't!*

The form walking away from them began to slow... and second by second, moved more slowly still. Nita closed her eyes and concentrated on being simply something for the power to pour through into the wizardry. Her brain felt like it was shaking itself apart, but Nita hung on, hung on. *Not—another—step! Not—another—*

In the distance, between one step and the next, Ronan froze.

Gasping, Nita opened her eyes again and looked at Kit across the spell diagram. He was still reading from his manual, finishing the last few phrases that would lock the stasis down. All around, the others were staring at her.

She looked around at them all. "What?"

Kit said the last couple of words of the spell, added the shorthand version of the words of the wizard's knot, and then slapped his manual shut and dropped it in front of him, next to Ronan's inert and unbreathing form. "You were kind of on fire there," Kit said.

Nita rubbed her eyes. "Tell me about it," she said. "I really need an aspirin."

"No, I mean on *fire* on fire," Kit said. "A lot of light..."

"I was?" She found it hard to care. At least the spell had worked.

"Yeah. And who else were you talking to?"

"Oh." She laughed. "My invisible friend."

Dairine looked horrified. "Oh, jeez, not Bobo!"

Nita laughed again. These days she couldn't remember the invisible friend she'd blamed for everything that went wrong around her when she was five or six, but her mom and dad had told her endless stories about "Bobo's" escapades. "Uh, no," she said. "Just wizardry."

Kit stared at her. "*Wizardry* talks?" he said. "Is this something new?"

Nita closed her manual and chucked it into her otherspace pocket. "Yeah," she said. "It took me by surprise, too." She looked down at Ronan. He wasn't breathing, but now that was normal. If he suddenly started breathing again, *that* would be a real sign of trouble. "Come on," she said, "we need to get back. This should hold for a few hours at least."

"Question is," Dairine said, "is that going to be enough?"

"Let's go find out."

Filif came gliding over to them with something held in his fronds. It was a drift of what looked like smoke, but it was shot through with glints of the dark green fire that characterized his wizardries. *This is a version of the mobility routine I use to get around on hard surfaces,* he said. *It will make Ronan a little more manageable until he's able to get around by himself.*

"Great," Nita said. Filif shook the cloud of smoke out like someone shaking a sheet out across a bed; the cloud thinned, drifted down over Ronan, and shrouded him like a see-through blanket. As soon as it had draped completely down over him, Ronan levitated gently up into the air to about Nita's waist.

"Handy," Kit said. He reached out and nudged Ronan's shoulder a little with one hand: He moved weightlessly through the air. "Okay, let's get him into the transit diagram."

The Yaldiv crowding around them made a little space for the wizards to pass over to where Roshaun had laid out their transit circle. As they made their way over to the diagram, one Yaldiv came up to them through the gathered crowd. To Nita's slight surprise, it was the Arch-votary. She could just barely see the old patterns on its outer shell, which had burned themselves pale in the overflow from the Hesper's transformation. "Friends of the Queen of Light," it said, "will you return?"

"If we can," Nita said. "There's a lot going on at home right now." It occurred to her then that there was something she wanted to do right away. She rooted around in her pockets until she found her cell phone. "But if we don't come back ourselves, we'll make sure somebody visits you when things quiet down."

Kit floated Ronan into the diagram. "Can he go vertical?" he said to Filif. "He takes up a lot of room in here."

"Certainly. I'll help."

While they were standing Ronan upright, Nita punched the "last dialed number" button on the phone, put it to her ear, and waited.

Nothing happened. She took the phone away from her ear and looked at it. Its dialing screen cleared and showed her a little message: DIALED PLANET UNAVAILABLE.

Nita's blood instantly ran cold. "*Planet* unavailable?!" Nita said. "What's *that* supposed to mean?"

She looked over at Kit, then at Dairine. Kit looked pale. Dairine's eyes were worried. "If it means that wizardry's failed completely back there—"

"I really, really hope that's all it means," Nita said.

"Unavailable?" Carmela mused, looking over Nita's shoulder at the phone. "I think you need to change your service provider."

"I think I prefer dealing with a monopoly," Nita muttered. She shoved the phone in her pocket, feeling herself starting to shake again. "You guys ready?"

"Ready now," Filif said.

To the Yaldiv surrounding them, Kit said, "Take care of yourselves, people, and go well. Meanwhile, stand clear—"

The Yaldiv crowded away. Nita took a last look around in that great dimness, which just a short time ago had been so bright. *Things looked really bad here, too,* she thought. *Just keep telling yourself that!*

They vanished....

The group came out into a Crossings that wasn't quite as frenetic as Nita had seen it last; and there seemed to be fewer Rirhait around...but she wasn't sure whether that was a good sign or not. The group got off the transit pad on which they'd arrived and looked around.

"Which way?" Kit said. "We should check with the Master before we head out."

"That won't take long," Nita said, and smiled just slightly. Away down the long shining corridor she saw a vividly purple shape pouring itself along toward them, followed by about thirty other Rirhait.

"You're back!" Sker'ret shouted at them, long before he got anywhere near them. The urgency of his manner was so much unlike Sker'ret's usual diffidence that Nita couldn't do anything but get down on one knee and grab him as he came up with them. Then she wheezed a little, because being hugged by someone with twenty or more pairs of legs can leave you a little short of air. "Oh, Mover without us and within," Sker'ret said, "I didn't know if we were going to see you again! I mean, 'when.' "

Nita just hugged him, then let him go. "We weren't real sure about that ourselves," Kit said, "so don't sweat it."

"The ceiling looks better," Carmela said, looking up.

"It's mostly back up where it belongs," Sker'ret said. "There's still some of it we need to regrow, but we've got other things to think about right now."

"Is wizardry working properly here?" Roshaun said.

"For the moment," Sker'ret said. "Though the manual functions went very strange there for a little while."

" 'Strange' has taken on many new meanings over the past sunround or so," Filif said, pushing his baseball cap around so that the front went frontways for a change. "We should be grateful that we've lived to see it do so. What about the Pullulus?"

"Its density in our neighborhood increased very noticeably a couple of hours ago," Sker'ret said. "Our star's not endangered yet, but the increase continues." He sounded nervous. "The odd thing is that Rirhath B seems to be affected much more severely than any system for hundreds of light-years around."

"Somebody's paying off a grudge," Kit said, "and it's going to take a lot of power to defuse it."

"So I thought," Sker'ret said. "All the wizards we have who're still functional are assembling to defend this facility and our star; and help is coming from the nearest inhabited systems where the Pullulus isn't any longer a threat. The local intervention force is assembling on one of our outer satellites, to distract attention away from the Crossings proper—because we're going to be using that to evacuate the planet."

Nita swallowed hard, wishing there was a way to do something similar for Earth. *And you will know it was all your fault,* said that cruel voice in the back of her mind. "Okay," she said. "We'll clear out of here and let you get on with it."

"I checked your local news not long ago," Sker'ret said. "Your world's wizards are doing something similar—those who're still viable. Not many, the manual says."

"Thanks," Nita said. "At least our planet's still there. We'll get going. But Sker', are you sure you're all right here? What about your ancestor?"

His eyes wreathed in barely concealed distress. "Still missing. There are many places yet to search. As for the rest of it, I'm not sure any of us are going to qualify for 'all right' any time soon. But we've all just got to cope."

"What is the status of the Pullulus beyond your local area?" Roshaun said.

"Its expansion has either slowed or stopped completely in most places," Sker'ret said. "Whatever you did seems to have worked."

"Believe me, it wasn't anything *we* did," Dairine said. "Or not directly."

Sker'ret pointed a couple of skeptical eyes at her. "I wouldn't be too sure," he said. "Never underestimate how connected things are: 'All is done for each.' But I suspect we've all got better things to do than start tallying up our scores just yet." He looked past Nita and Kit to where Ronan hung in the cloud of Filif's levitation field. "So come on over to this gate cluster and I'll reprogram as many as you need. Roshaun, Filif, what are your plans?"

"I think I should return home," Filif said. "My people have few enough wizards that they will need all the ones they have. The Pullulus is holding steady there, but there's no telling whether it might not soon increase."

Roshaun was once more holding in one hand the fierce little core of light that was his manual. He looked up from it with a slightly relieved expression. "So far," he said, "nothing untoward seems to be going on in or near Wellakh's system. In fact, the Pullulus seems to be receding." He looked over at Dairine. "I will therefore return with you and have a look at your star before making my way home, just to be sure the repairs we did are holding."

Dairine looked at Roshaun and opened her mouth

as if about to say something, then closed it again and nodded. Nita found this weird enough that she would have liked to get a closer look at her sister, but Dairine had turned away to put Spot down.

She let out a long breath and turned to Filif. "Fil," she said, and hugged him. His fronds tickled her back. "When you know that everything's safe at home, come on back and let us know. My dad likes having you in the garden."

"When I know," Filif said. He was as uncertain of the near future as Nita was, but he wasn't going to show it. He paused to look at Ronan. "Take care of him," Filif said. "He stood strong: He does not deserve to fall."

"We'll do what we can," Nita said.

The others crowded in close to say their good-byes. Finally Filif stood away from them. "Cousins," he said, "you're needed at home...and so am I. Till the journey brings us together again, *dai stihó!*"

"*Dai,*" they all said, and Filif made his way to the gate that Sker'ret had programmed for him. He glided out onto the pad, all his berries alight, and a second later he flicked out of view.

Nita let out a breath. *Will we see him again?* she wondered. *And more to the point...will he see us again?*

"There's one main area of activity on your world's satellite right now," Sker'ret said. "Should I drop you there?"

Kit stepped over to the console pad at which Sker'ret was working and looked over his top few sets of shoulders at the coordinates. "We know the spot," he said, and glanced over at Nita. "Let's go." He put an arm around Sker'ret, grabbed a fistful of eyes and wobbled them around a little. "Sker'—"

"Cousin," Sker'ret said. He looked up at the others. "Go do what needs to be done for your own world. One way or another, we'll meet again."

They all headed onto the same pad from which Filif had departed, and Roshaun and Dairine guided Ronan along behind them. At the control pad, looking very uncertain, very alone, even while surrounded by all his people, Sker'ret raised a single foreleg to them.

One way or another, Nita thought as she looked at him. He hit a control on his console. *Which doesn't necessarily mean while we're still alive.*

The Crossings disappeared from view.

There is no "dark side" of the Moon. In the course of its monthlong day, all of it eventually sees the Sun. But on the side of the Moon that the Earth never sees, just a shade below the spot where the lunar equator and its central meridian cross, there is a crater called Daedalus; and many of Earth's wizards know it well.

Almost dead center in the far side, the three-kilometer-high rim of the crater rises into the black and starry night. Normally Daedalus is where a moon-walker goes when he or she needs peace and quiet for some reason—in this case, "quiet" meaning complete isolation from the radio noise that Earth spills out into space. It's not a big crater—barely sixty miles wide.

Its floor is surprisingly flat and smooth for any feature on the far side of the Moon. But in the crater's broad center stand three small mounds, each about three miles wide, arranged in a triangle pointing southeast. At the top of the southernmost mound is a tiny crater, barely a half mile wide. There are many names for it, but most wizards call it the "Dimple."

Nita and Kit and the others came out just above where the smaller bowl of the Dimple dropped away before them, and paused, looking around. It was dark, the Sun well down behind the western horizon, and Earth, of course, was nowhere to be seen. Nita did a moment's calculation in her head. The Moon had just gone new when they'd left. Now, as seen from the Earth, it would be just past first quarter. *In "real time," we've been gone ten days, almost eleven—*

Just the thought started to make her feel shaky again, but she had no time for that right now. The Dimple below them was absolutely crammed full of wizards, faintly illuminated by hundreds of sparks or globes of wizard-light. Behind Nita, Roshaun and Dairine and Spot made their own lights, while Carmela looked around her in astonishment.

"Don't go more than six feet from us," Kit said to her, as Ponch went running and half bouncing off down the slope, scattering gray-white dust in all directions. "That's where our air stops."

"Doesn't seem to be stopping *him*," Carmela said.

"Ponch plays by his own rules," Kit said, looking down into the crater as Nita did. "So unless you can create your own universes, either stay close or get vacuum-dried."

"Kit, it's not a problem," Dairine said. "Look…"

He glanced up as Nita did. Over the entire crater a faint dome of wizardry was shivering. "Somebody down there roofed the whole thing over with an auto-maintaining life-support wizardry," Dairine said. "We can let the personal shields go as soon as we pass the boundary. Probably somebody didn't care to have to sweat the small stuff while there were bigger things to be doing."

"Makes sense," Kit said. "Come on."

They all stepped through the brief shiver of the spell's outer boundary and onto the downward slope of the crater. "Big crowd," Kit said. But the look on Kit's face reflected the worry that Nita was feeling. He'd noticed that though there might be hundreds and hundreds of wizards down there, there wasn't even one who looked adult.

"They've *all* lost it, haven't they?" Kit said. "Every single one."

Nita nodded, her mouth feeling dry again. It got drier when she looked up. Out in space, where there should have been nothing but a vast expanse of bright, unblinking stars, there was a huge blot of darkness, as if someone had spilled ink. At the edges of that huge, irregular patch, the stars twinkled and went faint.

Nita shivered all over. She had seen this in dreams, fleetingly, even before they got back from their trip to Alaalu—this darkness gradually and inexorably drawing across the stars. *I was hoping it was just a nightmare,* she thought. *I should have known better.* "So there's still nobody to deal with this but us," she said. "Question is, who's in charge?"

Kit shook his head. "Not sure it's the right question to be asking," he said. "But let's get on down there and see."

However, someone had seen them appear at the crater's rim and was already heading up toward them. Nita looked down, seeing the little blue cropped top and the cargo pants, and that long, long dark hair that she'd admired so much, and immediately recognized Tran Hung Nguyet as she bounced upslope.

"*You* guys!" Nguyet said, shaking her head in astonishment as she came up to them. "You dropped right out of the manuals for a long time. We thought we'd lost you."

"Were you waiting for us?" Nita said.

Nguyet shook her head. "A little too busy for that," she said. "But I felt the power pop out all of a sudden." She glanced over at Dairine, who was putting Spot down so that he could put his legs out and make his own way. "Is it him? He feels a lot different before. Which is good, because we need all the power we can get right now." She looked up at Ronan, hanging there in stasis. "What happened to *him*?"

"The Spear of Light," Kit said.

Nguyet looked stunned. "And he's still *here*?"

"I think he got some kind of special dispensation," Dairine said.

"Boy, he must have," Nguyet said. "Come on, we can use you. Almost all of us are back in-system

now—the ones who were away hunting a solution for
the Pullulus as a whole got word through the manuals
that its power supply had been 'withdrawn.' Then all of
a sudden that changed to 'abrogated.'" She gave them a
look that was peculiarly admiring. "You got lucky
again, didn't you?" Nguyet said.

"I don't know if 'lucky' is how I'd put it," Nita
muttered.

"Well, that's how my brother keeps putting it," said
Nguyet. "You should take it up with him, because he
keeps going on about how your part of the world is ruining everybody's statistical averages. Though just
what Mister Number Cruncher means by that, I have
no idea. If we all live through this, maybe one of you
can stay awake long enough for him to explain what
he's talking about." She rolled her eyes. "Better bring
some caffeine, or a stay-awake spell."

Dairine looked bemused. "*What* statistical averages?"

Nguyet shook her head. "This would *not* be my department," she said. "You want to know about skate-
boarding or weather wizardries, I'll tell you everything
you want to know. Math is Tuyet's problem. Meanwhile, let's get down there."

They all headed downslope together. "Where *is*
Tuyet?" Nita said.

"He's down there helping coordinate the group,"
said Nguyet. "There are maybe three thousand of us."
She shook her head. "Not as many as I wish we had . . .
mostly human, and a few of the heavy hitters from the
Affiliate species. Anyone Senior who's still functioning, and everybody else with any special skills, is down

on Earth. They're all busy keeping things from blowing up. Literally."

It was surprising how grim such a delicately pretty face could look, and Nita felt increasingly uneasy as they made their way down to the fringes of the huge crowd. Wizards of every height and shape and color were there, and of every age between eight or nine and maybe sixteen. There were several dolphins and small whales hanging in force-field–confined water jackets, and a few cats scattered about. Though it all looked disorganized, Nita could see a lot of the most central group standing around the huge spell diagram in the middle of the crater. Its characters and arcs were rippling with the subdued fire of a wizardry on "hold," completely implemented except for the starting command and the attachment of power sources.

Dairine and Roshaun and Carmela took a moment to guide Ronan off to one side of the crowd and put him carefully down. Then they made their way back to where Nita and Kit and Nguyet were examining the spell. "Complicated," Dairine said as they came up to the edge of the spell and everyone could get a good look at it. "A repulsor?"

"That's right," Nguyet said, as Tuyet came bouncing along to join them. "Seemed like the smartest thing to do was to concentrate on pushing the Pullulus as far out into space as we could. Increasing its distance minimizes its effects, and we may be able to buy ourselves enough time for it to lose power and die off, the way it's doing a lot of other places."

Nita wasn't sure how effective this was going to be,

bearing in mind what the Lone One had said to them before the Hesper had embodied. "You try anything a little more proactive?" Kit said.

Nguyet looked frustrated. "Are you kidding? Three or four times. We tried a couple of long-range transports, but you might as well try bailing a leaky boat with a sieve. More of the Pullulus just flowed right back into the same space. Then we tried just frying it, a wholesale denaturing of the dark matter out to about the orbit of Mars—"

Tuyet shook his head. "We didn't have anything like enough power. Leave even a grain of that stuff and it starts regenerating itself. And the kids who tried to channel that much power are just one big mental bruise. Seems like even though the Powers That Be can hand us nearly infinite power, the very biggest spells still have to be handled in groups to keep people from burning themselves out. They can change the rules, I guess, but not the way our brains work."

"Listen," Nita said, "do you have anybody else down here who's sensing the peridexis directly?"

Nguyet looked at her. "The what?"

"Oh, great," Nita said. "I guess it's just me, then."

"If I had the slightest idea what you were talking about, I'd be happier," Tuyet said. "Anyway, check the manual and see if anybody else here has what you need. Then find a place to plug your name in so you can feed the spell power, because we have to get it running. The main body of the Pullulus is already just outside Mars's orbit, and we really don't want to let it get any closer. The mass of it is already starting to screw up the Sun."

Nita glanced back at Roshaun. He had been standing and gazing, not at the spell, but at the ground. Now he looked up and nodded. "I thought that was what I was feeling when I arrived," he said. "You are right, and the effect is increasing every moment."

"That's right," Nguyet said, "you're one of the team who settled it down before when it started to act up. Can you do anything about it now?"

"I can try," Roshaun said.

"*We* can try," Dairine said, somewhat more forcefully than usual.

"Great," Nguyet said.

"Okay, pay up," said a voice from behind her.

Nguyet turned. "What?"

Darryl McAllister was standing behind her, with something folded and glowing in his hands. "You owe me a quarter," he said.

"I owe you a smack in the head," Nguyet said, "if you start bothering me with small stuff right now!" Nonetheless, she fished around in her pocket and handed Darryl a coin.

He stared at it. "What's this?"

"That's a whole two hundred dong, and right now you should count yourself lucky that our money doesn't come any smaller. Now tell me you've got the appendix for that spell ready!"

"Had it five minutes ago," Darryl said, flashing Kit the briefest grin. He opened the WizPod he was carrying, pushed it into Nguyet's hands, and turned to the others. "I had a feeling you'd be back around now."

"Should you be making *money* off that kind of thing?" Kit said.

"It wasn't a Feeling," Darryl said. "Just a feeling." He glanced at Ronan and bit his lip. "Sometimes I don't like being right, though."

"It's okay," Nita said. "It could have been a lot worse... and what you told us helped. How're you doing?"

"They're keeping me busy," Darryl said. "I'm not as good as some people at writing new spells from scratch, but I'm getting good at taking them apart and putting them back together in new ways if they're not working."

"Troubleshooting," Kit said as they moonwalked around the spell, carefully avoiding stepping or bouncing on the many other kids who were kneeling around the rim of the diagram and adding, or checking, their names in the Speech.

"Yeah. And this one's needed it, because we've been artificially increasing the spell's output."

Nita had already noticed the two large circles enclosed within the main one, each smaller circle bumped up against the outside of the diagram. "Nguyet goes in one," she said. "Tuyet goes in the other. And then they take the power that everybody else puts into the pool, and bounce it back and forth."

"You got it. Took us a few times to get it right when someone came up with the idea."

"'Someone'?" Kit said, looking at Darryl with good-natured skepticism.

"Oh, okay, it was me," Darryl said.

"I'm beginning to think you were worth the trouble," Kit said, sounding impressed.

"It's the way a laser works," Nita said. "But with all these separate power sources, it must get complicated."

"It did," Darryl said. "It does. Which is why I gotta go give them a hand with the final setup."

"Got any 'feelings'?" Kit said.

Darryl looked at him, and that small sharp face that was almost always smiling now lost its smile. He shook his head. "We're on our own," he said. "Later."

"*Dai,*" Kit said. Darryl headed off.

The wizards milling around the edges of the spell were now moving in closer to it. Kit knelt down and tucked his name into one of the open receptor sites; Nita did the same. Across the diagram, she saw small, trim Tuyet in his long jacket stepping into the diagram and carefully picking his way among the various statements and routines to stand in the farther of the two inner circles. Just in front of them, Nguyet was making for the other circle as Nita straightened up. "Nguyet," she said, "aren't there some other pairs of twins up here? You could increase the power feed to this even more—"

"Won't work," Nguyet said. "We've got three pairs of identical twins, but if identicals try to bounce a spell back and forth between them, it just cancels out. Only two-egg twins are far enough out of phase to keep the spell from canceling *and* close enough to make it augment. You ready?"

Nita nodded, and Nguyet headed off for her circle. Nita glanced down to her left along the outer arc, past

Kit, and saw Dairine and Roshaun kneeling about a hundred yards down, with Spot crouching just outside the circle, between them. A movement behind her caught her attention, and Nita looked over her shoulder to see Carmela sitting down cross-legged a little ways behind them. "I'll sit this one out," she said, looking out across the spell diagram with an intrigued expression.

Kit glanced at Nita with a resigned look. *Take my advice,* Nita said silently. *If any of us walk away from this…at your earliest convenience, get her another curling iron!*

He smiled slightly. *Yeah. And, Neets—if we don't walk away from this—*

Normally she would have said something reassuring right away. But she was desperately tired, and very nervous…and the darkness above them continued to grow. *There's always Timeheart,* she said.

Yeah.

Kit turned to look at Ponch, who was now sitting beside him, looking out alertly over the spell. *Big guy,* he said silently, *you need to promise me something.*

Okay!

If something bad happens to us, you need to get Carmela out of here.

Sure. And you, too—

I don't know about that, Kit said. *But make sure you get Carmela out, hear me? Take her home, and then get Mama and Pop, and Nita's dad, and take them away from Earth. Take them somewhere safe.*

Ponch blinked. *But why?*

*Look, explaining's going to take too long. Just prom-
ise me!*

Ponch started to look upset. Nita blinked hard at the
distress in his face and in his thought. *All right, but—*

"Okay," Nguyet said to all the wizards gathered
around the circle. She didn't need to raise her voice:
Anyone whose name was written into that spell could
hear her as clearly as if she were standing next to them.
"Let's do this just like the last time, but let's have this
one work. Start with the knot, end with the knot . . .
now!"

All the voices beginning to recite the spell—either
from the manual in front of each wizard's eyes or from
the larger diagram in front of them—made a silence
that swiftly drowned out all the lesser sounds associated with so big a group. All the many voices started to
sound like one gigantic one, and the universe leaned in
to listen, not once but a thousand times, three thousand
times, and more. Nita read along with everybody else as
far as she needed to, but her attention was on the line of
light that ran from where she'd put her hands down on
either side of her manual, out into the spell itself. Next
to her, she could see the light of donated energy running into the spell from Kit. Responding to the growing silence, Nita could feel the peridexis moving at the
back of her mind, growing, pouring energy out into
her for her use, and ready to give as much as she asked
of it. *But remember, if you ask it for too much, it'll give
you too much, and you'll burn yourself to a crisp . . .*

Nita watched Nguyet over at her side of the circle,
and Tuyet at the other. Both of them stood still as

statues, their hands held out toward each other. There was no other physical sign of what was going on with them, but Nita could feel the power that she and all the other wizards were pouring into the spell as they spoke, and could feel each half of the twychild taking that power, sending it along to the other one, standing briefly empty to receive what the other sent; then sending it back again, and again.

The power grew. The wizards finished speaking the spell, which was, after all, a fairly simple thing, describing how one wanted something to be farther away. Three thousand voices and minds, or more, said the last words of the wizard's knot together, and fell silent. But between those two out in the middle of the spell diagram, the power kept going back and forth. Nguyet's and Tuyet's outlines began to shimmer as if Nita were seeing them through a haze of heat. The sense of something actively dangerous going on started to build inside Nita, so that she very much wanted to get up and back away. But there was nowhere to back away to, and, anyway, everybody else, no matter how alarmed they looked, was holding very still. She shot a glance at Kit, who was sitting there with his fists clenched, tense but unmoving. Behind him, Ponch had begun to whimper softly.

Back and forth between the twychild the power went, back and forth. Between Nguyet and Tuyet, the air had begun to burst out in small sparks of power, wizardly energy looking for somewhere to discharge itself but not finding any way to escape. The power trapped in the air inside the spell-circle built and built, until Nita's hair started to stand on end and her skin prickled with it. *They can't possibly hold it in anymore!* she thought. *It's going to blow! They can't possibly—*

Inside the circle, the reflected and re-reflected power just kept building and building; the sparkles and flares of its attempted discharge got brighter and brighter, spreading away from the corridor between the twychild and right through the circle, beating right up against the boundaries of it like waves against a storm wall. The power climbed the invisible walls, held in by them and raving against them; it arched up and over until it completely filled the spell's dome. Inside the dome, the fog of concentrated, concentrating power thickened, the discharge flashes filling every cubic foot of air until Tuyet and Nguyet couldn't be seen at all. Whether she could see them or not, Nita concentrated on not even twitching, not doing anything that might distract the wizards inside the circle.

And then the spell boundary directly above them vanished.

Everything inside the dome went furiously, blindingly white. Nothing could have prepared Nita for the huge flare of wizardly fire that poured up and out of Daedalus crater, up and out into space, and fled, faster than any normal light, out past Earth's orbit—three thousand wizards' worth of wizardry, multiplied who knew how many times. Nita sensed rather than saw the wave front of the wizardry spilling out across local space like the expanding surface of a blown bubble, speeding away, spreading, pushing before it everything it met. A storm of the micrometeorites that followed

Earth around in its orbit vaporized as it impacted them; the ions themselves glowed and sheeted across the surface of the outward-speeding sphere like flattened-out auroras.

Nita tried to rub some sight back into her eyes, craning her neck upward. The spell went blasting outward, a rainbow bubble half the width of the sky, growing fainter as it went but not getting any less strong; it was accelerating as it got closer to the Pullulus. All around her, the other wizards were looking up, watching the spell get closer and closer to its target. A murmur of excitement started to go up among them as some of them started to feel what Nita did—a strange roiling out in the darkness, a sense of something that was darkly alive reacting with fear to something threatening that was coming at it faster and faster.

Nita looked out across the spell diagram, saw Nguyet and Tuyet standing there in their circles, shaking with effort, but watching what was happening with all the others. Out in the darkness, something was furious, something was frightened. *Come on,* Nita thought, *come on!*

She held her breath. There was a long, long pause, and then the outflung boundary of the wizardry flared as it struck the substance it had been intended for. Everyone who had been connected to that wizardry felt the resistance of that target in their bones. But the wizardry kept going. The light of it flared in all their minds as it hit the Pullulus, pushed it outward, farther outward. A second later, the wizards started to cheer—

—and the wave front flared out, vanishing.

Nita stared up, unbelieving. *No!*

The Pullulus was still there. That darkness swallowed the last of the rainbow, snuffed it out, absorbed all the power that had been poured into it...

...and plunged inward through the orbit of Mars, faster than light, faster than darkness, heading for the Earth.

Beside Nita, Kit looked up at the rapidly darkening sky in complete shock.

Ponch put his head under Kit's arm. *Was that it?* he said. *Can we go home now?*

Nita was hiding her face in her hands. Out in the spell diagram, Tuyet and Nguyet collapsed. Along with numerous others, Kit scrambled to his feet and ran across the diagram, heading for Tuyet. Ponch galloped after them. Darryl was one of those who wound up closest to Kit and who got to Tuyet first. Kit slipped an arm under his head, and Darryl boosted him from behind. It was shocking how light Tuyet felt, almost as if the power he and his sister had been channeling had burned him out from inside.

"Tuyet!" Darryl said. "Come on, guy."

"What about Ngu—," Tuyet said weakly.

Kit glanced over his shoulder. Others were helping Nguyet. "I think she's okay," he said.

"No, she's not," Tuyet said. "I can feel it. Burned. Burned out."

Kit shook his head. "It didn't work," he breathed. "With all that power, *how could it not work?*"

"It did work," Tuyet said, hardly above a whisper.

"It just wasn't enough." He sounded desperately tired. "Look," he said. "It's coming back."

Kit absolutely didn't want to look. He could feel perfectly well what was happening. He looked at Darryl. "Now what?" he said.

"Now, *this*," said a voice from the side of the circle. "And perhaps this will be enough."

Everybody looked over that way. Roshaun had stood up from beside Dairine and Spot. There he stood in that long, floppy T-shirt, his expression grim but not desperate. Around his neck, in the collar he had worn ever since coming back from Wellakh with Dairine, that great orange-amber stone burned like fire. As they watched, he slipped the collar off and held it in his hands.

Dairine got up, looking at him warily. "What're you thinking of?" she said, sounding slightly panic-stricken.

"It is what I did earlier," Roshaun said, "to fill in the cavern floor back on Rashah. But here there is no need to be so restrained."

"Are you *nuts*?" Dairine said. "Restraint is the *only* way to treat that spell! Moving little amounts of matter around is one thing, but you can't just pull out the kind of energy you'd need to deal with *that* and—"

"I have done it before," Roshaun said. "Not with a strange star, granted. But yours is no longer so strange. Also, this is your world's best chance now. If time is all we need to buy—"

"You're not doing it alone!" Dairine said.

His look got wry. "It had not occurred to me that

I'd be able to stop you," Roshaun said. "And perhaps Spot will also participate."

"Naturally," Spot said.

Kit threw a look back at Nita as he pulled off his jacket. *What are they up to now?* he said.

Nita shook her head.

Kit folded the jacket up and tucked it under Tuyet's head. Roshaun had stepped a little distance away from the spell diagram, and now was simply standing and looking down at that huge gem in his hands. A moment later he straightened up, settled the collar about his neck again, and began to speak quietly in the Speech. Dairine stood up a few feet away from him with her arms folded, her eyes half closed, as if trying to remember something; crouching on the dusty ground between the two of them, Spot put up a number of eyes, enough to watch them both at once, and held very still.

The silence of a listening universe came down on all the wizards near them. Kit watched, but for a long while nothing seemed to happen; Roshaun and Dairine spoke in unison, more and more quietly, as if they didn't need to hear each other speaking out loud. And, slowly, Roshaun began to stand out from his surroundings.

At least that was the way it looked at first. For the first minute or so, Roshaun simply looked more definite than the other wizards around him. But then it became plain that there was more light about him than what fell on him from the various wizard-lights hovering about. Then the glow became more obvious. The effect was strange, for it wasn't as if Roshaun himself was glowing; rather, he was merely the vessel for something else inside him that was the true source of the increasing light.

The light strengthened, slowly gaining a dangerous quality. Roshaun was less a vessel, now, than a crucible, resisting the power inside him, glowing as a result of that resistance. Kit found himself remembering the way the Champion had looked back on Rashah, like a statue of molten metal. This, though, was different, scarier, for at all times the Champion had seemed to be in control of what was going on. Looking at Roshaun, Kit got a clear sense of Roshaun's struggle with the terrible force inside him, something he was holding in check only with the greatest difficulty. That force was ready every moment to burst free, but Roshaun was spending all his energy to contain it until the moment was right. Behind him, Dairine was beginning to burn with some of that same fire, less violently, but also with a look of less concentration. Her attention was all on Roshaun now; Kit could tell it was, even though Dairine's eyes were squeezed tightly shut.

Very slowly, like someone afraid to lose his balance, Roshaun lifted his arms. All that hair of his was beginning to stir around him now, as if in a growing wind. His eyes were closed, too, and a look of utter concentration had taken possession of his face. He brought his arms around in front of him, put the hands together, and within them materialized the little globe of burning light that was the way he communicated with the Aethyrs; but for once it was the least bright thing about him, dim by comparison with the fire that burned in him.

Roshaun and Dairine both looked up at the sky. At the same moment, Spot's eyes all turned upward.

The little spark of Roshaun's manual-globe went out, and light burst upward from him.

It was like being hit in the face. Kit had to turn his head. The whole lunar landscape was lit as if by the light of day. But it *was* the light of day, the Sun's own light, borrowed, channeled, concentrated, and aimed like a spear at the inward-pressing tool of their enemy. That fire burned upward and outward and struck straight through the Pullulus.

It screamed. Where that beam struck, the Pullulus vanished utterly. Elsewhere, on either side of it, the darkness shrank away and left clean space and starlight showing. The beam moved slowly through the bulk of the Pullulus, shocking it backward and away, cutting through it like a knife.

But it's not wide enough, Kit thought, desperate. *This isn't going to do it, either. It needs—*

It was almost as if Roshaun had heard him thinking. Above them, the beam broadened out. Roshaun's expression and stance didn't alter in the slightest, but Kit could feel the strain on him increase. Dairine was perfectly still, but she was sharing more vividly now in that inward burning, and down on the ground, even Spot was beginning to glow from inside. The beam broadened. The silent screaming of the Pullulus got louder.

Roshaun's eyes opened wide. It was a look of complete surprise and, a second later, of regret, for something that should have worked, really should have—

Roshaun!

The cry was soundless. One moment he was standing there, a statue of burning gold. The next moment, the statue was a searing white, and the moment after that, there was no statue at all: just something falling through one-sixth gravity to bounce into the dust—a collar of yellow metal with a great colorless stone in it, as clear as glass.

The fire was all gone out of Dairine now. Spot's eyes had vanished; he lay as flat against the ground as if he wished he could bury himself in it. Dairine slumped to her knees. "Where is he?" she was whispering as she looked all around her, desperate. "What happened to him? *Where is he?*"

And the Pullulus began crawling back into the space that had been carved free of it, once more flowing toward the Moon.

Beside Kit, Ponch let out a single cry that wasn't so much a bark as a yelp of pain. He ran over to where Roshaun had been standing, and started frantically sniffing around the spot. He ran back to Kit, a horrified look in his eyes. *Where did he go?* Ponch barked. *What happened to him?*

Kit shook his head; his eyes were stinging. "I don't know," he said softly. The one thing he was sure of was that he couldn't bear to look at Dairine right now, the moment after she had picked up the fallen collar.

He turned and exchanged a glance with Nita. Then he dropped to his knees beside Ponch.

"You know you're the best, right?"

Yes, Ponch said, but he sounded dreadfully uncertain and frightened.

"Good," Kit said. He roughed the dog's ears up. "So now you have to go do what you promised."

I'm not going anywhere without you!

"Yes, you are. You have to take Carmela, and—"

No!

"You promised," Kit said fiercely. "Ponch, I'm a wizard. I promised I'd take care of the world, and that's what I have to do now. You promised me that you'd take care of Mama and Pop and Carmela, and Nita's dad—"

But I can't! Ronan couldn't, and then Tuyet couldn't, and now Roshaun couldn't, and if I go, you could— You'll—

"Ponch!" Kit said. He felt close to tears, but he didn't dare show it. "*This is what we have to do! Now go on.*"

He threw his arms around the dog. *One last hug,* he thought. *They have to let dogs into Timeheart, they have to.*

But what about you? What about Nita?! And what about Tom and Carl and—

"Ponch!" Kit cried. "Just *go!*"

Ponch stood and looked at Kit. He hung his head, and his tail drooped. Utterly dejected, he turned away. He started to vanish.

And then he stopped. Half there, half not, and wholly torn, Ponch sat down in the dust of the Moon and threw his head up and howled for sheer grief and pain.

The tears ran down Kit's face. *This is what it's like when your heart breaks,* he thought. *Good thing I won't have to feel it for long.* He looked up and saw the

Pullulus closing in tighter on the clean space that Roshaun had carved out. But then he heard something that distracted him.

It was still more howling.

At first it seemed a very long way away, but then the sound came to Kit more immediately. He realized that he was hearing it as Ponch did. Other dogs were howling. Kit stared all around, but there was no one there but all his fellow wizards, and the spell diagram—now burning low from lack of power—and Ponch, his howling briefly diminishing into a terrible moan of pain as he got up again, anguished, to do as Kit had told him. Desperately, Kit looked up into the sky and saw nothing but darkness, and a single pathway of seemingly lighter sky cutting through it—the dark of space with the stars still burning in it, while everywhere else, the Pullulus pressed in all around. Ponch looked up at that path and howled one last time, and it seemed to Kit as if somewhere beyond him, the voices of hundreds of dogs, thousands of dogs, hundreds of thousands, could be heard howling with him. *Or through him?* Kit thought. It was impossible to tell. The cacophony was unbearable: It drove all thought out of the mind that listened to it. All around them, kids were holding their ears, bending over double, trying to maintain some kind of control. *The air,* Kit thought. *The life-support—the spell won't hold for much longer; wizardry's starting to fail—*

Yet in this moment of utter terror, somehow the spell started to seem less important. For above them, the inward-pressing darkness of the Pullulus seemed to be taking form. Shivering, Kit blinked and rubbed his own eyes, certain they were fooling him. How could there be any blackness darker than what the Pullulus had already become? But there was such a blackness, and it took the form of eyes, burning in that darkness, embodying it. Kit started to think he heard something growling softly to itself in pleasure.

Did you hear that? he said silently to Nita.

There was no answer at first. Kit looked around for Nita and saw that she'd gone to Dairine, and was now kneeling down beside her, her arms around her little sister, while Dairine just knelt there looking dazed.

A little noisy, Nita said after a moment, wiping her eyes. *But is it just me, or is all this looking sort of strange to you?*

Kit glanced around him. There was more light here than there should have been, with the Sun completely blocked away from them, and the terrible potency of Roshaun's sunbeam gone along with him. The Moon had begun to look a lot less moonlike, almost more like a stage; it was as if something invisible was illuminating it from above. The howling was beginning to die away. Even Ponch had stopped now, and was staring up into the darkness, up into those eyes.

Very quietly, he began to growl.

"Kit?"

It was Carmela's voice, sounding thoroughly confused. He turned to see her looking at something off to one side. "What?" Kit said.

"Do you know any pigs?"

He stared at her. *"What?"*

"Over there," Carmela said.

Kit looked where she was pointing. Only a few feet away from them both, apparently unnoticed by many of the upward-gazing wizards, stood a large white pig that looked back at Kit with an interested expression, flicking one large pink ear.

Kit made his way over to that silvery-bristled shape and looked down at it in something like outrage. "What are *you* doing here?" he said.

"You forgot to ask about the meaning of life," said the Transcendent Pig. "That has to be a first."

"Yeah, well, it can wait, because there's other business," Kit said. He looked away from the Pig, back toward Ponch.

But Ponch was not there. In his place was a huge dog-shaped shadow that towered above them. It was looking up into that blank black darkness, its eyes trained on the darker eyes that stared down at them in fury from above. And it was growling, too.

Ponch? Kit thought.

The shadow-shape above him made no response. Stiff-legged, it took a step forward, its hackles bristling. That one step took it right past the edge of the Dimple. Its second step took it right over the edge of Daedalus, over that three-kilometer-high rim. The third step took it out into the roiling dark, and straight off the edge of the Moon.

The Transcendent Pig stood there beside Kit, regarding the two dark shapes that now stood in the depths of translunar space, eyeing each other through the endless night. "And why the surprise?" the Pig said. "You didn't think I kept turning up before just to see you and Nita, did you? I mean, not that it wasn't a pleasure; it's always nice to meet new people. But, as you say, there's other business."

And it gazed up at Ponch.

Above them all, the darkness grew and took shape as the Pullulus pressed inward. All around them, it beat against the orbit of the Moon as if against a seawall, and though for the moment it flowed no farther, Kit could feel that, at any moment, it might. Still, though, that pierced-through lane of normal space and starlight above them persisted ... and suddenly Kit realized what he was seeing. The memory of voices back in the cavern on Rashah descended on him, so that he might almost have been lying in the pup tent again; and a voice said, *No power more will come to you, and no new life, until you once more see before you the path you refused, and set out to walk it alone.*

This is my place, Ponch said to the darkness. *Go away!*

Make me, the Darkness said.

I will, Ponch said. *We said we would take care of them.*

You can't, said the being that was now wearing the Pullulus, in the shape of something huge and wolfish, with fangs as dark and deadly as its eyes. *And they can't save themselves, or you. You all get to die today.*

I have driven our Enemy out of time for just a little while, Memeki had said.

Kit swallowed. *I guess our time just ran out.*

You're just one more dog, the Darkness said. *You have no power against me, and your threats mean nothing.*

Ponch's gigantic shape merely stood there, growling softly in his throat.

I will always be here, no matter what you do, the Darkness said. *I will come for every one of your kind, sooner or later. That's the way this universe is.*

I think, Ponch said, *that I have had enough of you telling me how things will be.*

If you had, you'd be doing something about it. But you can't. I own this place, whatever you may think. And as I will come for all your people in time... I will come for all of his kind as well. And for him!

The growling stopped.

You came for Ronan, Ponch said very softly. *You came for Memeki. You came for Roshaun. But if you think you're coming for* him *today, think again. Today I choose a new way to go—and it goes through you!*

And Ponch threw himself at the throat of the Darkness beyond the Moon.

It was a "dogfight" in the same way that the meteor that killed the dinosaurs was an "impact." The stars shook and the Moon quaked with the tumult and the furor of it, and there was no telling how long it went on. The terrible growls and snarls of the Darkness were matched in their awfulness, and in a strange kind of splendor, by the righteous rage of the giant doglike shape with the starlight caught in its coat. Stunned, staggered, many of the watching wizards fell to their knees as the great battle slowly began to turn; others just stood gazing outward into that turbulent night, trying to assimilate what they were seeing. Kit, though, knew—for he'd heard the story beforehand. He watched as what had been foretold came to pass—the Hound taking His old enemy by the throat and throwing him down, yelping, against the floor of heaven.

The Wolf that ate the Moon slowly stood up from that downfall, still growling. There, in the darkness with which it had surrounded itself, It slunk a few steps away, head down, tail between Its legs, growling more softly... and then tried to dodge around and do Its Enemy one final harm. All at once, the Pullulus flowed past the Moon, heading for the Earth and past it, toward the Sun, trying to envelop them both—

The Hound opened His jaws and leaped at His enemy one last time.

The flare of power that had burst up from the group wizardry before was as nothing to this. All space went white as lightning in the flash of the terrible teeth. Kit closed his eyes and still could see nothing but that intolerable whiteness. In it, everything vanished. There was nothing to be felt or experienced but pure power and the eternity in which it was happening. In the face of that irresistible brilliance, the Pullulus burned away like so much ash.

In the white timelessness, Kit stood for some while, as blind as any other wizard on the Moon. But presently he was able to see something dark; and a wagging shape came wandering along to him, and put its head under his hand.

"I have to go," Ponch said. "But I wanted to thank you first!"

Kit got down beside his dog. "Thank *me*? For what?"

"You showed me what to do," Ponch said. "Now dogs have a new story, and a new way to be...thanks to you."

Kit shook his head, burying his face briefly against the glossy black of Ponch's coat. "I'm going to miss you," he said. "You're not coming back, are you?"

"Not like this," Ponch said. "I have another job now, and I have to get started. My people have been waiting for me for a long, long time. But I won't ever really go away." He looked up at Kit, and his eyes were full of starlight now. "And dogs won't really seem to change that much. Some old ways of being are good... while we work out what the new ones are."

Kit put his arms around Ponch and held him for a long time. He had no idea how long they remained like that, or when the light began to fade. But gradually it paled, like dawn in reverse, and Kit found himself kneeling in moondust. He looked up and saw nothing above him but starry night, untroubled by any darkness except the one that properly lives between the stars.

Nita was crouching down by him, looking closely at Kit. "You all right?" she said.

Kit let out a long breath and looked around him. What he had been holding was gone. "Yeah," he said. "I think so."

Nita sighed, too, as she stood, looking over to where Carmela was standing with one arm around Dairine. "And as for *you*...," she said to the Pig, which was standing on the other side of Kit.

"Tell me you're not going to ask me that question!" said the Pig.

"I was going to ask you," Nita said, "whether all that was what I thought it was."

"If you thought that dogs now finally have their own version of the One," said the Transcendent Pig, "then the answer is yes."

Kit was shaking his head. "I can't believe it," he whispered. "Are you trying to tell me that my dog— my *dog* was—"

"Is. Yes, it's the 'spell-it-backward' joke again," the Pig said, with some resignation. "The One just loves those old jokes. The older, the better." It raised its bristly eyebrows. "Making a big *BANG!* sound and running off to hide behind the nearest chunk of physical existence, like some kid ringing the doorbell at Halloween. And the puns. Don't get It started on the puns...you'll be there forever." It smiled. "Literally. But what did you expect? Your dog started making universes out of nothing. This wasn't a slight tip-off?"

"And not just making them," Nita said. "Saving them."

"Or saving one person," Kit said.

"It's the same thing, I'm told," said the Pig; and it vanished.

Kit looked around at the thousands of astonished

and exhausted wizards. Then he looked along the arc of the now-dimming spell diagram, and saw Dairine standing there, holding in her hands a collar with a stone that had gone as clear as water, and now was shading gently toward gold; and beyond her, off in the background, Ronan's still form. "This is going to take a while to sort out," he said, and wiped his eyes. "Let's go home."

Armistice

I T   W A S ,   O F   C O U R S E , not so simple. There was first
of all the matter of Ronan.

His problem was easier to solve than Nita had
feared. In the company of three thousand wizards,
there were always going to be many who were expert at
healing, and some far more so than Nita was. Within
a very short time, Darryl had introduced Nita to a
spiky-haired fifteen-year-old boy in jeans and a jeans
jacket. As he hunkered down by where Ronan hovered,
Nita found herself looking at the boy curiously, for he
was familiar somehow.

"Missed the heart by about a centimeter," he said
in an Aussie accent, running his manual up and down
over Ronan's chest and looking at the visualization of
the wound that appeared on the manual's pages. "Went
right past the right atrium into the lung, but below the
major bronchi, and cauterized the tissue on the way in,

so the lung didn't bleed or collapse. Missed the vena cava, too!" He sat back on his heels. "Couldn't have done it better with a scalpel, but that'd be the Spear for you. Whatever he might have had in mind, *it* didn't care to kill him. Or need to, I'm thinking—the trauma and shock did the job of letting the Defender out, not to mention his own intentions. I don't think he lost all that much blood."

"*Now* I remember you," Nita said. "We met in the Crossings!"

The boy blinked at her, then he grinned. "No accidents, are there?" he said. "Call me Matt, cousin. Get ready to pull this stasis off him, and we'll have him right as rain in no time."

It was a little longer than no time, and Matt looked a little pale by the time it was over. But fifteen minutes or so later, Ronan lay breathing quietly, and Matt was sitting in the moondust getting his breath back, his own wounds closing up. Like most healing wizardries, this one had needed blood.

"But he's not conscious!" Nita said.

"He won't be for a little," Matt said. "His body's still got to deal with the leftovers from the shock. Take him home, stick him in bed, let him have a few hours' rest. He's been through the wringer." Matt gave Nita a look, and glanced at Kit, who'd come to join them. "But so have you."

"He can be in my room," Dairine said from behind them. "I have some things to take care of."

Nita looked at Dairine with some concern. Her sister was holding Spot, which was normal enough, but so calm and flat a tone of voice was alien to her. Behind her, Carmela glanced at Dairine, then at Nita, and raised her eyebrows.

Nita nodded, and got up. "Sounds good. Matt, thanks!"

"No problem. Have him get in touch with me in a couple of days. I'll want to do a follow-up," Matt said as he stood up. "I'm in the book." He sketched them a small salute, and vanished.

They looked around them, watching the crater start to empty out. Nita looked up at that dark sky, full of stars again, and breathed out in relief. "Come on," she said.

They all vanished, too.

Her backyard looked so utterly ordinary that Nita could barely believe it, the late-afternoon shadows of spring lying over it absolutely as usual. But it was still much too clean for her to be used to as yet. She sighed. "We've got to go back and touch base with Sker'," she said. "See if he's found his ancestor yet."

Dairine nodded and went ahead of them, very quietly, unlocking the back door and vanishing into the house. Carmela glanced at Kit, then started after her.

Nita put out a hand. "Let her go," she said. "'Mela, maybe this is a job for you. Want to go check on Sker'ret?"

Carmela nodded, and roughed up the top of Kit's hair before he was able to do anything about it. "I'll go tell Mama and Pop that we're home," she said. "And that you're a hero."

"Spare me!" Kit said, but Carmela was already trotting down the driveway.

Nita and Kit headed for the back door. Just briefly, as they opened the back gate, Nita paused to look up at the Moon. There it hung, just past first quarter, looking utterly innocent, as if nothing of any importance had been happening.

"It's hard to believe," she said to Kit.

"I still can't believe it," Kit said. He was standing by the gate as if waiting for someone to run past him.

"Come on," she said softly. She checked to make sure that the wizardly screening field around their property was still in place, so that the neighbors wouldn't freak when they saw a body being levitated in through the back door.

They had gotten no farther than into the kitchen when Nita heard the sound of someone dropping newspapers by the easy chair. A moment later, her dad came around through the dining room and into the kitchen. Nita ran to him and hugged him hard. "Are you okay?"

"I feel fine," he said. "How about you?"

There were too many possible answers to that question, some of them contradictory. "It's going to take a while to tell you everything that happened," Nita said. "But are things okay here?"

Her dad sighed. "It looks that way," he said. "The political situation looked pretty bad late last night and early this morning, but now the news channels say that all the people who were threatening each other with nukes have begun to see sense and back down." His expression got wry. "One of the commentators said, 'Often you wait for one party or the other in a crisis to blink. But this time they all blinked at once.'"

Nita managed a very slight smile. "That would have been about the time," her dad said, "that every dog in town started to howl."

She put her eyebrows up at that. "Oh, yes," her dad said. "And it wasn't just here, either. Dogs all over the state, possibly all over the country. There are as many theories as there are news channels that are bothering to carry the story. The main theory seems to be that the government was testing some new kind of sound weapon... or early warning system."

Nita shook her head. "Ponch," she said.

Her dad had been looking at Kit, who was looking at Ronan. "I thought maybe it was something like that," he said. "Because all the other governments on the planet seem to have been testing the same weapon... Tell me later. What about Ronan there?"

"He needs somewhere to rest awhile before he goes home," Nita said. "Dairine said we should put him in her room."

Her dad nodded. "Fine. Neets... how is she?"

Nita shook her head. "I don't know."

Her dad sighed. "Okay," he said. "By the way, school called."

"Oh no."

"You all have to be back tomorrow," he said.

Nita was tempted to say *No, please, I need one more day!* But then she nodded, for it struck her that the utter terrible normalcy of school might actually be something of a rest, after all this. "Okay," she said. She turned to Kit. "Let's get him upstairs so he doesn't have to be floating around down here."

It took a few minutes to maneuver Ronan up the stairs and into Dairine's bed. When Nita got up to her room, Dairine was standing and looking into the closet with a very strange expression. As they came in, she turned hastily.

"Give us a hand here, Dair?" Nita said, pretending not to have noticed. Within a few moments they had Ronan settled, and Nita pulled off Filif's levitator field, wrapped it up into a small tight ball, and stuffed it in her pocket.

"Did Dad tell you about school?" Nita said quietly to Dairine.

"Yeah." Dairine gave Nita a look. "And don't even ask. Yeah, I'll be there. The last thing we need right now is more trouble. But I'm going out in a little while, and I might not be back till late."

Nita nodded.

"I'm lying on an effing Star Wars bedspread," said a dry voice behind them. "Will I ever be able to look myself in the eye again?"

They all turned.

"By the fact that I'm not on Rashah," Ronan said, looking around him, "but instead apparently in suburban hell and in contact with this dubious cultural artifact, I take it that we won."

Nita went over to the bed and looked down at him. "Mostly," she said, "because of you."

"Now why do I doubt that?" Ronan said. He started to stretch, and then scowled. "Janey mack, it feels like somebody's been performing Riverdance on my chest."

Nita spared a moment to wonder who or what "janey mack" was. "That would be because of the incredibly dumb stunt you pulled," she said.

"Wasn't so dumb, was it?" Ronan said. "We're here."

Nita found herself getting annoyed. "You scared us to death."

Ronan looked at her. "Oh, stop your whining," he said. "I couldn't go anywhere, the way you were yelling at me. Don't think I didn't hear you." He turned his head wearily to look at Kit. "What *is* it with these women? Always yelling..."

"They do that," Kit said, rolling his eyes.

Nita scowled at him, joined by Dairine.

"But it has to be a lot quieter in there now," Kit said.

Ronan snorted. "And sure now don't I miss Him," he said, sounding annoyed. "Typical. If I'd known I'd be rid of Him so soon, maybe I'd have appreciated Him more."

"But you didn't know," Nita said. "You thought He was going to be in there forever."

"*He* knew, though. That much I gathered as He was leaving. And *He* was just after gathering that the Spear hadn't been forged for me, *or* for Him, all that while ago. It was always forged for *Her*, for the Hesper, even when the Smith of Falias first made it, ten thousand years ago. And I thought I was just a spear-carrier? So was He." And Ronan laughed, then. "He thought it was a stitch. You should have heard Him laughing."

"I did. I mentioned about His sense of humor," Nita said, and rubbed one ear in memory of having been bitten there by the Defender, long ago.

"You did. But the whole bloody thing was a setup. The Hesper'd never have broken loose all the way unless the Lone One was there trying to stop Her. If It'd just ignored Her, none of this would ever have happened." He grinned that dark grin of his. "But wasn't that how They had it planned?"

He sighed, then, and glanced at Kit. "Where's the big fella?" he said.

Kit shook his head and turned away.

"It's a long story," Nita said. "You get some rest. We've got some things to do."

"And what's that big ugly thing on your face?"

Nita put up one hand, astonished. The zit stung her. She glared at Ronan.

"As soon as you're rested," she said, "go home, you ungrateful slob!"

Ronan grinned at her as they went out.

Nita paused just long enough to take the shower she had been desperately longing for and change her clothes. About half an hour later, pausing only to stop in at a shop in a little strip mall on the way, she and Kit were standing on Tom and Carl's doorstep.

Nita pushed the doorbell. She looked at Kit uneasily while they waited, and waited.

The inside door opened. Tom and Carl were standing there looking at them.

"Uh, hi," Nita said.

The silence lasted a few moments. Then Tom said, "We are on errantry...and, boy, do we ever greet you." He held the screen door open for them. Nita tackled Tom, and the hug went on for some time.

A few minutes later, they were sitting around the kitchen table. Nita shrugged out of her backpack, pulled out the little cup for which she'd stopped at the strip mall, and put it down on the table.

Carl picked it up, looking bemused. "Why thank you," he said. "It's been months since anyone brought me half a pint of mealworms."

"Tell Akegane-sama that I owe him one," Nita said.

"Her," Carl said.

"Are you guys okay now?" Kit said.

"If 'okay' includes being tragically embarrassed," Tom said, "yes. But we couldn't help it, any more than any other adult wizard on the planet could." He turned to Nita. "I remember saying exactly what I said...and I believed it." He shook his head. "It was terrible."

Carl was nodding; he ran his fingers through his hair. "Imagine not doing anything *but* work for the TV station." He shuddered. "It was a nightmare. Thank the One there's more to life. Meanwhile, let's see your manuals."

Nita and Kit pulled them out and dropped them on the table. They were both back to their normal size.

"So it's over," Kit said.

"Oh," Tom said, "I very much doubt that."

Kit looked briefly panic-stricken. "You mean the Pullulus could happen again? But It said—"

Nita shook her head. "It's never going to do that again," she said. "The whole reason for the Pullulus was to keep anyone from helping the Hesper wake up. It's too late for that now, and the Lone One won't waste so much energy again on an attack. This was a one-off."

"Is that a precognition?" Carl said.

Nita opened her mouth, closed it again. "Uh," she said. "I don't know..."

"Well, you'd better start keeping an eye on what you say," Tom said. "You started your Ordeal with a precognitive event, as I remember. At the time I wondered if that was going to be something that would develop in more detail later on. Looks like I was right; you may be changing specialties again. Better get back to your manual studies and make sure."

Nita shook her head. "And just when I thought things might get quiet now, stay the same for a while..."

Carl shook his head, smiling slightly. "There's only one part of this job that's the same for life," he said; "that everything's subject to change without notice."

Tom nodded. "Anyway, I'd agree with your assessment," he said. "The Pullulus itself is retreating rapidly everywhere now. Within days, even hours, perhaps, it'll be completely gone. And in the event on the Moon, it was burned clear out of space for something like eight light-years in all directions. As far away as Sirius."

"The Dog Star," Nita said softly, and smiled.

"There was also another interesting development associated with that burnout," Carl said. "It seems to have duplicated itself on a smaller scale in the neighborhood of Rirhath B. They burned clean at about the same time we did, the manual says."

Kit managed a small smile. "Probably someone saying 'thank you' for all the blue food," he said. "Carmela told us about that when she got back from checking on Sker'ret."

"Did they track down the Master, finally?" Tom said.

Nita nodded. "It took some doing, but once wizardry got working again in the neighborhood, Sker'ret found him and the Crossings staff on some little ice planet orbiting a brown dwarf in the Lesser Magellanic Cloud. I think the Tawalf and their masters had some idea that they might use them as hostages, or hold them for ransom, if the attack didn't go as planned. They were all suffering from exposure, but Rirhait are tough...they'll recover in a few months. Sker'ret will be the Master for the time being."

"Good," Tom said. "That place works best when a wizard's running it." He stretched.

Carl sat back, his arms folded. "Well, the universe is fortunate to have come through this with so little damage," he said. "Not that in other times and places the Lone Power won't attack in ways that are as awful, locally. But that doesn't change the fact that this was a victory of a kind we may never see again in our lifetimes."

Kit had been looking out the window into the backyard, his expression unreadable. Nita looked at him with some concern. "Is it true, you think, what we heard from the Powers?" he said. "That we're going to see more 'births' of the Hesper, and each one'll get stronger?"

Carl, too, had been wearing a brooding look. Now he stretched and stood up. "It seems likely," he said. "But the Powers, like the One, are cagey about their scheduling. They're not going to give away anything that will make it easier for the Lone Power to derail what They've got planned."

He went to the window, looked out to see what Kit was looking at: Annie and Monty, the two sheepdogs, playing out on the lawn, taking a bone away from each other and running around the yard with it. "But in the meantime, take a little while to feel good about what you've just done. Any victory that can be won in the physical universe is just a picture of the bigger, slower one that started happening outside of time ages ago, and will keep happening outside of time until it's all over."

"And we win?" Kit said. He sounded doubtful.

Carl put a hand on his shoulder. "As long as we don't stop fighting," he said, "we always win. Because what we do, They do."

"Not the other way around?" Nita said.

Tom shook his head. "It's a popular misconception."

He stood up. "You both look wrecked," he said. "You should go get some rest. I understand that tomorrow is a school day."

"Don't remind us," Kit said.

"And over the next week or so," Carl said, "we'd appreciate it if you went through the manual 'overviews' of recent events and annotated them. Your take on exactly what happened is going to be invaluable."

Nita nodded, shouldering back into her backpack's straps. There were already a number of things that were bothering her. The peridexis, for one thing, had gone silent, and she was wondering whether she was ever going to hear that voice again; the inside of her head was strangely lonely. She wished she had better understood the reassurance it gave her almost the first time it had spoken, when the shadow of the Pullulus first fell over her dreams: "There is only one to whom it will answer, and that one is not here." *It meant Ponch. But there've been so many other things it said that I still don't understand.* She still remembered the Transcendent Pig, on the Moon, looking at them all with an expression that suggested there was still something it was waiting for. *Or did I just imagine that? Having to study your own life is a pain.*

They all headed for the door. Tom looked at them as he opened the inside door. "You did good," he said. "But you know that."

"Yeah," Kit said. "I just wish it didn't hurt so much."

Carl nodded. "I know," he said. "*Dai stihó . . .* and hang in there. It's all you can do."

At around the same time, many light-years away, Dairine stood alone on the high platform outside the throne room on Wellakh.

Her clothes were much different than they had been when she came here last, and she didn't care. The only one for whom she would have willingly changed her clothes was not here now, though she was still wearing one thing from that outfit that she wouldn't willingly show anyone else.

Dairine stood there at the railing, looking out over the vast, blasted sunside plain. There was no sign of the huge crowd of people who'd been there before. They had had the Pullulus, Dairine's manual told her, as Earth had, but when Earth's infestation had been destroyed, so had theirs. Now they were probably cleaning up the local effects the same way that people were doing it on Earth. And like people on Earth, they'd be telling one another, for a long time, sad stories about the awful time the world changed, and how nothing now was the way it had used to be.

Eventually she heard the footsteps behind her on the stone. They stopped a long way from her. She turned, then, and saw the two tall figures standing there. Behind them, the great bronze doors stood open; in the great hall of the royalty of Wellakh, on the floor, halfway down that long, polished way to the throne, a single light burned. It was the same golden-yellow color of the planet's sun; and very alone it looked, burning there by itself.

Dairine stood there a moment longer, and scrubbed at her eyes briefly. She was probably kind of dirty, but she couldn't help it. If she'd stopped to take a shower—if she'd done anything except come straight here—she might have talked herself out of coming at all. And that would have been wrong. Slowly, she walked to them—Roshaun's mother, Roshaun's father, standing there together, waiting for her.

She could hardly bear their faces as she got closer to them. Wellakh's sun was behind them; they stood in the shadow of the uprising peak from which the castle was carved. Their faces were in shadow, and their eyes. But that didn't stop Dairine from seeing their expressions... and she wished she couldn't.

She stopped a few feet from them, and looked up into their faces. They were so calm, and that by itself made the tears come to her eyes again. The hollow sorrow in Roshaun's mother's eyes was terrible to see. His father—Dairine looked up into that cool, set face, and realized that his mastery of his own expression was not as total as he might have hoped.

"I think we know," Roshaun's father said, "why you are here... and why you are here alone."

Dairine looked up. "He did everything he could," she said. "He did everything that was asked of him. More than was asked of him." She gulped. "And it wasn't enough. But that never stopped him..."

Roshaun's mother stood very still, and only nodded, the tears running down her face. "Where did it happen?" Lady Miril said.

"In my solar system," Dairine said. "We solved the root cause of the Pullulus, but after that we decided to go back to my world..."

"*We* decided?" Roshaun's father said.

Dairine looked him in the eye. "*He* decided," she said. "You of all people should know that nobody made his choices for him. Not you; not me." Then she reached into her pocket. "But, afterward, this was left." She brought out the collar with the Sunstone, looked down at it, and then held it out to Roshaun's father. "Please," she said, "take it." *Because having it hurts too much—*

Roshaun's father looked at the Sunstone, and shook his head. "I will not wear it again," he said. "I think it's yours now. For look—"

She looked at it. The stone had been clear; now it had gone a much lighter gold than it had been. "It did that before," she said.

"It is a sign of the mastery passing to another," Roshaun's father said. "It seems to have become attuned to another star."

"Mine," Dairine said. "Ours is this color."

There was a long pause. Roshaun's father reached out to the stone, and then pulled his hand back. "It is still active," he said. "There are some routines that you should learn. He would have wanted to know that its power was not wasted, that it was safe with one he had—" Roshaun's father broke off. "That he thought worthy of his attention," he said after a moment. "Some of those usages you could be taught. With proper supervision…"

Dairine got a clear sense of what terrible control Roshaun's father was exercising over himself. She was determined to show that hers could be as great as his; here, in particular, at this point in a life that had been so much about control—and in which she'd lost so much control lately. "I'd like that," she said, "if you have the time."

"There'll be nothing but time now," Roshaun's father said. He gazed down at Dairine and reached out a hesitant hand to touch the necklace that just showed under the collar of her shirt. There, around her neck, where it would stay, was the fat, round, gleaming emerald threaded on a single sentence in the Speech. It was not until a little earlier, when Dairine had had a moment by herself, that she'd had time to read what that sentence was. She was determined not to think about it now. She'd just cry again. "And what we taught him—," Roshaun's father said. "That we can teach you, so that you can guarantee the safety of another world as he guaranteed his. Another star."

"Thank you," Dairine said. She was controlling herself very tightly, for right now, more than anything, she wanted to say to them, even to shout at them, *Stop talking about him in the past tense! As if he's*— But she couldn't say it. Part of her was certain that she was deluding herself. The thought, *You're just in denial!* was already coming up. To say out loud what she really believed would merely guarantee that other people would think she was in denial, too.

But I can't believe it yet. I can't say anything until I'm sure. Not until I've made that one last test.

Dairine looked from Roshaun's father to his mother. "Our world is going to need some straightening up after all this trouble," she said. "It's going to take a long time to get things back to normal. But as soon as I can come, I will."

She turned and looked across the vast plain of the sunside. "But he loved you," Dairine said. "Whatever else he would have wanted you to know, he would have wanted you to know that."

She had to go, then; she felt her control starting to slip. Back by the railing, Spot waited for her, silent. As she headed back, the darkness of a worldgate opened for her. Dairine stepped through, not looking back, and vanished from Wellakh.

No matter what Tom had told her to do, it took Nita a long time to get settled enough to rest. She walked Kit home, and talked to his parents, and reassured them as much as she could that they were both in fairly good shape. But all Mr. and Mrs. Rodriguez had to do was look at Kit to tell that there was a lot more that could be said on the subject. It was Carmela's mental state—thoroughly confused but still basically cheerful—that reassured them most.

And then everything started to catch up with Nita: She actually began to fall asleep on the dining room sofa while Carmela told them about what had happened on the Moon. Nita opened her eyes very wide and got up. "I'm so sorry," she said. "I've gotta go." She said her good nights to Kit's folks and headed out into the driveway.

He followed her out. They stood there together for a moment, looking at the Moon.

"I miss him already," Kit said. "It really hurts."

Nita nodded. "I know," she said. "Even though he's okay...more than okay." She shook her head. "It's not the same."

She yawned. "Oh, God, I'm sorry," she said. "It's not that— You know I don't—"

"I know," Kit said. "Go on, go home, get some sleep. We've got an early morning."

"Yeah," Nita said. But Kit didn't move to go inside.

"You've been hugging everybody else in the place," he said after a moment.

Nita turned around and gave Kit a hug calculated to be twice as emphatic as any she'd given anybody else. Then she held him a little ways away.

"You're not all right," she said in the Speech. "I'm not all right, either. But we will be."

"Is that a precognition?" Kit said.

Nita smiled very slightly. "Yes," she said. "Now get in there and let them know it."

Kit nodded, punched her lightly in the arm, and went inside.

Nita went home. Her dad was making dinner; she helped him, and was for a while blissfully happy with the simplicity of macaroni and cheese. Dairine arrived not long after dinner started, sat down, and was uncharacteristically silent. She ate, thoroughly but unenthusiastically, and then went up to bed.

Nita's father looked at her as they were finishing up. "I guess this means," he said, "that even after you save the universe, you can still feel let down."

Nita nodded. "It doesn't last," she said. "It keeps needing to be saved."

Her dad smiled at her a little. "Take your time," he said, as he got up to take his plate into the kitchen, "but I really want to hear all about it. Because it's worth knowing that it *can* be saved."

Nita smiled at that, stretched and yawned, then brought her own plate into the kitchen, kissed her dad good night, and went up to bed.

Dairine had gone to sleep holding the Sunstone, suspecting what the result of that would be, especially at a time like this.

The place through which she moved was one of light, and gathered around her was a huge crowd of inhuman shapes. Mostly little and low-built, shelled in light, they moved through a gigantic construction of fire that towered above and around them. Under them, as a floor, lay a spell diagram of incredible complexity, seemingly miles wide, a plain over which the low, shelled creatures moved casually while the uppermost fires of a star roiled and burned beneath them.

Dairine walked out over that wide floor of wizardry, and many of the shelled shapes accompanied her. *You're not supposed to be here just yet,* one of them said.

Dairine glanced over at Logo. "Neither are you," she said. "You're all still alive!"

Don't mistake this *for Timeheart,* Logo said. *This is just an anteroom—a portal area. But you brought us the data that made what's going to happen here possible. Causality therefore becomes something less than an issue.* And Logo gave Dairine a mischievous look.

You shouldn't be raising false hopes, Dairine said. *Everything dies eventually. Everything runs down. No exceptions—*

You'd be surprised, Logo said. *Everywhere it can, the universe breaks the rule, sometimes in the strangest ways. That's what wizardry's about, isn't it? Finding the unexpected way to foil the force that invented Death. Doing what Life itself does every chance it can. You've put the tools in our hands... and now the possibilities are endless.*

Dairine swallowed. *Let's see how endless,* she said. *Show me what I came to see.*

They walked a long time across the plane of wizardry, through the unending light. Finally, though, Dairine came to the place she'd known would be there. It looked a lot like Wellakh.

Here, though, the mighty spire of stone that reared up into the sky was not scorched barren. Here the red things grew, cascading down it, the hanging gardens of another world. Here that spire pierced right up into the darkness of space, not hubris or a challenge to the heavens, but a dream achieved. And all around it stretched an endless plain that was barren no more; Wellakh was healed of its old wound.

Dairine stood again high on that terrace above the world, looking down the mountain. She leaned over the railing as she'd done once before, seeing the beautiful red foliage of the native Wellakhit plant life stretching away for miles under the golden sun—not a garden, an artificial thing, but a natural reality, never destroyed by the terrible flare of the Wellakhit sun.

Dairine turned away from the railing and went across the terrace to the crystal-paned doors, and then through them, into the place where Roshaun's rooms had been. The decorations were much the same as they had been before—to her eye, rich and overdone—but the light that dwelt in every carpet or chair or piece of artwork told her that this was his idea of perfection, the place of his desire. And he wasn't here.

Dairine started to look around, taking her time. She went into every room in those apartments, explored every inch, but he was still not there. And in the last room she came to, a little place full of huge clothes-presses and nobly carved and decorated cabinets, Dairine found the one thing that could have surprised her. There was a darkness in one wall: the only darkening in that whole bright place—an active worldgate.

How interesting it was that the place of Roshaun's desire had a hole in it. . . .

Carefully Dairine ducked and stepped through the worldgate—and found herself in her own backyard, out among the trees right at the back of the property, where she and Roshaun had worked their second-to-last great spell together. There was no one here, either: nothing but silence and a faint smell of sassafras. Out past the trees, her yard was bright with moonlight. She stepped out into it, and saw lights on in the house, and all around her trees that seemingly reached up to the stars, and a full Moon above it all, turning everything silver—so strange a color, for someone whose own world had no moon.

Behind her, Logo, silvered by that same light, looked out across the strange place, the image of a Timeheart within a Timeheart. *Now do you understand?*

Yes, Dairine said softly. *We still have unfinished business...!*

She went back out through the worldgate, and back out through Roshaun's place in that virtual Timeheart, and back out to the railing. Then Dairine stepped back out of it all, across the plane of wizardry and back through the portals of dream to Earth's universe, to the real world, to begin the search for the one who was lost.

Watching this in silence from the shadows of the trees, Nita nodded slowly, then stepped back into her own dream.

She walked out of the shadows behind the dais in the great central cavern of the Commorancy. It was empty except for a pool of darkness that slowly began to draw itself up into human shape to look at her.

Nita laughed at it. "You lose again," she said.

"Oh, go on, delude yourself," said the Lone One, Its arms folded. "So your wonderful Hesper is here after all. Do you think that matters so far above your level of existence are going to have any effect on *your* pitiful lives? You won't live to see any difference her appearance will make. The worlds will seem to be doing the same old thing for millennia to come. And as for your 'victory,' you and your universe will be cleaning up its consequences for centuries to come." It sounded triumphant. Yet behind the triumph, Nita could clearly feel the rage: *None of this should have happened!*

"Maybe so," Nita said. "But for the time being, we'll keep our old promise to you... because that's what wizards do. We'll keep on fighting the little versions of you that you've left all over the place. And as for the long term...we have a new ally: the one who's doing what you should have done. So make what you can of what little time you have left."

"Little? *Little!* For millions of years yet I will rule this universe!"

"'Rule'?" Nita said. "Running around kicking over everybody's sand castles doesn't mean you own the beach. And as for 'millions'—in the bigger scheme of things, what's that?" She snapped her fingers, grinning. "Do what you can with it, because until you finally give up, we'll always be here to stop you."

It smiled again, one last time. "Wizards may always be here," the Lone Power said. "But will you?"

It vanished.

Nita shook her head. *Well?* she said to the peridexis. *Will I?*

Let's go find out, it said.

The next morning, Kit got up and did all the routine things that he did when getting ready for school. He got showered, brushed his teeth, got dressed, went downstairs. He ate breakfast, and washed the cereal bowl, and put it and the spoon away.

Then he sighed, and went to Ponch's bowls, and picked them up, and cleaned them. He rinsed out the water bowl and put it away. The dry-food bowl and wet-food bowls were empty. He washed them, too, and put them in a cupboard. And finally he went to the back door, to the coatrack where the leash was hanging, and took it down.

The front doorbell rang. His pop was at work already, and his mama was still in the bathroom, so that when the door opened, Kit had to smile, knowing what was going to happen next. He waited there by the back door for a few moments.

"Oh, wow!" Carmela yelled. "You shouldn't have! Or no; I take it back. Yes, you should!"

Very quietly, Kit went out the back door and down the driveway, swinging the leash. At the end of the driveway, he stopped, watching as the UPS truck that had delivered Carmela's new curling iron drove away.

There were no dogs in sight anywhere. Kit stood there and just felt the loss: the strange feeling of having Ponch's leash in his hand, but not having Ponch dancing around him and insisting that he hurry up and put it on him. It was much like the strange empty feeling of the braided rug beside Kit's bed, which had no dog lying on it with his feet sticking up in the air—the strangeness of a bed where there was enough room to stretch your feet out in the morning, because there was no dog taking up the whole lower end of it.

Kit started to walk, because there was nothing else he could do. *The only good thing about this,* he thought, *the* only *good thing, is that there won't be any more weird howling all hours of the day and night.* No more Hitchcock movie scenarios staged on his front lawn with dogs instead of birds. *No more,* he thought. *All gone.*

His eyes started to fill up, as he realized, on a different level, what Nita had had to deal with earlier in the year. The place where the other had always been...or for nearly as long as you could remember...now gone forever.

He kept walking, because that was what he did, this time of day, with a leash in his hand. There was no barking in the street. Even Tinkerbell, the slightly psychotic dog three doors down, stood quietly at his gate and watched Kit go by without the usual threats of bodily harm.

"Dai stihó," he said.

Tinkerbell just stood looking at him, then turned and trotted back behind his own house.

Kit sighed and kept on walking down the block toward the corner where he usually would stop and let Ponch do his thing. The only thing he was missing right now was the plastic bag he'd have picked up Ponch's doings with. There was no need for that now.

Kit stopped at the corner, looked around him, and let out a miserable sigh. *What am I doing here?* he thought.

That was when the sheepdog came trotting down the sidewalk. Kit just stood there for a moment, watching it come. It had been sitting on the lawn, weeks ago, and it wasn't a neighborhood dog: Kit's father had asked him where it had come from, and Kit had had no idea. His first urge was to turn away; the sight of any dog was a touch on an open wound.

Then he stopped himself. *I don't care,* Kit thought. *I want to talk to a dog, any dog, and get an answer back.*

The sheepdog crossed the street toward him, jumped up onto the sidewalk, and paused by him, looking up. Kit almost managed to laugh: The way its hair hung down in its face, it was amazing that it could see anything. He hunkered down next to it and ruffled it behind the ears, though the gesture made his throat go thick with tears. In the Speech, he said, "So listen, guy, just where did you come from?"

The sheepdog shook its fur out of its eyes and gazed up at him, its tongue hanging out. *That's sort of a funny question,* it said. *You should know. You were there, too!*

And Kit's breath went right out of him—because though the sheepdog's eyes were golden and not dark, *Ponch* was looking out of them.

Now the tears he'd been fighting so hard did come, and Kit didn't care. "But I thought— I thought that you—"

That me *did,* said the sheepdog. *But there's a lot more of me now. I'm more here than I ever was. I'm in every dog there is! Didn't I tell you I wasn't going to leave you?* The sheepdog grinned at him. *Some parts of the old Choice were worth keeping.*

Kit threw his arms around the sheepdog. *But I made another Choice,* Ponch said. *For all of us. And now we have a new story: how the Hound of Heaven defeated the Wolf that ate the Moon...but only with the help of the Wise One who knew that what you give away, you get back a hundred times more, and who brought the Hound to where he could learn how the sacrifice could be made. Now all debts are paid, and we can all be more than we were.*

And suddenly the street was full of squirrels, sitting upright on their haunches and looking expectantly at the sheepdog.

At least most of the time!

The sheepdog started wriggling wildly in Kit's arms and washing his face like crazy. Laughing, Kit opened his arms, and the sheepdog went lolloping off after the squirrels, barking his head off, tearing down the road and out of sight. One after another, all the dogs living up and down the street started to bark.

With the tears running down his face, and grinning, Kit turned back toward his house to get his things. As he did, he saw someone standing at the end of his driveway, watching him, as if she'd known exactly where he'd be.

Laughing, he ran to meet her.